LICENSE TO KILL THE LIGHTS

ELIZA BEGRAVE

Cover design by Nicolas Brown

ISBN: 979-8-9946505-0-9

TO NICK, SHANNON, AND STACY:
MY SURE THINGS,
WHO MADE LOVING ME LOOK EASY ENOUGH
FOR ME TO TRY.

Trigger warnings:

Graphically depicted violence
Gore
Pedicide (not depicted)
Substance abuse
Attempted SA
Child molestation (not depicted)
References to child abuse
Murder
Explicit sexual encounters (including LGBTQ)
Degradation
Consensual non-consent
Bondage
Torture
Venom
Lots and lots of naughty words

CHAPTER 1

ALI

Ali was no size queen, but even she would admit there were times when size mattered—paychecks, payload, and her current predicament: probable survival odds.

Hunched over, she shuffled around the end of a stack of weathered wooden pallets, hauling G's weary body like luggage. She slumped down behind the pile and peered around the corner, scanning for the henchmen who hunted them.

The golden light of the Kobe Port Tower and the jeweled glow of the city skyline shimmered off the glassy water, illuminating the docks. Six shadows prowled the aisles between the rusted shipping containers, their bodies slicing through the still air without disturbing it. Moonlight broke through the clouds, exposing the men, whose black cashmere suits would have styled them to perfection for a gala, were it not for the compact assault rifles glinting in the glow of the silent moon. The pack of hunters moved in wordless unison, stalking its prey.

Ali faced them with nothing but a pistol and a pain in the ass.

"You sure know how to show a girl a good time," she whispered, pulling the Beretta from the holster under her arm and twisting a suppressor onto the end of the barrel.

"Well, they say," G panted, "novelty is what keeps a relationship healthy." She attempted a casual tone, but her quivering lower lip betrayed her.

Ali would have paid a small fortune to transport them back to their first trip to Kobe. Just two teenage girls, tipsy on shōchū, sharing a first kiss under that tower—a kiss that launched them from friends to partners-in-crime-with-benefits. She missed those easy times before they were old enough to perceive their perils. Instead, she blew that small fortune getting to Kobe so she could risk her ass extracting G out of her quagmire of the month.

"Yeah, the dockside tour has been enchanting. I didn't expect our tattooed tour guide to be missing part of his pinky finger. You wanna explain to me why the Hasegawa-gumi is paying you such individualized attention?" Ali clicked the safety off and took another scan around the corner. Their cluster of slick pursuers felt closer than she preferred.

"They must still be bent out of shape about me taking Miko to Paris without asking," G said.

"Miko? As in Kimiko Matsuo? *That* Miko? Please tell me you didn't..." Heaviness compressed Ali's chest.

G shrugged.

Kimiko Matsuo was the favorite granddaughter of Akio Matsuo, the kumicho, or kingpin, of the most powerful organized crime syndicate in Japan—the Japanese Godfather.

"Do you wanna get katana-murdered? Because this is exactly how you get katana-murdered," Ali hissed.

She didn't relish the idea of being chased by the goons of a man who served eleven years of hard time for murdering a rival crime boss with an enormous sword in broad daylight. She grabbed G's hand and they took a crouched scamper toward another tower of metal containers.

"Fuck, man. Miko dumped me ten months ago," G said.

"You've been running from the Yakuza for ten months?!" Ali touched the back of her belt, wrapping her trembling fingers around her spare magazine. She calculated some quick math regarding her hollow points and their six-on-two dilemma. As far as she was concerned, the odds were six-on-one, with the one severely handicapped by an unarmed civilian with the worst possible taste in partners.

"Oh, give it up. I've been forging your identities for the last ten years. I'm pretty sure you're running from worse," G said, between breaths. "Pot, kettle, Babe."

G wasn't wrong. Helleborus was the most formidable and well-funded independent espionage organization in the world. Government overthrows, high-profile assassinations, dictator installation, and money market manipulation were all just a typical Tuesday for Helleborus.

According to the prevalent rumors, they emerged from an alliance of the oldest spy traditions of the greatest civilizations, dating back beyond the Roman Empire. Helleborus operated on the bleeding edge of modern-day espionage, leaving everyone else sprinting to catch up. CIA, KGB, MI6, Archangel: all watered-down intelligence built off Helleborus' sloppy seconds.

Ali was the only operative ever to escape the organization with her life.

"Well, I'm not going around kidnapping the Golden Princess of the Yakuza for a romantic getaway. Why can't you just pick up a girl at a bar?" Ali said.

"I did pick her up at a bar," G said defensively.

"Which bar?"

G's shoulders slumped, and her eyes avoided Ali's. "Dākudagā."

Unbelievable.

G met Miko at none other than the Michelin-starred restaurant reputed to be Matsuo's stronghold. Ali fixed G with an incredulous glare.

"They have the best udon," G asserted through her teeth.

"I'm sure it's to die for." Fear slipped inside Ali's sleeve cuffs and traveled up her arms.

"I was doing just fine before I came back," G hissed.

"Why in hell would you come back?"

Shame passed over G's face. "Miko still had something of mine."

"What, like your computer?"

G stroked a sleeve of her hoodie and sank down into it. "My favorite sweater," she whispered like a toddler caught covered in permanent marker.

Anger flared up Ali's face, burning and tingling against the cold. "You risked your life—and mine—for a fucking zip-up?"

"It's the softest and they don't make them any—"

Ali shhhed her.

She peeked around the corner. A bullet sliced through the air beside her cheek and pierced the glittering water. She forced a deep exhale as she pressed herself back against the relative safety of the container.

They were made.

G's dark brown eyes darted around as she trembled, pulling her hoodie tighter around her small frame. Ali knew if she had any chance of them escaping with both their asses intact, she needed to keep G from losing it.

Ali hadn't expected a sake-tasting tour when she received G's 911 message. G excelled at getting herself into these pickles, and Ali was always the best one to extricate her from them. But this was the Big Papa Pickle to rule them all. Ali zipped G's sweatshirt up to her neck and pressed a hurried kiss on her forehead, knowing a Yakuza assassin could corner them at any moment.

"I'm impressed you're still alive. You should've been sliced to sashimi the first week," Ali chided, grateful she caught G before she got royally screwed.

G stuck both her thumbs out and pointed them toward her face.

"Best hacker alive," she said, attempting to sound smug. "I owe you a steak dinner. Big time."

Ali grabbed G by the sweater and pulled her to her feet. "Less talk. More run."

Ali slipped into the cozy ramen joint. She stripped her beanie off, gathering her hair into a messy bun, and shed the heavy black coat, trading it for a soft brown suede cropped jacket she lifted off the coat rack. With a sly flick, she snatched the snapback off G's head and peeled her red hoodie off. G released a betrayed gasp which Ali met with a stern shake of her head.

The shop offered a small amount of merchandise, including a dark blue graphic zip-up that Ali draped around G's shoulders. She pulled the hood up over G's head, tucking her long, glossy black braid inside, and placed an arm around her. G snatched her favorite hoodie from Ali's fingers and shoved it under her new sweater.

Ali charmed the hostess with her radiant smile. She ordered a table for two, preferably in the back. She politely asked for the hoodie to be added to their tab in perfect Japanese.

The hostess escorted them to a two-top nestled near the bustling kitchen, where they could hear the energetic clatter of pots and the sizzling of food as it cooked. The aroma of braised pork and seasoned broth enveloped Ali like a warm embrace, reminding her she hadn't eaten since the okonomiyaki she scarfed when she landed yesterday. She ordered two bowls of Tonkotsu ramen from the server as two of their impeccably dressed stalkers passed by the glass storefront, scanning the interior for their quarry. G shivered despite the warmth of the restaurant, and her eyes darted to the windows.

"*Mierda,*" she whispered, her voice a barely-there breath of anxiety.

"Hey," Ali whispered with force, snapping G's gaze back to her. She tried to distract G with a playful grin. "Remember that month in Montenegro? We should go back sometime." She grabbed G's hand and caressed it.

"Go back?" G scoffed. Her eyebrows jumped up her forehead comically. "If memory serves, we polished off all of Marco's cocaine, and you stole his yacht. I'm pretty sure we're banned for life."

"Hey," Ali said, her voice tinged with hurt. G's eyebrows furrowed with concern. "I thought we agreed to call it—"Ali adopted her best Michael Caine accent—"Marcocaine."

G choked on her green tea. She cracked a small smile, and relief entered her eyes.

"And that twenty-nothing Albanian skipper was hiding a lot of goodies under that crew uniform," G admitted, loosening up.

The corners of Ali's lips lifted. "Hard agree."

The tremor in G's hand softened under Ali's squeeze.

The men seemed satisfied with their search of the restaurant and moved past the edge of the window. Ali's shoulders settled into a softer set.

"Don't you think it was a little impulsive and dangerous coming back here?" Ali said, a little more serious.

"Dangerous? That's why I have a... you. And I'm not impulsive. I'm spontaneous." G tipped her head up with pride. "It's one of the things Andy likes best about me."

"Andy? So, we've moved on already? Where did you meet her? The Cecil Hotel?" Ali allowed a little more bite to return to her tone.

"I met *him* at pottery class."

Ali lifted her eyebrows in skepticism. "You're taking pottery now? What happened to candle making?"

"I got bored."

Typical.

G burned through hobbies faster than relationships. Poor Andy had no idea what he'd signed up for.

"Do you ever wonder what it would be like if we could stop running?" G asked, her tone wistful.

Ali refused to entertain those thoughts. She assumed if she stopped running, Helleborus would find her in record time, and most likely kill her. She preferred that fate to the alternative: being turned into a murderer for them. She would rather die than become one of the monsters who raised her.

"We would need a fortress," Ali said, devoid of hope.

G clasped Ali's hand between hers, and inspiration flickered in her eyes.

"Don't look at me like that," Ali said. "That look is always expensive."

A police car crawled by with its lights off and stopped in front of the shop next door. The officer exited his vehicle, and spoke to one of their hunters. Ali's neck tensed.

Of course, Matsuo owns the Kobe cops.

The hits just kept on coming.

We need to get out of the city.

CHAPTER 2

DARWIN

Victor Everly peered through trifocals at the Pepto-pink aisles of stuffed kittens in an airport Sanrio store. As a seventy-two-year-old man in an expensive wool suit, he stuck out like a hot dog at a hamburger party. He would rather airdrop behind enemy lines than spend longer than five minutes poring over pink plastic pencil boxes wrapped in patterned cellophane.

Everly had quite literally written the book on evading detection while traveling. His textbook, *Deception Techniques*, was in its fourth edition. However, you wouldn't find it in the stacks at Barnes & Noble or a university library. It was required reading for all the cadets at Archangel Intelligence Academy, North America's most elite espionage training facility. AIA made the CIA's Camp Peary, affectionately referred to as "The Farm," look like a preschool. Everly had spent twenty-five years as tenured faculty at Archangel, the last ten of which he served as Director.

After his retirement and the loss of his wife, Lourdes, his twin granddaughters, Emma and Aubrey, were the only commanders he answered to. They had their "Poppy" wrapped around their tiny fingers ever since they came into this world six years ago. Those girls loved this Hello Kitty crap. If he arrived at his daughter's house empty-handed, he'd be deader than disco.

He plucked up a medium-sized Hello Kitty in a rosy, ruffled dress, holding a pink sprinkled ice cream cone, and turned it over in his hands.

$42.99? It's ridiculous what they charge for this crud nowadays.

Drops in the bucket if it made those girls smile. It wasn't as if Everly was hurting for money.

"I would've pegged you as more of a Keroppi guy. Serves me right for judging a book by its cover," a smiling clerk said from over Everly's shoulder. It was rare for anyone to sneak up on him.

You're slipping, old man.

Everly vowed to pay closer attention to his surroundings. He had to admit, this trip had left him more jet-lagged than usual—or maybe that was just a comfortable excuse for the deterioration of his abilities. Could he be getting that old?

The young man in the pink polo shirt picked up a stuffed green frog with round cartoon eyes and a V-shaped mouth. He squeezed it in his slender fingers and wiggled it in the air toward Everly.

Kids these days.

They treated you with too much familiarity, pretending you were old friends. It really ground Victor's gears. Practically no one in the world knew Victor in a significant way, which was by design. He found the false familiarity of salespeople saccharine, inauthentic, and annoying.

The clerk was an attractive young man, small-framed and clean-cut; Victor appreciated his allegiance to hygiene. The man's ivory cheeks pinked when he smiled. He appeared to be in his late teens or early twenties at the most. He carried himself with exuberant youthful confidence and an easy smile.

Everly selected a second cat plush. "I'll take two of these."

"Smart man. Always good to have a backup."

"Something like that." Everly didn't correct him. He was loath to divulge any personal details to strangers. Lourdes used to say that he could never stop being a spy, even when they were on vacation. Everly knew better than most that a surefire way to get information out of someone was to make a blatantly incorrect statement. It's called elicitation. The average person wants to be understood. They have a compulsion to correct others so that they don't make inaccurate assumptions about them.

Most people will choose to be right over being smart.

"I bet you could get away with one. You don't strike me as the type of man who's hard on his toys." The clerk maintained his playful tone and shot Everly a teasing smile.

Under normal circumstances, a chatty store associate would've annoyed the piss out of Everly. He detested small talk in all its forms. Something about the kid's good-natured ribbing amused Everly; it reminded him of someone. He followed the associate to the register, paid the boy cash, and headed out of the store to his gate.

He trudged up to the departure board. Next to his flight number, the word "DELAYED" flashed.

Sonofabitch. I miss flying private.

His former life had afforded him certain luxuries that had lapsed with the advent of his retirement. The best he could do nowadays was to book a first-class ticket. But even first class didn't guarantee your flight would leave on time.

The hired sedan glided to a stop in front of Adele Everly's brownstone. Victor checked his watch. His daughter would still be at the opera with her new boyfriend, Timothy. The benefit of a delayed flight meant that he didn't have to sit through dinner with that irritating idiot.

Although, it disappointed Victor to miss seeing *Rigoletto*. He rarely wasted an opportunity to see a favorite opera. It was past the twins' bedtime, so he would have time to wrap their gifts before seeing their cherubic faces.

Everly scaled the steps to the front door with his luggage, shoving the Sanrio bag under his arm. The heavy front door stood ajar two inches. He groaned. It must have been that awful au pair. His daughter's terrible taste in men was only eclipsed by her inability to select adequate staff.

The amber parlor lights flooded the entryway. Everly prepared himself to give that lousy nanny a piece of his mind for endangering his granddaughters when he saw them.

Duct tape bound Aubrey's arms and legs to one of the antique wooden parlor chairs. Her head drooped, and a tear-soaked fabric gag wrapped around her tiny, puffy, red face. She coughed and whimpered as she wept.

Next to her sat Emma, bound identically as Aubrey, except her gag had sagged down under her chin and rested on her shoulders. Sweat-drenched hair plastered her head, which was contorted back as far as it would go on her chubby neck. Her bulging, bloodshot eyes stared unseeing at the ceiling, and her mouth stood open in a silent scream. Broken capillaries littered her skin, which had ceased exhibiting a color that indicated life.

Victor dropped his bags and sank to his knees. Cold sweat broke out on his forehead, and his stomach tumbled. A sob surged out of his mouth, and he stretched a shaking hand out toward Emma's motionless form.

"Nice of you to join us, Poppy," a quiet voice said from the corner of the room, tightening Everly's shoulders and rooting him to the spot. A lean man rested on the ledge of the windowsill, turning over a stainless-steel letter opener in slim, leather-gloved hands. He had traded his pink polo shirt and khaki shorts for a black turtleneck and slacks, but Everly recognized him immediately.

Everly opened his mouth, but no sound came out. He couldn't process what he saw. A satisfied grin spread across the young store clerk's face, but the genial flush in his cheeks was absent.

Aubrey let out a squeak that rose into a piercing wail. The legs of the parlor chair knocked on the floor as she panicked and struggled in her seat. Everly wanted to go to her, but both fear and unpreparedness prevented him from acting. Had he been in his own home, he would have had several options for weapons to neutralize his opponent. He searched the parlor for anything he could improvise, but the man held the only implement that remotely resembled something dangerous. Adele was adamant about having no weapons in the house with the girls, so Everly lacked even a simple sidearm.

If Adele only knew that the use of arms paid for her entire privileged existence.

The young man clicked his tongue at Aubrey and crouched next to her with a menacing calm. He took her cheek in the gloved hand that still held the letter opener and rubbed some tears away with his thumb.

"Now, Aubrey, sweetie. You remember what happened

when Emmy couldn't stop crying. I had to give her a shot. You don't want a shot, do you?" he said with unsettling tenderness.

Aubrey choked out a faint "no" from behind the gag, shaking her head in a frantic refusal.

"There's my strong girl," the man said in a tone too soft and familiar. Aubrey dissolved back into muffled sobs.

"If you're really good, your grandpa has something special for you." His gaze flicked up at Everly, then back at the little girl who lay dead. He shook his head, then shrugged. "I tried to tell you to buy just one."

Everly's vision clouded, and his ears thrummed. Every piece of him wanted to shred this man beyond all recognition. No stranger to wet work, Everly was never one to shy away from taking a life. If there was ever a man to murder, the one who had just stolen his youngest granddaughter topped that list. Adrenaline electrified his veins. He scrutinized the room for any potential weapons. His eyes landed on his sweet Aubrey, whose face twisted in terror; her eyes pleaded to her grandpa for salvation as her tiny body quaked.

I still have a granddaughter left.

"P–ppy," she squeaked out through the gag. It tormented Everly not to be able to scoop her up in his arms. He inched his body toward her, every instinct screaming for action.

"Always good to have a backup." The clerk's words echoed in Everly's mind as if his granddaughters held the same value in that bastard's brain as a stuffed Hello Kitty.

Do something!

Find a weapon!

"Have a seat, Victor," the man in black gestured with the letter opener to a leather armchair. His tone remained buttery and casual, revealing nothing except a glimmer of amusement behind his eyes.

Everly forced his mind to quiet and his body to comply, dragging himself over to the chair. The room spiraled around him as he sank into the leather. This was no random crime. Everly's mind raced through a labyrinth of potential adversaries that stretched over his lengthy career. The level of calculation and skill this man possessed was unlike anything he had ever encountered, especially for someone so young.

"What do you want? If it's money, I can double whatever you're being paid." Everly understood the weakness of his offer. Although he was a wealthy man, his money ranked low on the list of his most valuable assets.

The young man's rich, mocking laughter punctured Victor's fragile resolve.

"These shoes cost more than the twins' tuition. It's adorable that you think I make house calls over money. You're better than that, Victor. I want what any man of my age wants: a thriving career, a happy home, the location of Archangel, and all the intel you have on Xiphos."

CHAPTER 3

ALI

Ali's toes tapped a manic merengue rhythm on the wooden floor of the dinghy. Her hand clenched around the tiller of the small outboard motor. G was supposed to go up to the village and acquire some food and water for the next leg of their trip, and she had been gone for longer than Ali was comfortable with. A deep unease churned her stomach. Ali wanted to put some more distance between them and the small harbor where they commandeered the boat. Their modes of transportation were constrained, considering that Matsuo's syndicate controlled most of the shipping out of Kobe. Conventional travel was out of the question; Matsuo's fingers extended into both the transit authority and law enforcement.

Ali spied G's little head bobbing over the hill. Her double braids bounced as she skipped up to the dock with several bags on one arm and a large wooden jug under the other arm.

"Fucking finally. Did you stop for a walking tour?" Ali snapped.

"Gimme a break. I had to go to a couple of places to get what we needed," G said, smiling. She wobbled as she stepped into the boat; G had the sea legs of a newborn giraffe. Ali pulled the starter cord. The motor sputtered and died, taking her hope with it. She tugged it again, and it sprang to life, reigniting her optimism. She puttered the skiff away from the dock.

The sun baked the river, drenching Ali's brow with sweat. "Did you find any sunscreen?"

"I don't think the locals use it," G smirked.

"I'll have them to thank when I fulfill my girlhood dream of growing up to be a Shar Pei," Ali mocked.

"I got you—" G whipped a wide-brimmed straw hat out of one of the bags— "this!"

Ali slapped the hat on her head and gestured toward the jug. G surrendered it with a dopey grin. What the hell had she been up to? Ali suspected she had found someone to give her some local liquor and wasted time in the village catching a buzz.

Ali took a large gulp of the liquid and coughed it back up. The syrupy taste clung to her tongue, and a putrid flavor assaulted the back of her throat.

"What the hell is that?" she croaked. "It's not fucking water."

"I got a bucket of mushroom tea from some guy at the village," G said with excitement.

"Holy hell." Ali wiped her hand across her forehead, suppressing a gag. "I am NOT drinking that." She clacked her tongue off the roof of her mouth.

"Oh, come on. Don't be a fun-sucker," G whined, pushing her lower lip out and shimmying her shoulders up and down.

"Oh, so escaping a grisly death by the skin of our teeth needs to have a fun component? Where's the water?" Ali asked sternly. G averted her eyes, fiddling with one of her braids.

"G... Where's. The. Water?"

"Tea is made with water!" G defended.

Ali twisted her wrist on the tiller and punched the throttle. The boat lurched forward, throwing G nearly out of her seat. She gave Ali a weak, guilty look, like a puppy caught chewing the fancy shoes.

Ali slowed the motor and took a deep breath. Thirst tickled her dry throat, and G tap-danced on her last nerve.

Fuck it.

Ali took a long draw off the jug.

The boat drifted a lazy serpentine path down the river. Ali lost her sense of urgency about half a jug back. She stared up into a shimmering tapestry of sunlight and clouds. Deep cerulean hues shattered into fractals that swirled and spiraled around each other in a dance of dreams. A profound peace comforted her battered heart. The river ferried her to her soul's birthplace, and the breathing trees that banked it midwifed her to the cradle of existence. The embanking palms swelled and shrank, whispering secrets of the universe for those brave enough to listen.

G's melodic ramblings composed a chaotic symphony across the fabric of consciousness for seconds, hours, possibly eons. The concept of time slipped away like water across river rocks as Ali's awareness strayed in and out of listening to her. Her mind skipped around the cosmos, leaving the worries of their frenzied flight behind. She dragged her fingertips up her arm, her skin like a dolphin's, leaving a sparkling rainbow-brick road of sensation in its wake.

G's tinkling voice took on a solemn tone, tethering Ali's awareness back to the boat.

"It's like, we all come into this world as perfect, precious babies. Then the world fucks us up. Somehow, we get tricked into doing shitty stuff and then, BOOM, we're all pieces of shit. I kind of feel like somewhere inside me, I'm still that perfect, precious baby. And like, what if that baby still deserves love and attention and all the things I want? When does that stop? At what age do our mistakes make us... irredeemable? When do we, like, age out of our worthiness? Does it happen all at once? Or is it a process?" G searched the sky's vast expanse for answers. Ali tried to wade through the tangle of her chatter, chasing the thread of meaning.

"What if we didn't lose it, though? What if we still are?" G asked, as if to the universe itself.

"Still are what?" Ali's voice sounded far away from her throat, like it echoed out of the clouds.

"Loveable. Worthy." The words throbbed and glowed.

Something in those words stilled the kaleidoscope in the sky. The trees fell silent; the voices of the universe were silenced by the shame that sharpened Ali's thoughts.

"Easy, Tiger. I think the shrooms are hitting you hard now," Ali said, apprehending the jug and bringing it back to her side of the boat. G would never understand. Ali could pinpoint the moment she aged out of her worthiness. There was no way a perfect, precious baby existed inside of her. Even under the expansive blanket of the spiraling heavens, when she became the river and the sky, she knew being a murderer made her beyond redemption.

Resolved, she set her sights down the river and fired up the motor.

"We're losing light."

G seemed not to notice the increase in speed. She sighed and lay back on the boat's edge, gazing up at the sky. Ali started a silent accounting of The Plan's next steps to get them back stateside. It wasn't much of a plan, but it was all they had at the moment to get them to safety. G, for all her charm, lacked reliability. Although G was the person she trusted most in the world, Ali didn't think she could ever fully trust her. Or anyone. Every time she trusted someone, she got hurt.

She could always trust G to fuck up, though. At least she was consistent in something.

Ali thought about how much money she would need to get them back. This trip hadn't ended up being exactly inexpensive. Before G sent out her 911, Ali was wrapping up a job that would allow her to make an offer on the off-grid cabin she lusted over. Their Japanese excursion had gnawed away at her hard-earned nest egg. Perhaps the owner would take her offer. Most of the money was intended to ensure his silence and discretion anyway.

A modest cabin sat tucked away inside enough acreage to permit the perimeter Ali preferred. Tall trees enclosed a landscape in which she hoped her soul would finally find some peace. She'd be short on the offer, but maybe she could negotiate.

Ali needed a break. Every job seemed messier than the last, and they had been wearing on her for years, weighing her down like an anchor to the depths of her own darkness. That last one would take a lot more than mushrooms and booze to wash away.

CHAPTER 4

DICKINSON

"Have you eaten lunch?" Faulkner grunted, pushing his short frame through the sturdy oak door of Dickinson's office. His wavy mane, more salt than pepper, splayed back from his receding hairline, and his trademark frown turned the corners of his skunk-striped beard down.

"No," Dickinson said, annoyed that the arrogant son of a bitch still neglected to pay her the courtesy of announcing his entrances. As the Director of Archangel Intelligence Academy, the educational branch of Archangel Directorate, she felt she was entitled to a modicum of respect, even from the distinguished Department Head of Program W.

"Good," Faulkner said.

"Why? Is there cake in the faculty lounge?" Faulkner would be the last of her colleagues to extend an invitation to lunch. He, as a habit, ate a cold slab of turkey breast on dry white bread, in the solitary privacy of his office. He enforced a strict "no visitor" policy between 13:00 and 13:30 so he could not enjoy his food in peace. Additionally, Dickinson and Faulkner had, at best, a civil professional relationship.

Dickinson respected Faulkner. His expertise as an

intelligence operative in his heyday was well-renowned across the agency, and he still served as a valued consultant for Archangel Strategic Command and assigned assets to the Advanced Recon Division. His skill as an instructor was extensive, even if Dickinson believed his students excelled predominantly out of fear.

She was also never convinced he respected her authority as a director and suspected it was due to her gender.

Faulkner ignored Dickinson's question. He barged over to her desk and flopped a file folder on top of her keyboard. She glared up at him.

"You do know everyone else knocks, right?"

The scowl she received told Dickinson he didn't give a sugar-frosted fuck what everyone else did. She opened the file folder. The words CERTIFICATE OF DEATH leered at her from the top of the document. She had encountered plenty of death certificates throughout her career. Death was part of the gig. What followed stopped her heart.

Dickinson's mouth fell open. Her blood pooled in her feet, taking all the warmth in her body with it. Freezing dread washed over her like deadly syrup, shaking her to her core.

"Is this a forgery?" she asked, raising her blurred gaze to Faulkner.

"Unfortunately, no. Darwin is dead."

An insidious heaviness seeped into Dickinson's chest. Victor Everly was the fourth former Archangel faculty or staff member to meet a gruesome end over the last three months.

"There's more." Faulkner gestured to the rest of the file. Dickinson turned the page, and her stomach turned with it. The images laid before her were so grotesque they threatened to twist her sanity into a knot. Her insides heaved, and she swallowed back the bitterness that crept up behind the back of her tongue.

"Dear God," she said, finding it difficult to look at the gruesome crime scene photos.

"Time of death indicates the twins died several hours apart, and the second one several hours before Everly. The au pair died first, but by garrote." Faulkner sounded grim, even for him. The crepey sallow skin between his eyebrows puckered. Dickinson forced herself to take a deep breath, hoping to suppress the wave of panic rising inside her.

"How were they... Who?" She struggled to string words together.

"Everly's daughter found them."

Jesus Christ.

"The agency has ordered full autopsies, but the preliminary investigation is congruent with the previous cases," Faulkner added. Realization wrapped its sticky, cold fingers around Dickinson's brain.

"The Deathstalker?" she gritted the words out.

"I hope so."

Dickinson gaped at him, appalled.

"If the alternative is that Helleborus has more than one sadistic psychopath hunting us," he said, his matter-of-fact tone offering no comfort.

Fair point.

"Do you think we're compromised?" she asked.

"There's no way to know for certain. Everly was the gold standard. He went through the program when they taught torture resistance practically. But that was before he had a family."

Everly also held the highest level of access to the entire academy as its director. Everly could give someone all of AIA. At least AIA as it existed at the point of his severance, which was still considerable. Even revealing the location would be devastating.

"Get with Fitzgerald. I want a comprehensive security diagnostic of the Keep. Every inch, every system," Dickinson ordered.

"Consider it done."

"I'm ordering level four psych evaluations for all faculty, staff, and students. We need to make sure we have no points of entry on personnel," Dickinson said, her mind racing to the next step.

"We're going psychopharmacological on the faculty?" Faulkner said, surprise sending his bushy grey eyebrows toward the shadow of a widow's peak at the top of his skull.

"Oh, do you think we should just polygraph the highly-trained liars?" Her sarcasm bit like glass. "If I'm being honest, I'd rather take the psych compound in the arm than scorpion venom. How 'bout you?"

CHAPTER 5

ALI

The door to Ali's apartment stood ajar. Splintered wood surrounded the lock meant to secure it. She pushed the door open with her boot. The curtain rod from the facing window slanted across the room, spilling the cheap curtain into a puddle on the floor. Anything that had previously been on a shelf lay broken and strewn across the carpet.

Ali entered, and the creep of panic danced up the back of her neck. A high-pitched ringing filled her ears, and her vision blurred as she trudged into the room.

Fuuuuuuuuuuuuck.

Ali shuffled through the debris toward her bedroom. Her heart slammed against her ribcage. Her mind transported her back to the apartment where she found Dominika.

Blood painted chaotic patterns across the already-stained carpet. The stench of death violated Ali's nostrils. Nika's body, dressed in Ali's dark clothes, contorted into a position that revealed the agony of her last moments. Nika's spine curled sideways over the floor. Her neck was pierced and swollen; her face unrecognizable. Ali looked into her eyes, and she could not find the girl she knew in the glassy abyss.

Dominika never deserved that.

Next to Nika's face, a face that Ali once wiped tears from, a face that now lay bloated and distorted beyond all recognition, resided a tiny red object. A shaft of morning light refracted through it, casting a small, orange pattern on the blood-speckled carpet. Ali reached out to pick it up. The miniature figurine curled into a J shape with claws on one end and a bulbous barbed tail on the other. Ali's blood cooled as she stared at the pinky-sized blown-glass scorpion.

The same feeling barreled her when she found an impeccable blown-glass octopus, covered in intricately crafted blue rings, lying next to the lifeless body of Borysko, her landlord in Prague.

By the third "gift" Ali received, a shimmering glass taipan snake, coiled in an eight upon itself, the assassin known as the Deathstalker, named after the venomous scorpion, had hit the European headlines. The espionage community buzzed with speculation over this elusive figure: a Helleborus assassin who slipped in and out of their kills with exasperating precision and skill—a ghost.

Since Nika's murder, the Deathstalker haunted Ali's steps, constantly encroaching upon her life. She felt their relentless advance, half a step behind her for ten damn years. Over the decade, she had received blown-glass lionfish, spiders, stingrays, catfish, several reptiles, and even a duck-billed platypus. All venomous creatures, most of them deadly.

Ali's thoughts swirled in clouds of despair, and she fell to her knees. Her breath abandoned her lungs. Nika was not here, nor would she ever be.

Snap yourself back to the moment, Babe. Be here now.

She assessed the room. Slashes covered the cheap sheets on the upturned mattress. The TJ Maxx art prints in plastic frames that once "adorned" the wall lay broken on the floor. Every book had been ripped from its home on her small bookshelf. Drawers of black, grey, and dark blue clothing appeared to have been launched in every conceivable direction.

Thankfully, Ali wasn't stupid enough to keep her stash inside a mattress. Or stuffed in a sock drawer. Or behind a painting. Or in a false book. Or inside the toilet...

Ali rushed to the bathroom. The toilet lid lay shattered inside the tub. Her eyes landed on the open doors to the cupboard under the sink. The $400,000 in hundreds that Ali had stacked in false maxi pad packages was gone. All the money she had saved over the last ten years doing dirty jobs for filthy people was gone. Her dream of buying an off-grid cabin in the woods, where it would be harder for Helleborus to track and kill her, was gone.

In place of her cash, a small object twinkled in the light: a blown-glass jellyfish the size of her thumbnail—another wink from the Deathstalker.

Tears stung Ali's eyes as cold devastation washed over her body. It was clear her apartment was no longer safe. Ali had nowhere to go. All she had left was the broken garbage in her apartment and the go-bag on her back.

"Double Maker's, neat. Please, Milo." Ali slumped onto a familiar wooden stool and rested her boots on the brass rail at her feet. Pain sliced into the space behind her eye.

Great. A stress migraine is precisely what I need right now.

"Shark Week again? So soon..." Milo's friendly gray eyes held concern as he slid the glass over the sticky bar. Ali lifted her eyebrows in defeat and cracked a sideways smile.

Milo would make a good operative. He had that knack, common among bartenders, for being intensely observant. Who else would remember, three years later, that you were the one who ordered a half-dirty Plymouth martini with five olives? But, then again, Milo would argue... who could forget?

The Pampered Pooch wouldn't earn any accolades for its culinary offerings or handcrafted beverages. Your choices were beer or liquor with a mixer. Still, it served as a lovely dive, far enough across town from Ali's demolished apartment. It wasn't much, but it was a little slice of home for those who never had one.

Ali occasionally tended bar for Milo between jobs. She usually didn't need the dough, but Milo let her keep her rusty employee locker in the dingy break room in the back. Right now, the couple of grand she had stashed there was the only cash she had left to her name. At least G managed to get a new passport for her when she dropped her off in Chicago.

Two tired, shabby men at one of the tables near the antique jukebox in the corner of the bar spit sunflower shells onto the grimy floor. Ali recognized the regulars, Arthur and Hank, who graced the bar with their presence every weekday from 4:10 pm until last call, and all-day Saturday. Their bleary eyes occasionally drifted toward the dusty TV that played *Logan's Run* on a silent, monotonous loop. The jukebox quietly slogged out "Friends in Low Places."

Milo knew that Ali saved bourbon for when she was in pain. Whiskey was the fastest avenue to numbness. She would order shots of Maker's Mark about once every month, like clockwork. Today, she needed something to dull the spear of pain in her brain. She shoved a greasy lock of hair out of her face. She hadn't showered since before Kobe.

With a decisive tilt of her neck, she gulped the shot back. The fiery warmth eased the cluster of despair in her chest. She took a deep breath, enjoying a moment of relief that vanished before she opened her eyes.

"And a beer back?" she pleaded.

Milo pushed the tap on a high-gravity beer with the largest glass he could find. Suds spilled over the rim of the glass and cascaded down the side. He flipped a coaster onto the bar top, salted it, and set the glass in front of Ali with the utmost care.

"What's up, buttercup? You look like something Guy Fieri shit out after three months of shooting Triple D."

A fair assessment since that's how she felt. She cracked her neck and wrapped her hand around the back of it, digging her fingertips into the base of her skull.

"You got any shifts?" She swigged a gulp of the cold beer, and the end of it hit the back of her throat, inducing a series of coughs.

"The place is popping," Milo sighed with a dry glance over at Hank and Arthur.

Ali nodded, resigned. The only hope she could find would be at the bottom of the beer she stared into. She rested her elbows on the bar and cradled her face in her hands.

Milo fixed her with a sympathetic gaze. "I could take this Tuesday off. Been working seven days straight for a few months."

Milo always worked seven days straight. He owned The Pampered Pooch.

"I'm exhausted." He drew a theatrical forearm across his head and faked a few labored breaths for Ali's sake.

"You'd give me ladies' night?" She desperately needed the cash.

Milo, if anything, was a generous soul. "You know I'm for the boys anyway."

CHAPTER 6

ALI

Ali was planted in a chair by the same two sets of strong arms that had pulled her out of the car. Even with a bag over her head, she could tell by the consistent pressure and the distinct, pungent colognes worn by both men that she was still in their grasp. Although she had spent most of the journey sedated, she surmised it had included both a private plane ride and a long drive.

Now, she found herself in a third location. Statistically, she had a bee's dick from zero chance of surviving this situation. Her head pounded from the lingering effects of the sedative and the bourbon she had consumed at The Pampered Pooch. She couldn't recall anything after being at the bar; she didn't even remember leaving.

Ali had no way of telling who held her hostage. The Yakuza? The Deathstalker? Given the levels of danger to consider between the two, she would prefer to see Matsuo on the other side of the shroud over her head. Death by venom or death by sword? Death by the sword should at least be quick. Or quick-ish. Disembowelment seemed a preferable improvement to the current cramping sensation in her stomach. Her thoughts spiraled.

Someone lifted the bag off her head, and she squinted, trying to adjust her eyes to the warm light in the room. Was it morning? Afternoon?

A walnut Hermle grandfather clock ticked away from the center of the opposing wall, activating a spasm at the top of her cheek with each soft click. Leather-bound books filled ornate varnished wooden bookshelves that ringed three walls of the room. The office smelled faintly of grass and vanilla, reminiscent of old books, combined with the fragrance of wood polish and leather, like so many libraries Ali had used as havens over the years. She equated the scent with safety, but she felt as safe as a knife's edge. All those smells mixed with the aroma of the freshly brewed cup of coffee that sat steaming atop the tooled leather surface of an antique mahogany partner's desk.

Ali was neither greeted by Akio Matsuo nor any of his lieutenants. Instead, seated at the desk was a well-dressed, handsome middle-aged woman. She appeared stern and accomplished, but the look in her eyes conveyed curiosity rather than hostility.

The woman stood tall and stately, wearing a Chanel skirt suit and costly makeup. Her glowing, cool beige skin wrinkled in places, indicating she may have once been a young woman who smiled. Her warm, dark blonde hair swirled into smooth, regimented sections, forming a gracefully precise chignon. Everything about her exuded power and sophistication. As she rounded the desk slowly and deliberately, Ali clocked a small knife in her hand.

"I can assume by the scant details in your dossier that the name atop it is no more than a current alias." The woman's rounded voice resonated with a choral depth, anchoring authority into every syllable. "And, as you won't be learning *my* real name, I figure that's a good place to start. I'm Dickinson, Director of Archangel Intelligence Academy."

AIA? How had Ali eluded the clutches of Helleborus for ten years, only to end up in the hands of the academic branch of its biggest competitor? Did they know what she was? How did she let this happen? She had no idea they had been tracking her.

Dickinson approached Ali, and a crisp shaft of crepuscular light infiltrated the window, reflecting off the blade. Ali tried to remain still, but every muscle in her body activated. She searched the room for a means of escape.

Dickinson bent down toward Ali and grabbed her hands, slicing the oversized zip ties that bound her wrists.

What?

"Congratulations. Your application has been accepted. I would like to welcome you officially to Archangel. This is Beverstone Keep, your new home."

CHAPTER 7

WILDE

Ali left the Director's sumptuous office with her scant belongings, a heavy dose of confusion, and a new identity.

"You'll go by codename Wilde now. The Program W wing is out into the hall and to the right," the Director had said. Ali couldn't believe she was still alive. Trying to appear casual, she slung her backpack over tight shoulders.

A polished marble hallway stretched out before her. Geometric black-and-white parallelograms wove their way across the glossy floor. Sunlight sent prisms through the graphic panels of stained glass, painting warm, rainbow patterns on the cool, white walls. Crystal chandeliers cascaded light over a masterwork of neoclassical architecture.

No shadows to hide in—only bright naked exposure everywhere.

The corridor bustled with people who looked like they both wanted to and expected to be there. Ali's gaze darted around, searching for an escape in this seemingly endless labyrinth of polished stone and grandeur. She needed to find a way out; she couldn't stay here.

A small body crashed into her, and tiny arms wrapped

around her waist. Ali's muscles activated in defense.

"You made it!" G gushed, nuzzling her face into Ali's chest. Ali pushed her back to arm's length. It was G, for sure. This wasn't some twisted hallucination.

Ali grasped her by the upper arm and dragged her around a corner.

"What the fuck?" Ali whispered. "What are you doing here?"

"I got accepted!" G beamed with pride.

"Of course, *you* got accepted. What the fuck am *I* doing here?" Ali demanded. The walls of the castle advanced around her like a thousand boa constrictors.

"You got accepted, too..." G's excitement faltered, dampened by the darkness in Ali's eyes.

"Accepted?" Ali squeezed G's arm. "I never applied."

G winced under Ali's fierce grasp.

"Well, *you* didn't..." G mumbled, her voice weakening. "But *I* may have on behalf of your new alias." Mischief sparkled in her eyes, a glint of defiance.

"Tell me you didn't... How?" Ali pressed, gripping G's arm harder.

"I forged some sexy merc credentials and military referrals on the Dark Web. It was like taking money from a well-funded militarized baby," G said, looking to Ali for approval.

"Why the fuck would you do that? Do you have any idea what this place is?" Panic bear-crawled up Ali's throat. She had no clue how she would get them out of this.

"You said we needed a fortress." G gestured around to the general area with her free arm, her enthusiasm standing in stark contrast with Ali's dread. Her shoulders drooped in disappointment at the lack of excitement on Ali's face.

A fortress? More like a prison.

Ali couldn't shake the fear of what would happen if Archangel ever discovered the truth about her.

G intercepted the worried look on Ali's face.

"Hey, best hacker alive?" G said, pleading for reassurance.

I'll be lucky if I can keep both of us alive in this nightmare.

"Well, can you hack our way out? How do we leave?" Ali asked, desperation creeping into her voice.

"Oh, there's no leaving. This compound is on like a bazillion acres and locked down like a motherfucker. No one's getting us in here," G chirped. Ali's heart sank. She didn't even know what state they were in. There was no guarantee they were even in the States.

"At least let me show you around," G whined, tugging Ali out of the corner with both hands. Ali allowed herself to be dragged into the hallway with reluctance. Every step felt like a layer of her skin peeled off, exposing her like muscles and sinew at *Bodies: The Exhibition.*

She knew how happy it made G to showcase her knowledge. There was no stopping her when she was in tour-guide mode.

Fucking fine. What do we have to lose? My fucking life. I'm fucked anyway.

"This is Beverstone Keep. The cybersecurity here is the Gibson! It fucking slays."

Great. I'm trapped in a high-security facility that's more secure than Fort fucking Knox. Slay...

"We're in the central hub of the Keep, where all the academic activities take place. Here, you'll find all the offices, lecture halls, laboratories, the library, and the infirmary," G said, looking to Ali for interest. Ali begrudgingly indulged her and attempted a look of attentiveness.

"Four wings extend from the hub, each designated for one

of the four programs of study inside Archangel," G continued. "What codename did they give you?"

"Wilde."

"Wicked! You're in Program W. Think of it like Hogwarts for spies. Except full of truly terrifying adults." G popped her eyebrows up for effect.

Ali felt a groan rising inside her. She never delved into wizard stories when she was younger. She didn't think the Archangel faculty would appreciate their selectively honed programs being compared to a mystical children's universe. But G's enthusiasm was infectious, so Ali tried to stay engaged despite her discomfort.

"Every cadet is designated to their program with a codename based on an author's name. From what I can tell, the names get recycled as assets move in and out of the programs. You're likely not the first, nor the last, Wilde," G said. At least Ali was learning. G, as aggravating as she could be, excelled at gathering intel.

"Your codename is Wilde because you're part of Program W. The Powers-That-Be don't come out and say what the letters stand for, but all the assets know what they mean. Program W is Weapons and Warfare. Classic mercenaries. Combat nerds. Bang and burn specialists," G continued.

She guided Ali through the disorienting corridor. Panic intensified in Ali's chest.

"I'm Capote now," G said, flipping her collar up with pride. "I'm in Program C: Cybersecurity and Cyber-warfare. It's where most of the cobblers go."

That tracked, considering G had been forging papers since she could use a computer. Ali attempted to push an expression of excitement out through her overwhelming anxiety.

"There's Program H, for honey trap. They're the hotties. You'll find all the sparrows and ravens there. Your roommate is in H," G said.

Roommate? Fuck me.

"Then, there's Program K, for—"G dropped into a whisper—"killers."

Ali still grappled for her bearings. They roamed multiple halls of wood and marble, all of which gave Ali the impression that she was being led deeper into a maze.

"They're the wet work specialists—stone cold assassins. At least, that's what they're supposed to be when they get assigned. Most of them give me the major heebies," G said, so eager to celebrate their entrance into what she thought was their salvation.

If her resume had been accurate, Ali probably would have been sorted into Program K. She was, after all, already a killer. She had been trained to be one since birth. Bloody memories poured into her mind, mementos of an existence of violence and survival. Her thoughts darkened, and her whole life's shame spiraled into her thoughts.

What the fuck did you get us into, G?

CHAPTER 8

WILDE

Third door down the fourth hallway.

Ali was mildly sure this was it. She rolled her shoulders back and cracked her neck to the side. She had been in plenty of hairier situations before. A big oak door with an entire mystery behind it? This was nothing, right?

Wilde balled her fist and knocked twice on the door, maybe a little aggressively, but it wasn't like Ali—or Wilde— had spent most of her life knocking on doors. Slipping in and out of them, sure. But knocking? No. She chewed her upper lip and glanced over her shoulder. It was just a castle filled with some of the most dangerous assets of her generation. No big. And she had to share a room with one of them. Unease settled into her bones.

Silence.

Wilde forced a breath. She rapped her knuckles on the door, a little louder this time, tugging on one of the straps of her backpack.

The door swung open.

Nothing could have prepared Wilde for what met her.

Wide-set almond eyes struck her, as the scent of gardenia

wafted from three feet of ginger waves that swept into the doorway like a living waterfall. A warmth spread over Wilde. Beckoning her was an enchantress who seemed as if she had been plucked out of time. A delicate button nose perched cozily between broad, pink, winsome cheeks. A tiny rosebud of a mouth sat beneath. It was as if all her features were fairy-sized confections on a vast canvas of perfect skin, peppered with freckles that cascaded across her face and chest like stardust. She possessed the face of a 1920s starlet stacked on a Jessica Rabbit body.

"Are you Wilde?" she breathed, like music carried on a breeze.

"Um, yeah," Wilde replied reluctantly.

"I'm Hemingway. It's a pleasure to meet you," the starlet said. Hemingway grasped Wilde's arm in both of her warm, tender hands and pulled her into the room.

The pleasure is all mine.

Gaslamp-style sconces and candlelight cast a tranquil glow throughout the room. Two mahogany canopied beds bookended the space, flanked by identical mahogany kneehole desks. Sage and ivory botanical-patterned jacquard drapes swept up to copper coffered ceilings. A varnished oak sideboard sat proudly between two long windows, allowing slivers of light to twinkle in.

The extravagance of the chamber bore a resemblance to some of the halls Wilde spent her late childhood in, mercifully absent of the agony screamed into the wallpaper.

Wilde took careful steps across the shiny wood-paneled floor, doing her level best to avoid tracking boot dirt across the buffed surface. An inviting fire crackled in the hearth. Wilde always felt grounded by a fire. In a way, Hemingway felt like that comforting flame, the essence of safety and serenity personified. Everything about her disarmed Wilde.

I guess that's how Program H does it.

"Program W, right?" Hemingway said.

"Apart from the codename, what gave me away?"

"Well, I don't know. The Jason Bourne backpack. And your clothes have such a... chic... 'lived-in' look." The perfect little bulb at the tip of Hemingway's nose scrunched in a teasing grimace.

Wilde shrank inside her skin. Her clothes served a specific purpose. But in this extravagant fairy's bower, insecurity crawled over her body like a shadow.

A mischievous look overtook Hemingway's face.

"Your little friend already filled me in when she dropped off your wardrobe," Hemingway said. Wilde could only assume she was referring to G.

"My wardrobe?"

Hemingway unleashed her whole smile, watering a bud of hope in Wilde's chest. She intertwined her delicate fingers with Wilde's and led her deeper into the suite.

"She was downright giddy when she dropped it off. When I told her I didn't have pink hangers, she showed up a few hours later with some. They're padded satin," Hemingway added with an impressed grin. "Honestly, you are *not* what I expected."

Hemingway guided Wilde to a walk-in closet filled with her worst nightmares. Pastel tartan miniskirts lined an entire wall. Cropped Angora sweaters hung above the skirts like layers of clouds. Cable-knit stockings in cozy patterns and textures filled artfully organized drawers. And of course, G had stocked several capsules to the brim with all the lingerie Wilde would never wear for her. This was the sexiest "Fuck You" wardrobe Wilde had ever seen.

Wilde's eyes scanned downward. G had also populated the collection with an epic selection of shoes: Louboutin, Manolo, Weitzman, McQueen. Most of these shoes cost several grand a pop.

"*Best hacker alive.*" G's words reverberated in her head.

I should invoice G for Kobe. Looks like she can afford it.

Wilde huffed a breath through her nostrils, thinking back to her wrecked apartment—all that money... gone.

G's gonna be stuffed satin when I get my hands on her.

Wilde surveyed the wardrobe, forcing a deep, steadying breath.

"Fashion show?" Hemingway offered, bouncing on the balls of her feet. A resigned sigh emptied Wilde's lungs.

Why did she have to dress me like a slutty Muppet?

CHAPTER 9

WOOLF

"Whitman has your key. He has left for the Outer Grounds today."

That was all the note on the door said. Woolf tried to push in. No luck. His body ached from the long journey to Archangel. They must have preferred their cadets completely spent on their first day, given the rigmarole it took to reach Beverstone Keep.

After five tours in the Army and some off-the-books jobs, he grappled with the awkwardness of civilian life. Archangel was a far cry from civilian activity, but this castle was a stark departure from the environments he had become accustomed to.

Follow the omens. Follow orders.

He hefted his pack over his shoulder, and trudged forward.

Slow is smooth, and smooth is fast.

He ignored the weakness in his legs, marching away from the room that was so close to salvation he could almost feel the soft pillow that awaited him.

The hallways extended with no conceivable end, making

it hard to gain his bearings. He followed the cascading light through the archways, thankful that he could at least navigate by the daylight until it receded.

Eventually, he found an archway that led to an expanse of grass. Hopefully, this was "The Grounds." So, maybe he could find his way to the "Outer Grounds."

Tall cypress trees stood sentinel along a grassy pathway. Large, irregular slabs of stone marked a pattern along the path. Dark clouds stirred above, and a slice of biting wind nipped at the cuffs of his shirt sleeves, sending an unwelcome shiver spiraling down his spine.

As dusk descended on the grounds, Woolf found himself out of breath from the hike, despite his considerable level of conditioning. He came upon a man.

The wind whipped the collar of the man's charcoal pea coat, which was pulled up as a shield. Dark curls swirled around his forehead, yet he remained still as a statue, staring at a distant point in the sky that Woolf's eyes couldn't follow. Nightfall encroached, and a battalion of dark clouds advanced across the sky. Still, the man in the wool coat gave Woolf no regard. His gaze into the darkening dusk endured, betraying no urgency.

Woolf, wearied from the wind and walk, plopped his pack onto the damp grass. He squinted his eyes against the relentless gusts that threatened to make his eyes water.

"Are you Whitman?" Woolf demanded through his exhaustion.

"I am." Whitman's minimal reply suggested Woolf's entire existence barely registered in his world.

Whitman's stare never diverted from some point in the gathering darkness.

What the fuck?

"The note said you have the key to my room," Woolf pressed, on the verge of losing his composure.

Whitman's eyes remained fixed on the sky.

"I *had* your key," he said, his tone as indifferent as the wind. "Now, Pattycake has it."

"Who the hell is Pattycake?" Woolf's frustration bubbled over. He was so exhausted at this point that he might just kill someone for a cot to sleep in.

Whitman whistled through his teeth, the piercing, high-pitched tone carrying over the howling wind as night fell. He offered a leather-gloved arm into the air.

A cloak of feathers and talons encircled Woolf's face, and he threw his hands up to defend himself. When he dared to lower them, he found a speckled white gyrfalcon landing with impeccable grace on Whitman's arm. She flapped a regal wing and dropped a key on the grass. Woolf marveled at the raptor, a creature of such impressive power and beauty.

Whitman fed Pattycake a treat, which she eagerly pecked at and swallowed. She nipped at his neckline, snagging the scarf that warmed his neck.

"Pats, baby, this is Tom Ford. We've talked about this," Whitman scolded, rolling his eyes. Woolf found it strange that Whitman spoke to the bird as if it understood English or had any idea who Tom Ford was. Woolf didn't know who the fuck Tom Ford was. How would a freaking bird know?

The bird nuzzled her head against the side of Whitman's face. He accepted the affection and stroked her along her back. In a swift motion, he raised his arm into the night. Pattycake took flight, her silhouette cutting through the dim twilight. Whitman watched until her wings disappeared, and a small smile spread over his lips.

CHAPTER 10

WILDE

"How are you today, Wilde?" Professor Frost said as she entered the room. A radiant smile accompanied her calm, soothing voice. Adjusting her cat-eye spectacles, she observed Wilde from behind winged eyeliner sharper than a scalpel. She smoothed a manicured hand across the side of her perfectly coiffed auburn French twist.

Wilde's eyes fell to the leather cuffs binding her wrists and ankles to the white, vinyl-upholstered dental chair. She sat in a stark, white cell with pyramid-shaped foam on the walls, so quiet that her desperate thoughts echoed. She struggled to calm the hellfire licking its way up her spine. There was no way to predict what the psych compound would bring out of her. If Archangel discovered her true identity or origin, a terrifying array of consequences would await her.

"Living the dream," Wilde said, meeting Frost's gaze and attempting a self-assured bravado far more confident than she felt. Nightmares are dreams, after all.

Of all the instructors at Archangel, Frost was reputed to be an absolute pussycat. Cadets breezed through her courses, bolstered by her renowned kindness and leniency. She served as Department Head of Program H, but it was an open secret that she graduated from Program K.

Beneath the surface of Frost's warm demeanor, Wilde clocked the calculated cadence of Neuro-Linguistic Programming and skilled hypnosis. She resisted the siren's song of Frost's weapon-grade charisma.

"Let's get started," Frost said, smoothing the front of her mauve pencil skirt with consummate grace as she took a seat.

Frost swabbed Wilde's forearm with an alcohol wipe. She lifted a syringe off the metal tray that sat on a small aluminum rolling table next to Wilde's chair. Wilde averted her eyes; needles were not exactly her favorite. She glanced back as Frost placed a round adhesive bandage adorned with a yellow smiley face on the injection site. Frost had injected Wilde with such precision that she barely detected the prick of the needle. She gave Wilde's arm a delicate pat on top of the bandage and smiled.

Wilde's vision blurred. Her head swayed as she struggled to retain consciousness. Her chest felt too heavy to take a breath, and blackness crept around her vision, circling until all light vanished.

Silence.

"Take me back to the beginning," Frost said, her voice fading away from Wilde with each syllable, as if it were echoing across a vast canyon. Ice slithered into Wilde's veins, and a wave of comfort washed over her body—maybe too much comfort. It felt like a cool, heavy blanket, like she could wrap herself up in a little burrito—a blissful burrito free from pain. Forever.

Fight it.

Wilde battled to keep her wits.

Wake up!

Wilde took a deep breath.

The breath reeked of beef stroganoff and vodka. The weight of Vasily's body bore down on her, anchoring her to the bed. His whistling breaths wheezed in and out, each one a labor. A bead of sweat dripped off his forehead into her eye.

He's done. Thank god.

Fourteen-year-old Wilde stared up at the ceiling. At this point, she was an expert at leaving her body behind while Vasily indulged his desires. Nevertheless, every one of these nights weighed heavier on her soul.

This was her mission: infiltrate the family. But Vasily had penetrated her very being. For four years, he had summoned her to his bed. For four years, she fulfilled her duty, not to him, to Helleborus.

With a grunt, Vasily rolled his clammy body off her.

"Where's Nika?" he rasped, his hot, fetid breath rushing across her skin like a blast from an oven. "I'm tired of you."

Vasily's daughter, Dominika, had recently turned the exact tender age Wilde was when she first arrived at their manor. Not a month passed before Vasily revealed to her his very particular tastes.

As Vasily heaved his mass toward the edge of the mattress, Wilde's thoughts spiraled about Dominika in her bed, pure and unprotected. Grief shook her ribcage as she struggled to suppress cries for her defiled childhood. She would NOT let this happen to Dominika.

"Stay," Wilde said, trying to entice Vasily.

Vasily, drenched in alcohol and perspiration, was not enticed. He grumbled and stumbled out of bed toward the door. Wilde slipped a pen knife out of the bedside table and hid it under a silk-covered pillow.

"Pretty please," she said, throwing her nightgown up and pushing her bottom toward him.

It worked. Vasily's eyes filled with lust. He grasped Wilde mercilessly and pushed her down onto the bed. His stinky breath invaded her nostrils, and his weight returned, pinning her down. Rage coursed through every cell in her body, but she held it back.

Wilde slid the knife surgically into the artery in his neck, and warm blood smothered her hand. She struck with such precision that it took him a few moments before he realized his life had started to drain from his body. He coughed and sputtered. His mouth gaped open in words he would never be able to speak, and his eyes widened with the impossibility of her betrayal.

Wilde pushed his heavy body off her and extracted the knife from his neck. Vasily's blood squirted out of the incision, spraying crimson patterns across her face, covering her in scarlet vengeance. Vasily reached for her. She expected his eyes to darken as life left them, but his eyes were wide open for the first time, filled with the horror of facing his sins. As the final traces of life departed his body, his bulging eyes stared into a void no one living could see.

A gasp came from the doorway. Her older brother, Pasha, stood there in stunned silence. Wilde couldn't imagine what she looked like; her blood-soaked nightdress stuck to her body, and her hand still grasped the knife. Kneeling over Vasily's lifeless body was Pasha's baby sister, the murderer. The horror on his face revealed everything she would ever need to know. She was a monster.

CHAPTER 11

WILDE

Wilde's fist trembled around the lollipop Frost had given her.

A fucking lollipop? After that? You just raped my fucking brain, you sadist.

When Wilde had finally cracked her eyes open, Frost scrutinized her with a mixture of curiosity, confusion, and sympathy. No, not sympathy. Pity. Rage roiled inside Wilde's belly. This well-dressed woman with her soft voice had needled her way into Wilde's darkest place. She felt utterly violated.

Frost had gently clasped Wilde's shoulders and ushered her into a standing position. Then she handed Wilde a lollipop, dared to smile, and thanked her for her cooperation before unceremoniously depositing her into a bustling hallway.

The bodies congesting the corridor suffocated her.

Wilde wanted to crawl out of her skin. Her experience inside the cell with Frost shook her to her soul. Even as the psych compound wore off, she could still smell Vasily's meat sweats. His blood flowed over her skin. Its tannic taste still lingered in the recesses of her mouth.

She wanted to vomit. She needed to cauterize that

memory from her mind forever, purging Vasily from her existence. After a decade of repression, all it took was a little shot and some soft words from Frost to put her right back in Vasily's bed, reliving the shame she had tried to drown.

Memories from after the murder flooded her mind: Pasha panicked at the sight of Vasily's corpse, explaining he had just received their directive to kill Dominika. Wilde knocked her older brother unconscious, woke Nika from a dead slumber, and escaped with her into the woods surrounding the estate.

And the cold. It was so cold.

The memories overwhelmed her. Wilde needed to hit something, or shoot something, or drink something, or even fuck something—anything to make this wretched cocktail of feelings disappear.

She backed into someone.

"Whoa, slow down, Babygirl," rumbled a voice from behind her. Wilde spun around to find that the voice belonged to a tall, hard-bodied creature of the night. Straight, short, glossy black hair overshadowed their brow. Tattoos of sigils and runes etched unknown stories into the shaved sides of their head. Coal-black lashes framed fierce blue eyes that oversaw an angular, narrow nose and a voluptuous mouth that suggested Israeli origins. But those wide eyes indicated they were also something else.

Beside the dark figure stood another gorgeous vision clad in black. Bleach-blonde coils sprouted from her head like an ethereal halo, contrasting with her ebony skin that glowed like a diamond. She wore a toothy Cheshire Cat smile that hinted she was like a cupcake with barbed-wire frosting.

These two had Program K written all over them. You wouldn't want to find yourself in a dark room with either of them, not if there was even a slight stretch of piano wire within reach.

Wilde had escaped Vasily's bed only to tumble into the laps of two strikingly stunning killers. Fresh panic stole the rest of her breath.

"I am so sorry," she panted. "I should've watched where I was going."

"Lucky for you, I don't take offense to beautiful women crashing into me," the towering one said, holding Wilde at arm's length with a grip so firm yet gentle that she felt simultaneously vulnerable and tethered. "Are you—"they assessed her—"okay?"

Barbed-Wire Cupcake tiptoed long, polished black nails up Wilde's arm and face, booping her nose. "She's on vibrate mode," she said, her voice dreamy and high-pitched like that of a child's ghost. Wilde fought the urge to recoil from the casual breach of her personal space.

Blondie's keen eyes fell to the lollipop quaking in Wilde's grasp. She squeaked a drooping puppy whine, nudging a sharp elbow into the big blue-eyed one's side, beckoning their gaze down to follow hers.

Sympathy colored the intense azure eyes fixated on Wilde's. "First time with Frost?" Blue Eyes squeezed her shoulders.

Wilde bobbed her head, allowing their unshakable grasp to steady her dizziness.

"I'm Koontz. This is King," the tall one said.

The vivacious blonde popped a grin and wiggled a dainty wave at Wilde.

"I'm Wilde." Ragged breaths returned to her lungs.

A quizzical expression flickered across Koontz's stony yet soft face. "Hmm. They usually put knockouts like you in H."

"Pretty little baby," King chimed, dragging a fingertip

down Wilde's arm. Wilde could tell she was fifty pounds of chaos in a five-pound bag.

"Bring it in, Babygirl. Let me squeeze some of those chihuahua shakes away." Before Wilde could react, strong, shapely arms enveloped her, leaving no hope for escape. She tensed.

Their embrace felt placid and assertive, like a tranquil mountain, remaining still until their steady frame eased Wilde's heartbeat.

No knife in the back. No strangulation. Wilde didn't know if she should feel comforted, creeped out, or turned on.

Koontz broke the hug and set Wilde steady on her feet.

"She smells like an angel," they mouthed at King, rolling their eyes back in playful exaggeration. "You know how much I love eating angel cake." Wilde couldn't tell if they meant cunnilingus or cannibalism.

King rolled her chest toward Wilde, taking a long, sweeping sniff. She hummed in approval.

"Come on, hon. Let's get you a stiff drink." She curled a finger on the underside of Wilde's chin, sending a shiver down her chest. That drink sounded like it might be a Roofie Colada, or perhaps a refreshing Mai Tai-you-up-and-steal-your-kidney.

"We have lecture," Koontz said in a flat tone.

King's shoulders sagged with a huff. "Play hooky?" she whined, eyes sparkling with mischief.

"Faulkner's subbing for Frost." Koontz's eyes dulled to the grey-blue hue of a rippling winter creek.

Frost clearly had a rigorous schedule of ripping people's brains apart. Unease invaded Wilde's shoulders once more, and she caught the scent of beef stroganoff in the air.

King pushed her lower lip out and stomped a boot on the tile.

"Rotten luck, darling," she said in a mock posh British accent, tapping Wilde's cheek. "You still need to blow off some steam. Can't leave all those little ickies inside." She wriggled a pointy nail at Wilde's chest.

The wicked little sprite was correct. Cortisol flooded Wilde's system, a wildfire desperate for quenching.

"Does this place have a firing range?" Wilde longed for the happiness of a warm gun.

"We can take you there. It's on our way." Koontz notched their thumbs into their belt loops and tilted their head, fixing Wilde with a tantalizing smile. Was this Program K's version of flirting, or had she just signed onto something she couldn't afford?

"Meet back up for happy hour after?" King said, her nails digging into Wilde's palm as she wrenched her pinky finger around Wilde's. "Pinky promise."

Wilde gave a tentative nod, fearful that breaking a pinky promise with this one might come with a deadly consequence.

Satisfied with the sacred girlish oath, King pointed at the lollipop. "Are you gonna eat that?"

Wilde arrived at the range and checked out a Serbu BFG-50 semi-automatic rifle. If she planned to shoot a pain this big away, she'd need a big ass gun. She hoped a .50 caliber would suffice in the absence of an RPG launcher. She headed out to the long range, where there was only one other shooter.

The sun shone high in the sky, and a light breeze wafted through the bulletproof glass stalls. Not the worst shooting conditions to lose oneself in.

Wilde's shoulders softened, the electricity in her limbs dissipating. She knew she needed to steady her trembling hands if she had any chance of hitting the broad side of a barn. The earmuffs blocked out the sounds of the range and some of her intrusive thoughts. She drew a deep breath and allowed the focus of an objective to clear her mind.

Wilde chose a stall and set the integral bipod of the rifle on the ground. She lay down on her belly and settled in. Nestling the stock close to her shoulder, she wrapped her fingers around the underside of the firearm, grasping the pistol grip with her other hand, and sliding her finger in front of the trigger. A sense of ease spread over her body. Gazing through the scope, she took a deep belly breath, exhaled, and squeezed the trigger.

The recoil reverberated through her small frame like a warm hug, softening her body. She always knew what to expect from a gun. Maybe, here on the range, she could shoot Vasily out of her thoughts.

"Fuck. Nice shot," came a voice from a few stalls away. Wilde glanced over; the other shooter's eyes remained focused downrange. She peered down her scope at her target. It was a kill shot.

"Thanks," she said back. Wilde took a closer look at the other shooter. He was shooting the Barrett—a solid choice. Judging by the Army-green t-shirt that showcased his granite-like biceps, he was probably former military. Wilde also clocked the perfectly formed ass filling out his tactical cargo pants. The Casio G-Shock watch wrapped around his wrist added to the Special Forces vibe. He fired off a round, and his solid frame hardly budged—the mark of a seasoned shooter. She squinted through her scope toward his target.

Not a bad shot yourself, there, soldier.

They exchanged shots, some of which were impressive, while others were less so. They volleyed casual compliments and expressions of disappointment. Mostly, they shared the silence between the shots, creating an unspoken understanding wrapped in the rhythm of their shooting.

There were no expectations, just a bit of friendly competition and quiet camaraderie. The experience soothed Wilde's restless heart. As the ammo dwindled, so did their conversation.

Wilde's gaze strayed from her target when the other shooter fired. She found herself captivated by the intensity in his piercing green eyes, how his copper skin crinkled around his dominant eye as he zeroed in for a shot, and how his full lips pursed during the crucial moment he exhaled and squeezed the trigger. The distraction was delicious, and for those effortless moments, everything beyond the range faded into the background.

CHAPTER 12

WILDE

Wilde rotated back and forth in front of the mirror. A skirt had not graced her figure in ten years. The pink Angora sweater clashed with her dark hair, a color her brother lovingly referred to as "librarian brown." Her shoulders slumped, and she wrapped her arms around the sliver of midriff exposed by the cardigan. She felt ridiculous.

Hemingway snapped Wilde's shoulders back. Wilde instinctively straightened her spine, a residual reflex from childhood ballet lessons.

"You know the difference between you and a spider?" Hemingway tilted her head to the side and appraised Wilde in the mirror. "A spider has *eight* hairy legs. You should think about shaving those babies sometime this century," she teased, giggling at the scowl Wilde shot her way.

Hemingway's wholesome warmth belied all the taunting she used to encourage Wilde to embrace this new look. Her eyes sparkled with delight when she saw the outfit, making it difficult for Wilde not to share in her joy. Since Wilde's arrival, Hemingway had shown her nothing but compassion and acceptance. The thought of disappointing her felt unbearable.

Eliza Begrave

Wilde had to admit she liked the way her legs looked in the skirt. She had never taken the time to consider them, or any other part of herself, for that matter. Mirrors were not something she had previously concerned herself with. Her legs, while not smooth to Hemingway's standards and pale from a decade of jeans, were shapely and well-toned. They matched the rest of her body: taut, lean, and athletic, thanks to years of training, fighting, and fleeing.

As Wilde inspected her reflection, she realized she was no longer a girl, despite being dressed like one. Her round face still carried youthful cheeks that flushed too readily at times, standing in stark contrast to the blue grooves carved under her eyes. She was certain Hemingway's makeup skills could help with that one. A little more sleep wouldn't kill her either.

Where was the harm in trying something new? Who would she be hurting if she embraced this new identity of Wilde? She needed to blend in anyway. She didn't want the wrong kind of attention from Archangel's Powers-That-Be. If they unearthed her past, she'd be proper-fucked. It served her best interests to make some new friends, though the thought of that made her stomach spasm.

She had crossed paths with few people since her arrival. Koontz and King had befriended, targeted, or adopted her; she wasn't sure which just yet. At least her range buddy was easy on the eyes and soothing to the nerves.

And then there was darling Hemingway. Thank the gods for Hemingway.

Wilde narrowed her gaze into the mirror. Who was Wilde? She began to explore the idea of actively crafting the person she wanted to be, instead of simply being who she needed to be. After years of operating in survival mode, Wilde had no idea where to find her true interests. She knew what she excelled at, but not what she liked.

Did she resist this new look simply because it was so foreign to her? When she thought about it, the sweater felt soft and warm against her skin. The skirt offered a sense of freedom intertwined with a hint of unfamiliar innocence. Could she recapture some of what she had lost here?

Wilde felt a little silly, but also a little sexy. Why should she care what anyone else thought about the look? The only person she knew from outside was G, and she couldn't wait to see her reaction. The outfit was such a departure from any of Wilde's previous aliases that it might benefit her.

No one had any expectations of her here, which felt liberating. She could choose how to enter this new world and any new relationships that might arise. An exhilarating sense of possibility blossomed inside her.

She could be whoever she wanted to be.

Hemingway tugged a lock of Wilde's drab hair out of her messy bun and manipulated it in angles around her cheeks, accentuating the shadows in Wilde's face.

Hem gazed at Wilde's reflection, her lips pursing in thought.

"Have you ever considered going blonde?"

CHAPTER 13

WHITMAN

"Open Mat, Baby! You ready to pound some ass?" Wells said, cracking his tattooed knuckles.

"As always, your word choice is beyond compare," Whitman said, pulling the grape-flavored sucker out of his mouth. He reclined on the broad bench that spanned the side of the gymnasium, propped up on his elbows with one knee raised. He knew Wells looked forward to this day all year.

Open Mat Practice sounded benign enough, but the upper-level assets knew better. This brutal rite of passage occurred every Orientation Week. It served as an aptitude test: Program W tryouts, where each new student would be classified into one of several specialized subprograms based on their skills. This gym session would determine an incoming asset's journey for the next one to four years. It was an opportunity for the first years to figure out their pecking order, and for the more advanced cadets to pummel some grit into the newbies.

Open Mat was the recruits' first sponsored ass-kicking, a time-honored initiation to a physically and mentally grueling program.

The format was simple: the faculty and upper-level assets ran the new cadets through a series of hand-to-hand combat circuits, each focusing on a different challenge, weapon, or discipline. Generations of elite spies designed each circuit to test the strength, agility, and mental fortitude of each incoming asset.

"Whitman," Faulkner said with a warning in his voice. Whitman missed him walking in. "I shouldn't need to remind you there's no food permitted in the gym."

"I guarantee this doesn't qualify as food. It is completely devoid of nutrition." Whitman threw a charming smile at Faulkner, who narrowed his eyes, unimpressed. With a dramatic sigh, Whitman took one last suck and whipped the sucker into a nearby wastebasket.

"Seeing as how it's only your second year as an instructor, don't you think it behooves you to at least warm up?" Faulkner questioned dryly, sizing Whitman up over his spectacles.

"The first ten cadets *are* the warm-up," Whitman said, interlocking his fingers and drawing his hands behind his head on the bench.

Faulkner regarded him with mild disappointment and marched over to the faculty contingent of the instructors.

"How do you get away with that? Most people are scared shitless of him," Wells said, bouncing on the balls of his feet and shaking his arms out.

"Fear is no fun. Anyway, if he pulls me from Open Mat, who's gonna do blades?" No one in Program W rivaled Whitman's expertise with knives.

"I could do knife defense," Wells said confidently.

"And give up the privilege of choking all the rookies?" Whitman countered.

Wells considered it for a moment. "Nah, you're right."

"That's a nasty habit of mine," Whitman said with a sly grin.

"You know what else I love..." Wells attempted to lead Whitman with a cocked eyebrow.

"Videos of people being tased?"

"Well, yeah. But that's not what I'm talking about."

"When Faulkner wears a bowtie?"

Wells choked on a laugh. "You know—the *thing*. Do the thing," he urged, incapable of containing his excitement.

"Not this year. I'm not in the mood." Whitman hoped this Open Mat wouldn't be a repeat of last year's snooze fest. It wasn't fun when it wasn't a challenge.

"Come on, man. Just a couple." Wells kicked Whitman's shoe. Whitman glared at Wells, who grinned at him like a dope, raising his eyebrows repeatedly.

"Fine," Whitman relented with a groan, smoothing the front of his black Gucci joggers as he shifted to a seated position to get a better view of the crop of quivering recruits.

"Mat One..." Whitman analyzed the two combatants for several moments. "Green Shirt is Jiu Jitsu—a Gracie school. She's not bad either. Her opponent? Muay Thai. Shitty Muay Thai." Right as the words left his lips, the opponent threw a failed low kick, and Green Shirt grabbed him, coiling around him like a boa constrictor, and trapping him in an armbar inside ten seconds. Wells' smile grew broader as he shook out his ankles.

Wells believed Whitman possessed some supernatural ability to detect a cadet's martial arts background at a glance. The reality was far less glamorous. After a devastating loss at his first Open Mat landed him in the infirmary, Whitman spent his recovery time immersed in books and videos of every fighting style he could find. As soon as he could travel on crutches, he spent his days in the gym watching other assets train. After he persuaded the physical therapist to clear him, he fought every person he thought he could learn from.

"Mat Two... Boxer on the right. The left? Shaolin Kung Fu. He's going to be fun." Whitman leaned over his knees to catch a closer look. "The boxer's fucked. He's just too cocky to know it yet."

"What about that guy?" Wells nodded toward a tall, heavily pierced and tattooed cadet who was stomping the stuffing out of a grounded kick shield with a worn combat boot. The man exhibited no discernible technique or training whatsoever.

Whitman rolled his eyes over to Wells. "Prison? Let's hope his talents lie in explosives," he said, unable to suppress a grin.

Wells chuckled, his smile widening. Whitman warmed to the game, infectious as it was to watch a guy as tough as Wells get the girly giggles.

"And the roomie?" Wells asked.

Whitman's eyes scanned over to Woolf. A swell of pride filled Whitman to find Woolf cranking away on a heavy bag instead of wasting his energy grandstanding with the other first years. His technique spoke for itself—brutal blows landing with precision and power. For someone who seemed to spiral into an existential crisis over a dry English muffin for breakfast, he certainly appeared to be in his element when violence was involved.

"SOCP," Whitman referred to the Special Operatives Combatives Program designed to train Green Berets. "And proficient kickboxing, it looks like."

"You better not take it easy on him," Wells said, continuing his calisthenics.

"Have you ever known me to take it easy on anybody?"

Wells raised his eyebrows and shrugged in a silent confirmation. Whitman never eased up, not since Kipling.

Whitman liked Woolf, despite their differences. Whitman was social, fun, and effortlessly charming. Woolf was reserved, surprisingly bookish for a trench monkey, and socially awkward. It was as if training and reading were his only solace from the suffocating pressure of social interaction.

Whitman was furious when Frost told him he'd be separated from Hawthorne after two years of bunking together. Whit and Thorne had been inseparable since their orientation, and Frost shuffling their sleeping arrangements would never change that. Besties are besties.

If there was one thing Hawthorne and Whitman had in common, it was that they bonded quickly. Both were social butterflies drawn to the glow of each other's light.

Constant transitions dictated the tempo of Whitman's childhood. He grew up being passed from one foster family to the next like a baton, with each new handoff renewing his sense of rejection. Every new "home" delivered a fresh set of horrors, but never safety. Expectations were erratic. Consistency was a myth. Chaos became his normal, and the concept of family faded to fiction.

His friendships always proved more enriching than any genetic connection, as if any of his blood relatives had ever sought him out. Even a brief, enjoyable friendship outweighed generations of family drama. He approached romantic relationships even more casually, like short courses in a prix fixe meal—intense and delectable, and whisked away just as the next course hit the table.

It came as no surprise that Whitman found himself quickly drawn to his new roommate, taking the sting out of his separation from Hawthorne. Whitman put Woolf through the Pattycake game to gauge his performance under stress, and Woolf delivered such an interesting first impression. He projected this gruff demeanor, but when you put four walls around him instead of a desert, he shrank into a ball of silent panic. Whitman felt instinctively protective and fascinated by him.

"What about the smoke show in the corner? She looks like she got lost on the way to Program H." Wells' words broke Whitman out of thought.

Whitman's eyes swept the gym until they landed on the little pixie Wells referenced. She sat perched on a pile of stacked mats, in a deep straddle stretch, eyes closed, bobbing her head gently to something that sailed over her earbuds. She stretched in a slow, relaxed manner, the sort of intuitive stretching that comes with being deeply in tune with one's body. Her toned legs extended outwards, toes pointed with impeccable turned-out precision.

Her ash-blonde hair was pulled back tightly into a bun, casting a striking contrast with her dark eyebrows and lashes. Her round ivory face radiated a youthful innocence and tranquility, making her seem exquisitely out of place. A serene grin played on her full lips as she stretched her arms out in front of her, pancaking her body onto the mat with feline grace. Her fingertips crawled farther along the mat with every rhythmic breath, demonstrating extraordinary flexibility that appeared effortless.

She sported tight green Lululemon leggings and a coordinating pink patterned sports bra with a peekaboo cutout that revealed the smallest amount of cleavage. At first glance, you'd assume she was warming up for a yoga class, not a six-hour mixed martial arts gauntlet.

Wells tore his eyes away from her to question Whitman

with them, awaiting his assessment.

"Pilates." Whitman grinned.

Whitman's gaze drifted back to her. She had sat up, opening her eyes to survey the room of nervous first years. Her face exhibited no trace of anxiety. She observed the sea of cadets with the detached curiosity of someone perusing the dessert menu. She closed her eyes again and fell back into the music.

Whitman sat transfixed as she methodically encircled both her wrists in well-worn boxing wraps that clashed with her luxury athleisure wear. Her hands orbited each other in a slow, meticulous rhythm, as if she had performed this ritual countless times. She rocked and rotated her hips back and forth as she wrapped, deepening her stretch.

She never opened her eyes to check what she was doing.

Faulkner's grunt broke Whitman's trance.

"For those of you new to the instructing staff, I trust you've reviewed the rules of engagement. The most important thing to remember is that you are permitted to hurt the cadets—"Faulkner's eyes shot to Whitman for a fraction of a second before landing on a new instructor—"but no intentional injuries. Understood?"

A chorus of silent nods rippled through the group.

"Break their spirits, not their bodies."

The little spitfire had some moves, that was for damn sure. Whitman hadn't known what to expect from the boxing ballerina. Right out of the gate, the little minx nearly decapitated him with a textbook Taekwondo spinning hook kick. Her hip and footwork revealed her training as a seasoned boxer, and her punches fucking stung.

She dead-armed him in the first minute. With the grace of someone who had at least a few belts in Jiu-Jitsu—impressively eclectic Jiu-Jitsu—she slipped out of every submission he threw at her. She nearly disarmed him twice with flawless Krav Maga and caught him off guard with an elbow strike over his left eyebrow that left him momentarily blinded. At times, Whitman forgot who was supposed to be running the knife defense drill. Despite his height, reach, and leverage advantage, his hands were full with this one.

Whitman had her on her knees from behind, with one arm secured around her waist in an ironclad grip, feeling like he finally had her at a disadvantage. The hot skin of her exposed belly warmed his arm. She held his knife hand on the ground by his wrist and steadied herself with her other hand. As she shifted her hips back into him, all thought and feeling he held in his brain shot down to the sensation of her firm ass pressing against his cock.

He tightened his grip around her, drawing her closer to him. His face brushed against the skin of her neck, and he inhaled her scent—lilies and a whisper of vanilla, mixed with their combined sweat. His focus tunneled to the raw sensation of having her locked in his arms.

In the short lapse in his concentration, she slid her hips to the side, grasping the hand on her waist, taking advantage of his relentless grip. With his arm trapped by hers, she rolled forward, launching him onto his back.

Whitman was in such shock at her deft maneuver that he hardly clocked the small hand disarming him of the knife as she spun him over. He found himself pinned to the mat, with the rubber knife kissing his carotid, straddled by the deadliest woman he had ever met.

She breathed heavily, and a thin gleam of sweat rested on her brow. Her deep brown eyes flashed with a concoction of hostility and amusement, like a predator at play.

Her eyes dropped to his mouth and lost their fight. A sparkle ignited in them, and her lips curled into a breathtaking smile.

"Sorry, handsome," she breathed. "Looks like I'm on top." Her eyes took on a mischievous glimmer, and she winked at him. She dismounted him and offered a hand to help him to his feet, sending an unexpected wave of disappointment through his body when her weight lifted off him. He took her hand, and she lifted him to his feet with what was no longer surprising strength.

She tossed the knife to him with a playful smile. "Thanks for the lesson."

Whitman gaped in bewilderment as she strutted away to the next station.

"I don't even know how she got the drop on me with that last move. It's like nothing I've ever seen," Whitman said, pressing the bag of ice into the rapidly forming goose egg on his forehead.

"Oh, that was so good," Woolf chuckled.

"Fuck me dead. You can smile?" Whitman said, flabbergasted at the transformation on Woolf's face.

"Of course I can smile." Woolf shook his head.

"Well, I'm thrilled you find joy in my defeat. We're really cultivating trust here, buddy."

"Oh, come on. That was the most perfectly executed Granby I've ever seen. No one could've defended against that."

"What the fuck is a Granby?" Whitman pulled the ice pack off and pressed a few fingers to the aching spot. They came back crimson; he hadn't realized he was bleeding. He stuck the bloodied fingers in his mouth.

"You're kidding, right? Didn't you ever wrestle?" Woolf asked.

"Wrestling?! You mean to tell me that little night terror finished me with a motherfucking wrestling move? Who the hell taught her to wrestle?" Whitman was too astonished to wrap his head around this, and his head was swelling in size by the minute.

"I dunno. Maybe Rulon Gardner's her dad or something."

"Who?"

"Jesus, dude. Really?" Woolf rolled his exasperated eyes at Whitman. Whitman hated the feeling of being blindsided, especially when someone had more information than he did.

We didn't exactly have a robust wrestling league in the group home.

In all his studies of fighting techniques, Whitman had glossed over wrestling in favor of what he thought were more effective forms of grappling, like Jiu-Jitsu, Judo, and Sambo. He realized he needed to revise his assessment of the sport.

"Looks like your little wrestling partner is in trouble," Woolf said. Whitman scanned the gym, eager to find a weakness in her fighting technique and maybe a little retribution for the instructing staff.

In the far corner, Wells had her at arm's length against the wall, both his gorilla hands wrapped around her throat. Her legs dangled a little over a foot off the ground, and her arms were well out of range to strike his face. She looked so tiny compared to him. Instead of the satisfaction Whitman expected to feel, his chest tightened with worry.

Wells better not hurt her.

Whitman's eyes traveled from her dangling feet up to her face. A flush spread from her neck to cover her cheeks. She glared down at Wells with untethered menace, refusing to yield.

Wells must have been enjoying himself so much that he didn't notice when she planted her feet against the wall. She threaded her arm between his forearms and drove her elbow down on the crook of his elbow. His arm bent just enough to get her in range to drive her other palm straight into his throat. He dropped her and doubled over, clutching his neck. She seized his shoulder with both hands and delivered a savage knee to his abdomen. Scrambling away, she positioned herself behind him.

Wells sliced his other hand across the air in front of his neck, signaling the end of the drill.

She approached him and put a hand on his back, gently rubbing as he fought to catch his breath. She said something to him, and he nodded. Then, to Whitman's surprise, he smiled at her and shook her outstretched hand.

CHAPTER 14

WILDE

Wilde shifted the front of her new, dove-grey cardigan and rolled her shoulders inside it, tugging at the hem of the black miniskirt. It was the most subdued ensemble she could find in the closet of fuzzy confections that G, or Capote now, had so hilariously purchased for her. These clothes would take some getting used to.

Wilde's options were limited. Her former wardrobe consisted of a handful of dark pants and hoodies, chosen for their ability to blend in. All she arrived at Archangel with was a single change of clothes in her go-bag, in tactical black.

She did find one advantage of the ridiculous clothes Capote chose: they afforded her the luxury of being underestimated, which had real value. It had already worked at Open Mat. Wilde was well aware that if people misjudge your potential, you have a better shot at outfoxing them. An additional perk to dressing like "Dark Academia Barbie" would be the look on Capote's face.

Hemingway had informed Wilde about the soirée, which was being hosted by Program H. Of course, they had the energy to host; after all, Program H probably spent their first week seducing each other in exotic languages and playing dress-up or some bullshit. They didn't spend the whole day getting the shit kicked out of them. To cover the bruises that were settling on her legs from the drills, Wilde had chosen some thigh-high stockings. They seemed to find every scrape and scratch as she stretched them over her tender skin. Her entire body ached.

As Wilde walked the halls toward the Program H Common Room, she envisioned herself stepping into her new persona. Who did she want to be? The last decade hadn't provided a lot of time to think about her identity beyond all the aliases. All she knew with certainty was what she didn't want to become.

She shook the darkness from her thoughts, focusing instead on where she was.

She admired the magnificent stained glass in this wing that echoed the windows in the hub of the Keep. However, the sharp lines and chevrons distinguished themselves from the soft, rounded, Romanesque curves and graceful arches of the panes she had seen near the lecture halls.

Warm fairy lights and patterned fabric lamps, dripping with antique fringe, cast pockets of glowing light across the Program H Common Room. Dark, jeweled-toned fabrics were draped over every surface, from floor to ceiling, begging to be touched. Gilded, heavily patterned wallpaper surrounded the room. The Art Deco styling of the Program H wing matched the unbridled sex appeal of its cadets. Add a few leather riding crops on the wall and a St. Andrew's cross, and this room would be a ready-made sex dungeon. Program H knew how to party.

Wilde scanned the bustling room for Capote, though she was probably engrossed in another online chat with her new boyfriend; things were getting serious between them. Instead, she saw several other members of Program W from Open Mat. Wells was there, surveying the room, nursing what Wilde assumed was a Jack and Coke. She searched for her range buddy, Woolf, only to be disappointed when she couldn't find him. She would have loved to see a friendly face. When Wilde left her room, Hemingway was only halfway through her several hours of makeup and hair preparation.

Wilde was on her own.

Clusters of assets in their twenties and thirties exuded confidence, talent, and style as they flirted and sized each other up. Wilde's cheeks grew hot under the scrutiny of all of their gazes.

For fuck's sake, where the hell is the bar?

Wilde hunted for any form of solace from her insecurities. No Capote, no Hemingway, no—*oh, thank god, there's the bar.* She made a beeline for something to dull the sharp edges of her reality. As she approached the beacon of salvation, her eyes landed on the two people behind the bar.

The first was an androgynous marvel clad in a captivating menswear ensemble—a tailored white dress shirt with buckled leather sleeve garters, cheeky suspenders, and a trilby hat. Dark brown waves spilled from under the hat, falling artfully over one eye and cascading down to their shoulders. Their style was impeccable yet effortless, evoking a young Johnny Depp vibe, were it not for their glowing skin and immaculate makeup. Judging by their command of the room, this was our host.

The other bartender was...

No way...Knife Defense?

He swapped the snug black tee and joggers for an outfit that surprised Wilde; he looked downright preppy. He wore a dark plum tailored dress shirt with a subtle botanical print, the sleeves rolled and pushed up to his elbows. Over the shirt, he layered a navy paisley waistcoat that complemented it to perfection. The colors stood out against his smooth almond skin. A half Windsor knot completed the look, loosened enough to accommodate the button released at the top of his shirt, offering a glimpse of his collarbone and the toned upper chest beneath it. Smooth, chestnut coils cascaded down over one of his thick eyebrows, while the rest of his closely cropped waves hugged his skull.

Distracted by the spirit of competition during Open Mat, all she had noticed about him was his slicked-back hair and heavy-lidded eyes set deeply into his serious face. She had never fully taken in the sight of him.

He seemed entirely in his element. His piercing hazel eyes, wreathed in envy-inducing midnight-black lashes, sparkled with easy charm as he engaged with people at the bar. The melodic quality of his laughter danced into her ears like music, contrasting sharply with the velvety baritone of his speaking voice. Having only seen him in a crouch to fight her, it astounded her when he stretched to his full height; he had to be over six feet tall with a few inches to spare. There was so much about him that amazed and intrigued her. If she had known she had *that* wrapped around her, she might have lost focus during the fight.

He must have sensed the weight of her gaze. When his eyes locked with hers, his demeanor cooled, stalling the cocktail shaker in his hands as he cast her a guarded glance.

Outstanding.

She finally found someone she knew at this party, and they fucking hated her.

Take a breath, Babe. You got this.

Wilde cracked her neck and strode to the bar with all the

confidence she could muster.

"I simply have to know your name because you look stunning," she said, extending an upturned hand toward the gorgeous bartender next to Knife Defense. The strategy of leading with a bold flirt rarely failed her. After years of flirting for sport, Wilde practically had a black belt in seduction. The barkeep placed their manicured hand into Wilde's with the grace of a queen. Wilde kissed it, gazing up at them from behind her lashes.

"I'm Hawthorne," the host said.

"It's a pleasure," Wilde said, laying it on thick. She chanced a glance at the other barkeep, pretending she hadn't noticed him before.

"Knife Defense?" she said, feigning surprise and exhibiting more cheek than she had confidence for.

"Most people just call me Whitman," he said through a bitter grimace.

"Oh, you lucked out with that codename. *Leaves of Grass* is a favorite." Wilde wasn't putting him on. Her battered copy of Walt Whitman's poetry was the only remaining possession from her time in Helleborus. It was the book her mother had read aloud to her, and she had stolen her copy from Vasily's study to soothe her on nights when she felt hopeless. Now that she was older, she read from it often as a source of idle comfort.

"How's the head?" Wilde asked, feeling a pang of guilt over the brutal elbow strike she landed on him during Open Mat.

"Never had any complaints," he said, his voice dripping with resentment. Hawthorne reached over to pull a tuft of curls away from Whitman's forehead, revealing a dark purple, swollen knot and a small break in the skin. Whitman flinched the curls back down.

The vision of those silky spirals between Wilde's legs flashed in her mind, and her breath stalled in her throat. Her hands tingled with the desire to bury her fingers in his hair.

"Well," Hawthorne chimed in, "what can I make for the cadet who creamed my bestie?" They appeared to be enjoying this.

"She didn't *cream* me," Whitman said, mimicking Hawthorne's tone insolently.

"What was that word you used? Flawless?" Hawthorne said with mock innocence.

Whitman fixed Hawthorne with a razor-sharp glare, nearing the edge of his patience. Hawthorne beamed back at him with smug satisfaction, a promise that they could do this all night. He redirected his gaze to Wilde.

"Well, you did pin me to the floor," he surrendered, a defeated smile tugging at the corners of his full lips. A swirling dimple pierced his cheek, betraying his caustic attitude. Those hazel eyes, even stained with disdain, penetrated Wilde in a deep, wet place.

"That was a huge mistake." Wilde leaned on the bar toward Whitman.

His brow furrowed as he retreated, struggling to find the error in her victory.

"You're supposed to pin a masterpiece to the wall," she said, running her tongue around the corner of her mouth.

Whitman's mouth spread into a dazzling smile, accentuating the cleft in his chin. Something shifted in his eyes, revealing a different man from behind his mask of scorn. His shoulders fully relaxed, and he chuckled, seemingly despite himself. Wilde couldn't help but fall for every tiny spiraling dimple that formed in his cheeks.

Hawthorne slapped the bar top. "Damn, girl. You sure

you're not from Program H?"

Whitman eyed Wilde with a mix of amusement and curiosity, which was an improvement over his contempt.

"That would be a reckless misuse of her talent. You haven't seen her fight."

A flutter of nerves stirred inside her at his mention of her talent. Was that a compliment?

"At least let me pour a drink for my worthy adversary. I've never been beaten by—"

"A girl?" Wilde challenged.

"An incoming asset," Whitman corrected, enunciating every syllable. "What's your poison?"

At the moment, it's you, sailor.

"How's your French 75?" Wilde challenged.

"Girl, he can whip you up a cocktail that would evaporate those panties right off ya," Hawthorne interjected playfully.

Wilde and Whitman locked eyes. "I guess I'll have to wear some next time." She drew her lower lip between her teeth.

Whitman tried and failed to stifle a smile, and his sparkling eyes marveled at her.

"Any preference for gin, Frenchy?" Whitman shifted into flirty bartender mode, flipping a steel cocktail shaker in his hand. She felt a sweet, melting sensation in her belly when he assigned her the nickname, so much more intimate than a codename.

"See if you can surprise me," Wilde purred, eager to pull him into her web. She had breached his defenses, but he held some in reserve. As he shook the cocktail vigorously, she found herself wondering what he looked like when he pleasured himself. What sounds did he make when he climaxed?

Whitman topped off the cocktail with cold brut champagne and carved a lemon twist to adorn the frosted champagne flute. He slid the drink toward her, leaned in, and folded his arms on the bar.

"Pretty fitting you'd prefer a drink named after a dangerous cannon," he admitted, just above a whisper. Wilde gripped the flute and took a sip. It was a damn good French 75.

"Well, I am Program W. Were I Program H, I'd probably be sipping a martini," Wilde said with a glance toward Hawthorne.

"Oooh, I love a martini," Hawthorne said, their eyes lighting up.

"Not the way I mix them." Whitman shot Hawthorne a rebellious stare.

"What, heavy on the gin and filthier than sin?" Hawthorne retorted, not missing a beat.

"Just like me," Wilde whispered to Whitman. Breaking his playful banter with Hawthorne, he fixed her with impressed eyes that pierced her swagger. She watched wariness dissolve from his face as genuine interest stepped into its place. Something about his probing attention made her feel more exposed than her miniskirt ever could.

He saw her.

Not her alias.

Her.

Deeper than she meant to be seen.

"I'm Wilde," she blurted, desperate to break the tension. Part of her yearned to remain connected with him, but she desperately needed to restore her emotional barricades.

"You sure are," he agreed, leaning toward her. His intense eyes flickered to her lips, which eased into a smile on their own.

"As in Oscar, dipshit," Hawthorne said, shattering the moment.

Wilde decided it was time to leave the party. She was a little too juiced up to be effective, and suspected Hemingway bailed on her. Gathering her wits, she steeled herself for the long walk back to the dorms. On her way, she peered back at the bar, hoping to catch one last glimpse of that handsome bartender, Whitman. Throughout the evening, her eyes found themselves drifting to him, mesmerized as he expertly shook cocktails and charmed everyone around him. Something about his effortless charisma drew her in.

She considered making a move after her third French 75, but chickened out.

"Hey there, Babygirl," a sultry voice seeped into Wilde's ear.

From the shadows, two figures emerged.

Koontz stood tall in a deep green dress shirt adorned with a leather body harness that accentuated their honed figure, and black slacks—pure, dark domination.

Tiny fingers entwined their way into Wilde's palm as King sidled up to her. Granny Smith apple, cedarwood, and Sicilian lemon flooded Wilde's nostrils. King laid her head on Wilde's shoulder, her shock of platinum blonde hair slicked in perfect finger waves. She wore a black lace Lolita dress and knee-high patent leather platform boots, exuding a captivating blend of danger and innocence.

"My liege," Wilde said, testing the waters. She lifted King's willowy hand, clawed in shiny black coffin nails, to her lips and kissed it. King bit her lower lip so hard it could have drawn blood.

King twirled a lock of Wilde's newly blonde hair around

a lace-covered finger. "I like this one. Can we keep her?" Her round anime-big eyes shot to Koontz, with a how-much-is-that-puppy-in-the-window eagerness.

"It's up to her, Sweetness. Always. Don't forget to ask first," Koontz drawled, then shot a heated glance at Wilde. "Forgive the doll. She's still learning," they said in a darkly reassuring tone.

"Sometimes they like it when I don't ask first," King spat in a defiant whisper at Koontz, then rolled her eyes and turned the sugar on Wilde.

"Would you, pretty please with extra cheese, like to come to a sleepover?" King said, theatrically batting her long eyelashes. The trio had flirted heavily at several happy hours, Wilde trying to gauge what kind of target she was to these two. Maybe it was time to find out.

Fuck it. Why not?

"I didn't pack my pajamas," Wilde said, purposefully coy.

"Perfect," Koontz almost growled, their voice a dark caress that sent Wilde's heartbeat racing. They snaked a strong arm around Wilde's waist, and the three of them slinked out of the Program H Common Room, wrapped around each other.

CHAPTER 15

WILDE

The path to the Program K wing was not nearly as straightforward as the path to the Program H wing. Every hallway leading to Program H radiated a warm feast for the senses, enhanced by its subdued, seductive lighting. As Koontz and King guided Wilde through the castle, the hallways darkened. Wilde took note of the several false walls they passed through on their way to the Program K wing. This tower was distinctly Neo-Gothic, creating a stark contrast to the Art Deco elegance of the H Wing.

Medieval torch sconces flickered through the passages, while moonlight cascaded through the stained-glass windows along the corridor. At first glance, they resembled those found in a European Catholic cathedral. Upon closer inspection, rather than chronicling stories of the Saints or the Stations of the Cross, they depicted scenes from Dante's Divine Comedy. Ornate candelabras splashed small pools of light across a seemingly unending, wide spiral stone staircase.

Wilde broke her handhold with King to catch her breath, her thighs shaking on the verge of giving out. The other two appeared accustomed to this hellish cardio. How many times a day did they have to scale these steps?

"Mind if I sit?" Wilde asked, slumping for a moment on the stairs without waiting for a response.

"Let me clean off a seat for you," Koontz said, licking their lips and dragging a thumb across their lower lip.

"That's no seat. That's a throne," Wilde gasped, now breathless for more than one reason.

"Well, a King needs a Queen, right?" King said as she backed herself against the wall. She wore a mischievous smile as she picked at her adorably crooked teeth with an inky pinky nail, looking comfortable enough to watch the scene unfold.

Koontz prowled into Wilde's space, and her heartbeat accelerated in the presence of this magnetic predator. She had never felt so at ease being inside another's crosshairs. Koontz's electric blue eyes ignited like wildfire. They pressed the palm of their hand into the center of Wilde's chest and wrapped their strong fingers around the base of her throat.

"You're tired? Relax, Babygirl. I'll help you." Koontz's words flowed like molten dark chocolate into Wilde's ears. One steady hand kept a grip on her neck while the other roamed down her body. Wilde yielded back onto the steps, the cold staircase supporting her as the overwhelming proximity of Koontz assaulted her senses.

A sly, strong hand glided down Wilde's ribcage. Rigid fingers canvassed her belly and journeyed lower. Wilde gave in, allowing her head to fall back against the cold stone step. Koontz's fingertips met the barrier of Wilde's panties, their eyes flashing with devilish recognition.

"You're a dirty little liar," they snarled.

"And you're a dirty little eavesdropper," she breathed back.

"Just collecting intel. Isn't that what we're all here for?"

they said, their voice dropping an octave as they lowered their face down between Wilde's legs. They slid one hand under her ass, grabbing her thong by the back, and dragging it down her legs until it slipped off her toes. They tossed it at King, who caught it with a giggle, like an excited puppy scoring a treat.

Koontz moistened two fingers in their mouth, never diverting their fierce gaze from Wilde's. They drew those fingers down Wilde's slit before slipping them inside her, sending shivers of excitement from the spot. Koontz's fingers curled and undulated inside Wilde. She couldn't snatch the moan before it escaped, echoing off the stone staircase. With masterful skill, Koontz finger-painted pleasure across her insides.

Wilde snuck a glance at King, whose hand hid behind a curtain of black lace around her waist. When Wilde met her gaze, King's eyes simmered with sensual promise. She raised the layers of tulle, revealing gartered stockings and no panties. She sank to her knees on the staircase, utterly irresistible.

Koontz locked lips with the lips between Wilde's legs, and all coherent thought left her mind. When she regained her senses, she glanced over at King, who lifted her ruffled skirt to reveal what she was doing to herself. She spread her spindly legs wide, planting her heavy black platforms on the stairs, and licking her middle finger. King lay back against the stone. Black nails carved along the skin of her thighs before diving inside, leaving a dotted trail of blood drops in their wake. Her spine spiraled like a King cobra as she gave Wilde a masterclass in self-pleasure.

Koontz placed a heavy hand on Wilde's stomach, swirling their tongue around her clit, teasing out a strong tug below Wilde's belly button with every swish. They pulled back and extended their tongue, licking Wilde like a cat. Wilde found it challenging to focus on anything but the exquisite sensation.

Wilde gave King a tip of her chin that said, "Come over here."

King shook her head, continuing her self-play, and shot a glare that said, "Make me."

"Get over here," Wilde commanded.

King's eyes sparkled with defiance.

"Get. The fuck. Over here, Brat," Wilde demanded.

King brought her fingers to her mouth and suckled the juices off them. She began to slide over toward Wilde, but Wilde gave one stern shake of her head.

"No," she told King calmly. "Crawl."

King complied, slinking down to all fours on the wide stairs. She prowled over to Wilde, her skeleton almost liquefying.

"Kiki, darling," Koontz said low between licks. Their blazing eyes held a warning, as their fingers treaded water inside Wilde.

King dipped her chin and scowled. "What?" She enunciated the t.

"Blades."

King rolled her eyes and gave an exasperated sigh. "Fine-uh." She rose to her knees and buried her hands in the ruffles. Looking up and to the side, she squinted her eyes and chewed her lip in thought. She removed one, two, three, four, and five razor blades from beneath the folds. She lifted the skirt and retrieved two small Gothic daggers, one from each of her garters. She dropped back down to her hands and shot Wilde a provocative glance.

Koontz clicked their tongue. "And the back."

King reached around and produced a pocket tomahawk from her dress. "Satisfied?"

"Not yet, but we'll get there." A smirk formed on Koontz's lips.

King returned to her sultry slink. She reached Wilde and sat up on her knees, ready for command.

"Have a seat, Your Majesty," Wilde said. King's eyes lit up, and she smiled a diabolical grin.

She brought a knee over Wilde's head and mounted her face, her juices instantly wetting Wilde's lips. She tasted like the best kind of trouble.

Koontz brought their mouth fully against Wilde's pussy and licked her like a fucking ice cream cone. They retreated their fingertips to about a half inch from her opening and applied pressure on the lower wall. Then on the upper wall. Down and up, sensitizing every nerve ending around the opening. Wilde lost her breath for a moment.

Wilde echoed Koontz's licking on King, who released a succession of short, high-pitched moans, like the sexiest squeaky toy you ever heard. She made little forward and backward grinds on Wilde's mouth. Koontz kept a low rhythm on Wilde, sparking a desperate craving for more.

Wilde struggled to focus on the task at hand as she felt her pleasure building. She slipped her hand under her chin and slid two fingers inside King's tight, drenched pussy. King chirped, and her breath hitched a few times in her throat. Wilde took the opportunity to hook her fingers inside, stroking the ridges on King's upper wall. King's moans grew longer and lower.

Koontz latched onto Wilde's clit and sucked her like a vacuum. She unraveled and moaned into King's pussy. King intensified her grinding, squeaking louder. Wilde felt King's tunnel expand like a tent around her fingers, signaling her proximity to climax.

Koontz slid the length of their fingers all the way to

Wilde's back wall, sending Wilde onto the crest from which she knew there was no returning.

King's wet pussy swirled over the whole bottom half of Wilde's face as ecstasy detonated between Wilde's legs. Her moans surged against King's clit, and King's cry echoed off the walls. Koontz held Wilde's hips tight to the stone as she trembled, her legs clenching around their face. Wilde clamped her arms around the top of King's thighs, holding on for dear life. Short whimpers shuttled out of King as she convulsed with her orgasm.

Koontz purred against Wilde's clit and slowed to gentle licks, sending little shockwaves pulsing with every pass. They slowed their fingers inside her.

King tilted her head down and smiled, running her tongue over a sharp canine. "Now, that was Wilde." She lifted her knee and dismounted, lowering her face to ravage Wilde's lips. Her long, slender tongue whipped and slashed around the inside of Wilde's mouth with ferocious passion. She bit down on Wilde's lower lip so hard it pierced the skin.

When King's face left hers, Wilde snuck a peek down at Koontz. They had an elbow propped up on her thigh with their head resting upon it. A slow, satisfied smile spread across their luscious lips.

"If you can't walk, Babygirl, I can carry you."

King clasped her hands together, and her hopeful eyebrows popped up. "Me, too?"

Koontz fixed her with a reproachful glare. "No." They lifted one side of their mouth. "You're going to do what Babygirl told you to do." Their eyes shot to Wilde's. "Crawl."

CHAPTER 16

WILDE

"Five shots. That's all it is. Two to warm up, three for real. I know you got five good shots inside you," Woolf said in a low voice. He lay prone on the mat right behind Wilde's elbow with his scope aimed downrange. He positioned himself as near as possible to her bore so he could track her bullet's trajectory. He was so close she could feel the heat radiating off his skin. Wilde had served as his spotter in an earlier heat, although she had to admit he was the better spotter. He performed well; out of the seventy-seven cadets participating in the Long-Range Competition, he was in tenth place.

If you could please stop saying things like "inside you" while you're wearing that shirt...

Wilde's focus abandoned her every time he opened his mouth. The unseasonable heat blistered the shooting grounds, prompting Woolf to shed his loose fatigue shirt, revealing a white tank that clung to his body like Saran Wrap. A thin sheen of sweat made his skin glisten like polished copper. He had spun his ball cap backward to get a better view through the scope, dark aviators shielding his striking emerald eyes from the unyielding sun. At least now he was situated behind her.

During his heat, she was behind him, front row to every subtle jiggle of those well-crafted muscles with each recoil.

"Just settle in and get a feel for it," Woolf said.

Wilde narrowed her eye down the scope, blocking Woolf from her peripheral vision. She took the shot. The concussion vibrated her whole frame.

"Nice. Good start. I'd bump it three mil toward five," he instructed.

Four more shots. Three mil to five.

Wilde wiped the sweat from her brow.

"Now, just take a breath and slip it in."

The crack of the shot echoed across the valley.

FUCK!

Woolf let out a long, low whistle.

"Well, there's a patch of grass in sector Three Alpha that's super dead," he chuckled. "In case you forgot, your target is in Two Alpha. What exactly were you aiming at?"

"I wasn't," Wilde answered.

"Thought so. That one was still for funsies, so you're good. My only advice: take up less slack on the trigger on your next firing sequence," he teased.

"Roger that, Sarge," she said, grinning behind the scope.

"It's Master Sarge, actually."

"Really?" Wilde said, impressed.

"Yes, ma'am," he drawled. She could hear the smile in his voice. Something about the calm confidence in his tone, combined with an unfamiliar charm, made her melt a little when he said those two words. He was so different when he was in his area of expertise.

"Okay, shooter. Let's refocus. You just gotta pump out three more and then it's beer thirty," Woolf said.

"Hooah," Wilde answered.

"By eye, find your target." Woolf was all business again.

"Eyes on," Wilde said.

"You sure?" he teased.

"Yes," Wilde said, dripping in sarcasm.

"Go to glass."

Wilde positioned her eye behind the scope.

"Check parallax and mil," Woolf instructed. Wilde adjusted the side turret on the scope until the focal planes aligned and the reticle settled on the target.

"One point six," she said. Woolf punched the information into the ballistic computer.

"Confirmed one point six. Check level," Woolf said.

Wilde double-checked to ensure the rifle was level. She inhaled.

"Ready," she said as she began to exhale. The last call she needed was a wind direction and speed reading from Woolf to signal she could shoot. She picked up the slack on the trigger.

"Left. Point four," Woolf said. Wilde finished her exhale and squeezed the trigger.

BANG!

"Now, that's what I'm talking about! Deadshot. Gimme two more of those," Woolf said. Wilde stared down the scope. The round pierced through the left half of the center dot of the steel silhouette. She pulled the bolt back, chambering another round. She settled back on top of the sandbag that steadied the rifle. She drew two long, steady breaths.

"Ready," she said at the top of her inhale.

"Left. Point eight."

Wilde exhaled into the trough between breaths and squeezed.

BANG!

"Just a hair right, but still really damn good. Watch your

wind," Woolf said. Wilde peered down the scope. The round pierced the steel a quarter inch to the right of the last shot. She chambered her final round, and the air stilled around her. She took two more breaths, initiating her firing sequence, listening for her heartbeat.

Inhale.

Thum-thump.

"Ready."

Exhale.

Thum-thump.

"Center," Woolf said.

BANG!

Silence.

"Holy shit," Woolf whispered, awestruck.

The recoil rumbled down Wilde's body as she peered downrange. The round pierced the small strip of metal separating her two previous shots, connecting them straight through the center bullseye.

"You Wilde?" a deep voice grumbled in a slow Alabama drawl behind Wilde.

"No, I'm Woolf," Woolf replied.

"I'm Wilde," she said over her shoulder without turning around. She still needed to check in her rifle from the competition, and that beer was sounding beyond delicious right about now. Her shots had catapulted her to the top of the leaderboard.

Nice to know I still got it.

She looked across the counter at the staff member

checking in her firearm. As she handed it over, he shook his head in a terse warning and directed her gaze behind her.

Wilde turned around.

The gruff voice belonged to a wall of a man standing at least two heads taller than her. Thick, roped muscles encased what had to be at least 350 pounds of solid mass. His shiny bald head contrasted with the reddish-blond beard that extended several inches down from a broad, sharp jawline. He held a Barrett MRAD that resembled a toy in his bear claws. He seemed more suited to tossing cabers across a green field or razing a small village rather than holding a .338.

"Hmmm," he grunted, sizing Wilde up with soulless, pale blue-grey eyes, from face to tits to hips to boots, back up to tits, then face again.

"What'd she shoot?" he asked the staff member, who Wilde had discovered was named Salinger.

"The Serbu .50 caliber, sir," Salinger said.

"Bullshit. Not at a thousand yards," the man scoffed.

"No bullshit," Wilde snapped with an arrogant flip of her hair. She had no patience to tolerate this horseshit on the heels of her win.

He took one long stride to close the four-foot gap between them. "You weren't shootin' Lapua?" His empty eyes turned to slits.

"I prefer the .50," she said. Considering she had been shooting .50 caliber rifles since she was eight, there was no reason to change things up now. She tilted her chin up in defiance. "I'm surprised a guy your size is that worried about a little recoil." Wilde felt a bit invincible after that win and wasn't about to let some misogynist spoil it.

"Lapua's way more accurate than the BMG-50," the man challenged, towering over her.

"At shorter distances, maybe. Some guys are comfortable with their short game. At a thousand yards, your undersized round might droop a little," she mocked. "And if the Lapua is more accurate, wouldn't that mean I won at a disadvantage?"

The man's cheeks flamed, and he rolled his shoulders toward her. Out of the corner of her eye, she saw Woolf's jaw flex as he took a step toward them.

"Mr. Kipling," Salinger interrupted, cutting through the tension. "The contest is finished. I must insist you surrender your firearm."

Kipling's eyes shot flaming meteors at Wilde before threatening Woolf with a glare.

The heavy metal doors to the armory swung open, and Fielding, Department Head of Program K, entered. Sweat covered her smooth olive face, and her chest heaved. Fury filled her dark mono-lidded eyes, a surprising divergence from her reputation of possessing nearly unshakeable chill. She ripped a pair of blue nitrile gloves off her long fingers and propelled them into the wastebasket. Glossy black, needle-straight strands escaped from her bluntly cut shoulder-length bob, falling across her face.

"Kipling!" Fielding's tone sliced through the air like a whip. Kipling met her with a dismissive, empty gaze. "You want to tell me what you know about your spotter being gurneyed away to my infirmary with a collapsed windpipe?"

"Sounds like I need a new spotter. Why? He say somethin' about me?"

"He didn't say anything. I had to trach him." Fielding fixed him with an accusatory glare.

The thought of a field tracheostomy turned Wilde's stomach. She shot a disgusted glance at Woolf. He shrugged, making it evident to Wilde that for him, cutting into someone's throat so they could breathe wasn't the goriest thing he'd experienced in his time in the Army.

"You're coming with me," Fielding ordered.

"See ya soon, Sugar," Kipling said, narrowing his eyebrows at Wilde. He shoved the firearm into Salinger's hands and stomped out of the room behind Fielding.

Woolf released an audible exhale. "Who the fuck is that guy?"

"Top of the Sniper Board, three years running," Salinger said, sweat breaking out on his face. His gaze shifted to Wilde. "You just unseated him. Congratulations, you've made a very formidable enemy."

"Is he that good?" Wilde asked.

"He's pretty good. He's also terrifying. Hard to tell what contributes more to his success," Salinger said.

Woolf grabbed Wilde's shoulders and squeezed. She hadn't realized how much the confrontation had tensed them.

"How about that beer, Champ?"

CHAPTER 17

WHITMAN

Whitman closed the copy of *Leaves of Grass* with more force than he intended and slammed it in his lap. Woolf's return from the Long-Range Competition had startled him out of the pages. Woolf swung the door closed, dropped his daypack onto his bed, and snagged a bath towel from his armoire.

"Were you just... reading for pleasure?" Woolf asked with skepticism, an uncharacteristic smirk tugging at a corner of his mouth.

"What?" Whitman feigned offense. "I read."

"Since when?" Woolf's amused smirk endured, his teasing mood an aberration from his typical dour demeanor.

"I have lots of free time to read while Pattycake is on the hunt," Whitman said, scrambling for any lie.

"I've been falconing with you. All you do is stare at the trees and sip scotch out of a thermos," Woolf challenged, stripping off his sweaty tank top.

"That's not true. It's bourbon. I would never put single malt in a thermos," Whitman admitted.

Woolf had a point; Whitman didn't read during falconry. If he were honest with himself, the main reason he got into falconry was the pageantry. Whitman preferred activities that bolstered his persona of opulence and sophistication, and he considered reading a bit mundane. As an unexpected bonus, he formed a close bond with his gyrfalcon and cherished that relationship more than most of his human connections.

"Well, how'd you do?" Whitman asked, genuinely curious.

"Thirteenth. I'm happy," Woolf said, a slight blush on his face. Had he been celebrating? Whitman was impressed. Woolf was such a homebody.

Whitman's thoughts darkened. "I assume Kipling is on his customary victory rampage." Whitman skipped the Long-Range Competition as a personal rule. That bastard always won, and Whitman favored blades over firearms anyway.

"Nope. Your wrestling partner took first," Woolf said, a proud smile spreading across his face.

"Wilde?" Whitman asked, pretending to be less familiar with her than he was, as if he hadn't been reading her favorite book because he couldn't stop thinking about her since the party. As if his pants didn't feel tighter every time he recalled that moment on the mat when he held her in his arms, her firm ass pressed up against him. And the sensation of her on top of him, her warm hips searing into his like a brand. He had been replaying his moments with her on a loop in his mind: her wink down at him as she held a knife to his neck, the moment she arrived at the party in that miniskirt, her sexy threat to pin him against a wall, and that lip bite that altered his brain chemistry. "You're joking."

"I swear. I saw it firsthand. Kipling was pissed," Woolf chuckled. The thrill of hearing about Kipling's loss and subsequent anger overshadowed the fact that Wilde had just earned herself a bigass bullseye on her back. He might be banned from touching Kipling, but if that fuckface hurt her, Whitman would make damn sure he kicked the breathing habit.

"She okay?" Whitman said, worry twisting his stomach and tightening his ribs.

"She's fine," Woolf said, flopping a dismissive hand at Whitman. "A little tipsy, but I made sure she got back to her room safely. Why?"

"Kipling has hospitalized people over less." Whitman spoke from personal experience.

"I think his spotter took the brunt of it. I'm pretty sure if Wilde lost, she wouldn't have crushed *my* windpipe." Woolf draped the towel over his shoulder and strode toward the bathroom.

"Wait, you're her spotter?" Whitman called after him, surprised to learn they even knew each other. They were drinking together, too? His eyebrows danced in confusion around his forehead as he struggled to process all this new information.

"We hit the range sometimes," came Woolf's voice from behind the wall as the shower sputtered on.

Whitman's mind swirled. He had hoped to have a chance with Wilde, but his jarhead roommate beat him to the punch. He supposed he could be happy for Woolf, but he wasn't.

CHAPTER 18

WILDE

Wilde shoved the office door closed and rested her back against it, breathing deeply for what felt like the first time in the last five minutes. Kipling had just barreled around the corner behind her in the hallway, eager for a confrontation.

"Ms. Wilde. What an unexpected pleasure. Although I won't flatter myself to assume you're here to see me. It appears like I am in an any-port-in-a-storm situation," Fitzgerald, Department Head of Program C, said, redirecting his gaze from the file on his desk to her. His half-moon spectacled eyes always held a certain warmth, regardless of the circumstances.

"Sorry, Fitz," Wilde said as she unglued herself from the door.

"Have they added hide-and-go-seek to the end-of-year competition?" he teased. Wilde gave a puckish glare back.

More like hide-and-go-seek-and-destroy.

Wilde didn't know how Kipling accessed her course schedule, but he seemed to be lurking outside of nearly every lecture.

"Well, you wanted out of the hallway. Mission: accomplished. Now that you're here, would you join me for tea?" An inviting smile beamed across Fitzgerald's round, tawny face, crinkling the skin above his cropped white beard. Wilde knew she needed to kill some time before venturing out again—Kipling could be waiting.

She nodded, scratching some of the prickling anxiety off the side of her neck. Fitzgerald poured steaming jasmine tea from an ornate cast-iron teapot and offered a plate of pastries. Wilde nabbed a chocolate croissant.

"What can you tell me about Kipling?" she said, plopping onto the tufted armchair across from Fitzgerald's desk and taking a bite of the flaky pastry. Fitzgerald's modest space was dwarfed in contrast with Dickinson's expansive office.

"Ah, is he 'It' in the hide-and-go-seek?" He slid a porcelain teacup and saucer across the desk.

"How'd you guess?" Wilde said flatly, reaching to retrieve the tea.

"Years of training." Fitzgerald sipped his tea, a knowing grin kicking the corner of his mustache up. "Taking his loss at the long range poorly?"

"You could say that." Wilde took a long sip. The heat traveled to her chest, unwinding the nervous coil there.

"Well, then, I think your current strategy of avoidance is your best plan of action. That one likes to play with his prey." Fitzgerald's genial dimples faded.

"How do you know that?" Wilde hoped a little more intel on Kipling might provide her with a strategic advantage.

"A few things I've witnessed. I've also had the unpleasant experience of reading his dossier."

"And?"

"You know I'm not at liberty to divulge that information." Fitzgerald's eyes held a playful scold behind them. "I see your course of study has not included The Art of

Interrogation with Frost."

The mention of Frost sent a chill tiptoeing across Wilde's scalp. "No. Thank god."

"Not a fan of her methods?" he questioned, his eyebrows slightly drawn.

"Not at all."

"Her predecessor's tactics were quite barbaric in comparison. Her approach seems a mercy." He shuffled the papers on his desk.

Wilde didn't want to consider what could be worse than Frost's psych compound.

"If you don't mind me asking, what did you see in your session with Frost?"

Wilde's thoughts blackened as they landed on Vasily. "Just a bad memory."

A long moment of silence passed between them.

Fitzgerald's sigh broke the gloom. "I wonder about the mass of tragedies this castle houses. Sometimes, it feels as if it thickens the air we breathe." His tone turned somber. Wilde's eyes lost focus as she gazed around her teacup. "It's no easy process to become a weapon. Even steel needs to be heated and hammered into shape. Sometimes, our greatest struggles unlock our greatest strengths. But only if we're open to engaging with the places that hurt."

Wilde finished her tea, Fitzgerald's words lingering in her mind. She had so many places that hurt, none of which she wished to revisit. She ran from her darkness with the same fear and fervor as fleeing Helleborus.

Wilde placed the teacup on Fitzgerald's desk. "I guess it's time to pay the piper. Thanks for the tea."

"Allow me to give you a head start," he said with a twinkle in his eye. He reached around the back of the bookcase, swinging it into the room and revealing a long stone hallway.

"Really? A secret passage?" Wilde raised her eyebrows.

"I wish I could say it was my idea. Someone before me had a flair for the dramatic. It may have heavily influenced my choice of office. You'll find yourself in the library—in the 230s."

"Religion?" she asked. After years of exploring the world's libraries, the Dewey Decimal System was practically a second language to her.

"Excellent, Wilde. Christian doctrine, to be specific. Somehow, it's not very popular in this castle, so I wouldn't worry about being seen."

Wilde peered into the narrow tunnel. "What, no suit of armor?"

"Oh, *that's* what's missing. Well, Ms. Wilde, I do have a birthday coming up..."

CHAPTER 19

WILDE

"Okay, okay," Hawthorne tried to cut through the raucous laughter. "Fuck, marry, kill—Frost, Faulkner, Fitzgerald.

"Kill Faulkner. Easy," Wells said.

"Fuck Faulkner. Are you kidding me? I would love to collar that bitch, and dog-walk him around my bedroom. I've got a strap with his name on it," Koontz said with a naughty gleam in their eyes.

"Cosigned," King chimed. "Mmm, that salt and pepper beard. I'm gonna soak that shit. Straight-up suffocate his ass." She paused, a thought crossing her mind. "Is there a fuck, then kill, option? Like, dead from the fucking?"

"Jesus Christ, King." Wilde nearly spat out her champagne, laughing. The tipsiness had settled into everyone at the unofficial end-of-midterms party. The Program H Common Room, usually pristine, sat in a delightful state of disarray. A mixture of under- and upper-level assets sprawled across couches and velvet pillows in a lazy circle, playing whatever games came to mind.

Something was soothing about being in the company of other fucked-up people, all indulging in some good, clean fun.

Wilde finally felt herself easing into her new life; Beverstone had begun to feel like a home.

Wilde scanned around the vibrant band of weirdos that had glued onto each other over the first half of the term. Hemingway beamed at Wilde from across the circle, her tangerine freckles practically sparkling from the champagne. Hem made such an adorable lightweight. Capote had pulled Hawking into an animated side conversation about blockchain, and Hawking was shooting Wilde the save-me eyes. Kafka and Whitman were in a deep, friendly debate over which faculty member was more suitable for marriage: Fitzgerald or Frost. Christie campaigned with Wells that Frost was the solid kill choice. After her psych eval with Frost, Wilde was inclined to agree.

"She's a total closet psycho. I'd rather marry the Deathstalker," Christie said.

Wilde's spine ignited at the mention of Dominika's murderer. She scolded herself for relaxing so much inside these walls. She yearned to forget everything about Helleborus and leave that life behind. Who was she kidding? The Deathstalker was probably still hunting her while she sipped champagne with her friends like an adolescent idiot.

"Oh, bullshit. The guy's a fucking myth," Wells shot back. He set his Jack and Coke down on the table and leaned back into the couch with a confident grin.

"No way. He's real. It's documented," Christie argued.

"Who says it's a dude? I doubt a man could pull off that stealth," King added, pulling her platform boots into a crisscross applesauce on her purple floor pillow.

"I bet she's hot," Koontz said with a tantalizing grin.

Wilde wished they would change the subject. Every mention of the Deathstalker added a boulder onto the mountain of growing dread pressing on her chest.

"I refuse to believe in some boogeyman. That's just a ghost story they tell to spook the cadets. 'Don't train hard enough and the Deathstalker will get you,'" Wells said, following up by imitating a ghost. "WoooOOOOoooo!"

"I'm telling you, I saw an article on the Dark Web chronicling his kills. They think his body count could be in the hundreds," Christie continued with conviction.

"Even if it's one hundred over ten years, that's almost one victim a month," Wells said.

"Well, like 83% of a victim," Capote corrected, smiling.

The conversation sent a shiver of apprehension spider-walking over Wilde's skin. She knew the Deathstalker was real and that he ensured anyone she cared about ended up dead. Capote was the only person in her life he hadn't gotten to yet. Wilde began to question her safety inside the castle, and panic knotted her chest.

Wilde's eyes searched the circle for signs of danger or sources of security. Her scan stopped at Woolf. He sat on the couch, arms crossed tightly, shoulders digging into the couch like he wanted to merge with the furniture. He attempted an occasional strained smile or response, but Wilde could tell his social overwhelm was growing. His eyes darted around the group as he progressively receded into the cushions. He might have been the only one as uncomfortable as she was right now.

Wilde had been surprised to see him at the party in the first place. Likely, Whitman had dragged him to it. Woolf had arrived in a hunter-green cable knit pullover that accentuated every one of his expertly toned muscles. The ensemble surprised Wilde, so different from the fatigues he wore to the range or the sweats he wore to their kickboxing dates.

Woolf was the best sparring partner Wilde ever had, which

was saying a lot since her regular Krav Maga partner was Koontz, a former member of the IDF. Woolf had an uncanny ability to read her, making his pad-holding skills unmatched. He challenged her, unafraid to attack with force. He instinctively understood her limits, allowing them to unload on each other. It was beautiful and comfortable.

Buddy check time.

Wilde sneaked behind the bar, mixed two gimlets—Woolf's favorite—and settled down next to him on the sofa. She handed him one of the cocktails, noticing the sweat droplets that covered his forehead. The heat from the fire in the hearth had inspired everyone in the room to remove several layers of clothing, except Woolf, who held out, probably out of pure fear. He stared back at Wilde with eyes that were both grateful for the libation and screaming, "Get me the fuck out of here."

"No way!" shouted Christie. "You can't kill Fitzgerald. He's a legendary graduate of Program C. He's forgotten more about espionage than any of us will ever learn. The loss of knowledge alone would be devastating. That's like the destruction of the Library of Alexandria."

The "Fuck, marry, kill" game was heating up.

Wilde placed a hand on Woolf's shoulder.

"You know you can take that off, right?" Wilde pinched a corner of Woolf's sweater. His skin looked like it might spontaneously combust. He grimaced at her, then resigned. He slid the wool up over his shoulders and head, freeing the scent of his cologne from its prison between his sweater and hot skin—sandalwood and cedar—like how she imagined her cabin haven would smell.

Underneath was a standard white t-shirt, so form-fitting and nearly translucent that it may as well have been crepe paper. Wilde saw every peak and valley of his artfully manicured landscape. Her eyes drifted down firm pectorals to pert nipples, which Woolf promptly covered with crossed arms. Wilde hoped he hadn't caught her gawking at him, but she couldn't help herself.

Woolf looked emotionally naked and terrified. At least the sweat on his brow reduced. He had traded one discomfort for another. Wilde tried to refocus her attention, and both of them gulped their gimlets in an attempt to reengage with the party.

"Not to mention, he's like the only actual human in this building," Hawthorne chortled.

"I said what I said," Kafka retorted.

"Who's up for a tour?" Whitman interrupted the argument.

Wilde cast her attention his way, surprised to find his eyes already on her. He shifted them to Woolf, and his mouth tightened around the edges. Wilde assumed Whitman was a little protective of his roommate.

She wished Whitman didn't avoid her so much. He fascinated her, and she craved more of him. Unfortunately, she couldn't take back beating him at Open Mat, no matter how much she hoped it would change things between them.

In truth, she didn't want to take it back. She never wanted to forget the feeling of his body beneath hers; in fact, she wanted more of it. All of it.

"Yay! I love a tour," Hemingway said, obviously tipsy. Hawthorne steadied her as she stood up. Wilde welcomed the opportunity to get to know the castle better, and the walk might ease Woolf's anxiety. She dragged him off the couch as the rest of the group collected each other and poured themselves into the castle.

CHAPTER 20

WOOLF

Wilde pushed the heavy oak door open, gasping at the sight before her. Woolf's gaze followed hers into the room, eager to discover what excited her. Warm light from standing candelabras and crystal sconces bathed an opulent suite decorated in the traditional French style. To their left stood a mahogany four-poster bed, its midnight blue silk sheets contrasting elegantly with the gold trim of the tufted velvet headboard. Gauzy tapestries cascaded from the posts of the bed, but the top of the canopy remained open for a good reason. Painted on the ceiling was a detailed mural of the night sky and the Milky Way. If you stared at it long enough, you might believe it was the real deal.

A deep navy tufted velvet chaise sat between tall narrow windows on the back wall. Heavy indigo tapestries, tasseled in gold, covered the windows from the ceiling to the polished parquet floor. Opposite the bed stood a varnished mahogany bar. Gilded oval insets sat flanked by intricate wooden carvings that depicted the signs of the zodiac. Behind the bar, glass-backed shelves showcased four rows of expensive liquor bottles.

Wilde slipped off her ankle boots at the door and skipped to the bed, flopping onto her back on the mattress. She took a deep breath and sighed. "This room is fucking amazing. I'm not leaving. I live here now."

She basked in the beauty of the room, while Woolf took in the sight of her: a beauty within a beauty. Her eyes sparkled upward with a startling pureness Woolf wanted to absorb himself in.

A flutter lifted his chest and spread down his abdomen, inflating him with a strange sensation of optimism. The slot where hope lived in him was filled with duty and expectation the moment he landed at boot camp. Wilde erased all that. Each moment in her presence filled him with the unfamiliar sensation that he could care about the future again.

Wilde had woven herself into his every thought since her first shot cracked across the landscape of his life. Her keen attunement kicked in the door of his fortified solitude. With every word, every glance, she teased him out of his protective shell.

Woolf glanced at Whitman, whose eyes stood transfixed by Wilde.

"Well, we're gonna keep going. There's loads more to see," Hawthorne said, nudging the rest of the tour group forward. Whitman paused, looking back at Wilde, who rolled around in bliss on the bed.

Woolf wasn't leaving. He would never leave her.

"You go on ahead, then," Whitman said. Hawthorne shot him a have-it-your-way-then glance, and skipped off with the others, giggling. Wilde rolled over and shot a naughty glance at Woolf and Whitman.

"Staying then?" she asked, kicking her feet playfully. She tipped her chin down and stared up at them with big, twinkling eyes. Woolf's brain lost its ability to process.

"It would be irresponsible of me to leave a first year here alone. Let alone two," Whitman said with a casual authority. Wilde sprang off the bed and tipped her toes over to him.

"Well, if you're going to stay—"she gazed up at him—"do you want to play?" She punctuated the last word by hooking her fingers into his waistband and pulling him close to her.

"IN," was all Whitman said before his mouth came down to meet hers. Woolf could only watch, but somehow, he didn't feel awkward. Instead, he felt rooted to the spot, watching a gladiator match between two skilled sensualists. Wilde's arms snaked around Whitman's waist, pulling their bodies closer. Compared to Whitman's six-two frame, she looked so small. His hands found their way into her hair as their tongues danced. They appeared to melt into one another, and Woolf's heart started to pound.

Woolf's fingers tingled with the desire to thread into Wilde's hair. He wanted to pull her up against him, but couldn't summon the courage. He could only watch.

After a time that could have been seconds or years, Woolf couldn't tell, Whitman came up for air. It was as if it just dawned on him that Woolf was still there in the room with them.

"A word of warning: this one's a little shy," Whitman said, nodding toward Woolf. Woolf didn't care for the dig, but Whitman wasn't entirely wrong. Woolf's sexual experiences amounted to four awkward attempts; he and his high school sweetheart had given up after that fourth encounter. Once he joined the Armed Forces, he stayed so busy that opportunities evaporated. It had been so long that he was starting to think celibacy might not be a bad lifelong goal.

The atmosphere of the room and Wilde's raw openness

ignited something in him. He was also "in."

Wilde left Whitman with a lingering look and padded over to Woolf, placing a warm hand on his chest. Time stopped, and he never wanted it to restart.

"You don't have to do anything you don't want to," she whispered, her gentle eyes imploring him. "If you want to watch, you can watch." She glared at Whitman with a promise of things to come. Wilde's gaze collided with Woolf's, offering an opportunity he could never deny. "If you want to play, you can play."

Sweat broke out on his palms as he tried to control his breathing. Was he nervous or excited?

Both. Definitely both.

Wilde's gaze drifted from Woolf's eyes to his mouth and back again. She tilted her head up and brought her lips to his. Before he knew what was happening, her arms were around his neck. Her soft tongue explored his mouth. The melting occurred with him, too. She smelled of vanilla and lilies and tasted like the perfect amount of champagne. His fingertips found the skin of her back. It felt impossibly soft and warm.

Woolf spent a significant portion of his life trying to stay grounded. Her kiss made him feel weightless, as if for those fleeting moments in her embrace, his pain no longer shackled him to the earth. She tasted like liberation—like release, as if muscles that had remained clenched for decades indulged in a moment of relaxation.

Her eyes remained closed for a moment after they broke off the kiss. She took a deep breath and sighed, basking in the moment. Woolf drank her in and felt, for once, like he was a character in his own story. He was no longer on the sidelines of his own life. When her eyes fluttered open, that deviant spark had returned.

"Now that's settled, ground rules. Standard safe words apply," Wilde said. Seeing the confusion on Woolf's face, she elaborated. "You're familiar with a stoplight. Red means stop completely. Yellow means you're getting into questionable territory. Anything else you can interpret as a green light. K?"

Woolf thought safe words were only for the whips-and-chains crowd. Quite a lot of time had passed since he had done anything close to sexual. Maybe they changed it. He nodded, pretending this was not-so-new information. The realization dawned that he might be out of his depth with these two.

Wilde grabbed Whitman's hand, pulling him toward the four-poster. She beckoned Woolf with a tempting glance. He hesitated a moment while she and Whitman fell back into each other. Watching them, you'd never believe it was their first time together. They anticipated each other's movements with a mesmerizing chemistry Woolf didn't even know existed. They were playing, trying to impress and outdo each other, and Woolf felt hypnotized by the display.

Woolf walked to the edge of the bed as Wilde pushed Whitman onto it. She started unbuttoning Whitman's shirt, her gaze locking onto his with playful intensity as she freed each button. He lounged, propped on his elbows like a compressed spring, his eyes devouring her with dangerous promise, like a leopard lying in wait.

"Cuffs," she said.

Whitman's mouth fell open in shock. "You brought handcuffs?" Woolf had never seen Whitman so off his guard before. His aloof mask dropped. If Whitman was in over his head, Woolf definitely was.

Wilde glared without losing the play in her eyes, and a sly smile played across her lips. "Your shirt cuffs, Love. If you lost one of those exquisite cufflinks, I'd never forgive myself."

A broad, genuine smile broke out on Whitman's face, and he unlocked his cufflinks from his shirt, eager to comply. The two of them tumbled back into a passionate kiss as Wilde slipped the shirt off his shoulders.

She sneaked a glance at Woolf. He felt naked under her gaze, like he was intruding upon their moment.

Wilde stopped and put a finger to Whitman's mouth.

"Hold that thought," she said.

Wilde pivoted to Woolf, and time swirled to a halt around them. She slid along the edge of the bed to join him and grasped the hem of his t-shirt.

"You don't need this, do you?" she whispered, her hot breath caressing his skin. She brushed a kiss onto his lips as she slipped his shirt over his head. Her delicate fingers glided up his body, igniting every nerve ending with a thrilling rush. Her lips were soft and wet, and every kiss made his body hum.

For years, his experience of intimate touch had only extended to brief backslapping hugs or high-fives. The only people he held in his embrace for more than five seconds expired before his arms relaxed. Touch starvation was too graceful a term for what he had endured.

Wilde's fingertips traced a path to the bullet hole scar on his side. His first. A somber softness flickered across her face, not pity or sympathy, but understanding—a simple acknowledgment of his grief he didn't know he needed. He wondered what scars she carried. In that simple moment, he knew she lived with a sorrow that either matched or exceeded the magnitude of his. Her eyes misted over, penetrating him with a tender clarity.

She cradled his face and kissed him again, lingering on his lips with longing. When they parted, Woolf caught a glimpse of Whitman, whose eyes revealed a mixture of awe and excitement.

"Anytime you want to join in..." Wilde whispered in Woolf's ear. She left a hopeful invitation in her eyes as she returned to Whitman.

"You're so gentle with him. I'm trying not to be jealous," Whitman said.

Wilde dropped to her knees in front of him and unbuckled his pants. "That's because different lovers need different things."

Whitman arched an eyebrow. Wilde grabbed Woolf's hand and pulled him toward her.

"He needs encouragement." She planted a soft kiss on Woolf's lips, pulling a piece of him away when she receded.

"And you—"she pulled Whitman's pants down and smacked his ass, hard—"need punishment—"shock and arousal passed across Whitman's face"—and reward." She wrapped her fingers around his cock and took him into her mouth.

Whitman moaned and wrapped a hand around the bedpost to steady himself. "Holy fuck," he whimpered as she thrust him in and out of her mouth. The sight of her kneeling in front of Whitman in a plaid skirt and fuzzy cropped cardigan made Woolf grow hard. She kept taking Whitman in and out of her mouth, locking eyes with him. Whitman's cool, calm demeanor became unknit with every stroke in and out of her lips, and his breath started to catch in his throat.

Every so often, she would sneak a furtive glance at Woolf.

Woolf found himself unzipping his pants as he watched them. He couldn't help but touch himself. Wilde was a goddess on her knees, lapping and sucking Whitman until he looked like he might explode with pleasure. She wrapped her hands around his ass and fucked him with her throat.

She glanced over, spying Woolf on the edge of the bed, hand inside his pants. She let Whitman slide out of her mouth, gaping in an open-mouthed smile at Woolf, lips wet. Whitman gasped, cut off on the edge of coming.

Wilde raised herself to Whitman's lips, kissed him, and shoved him onto the bed. Her eyes locked on Woolf's as she unbuttoned the first button on her sweater. He stared back, frozen, not knowing what to do. A goddess beckoned him into play, and he didn't know what to do?!

What the fuck, dude?

Wilde took two steps over, planting herself in front of him, and trapping him against the mattress.

"I assume you know how buttons work," she teased, presenting herself to him.

Woolf raised his fingers to the second button and released it. Wilde's eyes took on a pleased and encouraging sparkle. He freed the rest of the buttons and slid the sweater off, revealing nothing but her immaculate skin. Two perfect pink nipples emerged from behind the Angora, taut in the warm air, rising and falling with her breath. Woolf tore his eyes away from the sight to look up at her face. She gazed at him in anticipation, eyes feverish and expectant.

He was desperate to touch her, but was unsure how. She must have sensed his hesitation. She pressed her naked chest against his, the softness of her skin sending a shiver down his body. Her small, warm hands wandered his back, as her tongue slid into his mouth to meet his. After she broke the kiss, she offered a silent moment for him to make a move, which he conceded in his panic. Grace and understanding flashed in her eyes, as if she meant to tell him she was perfectly comfortable waiting until he was ready.

She melted back into Whitman as he eagerly removed her

skirt. They kissed on the four-poster, under the false night sky, looking like gods incarnate while Woolf watched.

On the edge of the bed, Woolf took it out. The vulnerability terrified him; he wished he could blend into the background until he blinked out of space and time. Yet, at that moment, he would go anywhere with Wilde. If she asked him to cut an arm off, he might. She made him feel alive, courageous, and sexy.

Wilde's eyes widened and flooded with a rabid playfulness.

"Holy shit, man," Whitman said, his expression a mix of surprise and admiration. There was something else in his gaze—was it envy? They were roommates, yes. But Woolf was pretty shy about what he had in storage. People tend to assume that if you have a massive dick, you know what to do with it— not the case for Woolf.

Wilde pushed Whitman down on the bed and mounted his face. Initially surprised, Whitman quickly adapted to the role, showcasing his skill after a few short moments.

How could I learn how to do that?

Wilde's head tilted back as she gyrated her hips to meet Whitman's mouth. His hands firmly gripped her ass, pushing her into his face, eliciting the sweetest little moans from her mouth. One of her hands glided up her ribs to grasp her breast while the other one traveled into her hair, gripping it into a bundle at the crown of her head.

The sound she made when her eyes met Woolf's sent him barreling toward his climax.

"Do you want to come in my mouth?" she breathed.

"Yes, ma'am," Woolf whispered, barely able to get the words out. Whitman moaned into her pussy, assuming she was talking to him, but her eyes never left Woolf's. One hand in

Whitman's hair, as her pleasure crested, she leaned over the bed and took Woolf into the back of her throat.

He lost himself.

Woolf came so hard he disappeared out of his own identity for the moment. Nothing existed, neither time nor place, only her—only now. She received each pulsating expulsion with eager acceptance, milking him of every tormenting thought, draining him of his pain.

He never knew such bliss.

Wilde moaned on his dick, slowly kicking his brain back online. She let him slide out of her, wiping a forearm across her mouth and licking her lips as she sat back up. Whitman must have ramped up his efforts; she lost her breath and could hardly make a noise as she buried both hands into Whitman's hair. Her whole body quivered as she cried out in rapture, her desperate moans sweeter than any symphony. Woolf was positive he was witnessing an angel in the flesh. Nothing he had ever seen rivaled her beauty. He felt an overwhelming desire to worship her.

Little droplets of sweat dappled Wilde's breasts and brow as she caught her breath, exuding radiance and power. The goddess opened her eyes, descending back to the world of man. The expression on her face convinced Woolf that she had invented satisfaction. She drew a long breath and winked at Woolf as she dismounted Whitman's face and settled on top of him. She planted a sweet kiss on Whitman's still-wet mouth, and his tongue eagerly met hers. She moaned as she tasted herself on his lips.

"It's time for payback. I want you to pin me and paint me like a masterpiece," Wilde whispered into Whitman's ear.

The look in Whitman's eyes was beyond carnal. He flipped her onto her back as if she weighed nothing, and she let out a little giggle. He pulled her by her hips down the bed toward him and gored her. It didn't take more than a few powerful thrusts until both of their cries pierced the room, announcing their climax.

They melted back into each other, and Whitman swept a damp lock of hair out of Wilde's face. She planted a slow kiss on his lips and rolled over toward Woolf. Wilde traced a lazy finger down Woolf's chest and smiled.

Whitman stretched his lanky figure across the bed and rested his curly head against the headboard. He was entirely on display, without a care in the world, like a marble statue. Woolf wondered if he could ever become so confident and suave. He doubted it. Whitman didn't need to give a second thought about who he was or what he wanted.

Woolf, on the other hand, couldn't pass a mirror naked without hyperventilating and breaking into a cold sweat. He wasn't ashamed of his body; he worked his ass off to hone it. But it was just an instrument to him.

Wilde leaned her head toward Woolf and kissed his shoulder, jolting him back to the moment. Her eyes shimmered. The way she looked at him made him feel invincible.

Well, fuck it, let's give it a shot.

CHAPTER 21

WHITMAN

Whitman felt utterly spent. He had a vague sensation that Wilde had rolled across the bed, but he could scarcely keep his eyes open. He heard hushed voices, and Wilde whispered, "Are you sure?"

She slid back over to Whitman and snuggled in under his arm. "Can I tell him?" she called back to Woolf. Whitman didn't open his eyes to confirm Woolf's silent answer.

Wilde tugged on Whitman's earlobe with her warm fingers, coaxing him back into the moment. Her sparkling eyes awaited him.

Absolutely fucking irresistible.

"Woolf has expressed an interest in using his mouth to pleasure me. He's a little concerned about his lack of expertise and could use some guidance." It sounded like the bedroom equivalent of an elevator pitch. The adorable false formality drew Whitman in. Wilde offered him a seat, and he was ready to ride.

"The way I see it, we have two potentially rewarding options. One: you watch while I walk him through what will please me. Or... you watch and provide him instruction," she offered.

"Oh, definitely the second one," Whitman said, not even needing to consider it. He sat a little taller and blinked his eyes fully open, his fatigue forgotten. If Woolf was down to learn, then buckle up, Buckaroo. School was officially in session.

Wilde's face radiated delight. She slinked over to the center of the immense four-poster, leaving everything on display for him on her way. Whitman's mouth gaped, lost in the view.

Good fucking gods.

She lounged on her back, propped up on her elbows, the candlelight kissing her skin.

"I guess I'm completely at your mercy, gentlemen."

Despite her words, Whitman knew she was the one holding the reins. Only his exhaustion gave him the restraint to keep from seizing her and claiming her once more.

Whitman drew a long, leisurely breath. If Wilde wanted him in the driver's seat, then she'd have to work at his pace. And he intended to prolong this.

It's playtime.

He was fully impressed with Woolf. Whitman couldn't imagine exhibiting the vulnerability it took to admit not having the foggiest idea of how to bring a woman to climax. Just the thought of that level of honesty made him want to puke a little. Whitman was a graduate of "Fake-it-Til-You-Make-It" University, expertly constructing a façade of confidence to mask a gnawing sense of inadequacy. He learned that you can live free of abandonment if you reject others before they have a chance to reject you.

Not Woolf. He was too awkward and accustomed to rejection. He disowned himself for breakfast every day. It imbued him with a strange boldness that Whitman envied.

Whitman had constructed an edifice of audacity, built on a foundation of expectation—expectations he set for himself so that others would perceive him as something marvelous, worthy of note. Unforgettable, or at least, significant... to someone.

He had to admit, the grunt had balls, that was for damn sure. Whitman had confidence. Woolf had courage.

At any rate, Woolf awaited Whitman's instruction, and Wilde anticipated his performance. He bent a knee and rested it against the headboard, propping his head up on a hand.

"The first thing you need to know is that seduction begins in the mind. If you want to wrap her around your finger, you have to get in her head," he said coolly. Wilde side-eyed him, her eyes a mix of suspicion and anticipation.

"I want you to slide your open palm up the back of her neck to the back of her head." Woolf placed himself between Wilde's spread knees. She shot him an encouraging gaze and settled deeper into the mattress. He crouched over her, sliding an unsure hand into her hair. She rose toward him, eager for his embrace.

"Now, close your fist."

Woolf grasped a handful of Wilde's hair, and she whimpered, her eyes smoldering. Woolf's eyes flared like he had just armed a nuclear warhead.

A flutter of victory flooded Whitman's chest. He knew what she wanted. "Now, you tell her in her ear what you're going to do to her."

Woolf growled something low into her ear that Whitman couldn't discern, and her eyes widened. His roommate was a quick study.

All Wilde had left on her body were her over-the-knee socks.

"Slide her socks off and kiss your way back up to her."

One, then two socks glided off her legs, and Woolf kissed a wandering trail up her thighs. Wilde gazed down at Woolf, her craving eyes transfixed. Anticipatory breaths lifted her perfect breasts as her elbows sank into the mattress.

"Now, hook your hands around the top of her thighs, and pull her down toward you."

Woolf grabbed her with more force than Whitman expected. Her eyebrows raised with excitement, and she shot an eager glance at Whitman. Woolf was surprising them both.

"Now, you can start sliding your tongue up and down her slit, slowly. You're just waking up the area. She'll want you to go straight to a spot, but make her wait."

Her eyes shot daggers, devoid of anger. She knew he was playing with her, but it didn't seem like she hated it—this was clearly why she made the game. Wilde lost her defiance as Woolf went to work, her eyelids drooping in pleasure.

"Now, find the button at the top." Whitman felt he needed to simplify things for Woolf. "Take it into your mouth and start sucking. Gently."

Wilde dropped off her elbows and fell entirely onto her back. She sighed, and her eyes slid shut. Woolf was adapting to this readily.

"I want you to slide your hands up the back of her thighs and grasp behind her knees." Woolf complied without looking up or diverting from his current task.

"Now, spread her knees wide." Wilde's legs offered no resistance as Woolf pressed them into the mattress. Her breath quickened, and her eyebrows rose and crumpled in a powerless surrender.

"Now, start tracing circles around the button, but don't stop sucking," Whitman instructed. Wilde started to moan.

Whitman saw her thighs tense as little shivers passed over her body.

"Alright, back it off a little. If you draw this out, she'll want it more. And she'll come harder."

Woolf slowed his pace.

"Oh, fuck you, Whitman," Wilde moaned, playfully frustrated. The sound of his name on her lips needled into him. He would kill a thousand people to hear her moan his name once more.

Woolf didn't back off for long. Once he ramped back up, Wilde lay back and her hands grasped the bedsheet. Whitman could tell she was getting close by her rapid breathing and those delicious whimpers. Woolf appeared to be doing just fine on his own now. If there was one thing he excelled at, it was following orders.

Wilde's body ignited. Her hips bucked toward Woolf's mouth. She buried her hands in his hair and began to grind into his face. Her cries grew louder and more desperate until she released one last breathless moan.

She collapsed back onto the bed, and her hands fell around her glistening face. She closed her eyes and seemed transported to another world. A quiet hum rustled out of the back of her throat. She looked so serene. Whitman wanted to reach out and slide his fingers down her cheek. He ached to touch the reclining goddess.

But Woolf was not finished. He hooked his hands around her thighs and pulled her to the edge of the bed toward him. Her eyes widened, and her jaw fell open. Whitman shared Wilde's shock. Woolf impressed them both with his boldness. Woolf spread Wilde's soaked lips and buried himself completely inside her.

He rolled his hips slowly into her, acclimating her to his

size. That thing looked like it could do some severe damage in the wrong hands; with great power comes great responsibility. Once she relaxed, he started thrusting deep and hard. She wrapped her arms around his shoulders, steadying herself, but she became quickly overwhelmed. Her breath reached a fever pitch, and her juices gushed out, drenching Woolf's cock.

Woolf stopped dead, breathing hard. Wilde's hand came to her mouth, and she let out a tiny giggle. She seemed as surprised as anyone else.

Holy Shit.

Wilde was a squirter. Whitman felt himself become hard. He couldn't fucking believe it. How the hell did Woolf pull it off? Part of it had to be attributed to Whitman's expert instruction on cunnilingus, right? Fucking Beginner's Luck? Or that goddamn horse cock?

What the fuck?

Whitman was impressed and envious something fierce. He hungered for Wilde. Watching her lose herself aroused him beyond anything. He yearned to be the one to make her gush. He was also feeling an uncomfortable twinge of inferiority inspired by Woolf's success. He was supposed to be the expert in this area. How did this game go so awry? He had been so in control.

Whitman reclaimed his command by seizing Wilde. He extricated her from Woolf's grasp and spun her ass into his lap. He locked his mouth onto her neck, snaking a hand up to her throat, and notching his cock at her entrance. He wrapped his fingers around her hip and started fucking her hard.

She was so fucking wet. Woolf stood in front of her, slipping his hand down between her legs and kissing her breathless.

The lingering pulsations of her orgasm squeezed

Whitman's cock tight, unraveling any sense of control. He came so fast he almost embarrassed himself.

Get a fucking hold of yourself, man.

He drew a few long breaths. Wilde panted on top of him, lips falling from Woolf's. Whitman drew a hand down her sweat-soaked spine and slipped out of her, flipping her toward him, and scooping her into his lap. He wrapped his arms around her tightly.

"Was I too rough with you?" he said, stroking her cheek with the back of his fingers.

She shook her head and grinned through one corner of her mouth, her eyes glimmering as she caught her breath. Whitman had never seen anything so beautiful. She brought her lips to his and snuck her tender little tongue into his mouth. He cupped her in his arms, so soft and precious. She wrapped herself around him like she had always been there.

CHAPTER 22

FITZGERALD

Charles strolled down the long tunnel, encompassed in a familiar sense of wonder. On the other side of the curved glass ceiling, schools of tuna passed by above his head, catching his curious eye. A small child in front of him burst into laughter, pointing in excitement as a spotted eagle ray swam by. Small groups and families loitered in clusters along the expansive hallway, giving Charles an excuse to take his time walking through the aquarium tunnel.

Charles exited the tube into a massive, dim room, illuminated only by the aqua light emanating from inside the water-filled tanks. To his left, small tanks covered the wall, and broad cylinders of plexiglass peppered the landscape. To his right was a floor-to-ceiling wall of glass with a wide banner beside it reading "Giants of the Deep." The space on the other side housed the largest marine organisms in the exhibit.

A sunfish the size of a smart car swam aimlessly around inside. Ten-foot manta rays kissed the glass. Sand sharks skimmed along the bottom of the enclosure. Out of the depths, a behemoth emerged. Speckled dark blue skin glided toward Charles—his favorite had arrived. The sole whale shark that resided in this tank approached the glass where Charles awaited her arrival, transporting him back through time.

When Charles was a boy, his mother would take him to the marine center on his birthday every year to see the whale shark. Without fail, she would swim right up to the glass, eyeing him. He believed that they celebrated a kinship. Since then, his affection for the animal and all marine life had only grown. The ocean captivated him to a level beyond a hobby; it became an obsession.

Here Charles stood once more, on his birthday, in the presence of an old friend. Although this shark was a different specimen from all those decades ago, the feeling remained the same. The extreme stress of the last few weeks of work began to dissolve out of his bones.

Dickinson had ordered Charles, or Fitzgerald as he was known within the walls of Archangel, to run endless tests on the security systems of Beverstone Keep. She had quietly elevated the security level of the stronghold twice, which was no small amount of work for him, considering he still had lectures to teach.

Also weighing on his mind was the psychotic assassin who had killed four of his former Archangel colleagues, and was still at large.

The whale shark slipped through the water, seemingly without a care. Charles, as always, envied her. The events of his life, and the loneliness that accompanied them, weighed like lead on his exhausted soul. Like young Charlie, watching the whale shark on his birthday, he never lost faith. Despite the inherent darkness in his line of work, he refused to abandon his effervescent sense of awe and unwavering belief in the power of kindness.

Shoals of people bustled around Charles as he made his

way closer to the glass enclosing his old friend. They clustered and scattered like sardines across the patterned carpet.

As Charles approached the tall glass wall of the tank, he encountered a young man. The man sat on a bench facing the tank, his gaze cast down to a point somewhere beneath the floor. Tears filled his red-rimmed eyes, and he couldn't contain the sobs that forced their way out of his mouth.

Children chased each other around the room, and their parents pursued them. Docents led small tours, spouting ocean facts to anyone who chose to listen. Altogether, they gave the young man a wide berth.

Charles wondered what the man could have done to deserve such avoidance. His distress threatened to quiver the very glass of the tank, tightening Charles' heart. He felt drawn to him.

"Are you okay, son?" Charles asked, placing a hand on the man's shoulder.

He startled, his wild eyes colliding with Charles'. "No," he choked out, returning his gaze to the floor.

"Mind if I sit?" Charles asked.

"Suit yourself. Everyone else in here is looking at me like I'm some alien," the man said, gripping the edge of the metal bench so hard it bleached his slender knuckles. One of his knees quivered so vigorously that it shook the bench.

"Do you mind if I ask what happened?" Charles kept his voice calm and soothing.

"I just proposed to my boyfriend in the middle of the tunnel, down on one knee and all that. In front of all these people. And he told me he wanted to break up."

"Oh, I'm so sorry to hear that." Charles' heart went out to the poor man. He couldn't relate on a personal level, having never been in a romantic relationship. It wasn't out of a lack of desire for love. He felt unable to fulfill the physical expectations that customarily accompanied romantic entanglements. It just wasn't in his wiring. So, he spread his love in friendship.

"And then he left me in the middle of this freaking aquarium. I'm sorry. You don't need to be listening to the problems of some stranger." The man's eyes darted over at Charles, then back down.

"Sometimes, strangers are the best people to tell these things to. That way you can feel what you're feeling, and you don't have to worry about what I think, because we'll probably never cross paths again," Charles smiled gently.

"I...I guess you're right," the man said, meeting Charles' eyes. His shoulders softened, and his brown eyes cleared a little.

"Tell you what: why don't you allow me to buy you a cup of coffee, and you can tell me some more?" Charles offered. This man was clearly in need of support, and Charles had a proven record of being an exceptional listener. Many of his students came to his office hours not just for educational counseling, but for emotional support, a service which he gladly provided. Charles believed everyone deserved to be listened to and feel heard.

"You don't have to do that. You don't even know me," the man said with reluctance.

"I don't mind at all. You seem like you could use someone to talk to. I'm Charles."

"Brian," the man said, shaking Charles' outstretched hand.

Charles paid cash for the two cups of "Brined and Grind" drip coffee from the aquarium cafe-slash-gift shop, resisting the urge to purchase one of the plush whale shark keychains at the cash register. He returned to the small table and slid one of the paper cups toward Brian, who took it with both hands. Brian had calmed a little since the bench, and the redness in his face subsided.

"He said I was smothering him, and that he's wanted to move out for a while. He said my codependency was 'toxic.' I thought we were gonna get married and make a life together. I thought he loved me. I feel like such an idiot," Brian said, wiping his eyes with the back of his sleeve.

"You are not an idiot for loving," Charles said. Brian looked up at him, unsure. "Your heart reached out toward someone, and you weren't afraid to love. And to love in a way that is true to who you are. That means everything," Charles said. Brian sniffled as the words landed.

"Some people live their whole lives without reaching out with their heart to capture that most real thing; they're too afraid. The act of love is inherently courageous. Some people have hearts full of love with nowhere to put it. You put yours somewhere, and it wasn't the right place. The right place might still be out there. Don't let this discourage you from looking," Charles encouraged.

Brian cracked a weak smile through his tears.

His voice cleared. "You are a very kind man, Charles. Thank you," he said, something unexpected passing over his eyes, like premeditated regret.

A wave of dizziness washed over Charles' head. He gripped the small tabletop to steady himself as the displays of science kits and colorful ocean-themed books blurred across his vision.

"Charles, are you alright?" Brian's voice began to sound distant. Charles' vision tunneled to black.

"Isn't she gorgeous?" Brian's voice drifted into Charles' ears. Charles' eyelids were leaden. He creaked them open to find Brian standing beside him. His demeanor had changed entirely; he was composed and calm, seemingly amused, appearing to be a completely different man.

Duct tape bound Charles to a rolling office chair in a cavernous room. He struggled to piece together the situation. The realization that Brian had drugged him began to emerge, but he could not, for the life of him, figure out when, how, or why. Charles had purchased the coffee, and Brian had never left his sight since they sat down. Had he put something on the tabletop?

The handshake. Rookie mistake.

In the black tank before Charles floated a ten-inch translucent bell with a flat top, illuminated in turquoise light. Clusters of long, spindly tentacles cascaded from the four bottom corners of the bell, extending across the tank like bedazzled spaghetti.

"This is the Australian Box Jellyfish, also known as the Sea Wasp. It's the most venomous marine invertebrate that we know of," Brian spoke in a calm, educational tone.

"Chironex fleckeri," Charles croaked the scientific name, scanning around the part of the room he could see. The two of them appeared to be the only souls in the jellyfish exhibit.

"Excellent, Fitzgerald. Your marine knowledge is just as impressive as reputed," Brian said with a warm smile.

The smile brought no comfort to Charles. A shiver worked its way through his body. The use of his Archangel codename and the fact that they were looking at one of the most venomous creatures on the planet confirmed his worst fears: Fitzgerald was staring into the hollow eyes of the Deathstalker.

How on Earth is he finding us?

Archangel took great care to protect the anonymity of its faculty.

"This beauty can kill a healthy adult human in minutes with a dose the size of a grain of salt. Now, speaking from your vast knowledge of marine biology, I want you to answer me one question: Where's the fun in that?" the Deathstalker smirked, the false warmth in his face twisting into something else.

He spun Fitzgerald around in the office chair until he faced a cylindrical tank full of moon jellyfish. The Deathstalker perched himself on the ledge of the tank and removed a two-inch-long clear tube from his pants pocket.

"I want you to meet a friend of mine." He brought the tube closer to Fitzgerald's face. Inside floated a clear mass the size of a sugar cube.

"Do you know what this is?" he asked. Fitzgerald knew immediately and nodded, swallowing back the fear rising in the back of his throat. It was an Irukandji jellyfish. This minuscule creature carried venom a hundred times more potent than a cobra. It was the second-deadliest box jellyfish after the Sea Wasp.

"Now, this bad boy probably won't kill you with one sting, and that's what I'm counting on. However, the people who have been stung by him experienced some impressively colorful symptoms. Some have reported back pain so severe they felt like power drills were penetrating their bodies, accompanied by violent nausea and relentless vomiting. Muscle restlessness made it impossible to stop writhing, while every movement of their bodies caused them excruciating pain. The effects usually lasted between twelve and forty-eight hours. Unfortunately, the aquarium employees will be back around 7 a.m., so our fun won't last quite that long. This little fella is the only toy I need to bring with me, and I love traveling light." His casual tone unsettled Fitzgerald to his core.

"If you think you can torture Archangel's location out of me, it's useless. It's undisclosed even to the faculty," Fitzgerald stated plainly. That wasn't strictly true; some Faculty members possessed the clearance, including program heads. Bluffing seemed like a viable option at this early stage of the situation. At least it would buy him time.

"Oh, Fitzy. Everly already gave me Beverstone. And I also know you're hiding Xiphos there. Why would I kidnap AIA's Head of Cybersecurity for a simple location? I need you to help me bypass the security systems, you silly goose."

CHAPTER 23

WILDE

Wilde had woken nestled between Whitman and Woolf, both still asleep on the four-poster. She didn't envy the conversation that would need to take place between them later. She felt exhausted and was grateful to be free of lectures for the day. Gathering her clothes and her composure, she tiptoed out of the Stargazer Suite—the name they had all playfully agreed upon—and made her way back to her room.

When she arrived, she found Hemingway at her desk, textbook and notebook open. Judging by the gallon jug of water next to an enormous iced coffee and the fleece blanket wrapped around her shoulders, Hemingway was also feeling the after-effects of last night's champagne. Wilde found the sight of Hemingway bespectacled and hungover adorable, knowing Hemingway would never allow anyone else to see her in such a disheveled state.

"Didn't see you after we split up. Have fun on your tour?" Hem said as if she was inquiring about the weather.

"The tour was... extremely stimulating." Wilde cocked an eyebrow, dropping her belongings on her bed. As a member of Wilde's current collection of lovers, Hemingway labored under no illusions of Wilde's chastity. So, Wilde knew Hemingway wouldn't take shock or offense.

"I'm desperate for a shower," Wilde said.

"I'm desperate for a play-by-play." Hemingway grinned and returned to her reading.

"Oh, don't you worry. You'll get one." Wilde winked on her way to the bathroom.

She took a long, scorching wash, her thoughts drifting to the night before. She had experienced a heaping handful of threesomes in her time, but last night surpassed them all. There was something so effortless and adventurous about it.

She dried off and put on a weekend version of her usual outfit: a fuzzy cropped sweater, a jersey skirt, and some long socks. A deep chill filled the castle, autumn's crisp cold heralding the coming winter's freeze.

Wilde searched her bedside for her copy of *Leaves of Grass*, but she must have misplaced it. She grabbed her current pleasure read from her bookbag and headed toward the Common Room. "I'll fill you in on my 'tour' when you're finished studying," she said, blowing a kiss at Hemingway. Hemingway mimed catching it midair, and the corner of her mouth lifted.

The fire popped, jolting Wilde from a doze. What time was it? The warm light from the window indicated it was midday. She craned her head around the arm of the leather couch to see the fire struggling. She added a few more logs and returned to her book, skimming a paragraph she had read maybe four times while drifting off to sleep.

The door to the Program W Common Room creaked open, and a showered and shaved Woolf walked in. His closely cropped beard had been freshly shaped and returned to a seventeen o'clock shadow. Memories from the night before flooded her mind, sending an exhilarating rush dancing across her skin.

"Hi," he said, taking a shy path toward the sofa. He bumped into the corner of the coffee table and mumbled, "Sorry," to it. The leather of the couch squeaked as he sat down, and he reacted, then tried to pretend like he hadn't.

Last night's confidence seemed to have faded, but Wilde found his awkwardness charming. It felt surreal to have been so intimate the night before when they had built their bond on mostly silence and violence.

"H-how are you?" he managed to push out, anxiety braiding into his voice.

"Tired," she said. "In a good way." She attempted to ease some of his nerves. He had nothing to be embarrassed about. "You?"

"It's safe to say this is the most unique roommate situation I've been in," he said with a wry chuckle.

Wilde shot him a playful "yikes" face.

"I guess I missed the window to take you to breakfast. Maybe next time..." Woolf rubbed his hands down his pant legs. "I mean, if there is a next time."

Wilde raised her eyebrows. "Do you want there to be a next time?"

"Hell yes." The words shot out of him. "I mean, yes, ma'am." He fiddled with the sleeve of his sweater.

She was both vicariously embarrassed for him and proud of him for summoning the courage to come to her. He had an innocence that she found endearing, paired with a real intrepid streak.

"When were you thinking?"

Woolf took a shallow, nervous breath. "What are you up to now?" Mischief flickered in his eyes.

She couldn't claim she was busy. She uncrossed her legs, and bands of soreness from the previous night wrapped around her thighs. She masked the pain and propped herself up on the arm of the couch, her interest piqued. "Well... okay. Where do you want to go?"

Woolf's eyes darted around the empty room. "We could stay here."

Wilde was sure this had nothing to do with the fact that Whitman was probably occupying their room.

"Here?" she asked, testing his resolve to fool around in a room where anyone in their program could catch them.

A daring spark ignited in his eyes as he nodded. His adventurous streak continued to impress her. Even she felt a little apprehensive at the possibility of getting barged in on, but the risk added to the allure.

She shifted on the couch and crossed her sensitive legs, excited for the challenge. "What did you have in mind?"

Woolf struggled to find his words. Wilde could wait. She wanted to see if he would take the reins.

"I was thinking maybe I could watch you," he said hesitantly.

"Watch me do what?" she teased with the desire to make him say precisely what he meant.

"I want you to teach me how you like to be touched."

Whoa.

The simplicity in his statement floored her, parting her lips in surprise. Her accelerating pulse traveled downward.

A slight grin spread over one side of his mouth. Wilde

Eliza Begrave

cherished every rare smile, no matter how small, that escaped from Woolf's somber face. He carried a graveness that excelled beyond his years, as if he had seen a century of sorrow. She wondered if his solemnity was a shield to keep the world at a comfortable distance. After ten years on the run from Helleborus, she knew better than most that safety can exist in solitude. Wilde felt privileged to watch his steel jaw soften. A small dimple formed on the side of his cheek, and youth emerged in his fierce green eyes.

There you are, Woolf.

The thirst in his eyes was irresistible. If he wanted to watch, Wilde could put on a show. She settled into the corner of the sofa and slipped her fingertips under her skirt, hooking them into the waistband of her panties.

Woolf entered her space. "Allow me," he whispered, wrapping his fingers around hers and pulling her panties down her legs. He slipped them off her toes and pocketed them in his corduroys, the raw confidence in his movements returning from the night before. A flutter of anticipation filled her stomach.

He reclined back on his side of the couch and fixed her with an expectant smile. "Teach me how you do it."

Wilde lifted her knees and spread them, her skirt spilling around her waist and leaving her on full display. She brought her fingers to her mouth, moistening them. Woolf ran his tongue along his lower lip, biting down on it. His breathing deepened.

Wilde lowered her fingers, spreading her lower lips for him to see. She toyed with them, tugging, teasing the opening. When she dove inside, Woolf's eyes locked on, studying every move. He stared, captivated, as if he were memorizing each moment.

136

Wilde pulled her wet fingers out and started to draw lazy circles around her clit. Tension eased in her legs. Sensation built in her belly every time she skimmed around the hood, and she closed her eyes, releasing a blissful breath.

"Eyes on me." Woolf's gentle command snapped her attention back to him. He had leaned closer to her, enraptured by the performance. She reached her other hand toward him and brushed her fingers against his lips. He took them in his mouth, coating them.

"Now the other ones," he said as they slid out. Wilde swapped hands, bringing the fingers covered in her juices to his lips. He wrapped his hand around her wrist and inserted them into his warm mouth. His eyes slid shut, and an entranced hum reverberated through her fingers.

A strong thrum built in her pussy as she watched him suck her nectar from her fingertips. She wouldn't last long at this rate, not with that hungry look in his eyes.

She slid those fingers inside herself, curling them, as she continued swirling her others over her clit.

Woolf took a sharp inhale, his eyes never diverting from her.

The door to the Common Room swung open. Wells strode in, catching sight of them on his way toward the dormitories.

"Hey, guys," he beamed.

Wilde startled, lifting her hands and shutting her legs. The back of the couch obscured them from Wells' view from the shoulders down, but Wilde couldn't help but feel busted. She delivered Wells a tight smile.

"Hey, man," Woolf replied casually, reaching over to gently nudge her knees back open. His hand filled the space hers had vacated, and she took a shuddering breath.

Is he fucking serious?

"What are you guys doing?" Wells asked, ignorant of what was happening just out of sight behind the couch's friendly shadow.

"Just talking," Woolf said, revealing nothing. Strong fingers slipped inside her, hitting deeper than hers could. He tickled the ridges along the inside wall and rolled his thumb in circles around her clit. Pleasure blossomed inside her.

Wells took a few steps toward them, eager to interact. "About what?"

Panic mixed with Wilde's pleasure, but she didn't dare stop Woolf. His touch felt electrifying, sending a thrill surging through her body.

"Exams," Woolf said, stopping Wells in his tracks.

"Oh, gross." Wells backed away with a grimace. "I'll be hitting the gym later, if you wanna join. The offer stands for both of you."

"Mmm-hmm," Wilde pushed out through her nose, her lips pressed tightly together.

"Sounds good, man," Woolf replied with a genial nod, nothing at all indicating how he was teasing Wilde into a frenzy. Pleasure spiraled in her core, and all she could give Wells was a smiling nod, unable to trust what sounds would escape her mouth were she to open it.

Woolf kept up his steady pace as Wells left the Common Room. The heavy door closed, and Wilde released a constricted moan. Woolf brought his body closer to hers. His loyal duplication of her techniques spoke to his attention to detail, but then he began to take creative license.

Woolf stretched his free fingers into the back of her hair, bringing his lips to her ear. "Like this?"

"Uh-huh," was all she could get out, all English words

having jumped out the window.

"Faster? Harder?"

She gave a desperate shake of her head. "Mm. Just like that."

He maintained his pace, searching her eyes for confirmation. A wave of pleasure built inside her.

"Oh, my god," she whimpered, clamping a hand over her mouth, afraid someone might hear.

He tugged her fingers from her mouth, and his lips replaced them.

"Let them hear. I don't fucking care," Woolf said, breaking the kiss.

His fingers maintained the perfect pace, as if he could read her mind, and she fell to pieces, moans escaping her. A proud grin danced on his lips as she quaked around his fingers.

He grasped her waist and spun her around, planting her knees on the couch, wrapping his arms around her from behind, and nuzzling into her neck, landing hot kisses on her skin. She glanced at the door, heart racing at the thought of another interruption, but it seemed Woolf didn't share her concern.

His firm palm slid up her spine and pressed her over the arm of the couch. The heat of the fire kissed her cheeks, and she melted into the leather, allowing her exhaustion to take over. Woolf lifted her skirt and flipped it up onto her back.

His warm tongue met her lips and glided in between them. He sucked on them, making out with her pussy. Wilde surrendered, no longer caring if anyone came in.

Woolf spread her knees wide on the couch. His hands grazed the back of her thighs, roaming upward. He sank his fingers into the skin of her cheeks and spread them, planting his mouth in the center.

Wilde experienced a moment of reservation, but it dissolved in a few delicious flicks of Woolf's tongue. She found herself entirely at his mercy. She sighed, resting her head on her arm.

"Is this okay? I can stop," Woolf's whisper came from between her cheeks.

"Don't stop," she begged. "Please."

Woolf wet his thumb and started to rub the outside, still licking. His other hand slid under her, up her belly, and inside her shirt. He grasped her breast, and his strong fingers started to knead. She had no time to stifle the moan that escaped.

Wilde heard his belt unbuckle. He entered her slowly, his cock spreading her pussy as he inserted his wet thumb into her ass. His remaining fingers grasped her asscheek as he circled his thumb inside her.

Fuck.

Woolf fucked her leisurely, so she felt every stretching inch. Wilde moaned into the fire as he plunged into her, and her ecstasy built. Her eyes closed, and her world was fire, leather, and pleasure.

Waves of sensation crashed over Wilde, as everything from her waist down pulsated with satisfaction. A bead of sweat rolled into her mouth, and she licked it from her lips, its taste salty and sweet. She took what felt like the first deep breath of her life as Woolf slid out of her, spent.

Woolf pulled her off the arm of the couch and placed her on her back. He planted a breathless kiss on her lips and buried his head in her chest. A deep sigh deflated his entire body, and his arms closed tightly around her waist. She stroked the sweat-soaked hair out of his eyes.

The sadness was absent in this face; in its place sat a novel serenity. There was a pureness in Woolf that Wilde envied. As much fun as it was to be a willing instrument in his corruption, Wilde wished she could preserve this perfect soul that emerged when no one was looking, the man he was when he didn't have his armor up.

Wilde felt the weight of the privilege of seeing his vulnerability and was unsure that she was worthy of it.

Am I awakening him or ruining him?

Woolf's arms tightened around her, and she pushed all thoughts from her mind.

Just be here.

The fire crackled, and Wilde relaxed on the couch, Woolf resting on her stomach. She stroked his head and stared at the ceiling. Emotions rarely crept into her sexual encounters. If she were honest with herself, emotions didn't come into play for most of her life. She had learned to compartmentalize as a toddler. She found this sudden rush of feelings both inconvenient and unwelcome.

They had been good friends, but now she didn't know what they were. She slept with a few of her friends but was always able to keep the sex separate from the friendship. She feared Woolf wouldn't be able to divorce the two.

However, it felt good to immerse herself in this moment. Wilde's heartbeat fell into step with Woolf's. So what if things got complicated? Her job was to assess and extricate herself from complicated situations.

I've got this. We're okay.

Her brain attempted to spiral into rationalizations. She shoved those feelings back into their boxes and shut the lids. She wanted them gone.

Am I ruining him, or is he ruining me?

CHAPTER 24

FIELDING

Twenty expectant faces stared at Fielding. She had been discussing the twentieth-century history of the L-pill, or lethal pill, when Faulkner poked his head into the lecture hall, a grimmer-than-usual expression on his face. He gave a stern nod out the door. Fielding sighed; she had only been teaching for ten minutes.

"Butts in seats, eyes in books. I'll return shortly," she announced. The sea of heads nodded in assent.

"You're all dismissed," Faulkner ordered to the room.

"Oh-kay," Fielding said, annoyed. The look in Faulkner's eyes left no room for negotiation. "We'll pick this up on Thursday." She waved the cadets out of the room.

Fielding had to speed-walk to keep up with Faulkner on the way to Dickinson's office. How did he move those short legs so fast?

Dickinson sat behind her desk, her eyes red behind her reading glasses as she pored over a file. All color had receded from her face except her signature lip shade of "only says no."

Frost occupied a corner of the leather couch to the side of Dickinson's desk. Her face was drawn and pale, and her eyes distant and vacant. She had crossed her arms, and one hand rubbed the upper part of her opposite arm. Faulkner placed a hand on her shoulder for a brief moment before taking a seat next to her on the couch. Confusion settled into Fielding's mind. Faulkner was not renowned for his gestures of gentleness.

Fielding took residence in an armchair opposite the couch. Dickinson's eyes had not left the file since Fielding walked in.

"Geez, who died?" Fielding said, attempting to pierce the thick tension in the air with a bit of dark humor. Dickinson's eyes snapped up. It was at that moment that Fielding noticed Fitzgerald's absence. A cold heaviness washed down her body.

"No," Fielding said, looking at Dickinson, hoping she would deny it.

Dickinson's mouth tightened. Fielding turned to Faulkner, whose gaze fell to the floor. Frost's chest hitched, and a small sob shot out of her nose.

"What happened?" Fielding said. Dickinson closed the file folder wordlessly and offered it across the desk. The unspoken message in her eyes said, "See for yourself." Fielding stood to retrieve the file. Inside was confirmation of what they all feared. The grotesque way they found Fitzgerald's body was identical to the M.O. of the Deathstalker. Fielding's heartbeat quickened, and an icy shiver ran down her spine.

"What I find most concerning is how he was compromised," Faulkner said. "The Deathstalker found him on the outside. It's unclear how, but he may possess intel on our identities. And if he does, where the hell did he get that information? Even Everly didn't have the clearance."

"Do you think we have a mole?" Frost asked.

"It's possible. It won't be easy to find out without

Fitzgerald. We need to consider a replacement as soon as possible. Without him, we're completely vulnerable," Faulkner said.

"Frost, I need you to search all the student profiles and flag any possibilities. We're launching Interrogative Inquiries ASAP," Dickinson said.

"We're going straight to I.I.s? Do we even have the doses to do them en masse?" Frost asked, shell-shocked. Fielding's mouth dried out. Even in practical training, she never had to endure a full I.I. dose. The possibility of administering it to any of the students, much less all of them, threatened to stretch the limits of even her extremely flexible code of ethics.

Looking around the room, she found no support in the eyes of Faulkner and Frost. Dickinson's directive was clear with no opposition.

"Fielding, get your team to start synthesizing the shots we need. Then consult with Fitzgerald's team and elevate us to Orange status. Do it quietly—strictly need-to-know. And keep your eyes and ears open for anyone who steps up from that team who might make a good interim replacement."

CHAPTER 25

WILDE

Wilde's head popped up from Hemingway's lap at the sound of the knock, and she blinked her eyes open. They had both drifted into a cozy nap on the couch after Wilde had come home, gushing about the night before and her subsequent interaction with Woolf.

Whitman filled the doorway, bathed in the amber light of golden hour. He leaned against the door frame, draping a casual arm above his head, and tapping his forefinger on the wood.

"So sorry to interrupt..." Sincerity and envy tinged his tone. He looked the two of them over, and a charming smile played on his lips.

"No worries," Hemingway said, propping herself up on her elbows, Wilde still resting over her lap.

"I need a study buddy," he said.

"Oh?" Wilde said, still shedding the sleep from her head.

"I have a fire going, some hot toddies, and an Escape Tactics practical to cram for. You free, Frenchy?"

Whitman's dark curls fell over his heavy-lidded eyes as he fixed Wilde with a tantalizing stare full of promise, coaxing her from the warm tranquility of Hemingway's lap. Wilde shot an impish glance at Hemingway, who cracked an approving smile back.

"As a bird," she said. Hem stroked Wilde's hair and gave her a playful push off the couch. "I'll get my stuff."

"Where's Woolf?" Wilde asked when they arrived at Whitman and Woolf's chamber.

"Training with Wells. Won't be back for hours," Whitman said, stepping to the sideboard and dripping honey into two steaming Turkish tea glasses, distinctive with their hourglass shape, ornate handles, and matching saucers. The corresponding teaspoon contacted the sides of the glass with a satisfying musical clink as he stirred with careful attention. Whitman couldn't complete a single task without exuding style.

Wilde slipped off her shoes and sat down on the rug, resting her back against the bed. The llama fur felt luxurious against her skin, its warmth enhanced by the fire. Whitman slid over, sat down next to her on the floor, and handed her a hot toddy.

"Have you... uh... seen Woolf today?" Whitman said, more tentative than Wilde knew him to be.

"Do you mean have I seen him? Or have I *seen* him?"

Whitman's eyes seemed to suggest that he was unsure whether he wanted the answer, but still needed to know. "Either, I guess." He attempted an air of nonchalance, taking a sip of his toddy.

"I *saw* him this afternoon," Wilde said, curious how

Whitman would react. "Truth be told, he saw a lot more of me."

"Damn, I'm impressed. Didn't think the grunt had it in him," he said.

"Are you jealous?" Wilde teased, a satisfied grin teasing the corners of her mouth up.

"No," Whitman answered, a little quickly. "Envious, for sure. Not jealous. Maybe... intrigued. People like us aren't the jealous type." He shot her a playful glance, his calm confidence returning.

"Too true," she said, still trying to get a read on him.

"What did you guys do?" he asked, with reluctance.

"You want all the gory details?"

"Maybe not *extensive* details. I'm just curious how Woolf's doing after last night. I am supposed to keep him under my wing, so to speak." Whitman lounged back against the bed.

"He wanted to watch me," Wilde said.

Whitman's spine stiffened. "You let him watch?"

"Wells almost got a show, too, when he breezed through the Common Room," Wilde said in a casual tone.

Whitman's mouth gaped. "You were in the..." He exhaled through puffed cheeks, losing his casual demeanor. "What else?"

"Just some light ass play and a slow fuck."

"That lucky fucker!" Whitman's eyes widened, and he ran a hand through his hair. "You guys didn't..." His eyebrows shot up inquisitively.

"Go to fifth base? God no! That thing would do irreparable damage. RIP my asshole," she chuckled.

Whitman sighed, relieved.

"I never would've pegged him for a public sex kind of guy.

I guess it's always the quiet ones." He took a long, slow sip of his drink and tipped his head back to rest on the bed.

Wilde wasn't sure why she was so comfortable sharing everything with Whitman. It delighted her to see the shock in his face and what looked like a twinge of jealousy.

The Stargazer had shifted the dynamic between them. Whitman had dropped his defensive caution around her, allowing a comfortable kinship to develop. Their chemistry felt effortless, as if they had always known each other. Wilde took a sip of honey and bourbon and leaned against him, resting her head on his shoulder.

He broke the silence. "How long do you think you'll keep it up with him?"

Wilde shrugged and shifted her legs on the rug. "I don't know. It's fun doing this stuff with someone who's never done anything. It feels sort of fresh and new." She curled her toes into the rug.

"If you start singing 'Like a Virgin,' so help me," Whitman teased. Wilde shoved a forceless elbow into his ribs, and he performed an adorable false wince. She eased her head back onto his shoulder, her thoughts wandering back to his question.

"I think breaking it off with him now would be a little cruel. I guess we'll see where it goes. Eventually, he'll get a girlfriend or get bored with me," Wilde said.

"He's more likely to fall in love with you," came the quiet response.

Wilde searched for answers in the flames of the fire.

"That concern has crossed my mind," she admitted. Wilde wanted to push the weight of Woolf's feelings off a cliff.

Who could be so stupid as to fall in love with someone like me? That's not MY fault.

"What if he asks you to be exclusive?" Whitman's voice cut into her thoughts.

"Well, that's a big fucking ask, and it's out of the question. I'll have to be transparent with him—let him know that if he catches feelings, he's on his own." Wilde noticed the sharp edge in her voice and vowed to rein in her feelings.

Whitman smiled, pleased by her reaction, but Wilde detected a tension behind it. In an instant, it vanished, and he returned to his easy charm.

"You just don't want to give me up, do you?" he said as he slid his fingers up the front of her thigh.

"Fuck no," Wilde flirted. "You're far too much fun. But that's only one piece of the equation."

Whitman lifted an eyebrow in inquiry.

"Well, for instance, I fuck my roommate on the regular," she said, eager to see his reaction.

"Hemingway? Isn't she dating that Biff douche on the outside?" Whitman seemed intrigued.

"It's Bryce. Anyway, she doesn't tell him. He's shit in the sack, but he's got wicked diplomatic connections and assloads of generational wealth."

"Assloads, you say? What's the current market conversion on an 'assload' in Euros?" Whitman taunted. Wilde smiled at the attempt to provoke her.

"And? There's gotta be more. I've seen the way you flirt. I can only assume your body count is almost as impressive as mine," he pressed.

"I guess there is the occasional tryst or fling..." Wilde admitted, grinning.

"Wait. You left the Orientation Week party with Koontz and King..."

"Oh, so you noticed," Wilde said, entertaining the fantasy

that he had been interested in her back then.

"A simple observation." Whitman defended with a half-grin.

"Uh-huh. Sure."

"And what about you?" He shifted to offense. "Hawthorne told me you couldn't tear your eyes away from me all night."

Wilde scoffed and spoke a few stuttered half-words, then resigned. Hawthorne sold her out. "Geez, god forbid a girl enjoy the view."

Whitman's face lit up with that gaze that Wilde found irresistible. He dropped all his sophisticated swagger, and his eyes sparkled at her as if he were witnessing fireworks for the first time—or a rocket launch. She wished she could inject that look directly into her veins.

Whitman licked his lower lip into his mouth. "So, Koontz and King?"

Wilde smiled and put her hands up as if to say, "You caught me."

"Damn, those two are fucking scary," Whitman said, not masking the shock in his tone.

"As long as Koontz is in the mood to enforce hard limits with King, it's possible to escape an encounter without permanent damage. You'd be surprised how many razor blades King can conceal in a petticoat," Wilde said.

"Wow. Anyone else I should worry about?" Whitman asked with inquisitive eyes.

"Well, Capote comes to me for a maintenance lay when she gets stressed about her marks, but not so much since things have heated up with her boyfriend. As you can see, exclusivity isn't exactly in my nature."

Wilde sipped her toddy, leaned against the side of the bed,

and closed her eyes for a moment. It was a relief to be honest with someone, even if it was just about one aspect of her life. She wondered if she would ever find someone with whom she could have full disclosure—someone who would learn about her past and still accept her. Someone who wouldn't leave once they discovered what she was.

Whitman had a remarkable talent for drawing details out of her. With his striking appearance and bulletproof charisma, he would have been an exceptional candidate for Program H. She had to maintain some guard; otherwise, she might blurt out that she grew up in Helleborus or something equally stupid.

Whitman's silken voice tugged her back from her thoughts. "What if I asked you to be exclusive?" By his tone, Wilde couldn't tell if he was joking or serious.

Her eyes interrogated him, and she chose a playful tone. "In that unlikely case, I guess we'll burn that bridge when we get to it."

A silence grew between them. Whitman sipped his drink, his expression unreadable.

"You'd tell me if you caught feelings..." she prodded.

He gave her a guarded smile. "If that's what you want. I could never say no to you."

A confusing itch tightened her chest at the possibility that he might someday want something more between them. Instead of mirroring the threat to her autonomy she felt from Woolf's growing feelings, the possibility of a future with Whitman gave her a sense of warmth.

"Nor get bored with you. What a ridiculous notion," Whitman continued, the seriousness fading from his voice and infusing the moment with a renewed sense of play.

"That's because you know how creative we can be

together." Wilde winked at him and leaned over to steal a kiss, eager to change the subject. "Now, what about this practical you need to study for?"

Mischief tsunamied over Whitman's eyes.

"After the mix-up about cuffs last night..." He reached over her to pull a pair of handcuffs out of the nightstand.

Escape Tactics test, indeed.

"The way I see it, we have two rewarding options..." Wilde said, noticing the heat filling his eyes as the callback to last night landed. "You can either cuff me spread-eagle, or cuff both my hands to a post like a damsel about to be put up for human sacrifice," she offered.

"Definitely the second one. I only have one set of cuffs, but we can save spread-eagle for later."

He coiled his arms around her waist and brought his mouth to meet hers. His arm slid under her knees, and he lifted and tossed her onto the bed. She giggled and rolled onto her stomach. He walked around to the foot of the bed and placed the handcuffs on the mattress between them. Button by button, he removed his shirt.

Alright, so it's a little theater you want.

Wilde gazed up at him and drew her bottom lip between her teeth. He took off his belt. She came up to her knees on the bed, locking eyes with him. She slipped her sweater over her head.

Your move, cowboy.

Whitman dropped his pants to the floor. The firelight kissed his bare skin. He was astonishing to behold, with every lean, corded, battle-toned muscle on museum-quality display. Wilde's eyes dragged down his firm chest, across his toned abs, to that V at his hips that pointed to exactly what she died to have anywhere inside her.

She started to slide her panties down her legs, but Whitman erased the distance between them and hooked his arm under her knees. She gasped as she fell back on the bed. He pulled her panties off and wrapped her legs around his waist, leaving her skirt on. He shifted her to the head of the bed.

Whitman snatched her hands, pulling them up above her head. He wrapped the handcuffs around the post of the bed and clasped them around her wrists, slowly, tooth by tooth.

Wilde was exactly where she wanted to be, at his mercy. Whitman's mouth and hands roamed her body. She squirmed and writhed to meet his touches. His mouth closed over one of her nipples as he slid a few fingers inside her, and her back arched.

"I love the way you look wrapped around my fingers. You are so fucking perfect," he breathed, his eyes regarding her with sensual awe. He explored inside of her, and his mouth traveled down to partner his hands.

Wilde's entire body pulsed. There was a deep tug in her belly that pebbled her skin. She tried to relax, but her thighs tensed around Whit's head with the overwhelming desire to bury her hands in his curls and pull him into her. The cuffs bit into her wrists as she tried to wriggle down closer to him. The more he licked, the more she lost control.

Her mind lost its sense of thought as ecstasy rumbled through her body, awakening every nerve. Wilde's pleasure overtook her, and she completely lost her breath.

As the contractions of her orgasm subsided, her entire body unclenched, and she exhaled into the softness of the bed. Whitman brought himself up to her, and she tasted herself on his lips. She ached to have him inside her.

With a lingering kiss, Whitman flipped her over onto her stomach. The handcuff chains crossed and pulled her farther up toward the bedpost. He grasped her hips, lifting her to her knees. He nudged her legs apart with his knee as his hard cock grazed the inside of her thigh.

Whitman leaned over and growled in her ear. "I want to fill this perfect ass."

"No!" Wilde squeaked.

"Oh shit! I am so sorry!" Whitman shot up and pulled his hands off her as if she had caught fire.

Her back arched, and she glanced over her shoulder at his frightened, bewildered expression.

"Love," she said, attempting to soothe his fear. "We have safewords."

His alarm shifted to confusion.

"What I said was..." she batted her eyes with feigned innocence and used her best damsel voice... "no."

Comprehension and relief spread across his face at the same time. As he sank his fingertips into the flesh of her hips, she buried her face into the soft sheets.

He traced his fingers along her spine and took hold of a handful of her hair, gently pulling her head back toward him.

"If it gets to be too much, I'd better hear a 'red' fly out of that mouth," he warned, his voice a mix of authority and concern. Even in the heat of the moment, his protective nature made her melt. His warm lips found their way to her neck, drawing a soft moan from her as his fingertips glided down her back.

He spat into her asshole with remarkable precision and then kneaded the moisture in with his thumb. Her memory transported her to a couple hours earlier when Woolf had worshipped that hole. Her back arched, opening herself up to him.

Wilde heard a squirt and then the unmistakable sound of

Whitman coating his dick in a generous quantity of lube. He notched his cock at her asshole, rubbing the moisture in gentle circles around the gate, knowing exactly how to use his firm head to tease her into submission. As he pushed in slowly, she tried to focus on her breath. The sensation was intense, but not unpleasant. Whit slid a hand around her waist and sank it between her legs, easing her tension by teasing her clit. All she could feel was his fingers, and that delicious pushing. When his whole crown popped in, everything relaxed.

"Are you okay?" Whit whispered into her ear. Wilde could not be better.

She flexed her asshole around his cock.

He gave a fragile moan, grasping her hips to steady himself, and releasing a feathered breath that unraveled her mind.

"I want you to ruin me," she whispered.

Whitman buried himself inside her, their hips rocking toward each other in rhythm. She felt completely vulnerable and entirely his. She pulled on the cuffs and they chafed her skin, as he slipped in and out of her.

His pace and breath quickened. His fingers never stopped bringing her closer to her moment of passion.

Whitman brought her to climax, and the pulsations that it caused made him moan and tremble. Wilde's entire frame quivered, and it felt like she left her body for several pulsating moments.

He wrapped his steely arms around her. "I've got you, Baby," he breathed in her ear as she returned to Earth.

Drenched in sweat, both of them struggled to return to reality. Whitman planted a soft kiss on her shoulder, then reached over to retrieve the handcuff key from the nightstand. He unlocked the cuffs, kneading and kissing her wrists as he freed them.

Whitman slid his body down beside Wilde and wrapped her legs around him. She placed her hands on his chest, their bodies intertwined. He gave her those fireworks eyes as he brought her hand up to his mouth and kissed her palm. After that, with the same amount of tenderness, he brought her other hand up and kissed it as well. Then, he wrapped his hand around hers and drew it down his cheek, closing his eyes.

In that moment, it was as if she could see beyond all the trauma and conditioning. She could see who he truly was. He looked so at peace—no personas, no agendas—just pure, here with her.

CHAPTER 26

WHITMAN

Wilde's skin glistened with a light coat of sweat as she threaded her arms into her sweater, flashing Whitman a coy smile over her shoulder. He longed to reach out and draw his fingertips down her back, sneaking in one last touch before she left. For a moment, he considered asking her to stay, but then thought better of it. He wanted to avoid the awkwardness of being found in bed with her when Woolf returned.

Whitman wished she could stay. He'd had some accomplished lovers throughout his life, but none on her level—none even came close. Calling sex with her mind-blowing would be a gross understatement. Wilde was a supernova.

He found her incredibly fascinating. She projected this effortless femininity, but it was risk wrapped in ruffles. Wilde had an edge, much like a marshmallow that becomes more delicious with a singed outside.

When she opened up to him, he discovered a new side of her. Her defenses fell away, revealing a raw, wild, and wanton spirit. She embodied both danger and desire, like a warm pillow lined with hot knives.

Yet, in her eyes resided a tranquil stillness that calmed Whitman. When he gazed into those deep wells, he felt understood. She seemed not to expect him to be anyone other than who he was.

Wilde revealed a vulnerability he had concealed for years. Whitman had never entrusted anyone with the depths of his true self, but she tempted him to trust her. No one had ever dared to venture close enough to his core to even notice the tenderness that lay within.

Whitman came to his senses. The moment had almost swept him away.

Wilde crawled back across the bed for a goodbye kiss. Her lips lingered on his for a moment longer than he thought they would, and a moment shorter than he desired. Without a word, she popped off the bed, retrieved her bag, and headed to the door.

Before she reached it, the door opened, and in walked Woolf. Well, not entirely in—he stood there dumbfounded, staring at Wilde, clearly at a loss for words.

Jesus god, man, say something.

What was Whitman going to do with this poor doofus? Woolf was a total savant with weapons and a skilled fighter—a perfect fit for Program W. But he had no finesse. Still, he had caught Wilde's interest, and it didn't seem to be solely because he had a dick longer than a Monday.

There's a lot to be said for novelty, I guess.

As Wilde crossed the threshold, Woolf took her hand. He whispered something to her that Whitman couldn't make out. She paused, then smiled at him and said just above a whisper, "Come find me."

Whitman's chest flared white-hot, and his jaw tightened. *Are you kidding me? This fucking guy?*

There was no way this jarhead stood on anything resembling level ground with him. Whitman had spent years honing his charm. He owned a perfectly curated wardrobe and possessed a diverse set of marketable skills, both soft and hard. He was more sexually experienced, savvier, and more attractive. What could she possibly see in this blunt instrument?

Whitman took a deep breath as he noticed the conflict beginning to spiral his thoughts. He was skilled at stepping back to examine his emotions. He had mastered the art of rationalizing, categorizing, and compartmentalizing every passing feeling. In doing so, he managed to avoid truly experiencing them.

She's a big girl. She can fuck whomever she wants.

He knew he wasn't angry with Wilde. Her choices were her own, and while he might lightly judge her taste, he was also among her current interests. He couldn't be jealous—no, that was impossible. People like Whitman and Wilde were above such feelings. Jealousy would imply that Woolf posed a threat to something Whitman considered his own. But Wilde didn't belong to him. She gave off the impression that she would never belong to anyone. She was untouchable, more elusive than trying to catch a forest fire with your bare hands. To possess her would be like trying to own a constellation.

Jealousy was out of the question. So, why did Whitman feel the overwhelming urge to walk over to Woolf and knock him the fuck out?

CHAPTER 27

WILDE

"Have a seat, Wilde," Dickinson said, motioning toward the leather armchair in front of her desk. Rather than sitting behind the desk, she perched on the edge of it. Wilde felt both relieved and cautious about the more relaxed atmosphere of this meeting compared to their last one.

"Thank you," Wilde said, observing the Director. Dickinson adjusted her position slightly on the front of the desk, crossing her legs at the ankle.

Wilde let the silence hang in the air between them.

"How are you settling in?" Dickinson asked, stretching her hands out on the desk beside her.

"Not bad. I mean, no one's thrown a bag over my head in a couple of months," Wilde said with a slight grin, noticing the sharpness in her voice. She hadn't meant to sound so aggressive, but she couldn't shake the feeling that this was more of an interrogation than a friendly check-in. Dickinson's spine stiffened, and she forced a smile that came across as neither warm nor confident.

"Your marks are looking good. And you're certainly keeping our upper-level students on their toes on the marksmanship board," Dickinson said in a congratulatory tone.

So, it's flattery now? What is she after?

Wilde felt increasingly anxious to escape her current situation. The longer she remained in the room, the more likely it was that the Director would grow suspicious of her. She couldn't afford to draw more attention to herself. Looking back, she realized it had been a mistake to showcase her talents so openly. From now on, she vowed to adopt a more modest approach. However, mediocrity was never her forte.

"Guns are a good stress-buster for me." Wilde hoped that admitting her stress might come across as an admission of vulnerability, weakening her in Dickinson's eyes. She attempted a shy smile.

"Making friends?" Dickinson asked, attempting to break the thick, awkward silence.

Wilde's thoughts strayed out of the room to Whitman and Woolf. "You could say that."

"Well, if there's anything that you need from me, please don't hesitate to ask." Dickinson awaited Wilde's response.

"K."

While Wilde was in here, she might gather some intel on something that had been bothering her. Fitzgerald had been absent from three lectures in a row, and his office hours had been dark. Wilde was starting to worry that he might have fallen ill.

"Do you know if Fitzgerald's in lecture or his office? I found a book I think he'd enjoy. I'd like to drop it off."

Something unexpected passed over Dickinson's face for a millisecond before she plastered on a warm smile. "Fitzgerald is on assignment. I can take it."

Wilde sensed something was off. "I can wait until he gets

back."

"Very well," Dickinson attempted a smile, but it fell flat. "Thank you for coming in, Wilde."

Wilde gave a tight-lipped nod and stood up from the armchair. She turned toward the door, her hand a foot from the ivory door handle, when she heard Dickinson call from behind her.

"Oh, and if you don't mind, Frost would like to see you on your way out."

FUCK.

"Another visit to the Penthouse? How does a girl like me get so lucky?" Wilde's voice dripped with sarcasm. She was beginning to believe that being caught by Helleborus might not be so bad when compared to another encounter with Frost.

She felt defenseless. The thought of reliving that moment with Vasily every time Frost strapped her to this ridiculous chair was unbearable. The hairs on her forearms stood up, and hot fear burrowed under her skin.

Frost smiled and sat down next to the vinyl chair, sliding the silver cart to her side and picking up a full syringe. Wilde couldn't tell if it was anxiety or her apprehension about needles, but she swore this one looked bigger.

Every slight sound broke the eerie silence of the room—a quiet so profound that Wilde felt as if the echo of her blood surging through her veins could deafen anyone within a twenty-foot radius. She attempted to dampen any resonance emanating from her body that might reveal her nervousness.

The ringing in Wilde's ears bellowed in the moments between the faint clinks of Frost's actions.

"You're always in such good spirits, Wilde. I enjoy that about you," Frost said. If Wilde didn't know better, she might have almost believed Frost. It's no wonder she was so successful at training honey traps.

"So, it's not just my rugged good looks and boyish charm?" Wilde stalled with a dazzling grin, hoping to buy herself some time.

Frost smiled.

Program H could disarm you as easily as breathing. Wilde's thoughts drifted to Hemingway. Was she sincere, or was it just a matter of her training? Could Wilde trust any of her relationships to be genuine? Were they all in this castle to learn how to deceive one another? How could anyone honestly know if someone cared for them or if they were merely a tool—a means to an end?

Wilde realized she had been staring into the pyramid foam, lost in her thoughts long enough to miss Frost injecting her arm with the psych compound. When she finally looked back, a round bandage with a banana on it stuck to her arm. Frost surveyed her expectantly.

A cold numb wave spread from the injection site up her arm and across her chest. Wilde didn't remember that from the last dose. A blanket of darkness rose from her neck over her face, blocking out the world.

The silence and blackness returned for an immeasurable time.

"Let's go back farther this time, Wilde. We'll go together," Frost's voice echoed from a distant realm.

Wilde didn't want that; she wanted to remain in nothingness.

"I don't want to leave," she said.

"You will do as I say," Mama ordered from across the kitchen table, her eyes fixed on the front window, as she shuffled the papers into a stack. Wilde had spent the last hour decoding that cipher and felt like she was on the verge of solving it. Try finding another ten-year-old who could do that. In a rare moment of resistance, she shot a hand out for the papers.

"But I'm almost done!" Wilde protested. She didn't make it a habit to be disobedient, but Mama never paused their training sessions. They would continue until Wilde mastered the skill, and she was close to getting it right. She would get it right. She just needed a few more minutes.

Their studies, combined with her father's training, were crucial for the mission. If she didn't prove that she could execute her directive, the company men would come for her. Her mother had warned her that she couldn't shield her if they did.

Mama seized the papers and returned them to the file folder with a stern look that punctured Wilde's defiance. There was no ignoring that look—the one that said, "Don't make me tell your father." Frustrated, Wilde sprang up and stomped to her room.

"You have five minutes," her mother called after her. As Wilde glanced back, she noticed the worry etched on her mother's face. No, it was more than worry—Mama looked scared.

In her room, Wilde stuffed a few changes of clothing into her backpack. Her eyes fell on the leather-bound copy of *Leaves of Grass* resting on her nightstand. Wherever they were going, Mama would surely want it taken with them. After all, what would she read to Wilde before bed?

That was Wilde's favorite time of day—listening to Mama's voice at bedtime. Even Pasha would quiet down and listen when her voice softened. There wasn't much else you could do to get him to shut his big mouth, even for a minute. Wilde carefully tucked the book into her bag.

From across the house, Pasha's voice erupted, but Wilde couldn't make out his words. Their father's thundering reply shook the walls, as always. The two of them fought constantly.

Pasha was so defiant, while Wilde preferred to follow the rules. She wanted to keep Mama and Papa content so they could all stay together. Pasha, on the other hand, seemed determined to ruin that for both of them. All it earned the stupid asshole was more punishment.

Wilde thought he might secretly hate her for how easily she excelled in her exercises. Training came naturally to her, while Pasha had to work twice as hard to achieve half as much. He was always driven more by his emotions than by discipline or skill—and it felt like right now was one of those moments when he couldn't contain his "sensitivities," as Father would call them.

Wilde trudged into the living room with her bag.

"Where are we going?" she asked, but her mother didn't respond. Wilde followed Mama's stare to the front yard, where three black SUVs blocked the driveway. Two men dressed in black dragged a screaming and kicking Pasha out of the side door and across the grass, his feet carving grooves in the dirt.

They're taking my brother away.

Wilde started to panic. They couldn't take Pasha. Even if he was a total butthead. She would get him to study harder. She could talk to him. They could work this out.

Don't take my brother.

The strap of her full backpack dug into her shoulder, and Wilde realized that she was going, too. Her stomach tumbled.

"Where are they taking us, Mama?" she croaked in a brittle whisper, her chin wobbling.

Her mother ignored her. Tears stung Wilde's eyes as she rushed to her mother, grabbing at her shirt.

"Stop that," Mama hissed, pulling her shirt free from Wilde's desperate hands and pushing her back. She wiped the tears from Wilde's cheeks without gentleness and roughly straightened her dress. "Don't embarrass yourself."

Three more men barged through the front door and marched straight toward Wilde. The first one had a hooked nose and a fresh red scar on his cheek that resembled the Crown of Thorns starfish Wilde had seen in her oceanography book. She dashed backward across the kitchen tile, kicking at him as he closed his strong arms around her struggling body.

He lifted her off the ground and began carrying her toward the exit. In the process, she dropped her bag, causing the book to spill out and fall to the floor. Mama's glare shot to the book, then at Wilde, her expression filled with disappointment and anger.

Wilde was angry, too. Why would Mama let them take her? She scrambled to the floor and snatched the book, holding it tight against her chest as the man carried her out of the house.

The sunlight blinded her as the man lugged her across the lawn. She caught a glimpse of Pasha's limp body in the arms of one of the men.

Oh my god, is he dead? Are they gonna kill me, too?

The men crumpled Pasha's body into the backseat of the middle SUV. Wilde looked back toward Mama for help, stretching her arms out, one hand still grasping the book. Her mother stood unmoving, watching as strangers took her children away.

A flicker of Wilde's fight response fought its way through her heavy grief, fanning into a flame.

"But I've done everything right!" Wilde screamed in justified outrage. Loving obedience, yearning diligence, and stringent devotion had only earned her abandonment?! "I've done anything you've ever told me to do. Why do I have to go?" Her voice cracked as she kicked and nearly broke free from the iron grip that held her.

Wilde's mother crossed the grass toward her, offering a glimmer of hope that she would save her children from their captors. As she reached her daughter, her eyes darkened. She wrenched the book from Wilde's extended hand and struck her hard across the face with it, sending a shockwave of pain that blinded Wilde with rage and confusion. A scream tore from Wilde's throat, a raw, haunting symphony of physical agony and emotional torment. A strong arm encircled her neck, and her vision dimmed to nothing.

CHAPTER 28

WILDE

Wilde rested her feet in Whitman's lap as he gently massaged them.

"Whit, I really need to focus on this," she said, attributing her anxiety to schoolwork rather than her interview with Dickinson and the subsequent visit with Frost. She had left Frost's office with a voice hoarse from yelling. She didn't want to confront what she could have said in that cell. Frost's face had been a mix of confusion and alarm.

"That is all, Wilde. You're free to go," Frost said. No lollipop this time. As Wilde was leaving, Frost called her back and retrieved a full-sized chocolate bar with seventy percent cacao from her desk drawer. She handed it to Wilde with a concerned look in her eyes that made Wilde's heart twitch.

Now, back in her room and safe on the couch, she struggled to distract herself from the memory of the expression on her mother's face so she could focus on her studies. Instead of reading the words in her textbook, she found herself staring through them.

"I promise I'll behave." Whitman raised his eyebrows in mock innocence and batted his lustrous eyelashes. "See? Good study buddy."

Wilde shot him a glare that was half disbelief, half amusement.

"What's it for?"

"Deception Techniques. With Faulkner," she groaned.

"Yeesh. Faulkner's classes are hell," Whitman said with a sympathetic grimace.

"Exactly." Her brow knitted.

"We can do this," Whitman said as he shifted into fix-it mode. "I aced DecTech last year. Granted, I had Frost. But the course material is the same. I can help if you get into a tight spot." He tickled the bottom of her foot, and the innuendo was not lost on Wilde.

Whitman's slightly unbuttoned shirt revealed a patch of his chest, and his cologne radiated off his skin. His presence was more than distracting, but it was the first thing to take her mind off the psych compound that still clouded her mind. She needed to study; anyone who didn't pass would be cut from Level II next term. Faulkner was ruthless.

"I just really need to go over this chapter," she sighed, trying to refocus. Whitman fell silent and returned to kneading her feet. His hands migrated to her calves. Wilde dropped her pen, closed her eyes, and wrapped her hands around the back of her neck, gently cracking it back and forth. The stress of these exams, coupled with her unease about Dickinson and Frost, left her body wracked. It had been a decade since she last needed to study—ten years of nothing but survival mode.

"You're so tense," Whitman said. "You really need to relax."

"I don't have time to relax," she snapped, her tone sharper than intended. Her eyes met Whitman's worried face, and she grabbed his hand. "I'm sorry."

Whitman smiled, and Wilde's heart sighed in relief. His smile was impossible for her to resist.

"I can help. Relaxation happens to be a specialty of mine," he said through a flirtatious grin.

"Would you two keep it down? I have back-to-back Hungarian and Ukrainian exams, and my brain is a fucking pretzel," Hemingway huffed from her desk in the back of the room.

"Aye, aye, Captain," Whitman said with a mini, two-fingered salute and a snicker. Hemingway shot him a fuck-off smile and made a dramatic display of putting her earbuds in.

Whitman and Wilde exchanged smiles.

Busted.

A playful glimmer sparkled in Whitman's eyes, while Wilde's offered a weak warning.

"Lie back," he whispered. "We can multitask. You study, and I'll make sure you relax."

"Whit…"

"Shhhhh," he fake-scolded. He nodded toward her textbook. "You need to focus."

Wilde returned her gaze to her book and tried to process the words on the page. Whitman spread her thighs and placed his head between them. He slipped her panties to the side with a feather-light sweep of his fingertips. Wilde stifled a gasp, grateful the back of the couch blocked Hemingway's view of them. His mouth locked on, scattering her anxious thoughts like leaves in the wind.

I hope those earbuds are noise-canceling.

CHAPTER 29

WILDE

"Been lookin' for this?" Kipling drawled from a dark corner in the back of the room. He held up Wilde's copy of *Leaves of Grass*. So, it *had* gone missing.

"What the hell could you want with that? It's not illustrated," Wilde said, furious to discover that he had broken into her chamber while she was out.

"There's that smart little mouth. Can't wait to put it to use." A malicious grin spread across Kipling's face.

Wilde took a few steps toward him. "Give it back."

"Nope. It's real educational—especially the part where it's stamped, 'From the library of Vasily Volkov?' A friend of yours?"

Wilde straightened her spine and glared at him.

"Not a friend, then," he observed, clearly enjoying this. Wilde felt foolish for reacting emotionally; now he knew even more.

"I did a little diggin'." He took a few slow steps toward her. "Volkov was a hit job ten years ago that Helleborus took credit for. You would've been just a wee girlie back then. So, I'm wonderin': what's your connection to a dead man? Or

Helleborus? I'm sure Dickinson's gonna wanna know, too."

"Fuck you," Wilde said. She marched over to him and attempted to snatch the book from his hand. He lifted it high above her reach.

"Mmm. Now, that's a good idea," he sneered, cornering Wilde between his hulking frame and her bed. Fear jolted up her spine. "Bet it would chap the shit outta Whitman's sissy ass if I stuck it to his little fuck buddy. I'm lookin' forward to gettin' you to do everything I say. Just shut that smart little mouth with my pecker."

Kipling's intentions crystallized in Wilde's mind. She weighed the option of allowing him to carry out his threat. Would she come out the other side of this less injured if she chose not to fight back?

She thought of Whitman. Some part of her couldn't bear the idea of being with someone else, even if it were against her will. She made the only choice she felt she had in the moment.

Wilde drove the heel of her palm upward, slamming it with all her strength into his face, breaking his nose with a satisfying crunch. He barely flinched as the blood poured from his nostrils, dripping down his moustache and soaking his beard.

Kipling shoved her back onto the bed and pinned her legs down with his knees. Pain shot through her thighs under his weight. He trapped her wrists on the bed, pulling them painfully above her head, squeezing them so tightly that she feared they would snap.

"Just for that, I think I'll make you call me Vasily," he snarled in her ear. Adrenaline flooded Wilde's ribcage and raced down her arms and legs. Scorching rage crept up her neck. She fought against him, but he wouldn't budge. Droplets of blood fell from his nose onto her.

"Ooh, it makes my dick tingle when you squirm like that," he chuckled. "Struggle as much as you want, Sugar. I'm gonna break you like a horse."

"You wish, you fucking psycho," she spat.

He wrenched her arm down and bit her shoulder, piercing her skin with his teeth. She held back a cry, though some of it escaped.

"You wanna see psycho? I'm gonna love making you regret callin' me that," he said, hooking his paw into the waistband of her leggings, preparing to yank them down.

Hemingway cleared her throat. "Sorry, am I interrupting something?" she said, bewildered, from the doorway. Kipling's head snapped toward the door, and his grip loosened for an instant before ratcheting even tighter. A frustrated growl bubbled from his bloody nose.

"That's enough foreplay," Kipling sneered at Wilde. "I'll skip it next time." He thrust his hips hard into hers. "If you miss me too much, just check your six." He crumpled a handful of the duvet cover and mashed it against his face, blowing a gurgling, bloody snotball into it. He left a gory red stain on the fabric as he lifted off the bed.

"Hey, Toots, nice legs. When do they open?" Kipling leered at Hemingway as he walked past her.

"I have repeatedly told you not to call me that," Hemingway's words trailed off when she turned and saw Kipling's bloodied face. Her already large eyes widened in shock, and her head receded on top of her neck.

Kipling stuffed the book in the back pocket of his jeans and lumbered out the door.

Wilde managed to shake herself from the frozen state she had been in on the mattress and sat up. Her body trembled with a mix of shock, fear, anger, and relief. Thank goodness

Hemingway had arrived when she did; Wilde shuddered at the thought of what Kipling might have done next.

Hemingway's eyes filled with worry, and she rushed to sit next to Wilde on the edge of the bed.

"Honey, you're bleeding," Hem said.

Wilde followed Hemingway's eyes to her shoulder, where crimson droplets seeped out of the two rows of teeth written on her skin in blood. The flesh around the cuts had already begun to purple and swell.

"Is that what I think it is?" Hemingway asked, her eyes wide in horror.

Wilde shuttered her eyes, letting the first tear fall down her face, and nodded once.

"That fucking monster. Did he..."

"Almost," Wilde murmured, her voice trembling along with her body.

"Oh my god," Hemingway sniffled, wrapping her arms around Wilde and cradling her head. "I'm so sorry, Sweetie," Hemingway gently smoothed Wilde's hair away from her face. Wilde could hear the emotion choking Hem's voice and knew she had started crying as well.

The hand that soothingly rubbed Wilde's back stopped. Hemingway lifted Wilde's face, and her light eyes darkened.

"You have to take this to Faulkner. Or Dickinson," Hem said, her voice dropping an octave. Wilde shook her head as she choked down a sob.

"They need to know. Kipling is dangerous," Hemingway insisted.

"I can't... You can't. Promise me you won't tell anyone about this," Wilde pleaded. Dickinson and Faulkner couldn't find out. Kipling would expose her in an instant, and she would be reprogrammed or killed. Hemingway's eyebrows furrowed in worry and confusion.

"Hem, please," Wilde begged.

"Maybe they can keep you safe," Hem suggested. Wilde knew they couldn't. What if he tried again? Would it be easier and less painful if she granted him what he wanted? Her skin tightened, and she swallowed the sour taste in the back of her throat at the revolting thought.

She feared Kipling, but she was even more afraid of what would happen if her cover were blown.

"He shouldn't even be here, not after what he did to Whitman," Hemingway said. Wilde's demeanor shifted. She knew they didn't like each other, but clearly, there was more to the story.

"What is it between them?" Wilde asked.

"They hate each other. They shared a room during Whitman's first year. Kipling used to be in Program W; he was Wiesel back then."

Whitman had never mentioned anything about this. How much more had he kept from her?

"Wiesel thought Whitman needed to toughen up," Hemingway said.

"Whitman?!" Wilde scoffed. "He's one of the toughest hand-to-hand fighters in the Academy."

"And he was when he arrived. Kipling didn't like that Whitman made friends so quickly and actually had feelings. It didn't help that Whitman and Hawthorne were thick as thieves from the start."

"What's his beef with Hawthorne?" Wilde asked. Hawthorne was a delight.

"He dislikes anyone who identifies as 'they.' He's squared off with Koontz a couple times over it, but even he's not stupid enough to take them on with King at their side, considering how lethally protective she is."

"So, Whitman is defensive of Hawthorne. They're best friends," Wilde said, trying to piece everything together.

"That's not all." Hemingway's grim eyes filled. She wrapped her fingers around Wilde's hand, bracing her for what came next. "Kipling put Whitman in the infirmary in the first week. He broke Whitman's femur at Open Mat. And he laughed when Whitman passed out from shock. Everyone in Program W saw."

"I thought the rules of engagement prohibited instructors from intentionally harming the cadets," Wilde said, shocked and enraged. She would fucking kill that guy.

"They do now. Kipling got evaluated, then transferred to Program K, and he's never had a roommate since."

Hot rage grew in Wilde's chest.

"I guess the Powers-That-Be considered him too dangerous to set loose as a free agent," Hem said.

"Jesus suffering fuck," Wilde said, massaging her eyebrows. She couldn't give in to Kipling now. She would never forgive herself if she did that to Whitman.

"Now, will you please go to Dickinson?" Hemingway pleaded.

"I can't do that," Wilde whispered.

"Why not?" Hemingway's eyes implored her.

"Please don't ask me to tell you." Wilde couldn't afford to divulge her history to anyone, not even Hem. She lacked the emotional strength to address that topic now, anyway.

Hemingway's shoulders slumped, and her lower lip quivered in resignation, twisting Wilde's insides with guilt.

"At the very least, promise me you'll steer clear of him," Hem said, squeezing Wilde's hand.

"Oh, guaranteed I'll be avoiding him. But I don't think he

has any intention of leaving me alone."

CHAPTER 30

WHITMAN

The navy-blue silk wrap dress accentuated every one of Wilde's curves as she poured three flutes of champagne. With her back to Whitman, he felt free to admire her to his heart's content. He couldn't tear his eyes from the outlines of her body. Every graceful bend beneath the silk reminded him of the soft crests and slopes of her skin—landscapes he longed to explore.

The dress was a detour from the pleated skirts and cozy sweaters she usually wore. As much as Whitman enjoyed those outfits, there was something about this sleek silhouette that made her shine in a way that felt authentically her—like the Wilde he encountered when they were alone together. Not the Wilde she presented to everyone else. The rich color transported Whitman back to their first night together in the Stargazer; he wondered if she had chosen it to evoke the memory.

He hoped she had.

"What's the occasion?" he asked from the couch. He had been studying when Wilde came in looking sixteen shades of distracting.

With a playful spin, Wilde turned, two glasses cradled in

her hands, a radiant grin lighting her face. "I aced my DecTech final."

A swell of pride filled Whitman's chest. "See? I told you you'd be just fine if you relaxed a little."

Wilde glided over to him and sat across his lap, handing him one of the flutes. Her warm skin melted into his, separated only by a whisper of silk. She clinked her glass with his in celebration and took a sip.

Woolf had his backpack slung over one shoulder as he headed toward the door.

"Woolf, stay! I poured you a glass," Wilde called after him from Whitman's lap.

"I can't. I have a prior commitment." Woolf's eyes reflected a blend of longing, duty, and a hint of disappointment. "Um, congratulations, by the way." He took two steps past the sideboard, hesitated, then walked back to it. He lifted the flute toward Wilde in an air-cheers, downed a big swig of the champagne, gave her a stiff grin, and headed out.

The heavy door latched shut behind him.

"Jesus, he can be such a buzzkill sometimes," Whitman said between sips of champagne. "He seems the type that grew up in a house with wooden signs that said "Live, Laugh, Love." And his cold suburbanite parents never bothered to teach him how to do any of the three."

"Take it easy on him. He's still so young," Wilde mock scolded.

"He's older than both of us."

"Well, he's a young 'older than both of us,'" she crinkled her nose at him. She was right, of course. Woolf had an easy five to seven years on Whitman, but Whitman was worldly. He had spent the several years prior to Archangel globetrotting and weaving a tapestry of opulence and charm. Woolf likely spent those years scraping his war buddies out of the sand.

Whitman took Wilde's champagne flute with the same hand that held his own and set them both on the side table. He tightened his arms around her waist and pulled her close, enveloped in the fragrance of lilies and vanilla—her signature scent that awakened all his senses.

"At least I don't have to share you now," he said.

"Well, the champagne and the dress were meant for you, anyway. I just didn't want to be rude," Wilde said, naughtiness sparking in her eyes.

"Aw, but I like it when you're rude." He sank his fingertips into the soft skin of her sides and planted a firm, searing kiss on her lips. She melted into his lap, evicting every thread of tension from his muscles.

Whitman slid a hand up Wilde's thigh. It was the first time he had seen her wear silk stockings, and they felt luxurious beneath his fingertips. His hand wandered higher, slipping under the hem of her dress until the stockings came to an end. His fingertips brushed against the tender skin of her thigh.

Whitman gave Wilde a questioning look. He untied one side of her wrap dress and opened it, revealing the small strap of a garter belt.

Holy fuck.

Garter belts were somewhat of an Achilles' heel to Whitman. He bit his lower lip and slid his middle finger underneath the strap. Wilde's eyes followed his finger with sultry anticipation. He lifted the strap and released it, giving it a little snap. Wilde bounced and giggled as it stung her skin, every inch of her perfect body jiggling in delight in his lap.

This fucking woman will be the end of me.

Whitman unfastened the other side of her wrap dress, revealing an exquisite midnight-blue lace lingerie set. Delicate straps crisscrossed her breasts, which threatened to overflow the cups of the balconette bra, while intricate scallops of lace obscured what his tongue yearned to taste.

Fuck me.

Whitman drew a sharp inhale. "Remind me to do nice things for you more often."

CHAPTER 31

WILDE

Wilde was nearly shivering; the paper-thin silk no longer protected her from the chill in the room, and her body vibrated with anticipation. Whitman explored her with those fireworks eyes, leaving her feeling profoundly powerless. Goosebumps began to form on her skin as she wrapped her arms around his shoulders. His warm hands moved up the backs of her thighs and grasped her hips, pulling her molten body over to straddle him. Her spine uncurled like an awakening fern as she wrapped her hands around his perfect face.

She felt him swell beneath her, pressing against her lace panties, and a pulse began to grow at that point of contact.

Whitman's hands roamed across her skin as he slid the rest of the dress off her shoulders, the smooth fabric leaving a silken imprint on her skin. She felt the warmth of his mouth on her neck, his lips and hands tracing delicate trails. She surrendered to the moment.

Whitman's fingertips grazed her shoulder and paused. Wilde lifted her head to find him examining the fading green oval bruise that marred her skin, remnants of Kipling's bite.

Whitman traced the top of it with his thumb, concern filling his eyes. The scabs left by Kipling's teeth had thankfully fallen off over the last few days.

"Training," she said, hoping the excuse would suffice. The worry in Whitman's eyes lingered for a moment. She brushed a curl from his creased forehead and attempted to dazzle him with a seductive gaze. A faint growl emanated from the back of his throat as he buried his face in her neck.

One of Whitman's hands slid up the back of Wilde's neck, grasping a handful of her hair with gentle control. He tilted her head forward and filled her mouth with his tongue. A small moan fell out of her mouth into his.

Intoxicated with him, she forced herself to come up for air. She needed to gain some control, or she'd lose herself.

"You have me at a slight disadvantage," Wilde gasped, panting. Whitman paused reluctantly, his breath heavy and ragged. She cast a suggestive glance down at her state of undress.

Wilde released the top button of his shirt, and a knowing smile spread over his lips. He eagerly freed the rest of the buttons and untucked his shirt from his pants.

Wilde slid herself onto the floor, kneeling between his legs. Whitman caught his breath and marveled at her with those rocket-launch eyes, overwhelming her with a feeling much more profound than lust—beyond mere attraction.

She unbuckled his belt, and his breath stalled. Inspired by his vulnerability, she lowered his zipper, releasing his hard cock.

Wilde grabbed it by the base and slid her hand up to the tip, locking eyes with him, smiling and licking her lips. She longed to taste him, but she wanted to take her time. She fixed him with her most provocative gaze, opened her mouth, and rested the head of his cock on her tongue.

His mouth hung open in astonishment.

Wilde took his crown into her mouth and started licking, lapping, and gently sucking. Her hand stroked his shaft while she let her mouth run wild over the tip, gliding her tongue around the rim. Whitman's breathing deepened.

She glanced up to catch his eyes before his head fell back against the couch with a groan. She took this as her opportunity to slide his full length down the back of her throat. Whitman's breath hitched. Wilde felt his thighs contract and then relax as he let out a low moan.

Wilde began to pump Whit's cock in and out of her throat, now letting her tongue tease his balls. She felt his muscles tense with the desire to take control of the pace. She reached up and seized his hand from the armrest, placing it on the back of her head. The relief spread down his legs as his fingers carved into her hair. His hips began to move and rise to meet her, slowly beginning to fuck her face.

Whitman's pace quickened as he began to lose control, his other hand entwining in her hair next to its pair. As she sensed he was getting close, he stopped with a sharp inhale. He took a deep, controlled breath.

He slid out of Wilde's mouth, and she looked up at him, both of them catching their breath and trying to regain their composure. Whitman gently tipped Wilde's chin up with two fingers, leaning down to steal a kiss. It seemed as though he didn't want this moment to end so soon.

Wilde couldn't help but watch him surrender to his pleasure. She wanted him to explode inside her mouth and hear the sounds he made when he finally lost control.

He wants to take his time. Fine. Two can play that game.

Wilde stood and turned her back to him. She bent at the

waist, slipped her panties down to her ankles, and stepped out of them, giving him a full view of what she revealed. The moment stole her breath. When she turned around, Whitman gazed up at her with eyes that still lacked complete control over his desire.

She yearned to sink back into him.

Wilde closed the distance, straddled his lap, and spread her lips. She lowered herself, inch by inch, onto Whitman's throbbing cock. She sat down on him, savoring every moment of him spreading her open. When he hit her deep, her control evaporated. She began to rock back and forth, grinding on his lap.

Whitman lifted her hips and rose to meet her thrusts.

Wilde felt a pleasurable sensation rising from the base of her spine, spiraling up from her tailbone to the skin on her scalp. Every hair follicle on her head stood on end, and waves of sensation cascaded back down over her body.

CHAPTER 32

WHITMAN

Whitman was barely maintaining control over his pleasure watching Wilde buck and rock on top of him. She looked fucking magnificent, sweat dappling her skin, head falling back in rapture. Her breathing quickened, and her moans pierced the air. He felt her moment of climax as the muscles inside her tensed and relaxed in rhythm, squeezing around his cock, and bringing him to join her in ecstasy.

Whitman couldn't remember a time when he had come so hard. The sensation alighted each nerve, sending reverberating shockwaves over every cell of his body.

Wilde collapsed onto him, wrapping her arms around his head and shoulders. He loved hearing the sweet sound of her moan as she settled on top of him. He remained inside her, his cock pulsating with the remnants of his orgasm, sending skitters of electricity up his spine.

He tightened his arms around her and buried his face in her breasts, planting a wet kiss on her skin. Her scent intoxicated him. Even though he thought it was simply the fragrance of her perfume, a lingering sensation convinced him that he could taste the rich sweetness of vanilla on her skin. He wished they could remain in this moment for eternity, wanting nothing more than to stay in the blissful embrace of his Valkyrie.

Wilde placed a kiss so small it was almost imperceptible on the top of Whitman's head. Yet he sensed it, and it demolished him. It filled him with the unfamiliar sensation of belonging. At that moment, he felt indivisible from her. Their skin blended, and he lost awareness of the barrier between her body and his.

She made him feel truly wanted; he had a home in her arms—a real home for the first time in his life.

He belonged to her.

And that's where Whitman wanted to stay—with Wilde. Whether it was by her side, watching her six, or in her arms, he would never leave her. He would accept whatever percentage of herself she was willing to give him and offer his whole self in return. He wanted to be her champion.

CHAPTER 33

WHITMAN

The chains of the heavy bag rattled as Whitman hailed heavy punches, finding a pocket of focus in an otherwise aimless training session. His concentration had vanished the moment Wilde and Woolf arrived at the gym together.

Wilde's royal blue sports bra and form-fitting leggings screeched Whitman's thoughts to a record scratch halt. Woolf could stomach training with her, but the idea of bringing her any harm would send Whitman on a one-way trip to a toaster bath. He was confident Woolf wouldn't hurt her, but he couldn't keep his protective eyes from drifting to them.

Kipling's putrid breath heralded his arrival from behind Whitman's back. Whitman slammed a few more blows into the bag, ignoring the aggravating presence.

"Look, it's Wimpman," Kipling said in a dull, mocking tone. Whitman's shoulders slackened as he caught his breath and wiped the sweat from his brow.

Can't even train in peace with this dickhead around.

"Wow, in three years, you haven't come up with anything better. Wait a minute, if you're here, then who's threatening billy goats down at the bridge?" Whitman shot back. He turned to face Kipling, who sported a broad white splint across the bridge of his nose. "Oh, thank god you finally did something about that. Now all you need is a personality implant."

"In the market for another broken leg?" Kipling rolled his shoulders forward.

"If you're up for getting kicked out of another program. Maybe with your new nose, they'll consider you pretty enough for H," Whitman taunted, filling his chest and lifting his chin. "C probably requires you to be able to type and read without mouthing the words." He ripped off his boxing gloves, dropping them one by one on the mat at Kipling's feet. He glared up into the ogre's gnarled face with unbridled hatred.

No need to hold back on shit-talking, considering they were both banned from sparring with each other since the incident during Whitman's first Open Mat. Shame, because he itched for another shot at the asshole. A shot at redemption. The leg injury and rehab set him back most of his first year, and he had trained his ass off ever since.

"You're tough to understand. I don't speak Little Bitch," Kipling said, the corners of his thick, ginger mustache ticking up. He took one giant step toward Whitman and tilted his chin to his chest, splaying his beard. They stood nose-to-busted-ass-nose. Whitman wished he could shake the hand of the person who had broken it.

"I know it's hard when the sentences are more than two words. Right, Big Guy? And since your Great Pumpkin-ass head could have only been pushed out by a lady who turns green when she's angry, it makes sense that your native tongue would be Big Dumb Cunt," Whitman challenged.

Without warning, Kipling swung an uppercut at Whitman's face, clipping his jaw. The mat rushed up to meet

Whitman, as he caught himself on his elbows. His skull buzzed, eyes blurred, and jaw throbbed. He tasted sand and pennies.

That motherfucker sucker punched me! Oh, it's fucking ON.

Whitman's fingers fell on the handle of his warm-up jump rope. He slashed blindly with it in Kipling's direction, hearing a crack as the big dumb brute hissed.

He dashed and spun a kick at Kipling's ankle, dropping him to one knee. Rising to his feet, he stomped on the side of Kipling's vulnerable thigh, hoping to hear the same snap his own leg had made. He jump-punched Kipling across the face while he was still down.

Fuck!

Even with his boxing wraps on, it felt like punching concrete. Whitman wiggled his knuckles, hoping the blow hadn't dislocated them.

Kipling rose, unfazed, and stalked toward him with a surprising quickness and a discouragingly slight limp.

Shit. Plan B: Defense.

Kipling threw a heavy hook. Whitman ducked it as a vicious kick landed on his bad leg. Agony detonated across his thigh. He bit back a howl.

Fuck. Plan C: Don't die.

"Ow! Shit-damn, Wilde. Take it easy," Woolf yelled from across the gym, stealing Whitman's precious focus and forcing his attention to Wilde.

"Shit, sorry," she said, grabbing Woolf's arm in both her hands.

Taking advantage of the distraction, Kipling spun Whitman's world as he whipped him to the floor. Whitman snuck his forearm up, blocking a full choke hold, as one of

Kipling's tree-trunk arms wrapped around his neck. Darkness rushed into the periphery of Whitman's vision.

"Ooooh, there's my little whore, Wilde," Kipling murmured in Whitman's ear. "I wanna catch up with her again, later. She's a feisty little lay, ain't she?"

Whitman's jaw clenched. "You're fucking dreaming, Big, Dumb and Ugly. Wilde wouldn't touch you with a ten-foot pole," he ground out as he fought against the creeping darkness.

"She sure does like suckin' on *my* ten-foot pole. She loves riding a man that don't break easy, like you. Idda thought you'd be tougher by now with how rough she likes it."

"You're so full of shit," Whitman squeezed out. In his fading vision, he saw Woolf take Wilde's hand. Fresh jealousy and anger strengthened his spine.

"Imma find that little cumdumpster after I whoop your ass. She tastes just like vanilla ice cream. Sweet as sugar, that one."

How the fuck would you know?

Fury flooded Whitman's veins as a runaway truck of realization struck him.

Unless he's telling the truth.

Whitman's rage soared, and his strength returned. Taking the risk of Kipling knocking him out in seconds, Whitman removed his arm from protecting his neck. He locked his hands and used the force of both arms to drive his right elbow into Kipling's ribs, loosening the overpowering grip, and breaking free. He scrambled up, lungs scorching inside his chest.

Kipling lumbered to his feet a hair slower than Whitman. It was just enough time to take one full breath and attack. He steeled himself and drove the full force of his forehead into the center of Kipling's bandaged nose. Kipling roared and cradled his face as blood gushed from his nostrils.

Those few moments were all Whitman needed to summon his remaining strength and deliver a kick squarely into Kipling's solar plexus, emptying his lungs and knocking him off his feet. Big, Dumb, and Ugly landed on the flat of his back, gasping and choking.

Whitman pounced on him, bludgeoning his face with repeated elbow strikes. Blood dripped down Kipling's beard and the sides of his cheeks. He gurgled as it filled his throat.

Choke on it, motherfucker!

Whitman wrapped his palms around Kipling's bloody head and prepared to drive his thumbs into his eye sockets.

"That's the last time you're gonna even fucking LOOK at Wilde," Whitman snarled.

"WHITMAN!" Faulkner barked from the side of the mat. Whitman paused, the squishy roundness of Kipling's eyes squirming under his thumbs.

"Stand down," Faulkner said in a lower grunt. Whitman lifted his hands from Kipling's face with a wrathful growl. His chest heaved as his burning breaths caught up.

"Go wait in my office. Now," Faulkner ordered.

Kipling's breath snorted in and out of his obliterated nose and mouth. A tobacco-stained tooth dangled from his bloody grin as he stared up into Whitman's rage filled eyes.

"You." Faulkner pointed an accusing finger down at Kipling. "Come with me."

Whitman found Wilde across the gym as she whipped her hand away from Woolf's. Her eyebrows scrunched in a silent question, and concerned eyes penetrated him. Was she worried that he knew the truth? Not only was she fucking his new roomie, Woolf, but she was nailing his former roommate and worst enemy, Kipling. Whitman glared at the two of them as he swiped his boxing gloves off the mat on his way out of the gym.

Why Kipling?

Whitman's chest ached from more than breathlessness; Wilde was his oxygen. Despite wanting her for himself from the center of his heart, he'd known he needed to abandon hope that she would ever be his alone. It was difficult enough sharing with Woolf, and whoever else. Now, Kipling?

He was stupid for believing he had meant something to Wilde.

He was only one of many.

Allowing himself to develop feelings for her was just a countdown to pain.

Why did she have to fuck HIM?

CHAPTER 34

WOOLF

"Do you think he's okay? Did he look injured?" Wilde asked, her fingers tapping an erratic rhythm on her thighs. Woolf brought her a gin and tonic from the sideboard to calm her. He took a seat and a sip of the one he had made himself.

When Whitman had stormed out of the gym, anger wasn't the only emotion on his face. He looked devastated.

"I think he was disappointed to leave Kipling alive," Woolf said. Wilde's eyes glazed over with a mix of emotions Woolf couldn't decipher. She trembled.

Woolf slipped his arms around her, tucking her into a hug that he hoped would soothe her nerves. She melted into him, gripping the back of his t-shirt and nuzzling into his chest. His fingertips met the soft skin of her back, exposed by her gym outfit. She felt like heaven in his hands.

When Wilde started kissing him, Woolf didn't stop her. He surrendered to her touch. She fed her soft tongue to him, and he cupped the back of her head, weaving his fingers into her hair.

She poured herself onto him like a waterfall, but something wasn't right. Her anxious lips painted desperation on his mouth. She wasn't here for him.

He dreaded what he needed to do, fearing it might make this the last time they would be together. As his heart cracked, Woolf took one last taste, delving into her mouth with abandon. He gasped between kisses, teetering on the edge of losing control.

It destroyed him to push her away.

"Fuck," he whispered, breaking the kiss and taking a deep, feathered breath. He settled his hands on her perfect hips, keeping her at a distance.

"What is it?" she asked, her irresistible eyes glistening. Those damn eyes.

He could easily continue. He could do the wrong thing that felt perfectly right. He could stay here with his angel.

"Look, I want this." He squeezed his fingertips into the meat of her sides, the soft skin yielding to his touch. "Fuck, I want this," he muttered.

"Then what's stopping you?" Wilde flirted, leaning back in. Woolf held her back with all the emotional strength he could summon. He withered inside. He could refuse her, but he would never stop wanting her.

"I only want this if you want *me*. And it doesn't feel like you're here with me anymore."

Wilde's eyes fell. "What do you mean? I'm right here." She clasped his hand and pressed his palm over her heart. Woolf clung desperately to the shreds of his self-control.

"You came here to wait for Whitman," Woolf said, pain lacing his words. "I don't want to be a placeholder. Or a distraction." If he could have her, he wanted all of her. If he couldn't have her, he wouldn't keep her from the one she desired.

The right thing for him wasn't the right thing to do.

He recalled the fury in her eyes when Kipling struck a strangled cry out of Whitman. For the first time, Wilde had unleashed her full strength on Woolf, roundhousing him on the upper arm.

"We have to do something," she said, keeping her eyes fixed on Whitman's face as it changed colors from red to purple. She stepped toward the fight, but Woolf reached for her hand, holding her back.

"Are you crazy? What are you gonna do, break it up?" She would end up injured if she tried.

"He's hurting him. He could kill him!" Emotion shook her voice, and she lunged forward, but Woolf held her tight. Whitman had been waiting for this opportunity.

"I believe that's a chance he's willing to take. Let him have this," Woolf said.

"I saw your face when Whitman was in that fight. You were scared. You weren't even scared when you faced down Kipling yourself," Woolf said.

"Of course, I was scared. It's Whitman," she said.

"It's *your* Whitman." He searched her eyes for any sign of contradiction.

"He's not mine." The despair in her voice crashed into him.

"Then why do I feel like he secretly hates me the more time I spend with you?" It was true. Whitman's attitude toward Woolf chilled as things with Wilde heated up. They barely shared words anymore.

"Why do you think that?" she said in a doubtful tone.

"There's a palpable vibe. If he walked in here right now to find you in my arms, how do you think he'd take it?"

Horror filled her eyes.

"And you feel the same for him," Woolf said, wishing for

a sliver of chance she'd deny it.

Wilde sank back into the couch in speechless dismay. Woolf's heart plummeted at her silent confirmation. A fist formed in his throat.

She opened her mouth to speak, but he cut her off.

"You call him 'Love.' You call me Woolf."

Wilde's shoulders curled forward like he had struck her in the chest. Her gaze scoured the floor for answers. In the moment her eyes rose to his, Woolf knew that she hadn't previously realized how deep her feelings for Whitman ran.

A shadow of panic fell over her face. Her eyes darted to the door, and her trembling breaths quickened.

Woolf activated. "Hey, hey, hey. It's okay. Just breathe, it's gonna be okay."

"No, it fucking isn't. I don't know how to do this. I'm not the fall-in-love girl." Wilde breathed hard, and tears filled her eyes. She raked them away before they could fall.

Woolf grasped her shoulders and sat in the moment with her, trying to steady her with his soft, supportive gaze.

She drew a stuttering breath and met his concerned eyes.

"I can't do this. Love is a liability," she said, defeat weighing her words.

A profound ache clutched Woolf's heart. He wondered what horrible experiences had taught her that lie.

"You really believe that?" he said with a soft scrutiny.

"The people you love always end up hurting you." A distance grew in her eyes as she spoke.

"Apart from giving me a dead arm, you've never hurt me," he said.

Wilde considered his words for half a moment before her eyes flashed in recognition.

Oh my god. Did I just fucking say that?

Woolf's face twisted into a grimace. "Shit," he muttered.

"Wait, so you…" she asked, nervousness tinging her voice.

He sealed his lips and squeezed his eyes shut, kneading a temple with his fingertips.

"Yes, ma'am," he whispered, mortified.

Of all the ways he'd imagined telling her how he felt, blurting it out in the same breath as endorsing another man had never crossed his mind.

Real smooth, dumbass.

He loved her, not only when they kissed or made love. He loved her in the small moments. In her sly smile that came after she caught him telegraphing a punch. In every log that kept a fire from dying. In the playful way she kicked her feet back and forth when she racked up another killshot at the long range. In the horses she doodled in her notebook when she was bored in lecture. How he always knew she kept a book on her, and, nine times out of ten, it was one of his recommendations. She would return it to him, stuffed with colorful annotated sticky notes, each one feeling like a glimpse inside her mind—a tiny love letter from her inner world.

He loved how she linked arms with him on the way to the gym when she was in a good mood, even though he knew Whitman inspired her giddiness.

He loved that in the quiet moments by himself, when he previously ruminated on the pains of the past, the thought of her flooded that space, and he no longer felt so alone.

He loved her too much to sacrifice her happiness to save his own.

"What does this mean… for us?" Wilde's voice quivered with uncertainty.

"Well, no more hot sex, unfortunately," Woolf sighed, resigned. "I'll step aside."

Tears returned to her eyes. "I can't lose you."

"I'm not going anywhere. I'd like to keep watching your six, if you're okay with that. Such a nice six," he cocked his head to the side and crinkled his nose at her.

Relief washed over her face, and her invigorating sense of mischief returned. "So, friends with flirtation?"

"Yes, ma'am. As long as it's alright with you."

Wilde curled her arms around Woolf's waist, and he swept her into his lap. She rested the side of her face on his shoulder, her nose nestling between his collarbones. He let out a deep, contented sigh as he squeezed her tighter.

"Yes, please," she breathed against his chest. Woolf planted a small kiss on her forehead and rested his cheek on the top of her head. He wished they could remain here forever.

After a few moments, Wilde's body grew stiff in his arms. "I have to go. I can't be here when he gets back. I don't know what to say."

Woolf released her, knowing that it might not be the worst idea for her to leave. He had never seen Whitman so furious. "I can let you know when he's back. You two need to talk. I'll make myself scarce for a while."

Wilde nodded. She gazed into his eyes with deep affection. Woolf placed his hands on the warm small of her back. She wrapped her fingers around his face and kissed his cheek with exceeding tenderness. The skin of the side of his face crinkled into a smile beneath her lips.

Woolf clocked her reluctance as she separated her mouth from his cheek, a small farewell to their potential.

"Please, let me know that he's okay," she pleaded.

"Yes, ma'am."

CHAPTER 35

WILDE

Wilde wiped the sweat from her palms on her skirt. The two gin and tonics she drank with Hemingway had barely taken the edge off her nerves. Hemingway agreed that Whitman deserved to know how she felt about him.

How do you tell someone you're falling for them?

She prayed the words would come to her in the moment. She would see him and know what to say. Who was she kidding? She had never done this before.

Oh, come on. How hard could it be?

She had been in way hairier situations.

What if Whitman didn't feel the same way about her? What if she were only a fuck to him? They both weren't the falling-in-love type. People like them couldn't afford to fall in love. Love was an exploitable weakness.

What the fuck am I doing? This could ruin everything.

She had to know, either way. At least if he didn't reciprocate her feelings, she could move forward. She wouldn't be endangering anyone with her inconvenient emotions.

Why did the thought of losing Whitman feel like it would annihilate her?

She couldn't believe she had been reduced to an anxious, blubbering, love-drenched mess. It was embarrassing. She needed to get her shit together.

Just breathe.

She cocked her chin up. She would do what she always did in unpredictable situations: improvise.

She knocked on the door. Nothing.

She pushed it open a crack. Dim lighting cast shadows across the room. Maybe Whitman wasn't in.

"Whit?"

No response.

She opened the door wider and blinked as her eyes adjusted to the low light. As she scanned the room, she detected the smell of pipe tobacco. Or was it cigar smoke? In the back corner of the room, behind the antique desk, glowed a circular ember.

He *was* in.

"Hey," she offered as she tiptoed over the threshold.

"Hey." His voice was gravelly and slightly cold. Was he brooding? That wasn't like Whitman. She was used to him being playful. Had he been injured in his fight with Kipling? Silence hung in the smoky room between them.

Maybe he was angry with her.

"I can go if you want to be alone." Wilde backed a step toward the door.

"Stay."

The air stilled in the room. Wilde recognized a command when she heard one.

Oh, so this is a scene.

Wilde was down to play along. After all, the muted lights and curling wisps of cigar smoke imbued the room with a sultry ambiance and a hint of danger. They could talk after; she was eager to discover where he was about to lead her. Relief settled her bones, and the possibility of what was to come heightened her senses.

She complied, dropping her bag on the floor and slipping out of her shoes. She took a step forward.

"I said," his tone was quiet but deliberate, "stay."

Anticipation pulsed in Wilde's body, and her fingertips trembled at her sides.

Whitman took a long drag from the cigar and twisted it into the ashtray. He stood and prowled toward Wilde while she remained frozen in place. His curls splayed in a disheveled crown around his dark brow, and his shirt lay partially open. Had he been drinking? The empty lowball she spied on the desk confirmed her suspicion.

Whitman's expression darkened as he stalked her like prey, his lips pressed into a firm line. He approached her and pushed her back against the oak door. His strong hand grasped her chin, tilting her face up. The cigar smoke mingled with the fragrance of his cologne and the scent of whisky on his breath. Whitman turned her face to the side and nuzzled into her neck, raking his teeth against her soft skin and leaving playful love bites. Wilde gasped at the sensation.

He tipped her chin down with his thumb, opening her mouth and sliding his fingers inside. She sucked and licked them, hoping to drive him as wild as he was making her.

Whitman brought his hand under her skirt and found the space between her legs. He slipped her panties to the side and sank his fingers inside her.

A deep, pleased groan rumbled out of his throat. "My little slut is already so wet for me," he growled in her ear.

His eyes betrayed no change in emotion, just that same stern heat, as he slipped his fingers out of her. He grasped her shirt and tore it open, sending the buttons shooting across the room. He pulled the cups of her bra down and clasped both his hand and his mouth on one of her breasts. His warm lips sent shockwaves of sensation across her skin, and she moaned. The fingers of one of Wilde's hands curled into his hair by instinct. Whitman snatched it by the wrist and pinned it firmly against the door above her head. His hot mouth rained kisses and bites across her skin like shellfire. Wilde's grip on her self-control started to slip.

Whitman unbuckled his belt and tugged his pants down with one hand. He grabbed her leg behind the knee and pinned it up against her body as he entered her. He pumped in her hard and slow, pressing her against the heavy door with every thrust. She surrendered to the feeling and wrapped her other arm around him. He grasped it and pinned it with its pair, holding both her wrists against the door above her head with one fierce hand.

"You like getting fucked rough in this needy little cunt, don't you?" he rasped.

Holy fucking hell.

"Mmh, hmm," was all she could push out. Whitman wrapped Wilde's leg around his waist, and her moans grew more desperate.

He smothered her mouth with his hand and fucked her harder. "Then shut the fuck up and fucking take it," he whispered. Wilde turned molten. She found the degradation delectable. This darker, more primal side of Whitman was a new experience for her, and it was sweeping her away.

Her body sprinted toward climax when Whitman stopped short. His fingers fell from her lips, and she struggled to catch her breath. His iron grip on her hands eased, allowing her arms, tingly from being held up, to fall lazily around his head. Her fingers found home in his curls as they had so many times before. He wrapped her legs around his waist and lifted her, still inside her.

Grasping the meat of her ass with firm hands, Whitman walked them both over to the bed. Wilde buried herself in his sweaty, musky skin. His muscular arms tightened around her for a moment, embracing her tenderly, a brief departure from his feral persona.

He let out a throaty snarl and tossed her onto the bed, flipping her onto her belly and yanking her by the ankles to the edge of the mattress.

He was back inside her before she realized what was happening. He spread her legs wide across the sheets. He bucked inside her, unstoppable, threatening to push her ecstasy over the brink. His pleasure overcame him, and he unloaded inside her, his moans piercing the smoke in the air. His cock pulsed inside her, and she lost any shadow of the control she had long since surrendered to him. The pulsations spread to the muscles inside her, and ripples of satisfaction rolled across her body. Her consciousness lifted out of her body, and her vision washed white.

Whitman collapsed onto Wilde for a few moments, his hot breath tickling her ear as they melted together, just as they always did. She knew she could tell him how she felt; it didn't matter if she couldn't find the perfect words. They had to share the same feelings. She reached back with her hand to stroke his skin, but then he lifted his body off the bed and walked away.

Wilde was still regaining her senses when she heard the clink of a whisky decanter meet the rim of a glass, followed by a few glugs of liquid. She rolled over toward the source of the noise and brushed some hair out of her face.

"Are you pouring two of those?" she said, injecting some

play into the tension hanging in the air. She could use a bit of liquid courage for what was to come next.

His back faced her, and he remained silent. He tipped the glass up and swallowed the entire dram in one gulp before setting it on the desk.

"You can go now." It was a command, but it felt different this time. This didn't seem like a scene anymore.

Wilde's stomach dropped. "Whit—"

He raised a single finger, silencing her without turning around.

"I assume you're familiar with the location of the door," he said as he poured himself another drink.

Wilde struggled to understand the situation. This wasn't right. She had thought it was roleplay. Was he serious all along?

What the fuck just happened?

Whitman was never like this. Even when they dabbled in rough stuff, he never neglected aftercare. What had she done to deserve this? Tears stung her eyes, and she was grateful for the moment that his back faced her.

She felt used. Her cheeks burned with embarrassment, and strength abandoned her legs, but she needed to get out of the room.

Wilde pulled the cups of her bra over her exposed breasts and tugged her shirt over them. She picked up her bag and marched towards the door.

That fucking door.

She would never be able to look at that goddamn door the same way again. As she struggled to fasten the front of her buttonless shirt, she reached for the heavy handle. Just before she could grasp it, the door swung open.

Woolf stood there, his mouth agape as he took in the sight of her, half-dressed with tears smeared across her face. Without a word, she shoved an arm across her face and pushed her way past him. As she walked away, she heard him call out something after her, but she didn't care. She needed to get back to her room as quickly as possible. She couldn't bear the thought of anyone else seeing her like this.

Her emotions poured out in barely contained sobs, and the tears wouldn't stop. They kept seeping out of her eyes like the remains of Whitman dripping down her leg.

CHAPTER 36

WOOLF

Woolf could never have prepared himself for what faced him on the other side of that door. It was Wilde, but not as he'd ever seen her. Heavy black tears rolled down her face from her red eyes. Her shirt lay open, and she pushed the two sides of it toward the center with little success. Her bare toes kissed the cold hardwood as she shoved her handbag under one of her arms. She looked up at him with bulging eyes, averted her gaze, and shoulder-checked him on her way through the doorway.

"Wilde, wait up!" Woolf peered into the room, trying to ascertain what had just happened. He could make out Whitman's silhouette beside his desk.

What the fuck did you do to her?

There was no time to confront him. Wilde was already halfway down the hallway. Woolf ran to catch up with her.

She had almost closed the door to her room when his hand shot out to stop it.

"Wilde, come on." The heavy door pinched his calloused fingers, and he released a hiss. He pushed through the pain and into the room.

Wilde's bag exploded upon contact with the floor,

Eliza Begrave

sending her belongings skipping across the parquet. She
collapsed onto the loveseat and buried her face in her hands.
Hemingway rushed toward them, her face awash in alarm.

"What is it? What happened?" Hemingway sat down
beside Wilde and wrapped her arms around her. Wilde's
frantic hands shook as she squeezed the useless remains of her
shirt around her body as if she wanted to fold herself into
nothingness. Hemingway grabbed a wool blanket off the edge
of the couch and draped it around Wilde's trembling
shoulders.

Woolf knelt before Wilde, placing his hands on her shaky
knees. "Breathe, okay? Just breathe. You're safe now. I've got
you," he urged, his voice steady.

Wilde attempted some shaky breaths between sobs,
breathing in and out with Woolf guiding her. Hemingway
rubbed her hands on Wilde's back, shh-ing her gently. Woolf
gave her a few moments to catch her breath and calm down.
Hemingway's eyes searched Woolf's for answers.

"I need you to tell me what he did to you," Woolf said.

"Kipling?" Hemingway's voice quivered with panic.
Woolf set his confusion aside to make sense of what was
happening with Wilde.

"Whit..." Wilde choked out.

"It was Whitman?" Hemingway's face went ashen. Woolf
squeezed her knee, a little firmer than he intended. It was
instinct, but he realized he had never touched Hemingway
before and hoped he hadn't crossed a line. He would worry
about that later. Right now, he needed answers.

"What happened?" he said.

Wilde swallowed hard, her eyes clenching shut as fresh
tears cascaded down her cheeks. "I went over to tell him..." she
began, but her voice faltered, a sob wrenching free.

"Did he..." Woolf's blood threatened to boil over. If Whitman had forced himself on her, they were going to find out if his dick could split a bullet.

"No, no. Not like that... Before we could talk, we just sort of fell into it. I... I thought it was a scene. I mean, it was rough, but it was hot. I was into it. I thought that he was..." She swallowed, and a tiny sob came out of her nose. She sniffled. "But then he finished. And he..." she choked down another whimper, "...he ordered me to leave."

"What?!" Every one of Hemingway's freckles flashed red with rage.

"He was so cold. So detached. I'm just some fucking slut to be used and thrown away," she cried, her voice a shattered whisper. "I feel like he just anger-fucked me. I don't even know what I did. He's never been like that. I... can't..." Wilde's tears carved rivers down her cheeks, her sobs transforming into uncontrolled cries. Hemingway cradled Wilde's head and rocked her, her own eyes glistening with unshed tears.

"I'm gonna fucking kill him." Woolf's face heated, and he made to stand up. Hemingway grabbed his hand and squeezed, her pleading eyes imploring him to stay. His gaze landed on Wilde. She was broken.

Hemingway was right. There was no way he could abandon her in this state. He swore to himself not to leave her side until she was better. Whitman had a reckoning coming, but right now, Woolf needed to take care of his girl.

CHAPTER 37

WILDE

Wilde woke swaddled in Hemingway's soft embrace. The tender rise and fall of Hem's slumbering breath provided comfort, but it was the only solace she felt at the moment. She slid out from under the arm that she was wrapped in and placed it with care on the pillow top.

Quiet embalmed the room. Woolf's body lay slanted on the couch; his head lolled over onto the armrest. He hadn't removed his jacket and shoes. Wilde's belongings lay strewn across the floor. She exhaled forcefully.

What a mess.

She picked up a bottle of gin from the sideboard on her way to the bathroom. She squeezed the cork out of the neck of the bottle with her teeth and took a long gulp. She opened the tap on the faucet and leaned toward the spout, splashing water onto her face and into her mouth. She was wiping the drips off her lips when she caught herself in the mirror.

Her eyes were red, their sockets swollen half-shut. The remains of her makeup smeared a canvas of regrets across her face. The corners of her mouth turned down, echoing every disapproving glare she'd received in her life. She took a deep breath in and out through her mouth, her nose still clogged from hours of weeping.

No wonder nobody wants you.

How could she blame Whitman for sending her away?

Just look at you.

This moment was only one of the hundreds of times she had seen this girl in the mirror and wondered what the fuck was wrong with her. The same eyes stared at her since before she could remember. The only difference was that this time it hurt more. Whitman had made her feel like she was more. More than what she could do. He had made her feel like she was someone to him. Significant.

But she was wrong. She was no one to Whitman. Nothing. She was a toy, a tool, just like she was to everybody else. How did she let him fool her into thinking anything different? Now she knew. She wouldn't make that mistake again.

Every person in this castle was an agent, a trained deceiver. How could she have let her guard down with anyone here? What was she thinking trusting any of them?

She met her own eyes in the mirror, the same eyes she'd seen her whole life. A girl's eyes. Part of her had never changed. Years and experience had hardened her. People and choices had shaped her into the woman she was. But she was still the same, in a way. There was still a little girl inside, afraid and alone.

And worthless.

She searched her face for the markers of unworthiness. Which mole, which wrinkle, which freckle was the one that signaled everyone to her uselessness? That only by being hardened in the crucible of training could she gain worth? Was she born worthless? Were we all? Was the sum of our existence only equal to the weight of our accomplishments? How much did she need to achieve to be lovable? Tears filled her eyes again.

Her weakness enraged her. She raked her hands across her cheeks, punching the tears out of her eyes. If she could discover what it was that made her unworthy, she could find a way to work hard enough to erase it. The clarity of her self-inflicted wrath cleared her sinuses.

But what would it mean if Whitman still didn't want her? Her chest tightened, and her chin quivered. The strength drained out of the girl in the mirror, and Wilde could no longer stand to look at her. She took several long chugs from the bottle of gin on her way back to the bed.

A deep rumble drew her attention to the window. She walked over and pulled the heavy velvet curtains back. Grey skies cast walking shadows over the grounds. Lightning crackled across the dark expanse. Thunder rolled through the hills.

Storms always brought Wilde comfort, as if the sound and fury outside echoed the chaos in her soul. She wished she could unleash the rage inside her body like nature did. Nature had permission to scream anger into the heavens and shake the earth, raining down endless tears that turned into landslides, swallowing everything in its path.

Lightning flashed across the sky, followed by a crack of thunder that shook the windows. The storm closed in. Wilde glanced back into the quiet room. Hemingway slumbered unperturbed. Wilde envied her; she could sleep through an airstrike. Woolf stirred and mumbled on the couch but remained asleep. Gratefulness filled Wilde that she could enjoy the storm alone. She closed her eyes, falling into the symphony of the tempest. Heavy raindrops battered the windows, their staccato easing the heartbreak in her bones.

Wilde drew a long breath. At the very least, if sleep

escaped her, the soundtrack would satisfy.

CHAPTER 38

WOOLF

Woolf woke up on the couch. The amber light of morning crept over the room, replacing the grey of dawn's twilight. His neck ached, and his head pounded. All the stress and anger from the night before had put his body through the ringer.

He checked the bed. Hemingway and Wilde were two fully clothed little spoons, Hem's arms wrapped around Wilde. They were finally asleep, thank god. Wilde had cried most of the night while Hemingway whispered lullabies to her and tried to keep her own tears at bay.

Hemingway stirred as Woolf padded across the room.

"Are you going to class?" she whispered, her morning voice high and hoarse.

"No. I just need to pick up some fresh clothes. I'll be back."

"I'm staying, too. I don't think she should be alone." Hemingway slid out from behind Wilde, taking great care not to wake her. "Let me make you a cup of coffee before you go." Hemingway's hospitality held no match. She tiptoed to the sideboard and started a pour-over in near silence.

Woolf admitted to himself there was no rush, and a cup

of coffee sounded heavenly after the night they had endured.

"How would you like it?" she asked.

"Black is fine," Woolf said.

"I didn't ask how you *take* your coffee. I asked how you would *like* your coffee," she pressed. Woolf eyed the vanilla creamer on the sideboard. Hemingway intercepted his glance and poured some into the steaming cup. She handed it to him with a warm smile.

Woolf marked the deep blue grooves under her eyes. Despite the exhaustion that weighted her eyelids, those sparkling touchstones still burned true. It was almost as if Hemingway's eyes couldn't help but glimmer, no matter what.

"It's kind of a secret superpower. Sometimes we need someone to help us figure out what we want... in our hearts." Even exhaustion could not snuff out Hemingway's pure, wholesome kindness.

"How long has she slept?" Woolf asked, taking a sip of the scalding brew. The creamer had cooled the coffee enough to prevent it from burning his tongue, and the vanilla tasted reminiscent of Wilde's skin. It wrapped around his insides like a warm hug.

"Just a little. She was up most of the night. She finally went down after sunrise." Hemingway cast a concerned glance at Wilde asleep on the bed.

Something ate at Woolf. "About yesterday. You mentioned Kipling."

Hemingway evaded his eyes, tinkering with the items on the sideboard.

"He's been kind of stalking her," she whispered. "Look, it's not really mine to tell. I was afraid he got to her on her way to tell Whitman."

"Tell Whitman..."

"That she's falling in love with him."

Woolf's mind raced, and the word "love" needled into his heart. He would find a way to deal with Kipling, but right now, chest-bursting outrage consumed him.

She loves him. And he did this to her.

Whitman had it coming.

CHAPTER 39

WHITMAN

Morning light sliced through a crease in the curtains, piercing Whitman's eyelids. He had passed out, half-naked, face down on the cherry desk. It felt as though someone had welded a steel band around his skull. A vile combination of stale tobacco and scotch vomit rotted in his mouth.

It wasn't long after Wilde and Woolf left that all the booze Whitman had consumed the night before exacted its revenge.

After his fight with Kipling, and the subsequent ass-chewing from Faulkner, thoughts of Kipling fucking Wilde had launched him into a fury. He couldn't stand it. He wanted to jump out of his skin—or a fucking window. Hawthorne had annoyed him further by suggesting his actions were motivated by jealousy. Whose side were they on?

Whitman had retreated to his room and attempted to numb his anger with expensive scotch and a Dominican cigar. He never expected Wilde to come to him. By the time she dropped by, he was well inebriated.

Had she come straight from fucking Kipling? Would he smell Woolf on her skin? Did she touch them the way she touched him? The thoughts splintered through his brain like ice crystals of insanity.

And there she was, the cause of all his anguish. He wanted her. His body responded at the very sight of her. But he also wanted to hurt her. He wanted her to experience at least a fraction of the pain she had caused him. She wasn't the only one who could play games with hearts.

He wanted her. Oh, yes. He wanted her on her knees, wearing nothing but a prayer.

But when she crossed his threshold, every cell in his body awakened to her presence. Over the cigar smoke, he could smell her. He didn't detect Woolf or Kipling—only vanilla and lilies and that visceral essence that was uniquely Wilde. He swelled within his pants, and his mouth watered at the thought of her skin. All he wanted to do was melt back into her.

And she was all his. She offered herself so enthusiastically to him, so compliant. Those dark eyes pierced right through him, and she melted into him like she always did. He had to battle himself to keep from giving in and falling at her feet.

He still worshipped her.

He couldn't get caught up in all that. He convinced himself that it felt good to dominate her. It gave him a brief, artificial sense of authority. He couldn't control what she did with all her other lovers. She was untamable. She would never be his. But, in those moments, he could feel like he owned her. He couldn't let her find out that she owned him with a mere glance.

He thought rejecting her would make him feel better, hoping he could regain his power. But those moments when he almost gave in to her made him feel more powerless than ever. He felt profoundly out of control, desperate to lose himself in her.

Wilde spoke the language of his body, knowing

instinctively how he needed to be touched. Each moment his fingertips grazed her skin, she electrified his soul. Every moment he filled her, her spirit filled him in a remote, unfamiliar place her presence granted him access to for the first time.

She saw him and knew him in a way no one else ever had. He felt raw and vulnerable, like the fresh pink skin replacing a long-healing wound. And when she was not near, the rawness that remained was too much for him to manage.

When he told her to leave, instant regret sent a shockwave through his chest. He crumpled, but the damage was done. The quiver of hurt in her voice tore through his body. How could he have done this? He wanted to run to her, fall at her feet, and beg for forgiveness.

Please, Baby. Please, my Love, my Frenchy. I'm so sorry. Please, let me take it back.

But he couldn't even muster the courage to look at her.

And then Woolf had to swoop in on his white charger.

Well done, Whit. You drove her right into his arms, you blue-ribbon idiot.

They probably went straight back to her room, where Woolf dried her eyes and fucked away all her problems.

Whitman's thoughts snapped back to the moment. He checked his watch.

Shit-fuck.

He had a lecture in thirty minutes. He pulled a drawer open, shook out a few painkillers, and swallowed them with the leftover whisky in the glass on the desk.

The door swung open, and Woolf strode in.

Great, just who I wanted to see.

Woolf glared at him and stomped straight to the dresser, stripping off his clothes. He yanked a fresh outfit on and crammed more clothing in his bag.

Packing for a romantic getaway?

Whitman's neck grew hot, and his teeth clenched. "Long night?" he said in a caustic drawl.

Woolf's eyes shot poisonous blow darts, and he balled his fists.

"Don't," was all Woolf said. A large vein bulged in his neck. He took a deep breath and continued shoving clothes into the bag.

Why was he holding back? A warm bed to get back to, likely. Whitman was in no shape for a scrap anyway, and Woolf looked like he was one more sarcastic comment away from exploding.

Whitman shrugged and sat back in the chair. No sense in pissing off 180 pounds worth of Special Forces this early in the morning.

Woolf zipped his pack like it had stolen his wallet and stalked toward the door. Before he reached it, he paused and turned around. He took a few steps back and plucked Wilde's shoes off the hardwood. He marched out of the room, slamming the door and leaving Whitman with his thoughts.

CHAPTER 40

WILDE

Light poured into the room, and someone stripped the covers from Wilde's body.

"Alright, enough is enough. Get out of bed," Hemingway attempted to sound stern. Wilde groaned something to the negative and blocked out the world with a pillow.

"You've missed three days of classes, and I can't make excuses for you anymore. Get up," Hemingway insisted. The light sliced through Wilde's shuttered eyelids.

"It's Friday. Like you said, I already missed all my classes. Leave me alone," Wilde shot back with a failed grab at the coverlet. Hemingway held it just out of her reach.

"You are going to the Program H party tonight," Hemingway ordered. Wilde shot as much of a laser glare as she could out of squinted eyes. She was in no one's mood to be taking orders.

"Like hell I am. Hawthorne's hosting, so Whitman's guaranteed to be there." There was no way in hell she was in a state to go to a party and face him.

"That's the point. You need to show that prick what he's missing and remind everyone who the fuck you are,"

Hemingway said, impressing Wilde with her champion's spirit. Hem breathed with force from her nostrils, having the effect of a teddy bear trying to be a British governess. She was adorable, and Wilde was touched at how much Hem cared.

Wilde sighed, and the reserves of rebellious energy drained from her body. She was fresh out of fight.

"I'm not ready," Wilde said, nuzzling her face into the pillow. She allowed herself to look as pathetic as she felt, for once. Maybe it would garner some sympathy.

Hemingway's expression softened.

"That's why I brought reinforcements," Hemingway said with an uncharacteristic sense of mischief.

Koontz emerged from a dark corner, startling Wilde.

Jesus, where the fuck did they come from?

They took a few steps into the room and ran a slow hand back across the freshly buzzed hair on the side of their head.

"Get out of bed, Babygirl," they said, their voice a cool, weighted blanket. "We're getting you Revenge Hot." They chucked a leather jacket on the bed in Wilde's lap. Wilde shot a questioning glance at Hemingway, realizing she wasn't the only one in this suite who benefited from being underestimated.

"I knew none of my stuff would fit you, and this calls for something a little more high-octane than that schoolgirl shit Capote bought you." Hemingway's half-smile was less than half an apology.

"Can't bring a cheerleader to a bad bitch fight," Koontz purred, hooking their thumbs behind their belt.

King clomped out of the bathroom, slurping her trashcan-sized cold brew with a devilish grin. She twirled a makeup brush in her other hand and fixed Wilde with wicked eyes.

"I heard we're gonna make a motherfucker wish he was never born." She drew her tongue over one of her whetted canine teeth. "Who's the target?"

CHAPTER 41

WHITMAN

"Are you gonna get over yourself and have a good time, or what? You're at a fucking party," Hawthorne said, jolting Whitman out of deep thought.

"Yes, geez, I'm fine." Whitman kneaded his forehead. The migraine he had since he last saw Wilde refused to fade. He was hoping the two Old Fashioneds he downed would have taken the edge off, but no luck.

No one had seen Wilde or Woolf for nigh on three days, and Whitman was spiraling. He had been so cruel to her. He overanalyzed every moment he remembered from that night and had been using them as weapons to slice and stab at himself. He spent days oscillating between self-loathing and jealousy, finally landing on worry. He needed to know Wilde was okay.

Hawthorne was beyond annoyed with him. "If you're that worried, why don't you just grow a pair and go knock on her door? Then, at least you'd know. Hell, maybe they'd invite you into their orgy."

"Shut the fuck up, Thorne." Whitman took another swig of his cocktail. "Anyway, I'm not worried. And I'm not jealous.

I just have a splitting headache and could do without the lecture."

Hawthorne tipped a few more ounces of whiskey into Whitman's glass as a peace offering. He accepted, knowing he didn't have much of a choice in his state. He knew he needed to take as many edges off this pain as he could. Hawthorne meant well, even if they had an atrocious bedside manner.

They slammed the bottle down on the bar, aggravating Whitman's headache.

"Ho. Lee. Shit," they whispered.

Whitman opened his eyes and looked up at Hawthorne, whose eyes and mouth stood wide open as they stared at the entrance.

"Incoming," they said. Whitman followed their gaze toward the door.

Wilde strode in, flanked by Koontz and King.

Fuck me.

"She looks..." Whitman started.

"Fucking unbelievable," Hawthorne interrupted. The undead Queen of England could have galloped in on the back of Santa Claus, bathed in Aztec Gold, and Hawthorne would have yawned. Impressing them was nothing short of the tallest of orders.

Wilde had poured herself into a pair of black, ripped jeans. She prowled into the room in lovingly seasoned Doc Martens. Her leather jacket opened enough to reveal a skin-tight red crop top that showed vast swathes of skin both above and below. She had swept her hair into a messy ponytail, with blonde strands that dropped down over smoky black eyes that made her cocoa irises sparkle unpredictably. A garnet choker wrapped around her neck and Whitman's thoughts. Craving stirred in his pants.

Wilde's eyes exhibited a savagery Whitman had never seen outside the confines of Program W training. Usually, that intense stare was trained down the barrel of a Beretta. He had been on the receiving end of those eyes only once before, from the flat of his back, with a rubber knife at his neck. She looked lethal.

King and Koontz planted kisses on her cheeks, slinked away, and became the darkness of the room. Wilde trained her sights on Whitman, who stood transfixed behind the bar. His breath abandoned his lungs, and he adjusted his pants. Every step she took seemed to freeze time. She was a force of nature.

Oh god, she's coming this way.

"Nice party, Hawthorne," Wilde said, her seductive voice slipping into Whitman's ears like the most delicious poison.

"Have you come to expect any less? Haven't seen you in a spell. We were starting to worry," Hawthorne said.

Whitman stomped on Hawthorne's foot under the bar. They winced but barely showed it.

"I just couldn't drag myself out of bed. Sometimes, you get caught up in a moment and it kind of takes over your life, you know?" The sweet timbre of her voice masked a restrained menace that chilled Whitman's blood. "But I wouldn't dare miss a Program H party." Her voice dropped an octave, and she shot Whitman a sharp glare.

"And you are looking extra delicious," Whitman finally pushed some words out of his throat, forcing a playful tone as he dipped his toes into potentially dangerous waters. Maybe she had forgotten about the other night. A waft of her perfume sailed across the bar, and he longed to have his fingers and mouth on her skin.

"Delicious, hmm? Want a taste?" A predatory challenge waded behind Wilde's suggestive eyes. Whitman knew that taste would probably go down about as smoothly as a cyanide pill. He cleared his throat and pivoted.

"What can I get you to drink?" he asked.

Wilde gave it a brief thought. "I'll have a gimlet." Her fierce eyes chafed Whitman's already shaky confidence.

He shook up the cocktail and slid it across the bar. Glossy cherry-red lips wrapped around the rim of the glass. Her cheeks hollowed as she sucked a sip into her mouth, reminding him of every time her lips had wrapped around his cock. Wilde's eyes sized him up behind long black lashes. He felt like he was naked and being prepared to be spit-roasted.

"Looks like you've got company," Hawthorne said, breaking the stare-off. Whitman scanned over Wilde's shoulder to see Hemingway waving at them. Woolf stood next to Hemingway, glaring at Whitman, hands in pockets and murder in his eyes.

"Duty calls," Wilde said with a fake sigh and a half-grin. "A slut's work is never done," she added, her gaze falling to the bar top. For the briefest moment, her lips tightened, and a flash of sorrow passed across her eyes. She blinked it away, regaining her haughty demeanor.

Guilt pierced Whitman's gut. He hadn't been able to evict the other night from his head—what he had done to her. Maybe she hadn't forgotten about it after all.

With an arrogant smile, Wilde scooped up the cocktail and strutted toward Hemingway and Woolf. Whitman stared after her, watching her lift one of Hemingway's hands to her lips to kiss it. She turned to Woolf and tipped a sip of the cocktail into his mouth before taking them both by the arm and walking away.

"Now, I'm terrified *and* turned on," Hawthorne quipped.

Whitman knew the feeling. Even through the thick haze of guilt tightening his whole body, he could feel the familiar hum of lust rushing through his veins at the sight of Wilde. The slicing pain in his head intensified.

"I'd sleep with one eye open. Looks like G.I. Jackass over there would love to knife you in your sleep," Hawthorne said. Woolf's eyes shot missiles at Whitman.

Whitman could probably take Woolf in a fight. But if Wilde wanted him dead—and judging by the murderous way she just eyeballed him, that was a fair assessment—he didn't stand much of a chance. She bested him at play. Every weapon she picked up, she wielded with deadly precision.

Her intellect was equally impressive. She excelled in her studies with minimal effort, as if it were all a review. Whitman knew she tutored Hemingway in at least four languages. The thought of what she could achieve if she fully asserted herself both frightened and excited him.

"I thought she drank French 75s," Hawthorne observed. Whitman's forehead broke out into a cold sweat, and his throat caught fire. His mouth went dry, and he pulled out four shot glasses.

"She does. Fucking Woolf drinks gimlets." Jealousy tightened his ribcage.

Whitman poured a shot of bourbon into each of the glasses.

"Guess we're getting wasted tonight," Hawthorne said. Whitman downed all four shots in succession, slamming each glass down on the bar one after another. His elbows crumpled on the bar top, and he kneaded his forehead.

Hawthorne sighed. "Guess *you're* getting wasted tonight."

Whitman's buzz had kicked in, but his headache still lingered after six shots of whiskey. His concern over Wilde's welfare faded the longer she laughed and mingled around the room. She seemed to be doing just fine without him. He, on the other hand, struggled to disguise his misery with nonchalance. He retreated to the men's room to splash some water on his face and get his shit together.

His jaw ached from clenching his teeth when Woolf repeatedly placed a hand on the small of Wilde's back; the one time it slipped under her jacket, grazing her bare skin, Whitman's ears had rung.

Wilde seemed incapable of carrying on a conversation without bestowing some touch on the other person, renewing Whitman's sense of betrayal with each casual caress. Whenever she grabbed one of Woolf's aggravatingly muscled arms, hostility hardened Whitman's stomach.

He closed the door to the restroom and collided headlong into Hemingway.

"Another crisp Pinot Grigio for the lady? I'm on my way back to the bar," he offered.

Determination and anger sprouted two lines between Hemingway's uncharacteristically harsh eyes.

"No. I think I'll have a vodka cranberry, so it'll ruin that pretentious silk shirt when I throw it in your face," she spat. Embittered breaths blasted in and out of her nostrils. She resembled a fiercely enraged kitten. "I'm glad you weren't this much of a prick when we were dating."

"Pri-hi-hick?" Whitman erupted in laughter. "Language, Hemingway. What would everyone in the Hamptons think

229

about that tone?" he teased. "Wilde's potty mouth is rubbing off on you."

His thoughts strayed to Wilde's foul little mouth. Those perfect lips could twist his thoughts with a simple turn of phrase. She whispered the filthiest things in his ears when they shared a bed, making every inch of his skin zing. How could he tear himself away from wanting her?

Whitman glanced across the room to find Wilde beaming her irresistible smile. She looked so perfect. She draped an arm around Woolf, whispering something in his ear. Whitman suppressed a hiss. The thought of her being with someone else felt like a burning knife in his soul. He refocused on Hemingway, holding back his ire.

"When we were dating, I was recovering from an injury. I was tender." Whitman pouted his lower lip in mock vulnerability.

"Injure your brain this time?" Hemingway scowled. She impressed him with how defensive she was of Wilde, unaware of how cruel she could be.

"So vicious, Hem." He clicked his tongue, casting her an arrogant, sideways grin as he peeked back toward Wilde.

Kipling's hulking frame came into view, pushing into Wilde's circle, making Woolf look comically small in comparison.

Great. I have to see them together now?

"Also, you weren't fucking my worst enemy," Whitman added in an acidic tone.

"Enemy? That's a little dramatic. Woolf's just being protective," Hemingway said with a dismissive roll of her eyes.

"Not him." Whitman directed her attention across the room to Kipling.

Hemingway's eyebrows snapped together, and her voice

lowered, filling with venom. "What?! You think she—? She would never do that to you. If that's how little you think of her, you didn't deserve her in the first place."

Whitman guessed Wilde hadn't been honest about her relations with Kipling. "Well, maybe I dodged a bullet," he said, ruefully.

"How fucking dare you?" Hemingway's voice was ice. "That bastard assaulted her."

She slapped her hand over her mouth, and her eyes flared in horror at her confession. She was always shit at keeping secrets from him.

"He... fucking what?" Murderous intent flooded Whitman's veins at the possibility that the statement held an ounce of truth. The thought of Kipling attacking Wilde activated every filament of rage within his body, extinguishing his migraine. His heart thumped a war drum in his ears.

A look of panic replaced Hemingway's fury. "I wasn't supposed to... She made me promise I wouldn't... You can't tell anyone. She'll hate me," she pleaded.

"Everything you know. Now," Whitman threatened.

"I can't."

"You already did. May as well fill in the details," he said, grasping her arm and steadying her against the wall. "What did she tell you?"

Hemingway's eyes fluttered and darted as she sought an escape from the moment, a single tear dropping from her lashes. Whitman grasped her other arm and pressed her back, compelling her to meet his gaze.

Her big doe eyes filled with guilt and sorrow, reflecting her unintended betrayal.

"She didn't need to tell me. I saw." Heavy tears tumbled from her eyes.

"Saw what?" Whitman pressed. He tried his level best to set Hemingway's emotional reaction aside, but it burrowed beneath his callous swagger.

"He had her pinned to her bed."

Whitman lifted his eyebrows to insinuate Hemingway was only confirming his suspicion.

"That maniac fucking bit her," Hemingway said, terror in her eyes. Her breath hitched.

"Well, Wilde is into some freaky shit," Whitman said aloofly. Kipling said she liked it rough.

Kipling towered over Wilde and backed her against a wall. Whitman braced himself to see her gaze up at him with those playful, seductive eyes she often turned on him.

"I don't see *you* with a broken nose."

"What? Wilde did that? How do you know?"

Wilde raised only her eyes to Kipling, and her jaw solidified, exhibiting no trace of flirtation or playfulness. Her face was a mask of hatred, obscuring something Whitman had never encountered in her: fear.

"Because I saw him moments after she gave his face a hard reset. She had both of their blood on her." Tears followed their established streams down her cheeks. "I saw her. I saw her face," Hemingway sobbed.

Kipling leaned in farther, and Wilde pulled her head back so far into the wall that it seemed she wanted to dissolve into it. Woolf took a protective step forward.

The full weight of the situation descended on Whitman. A memory of the oval, healing bruise on Wilde's shoulder surfaced in Whitman's mind. She said it was from training. Kipling had bitten her hard enough to break the skin? Now he wished even more that he had killed the bastard when he had the chance.

Hemingway was right; Kipling lied to him. What the fuck had he done to her? Whitman didn't want to face the fact that something terrible had happened to Wilde. His collar tightened around his neck like a noose, and his face went hot.

"Did he...?"

Rape her?!

He couldn't choke the words out. Hemingway shook her head a fierce "no" so he didn't have to.

"Almost."

Why didn't she tell me?

Whitman loosened his grip on Hemingway, and she wrenched her arms out of his hands.

Whitman's jaw set, and his chest blazed. He was so enraged he could shit fire.

He's fucking dead.

Before Whitman could make a move toward Wilde, Koontz and King emerged from the shadows and stationed themselves behind Kipling. King reached up and wrapped a claw around Kipling's massive shoulder, digging her talons into his skin. He whipped around, threats shooting from his eyes. King bared her sharp canines, tipped her chin up, and reached a skinny arm behind her back. Whitman could make out her saying, "I triple dog dare you."

Koontz crossed their arms across their chest and arched a fuck-around-and-find-out eyebrow.

Kipling exhaled forcefully, assessing the threats surrounding him. His shoulders lowered as his eyes darted between Koontz and King. He wheeled on Wilde.

"Soon, Sugar," he growled and strode out into the hallway.

Wilde released a shaky breath, and the corner of her mouth ticked up in a nervous smile. Koontz stepped over and enveloped her in their embrace.

Hemingway crossed her arms and jutted her lower jaw, sizing Whitman up with fierce judgment.

What a colossal misread. How could I be so damn stupid?

"I didn't..." he started. "I'll get you another wine." Resigned, he took a step back toward the bar.

"Don't bother. I'm leaving," Hemingway huffed, a small, choked sob escaping her at the end.

Whitman returned to the bar next to Hawthorne.

"Have a nice chat with the ol' ex?" they pried, eyeballing him.

"Just peachy. She called me a prick," he grimaced.

"Wow. Strong words from the pride of Program H," Hawthorne smirked. They threw a nod toward Wilde. "I thought you said she was fucking Kipling. Things go south?"

"You'll enjoy this. I know it doesn't happen very often, but it appears that I was wrong," Whitman admitted. "So fucking wrong." He had allowed his jealousy to blind him, hurdling right over logic to think the worst of her.

Memories of the other night flooded his brain, and his stomach heaved. He had been so cruel to her. Not only was she innocent of his accusations, but Kipling attacked her, and he wasn't there to protect her. His throat thickened, and he dropped his head into his hands, shame spiraling his thoughts.

What the fuck is wrong with me? I just fucked up the best thing to ever happen to me.

"What's your deal, man?" Hawthorne said.

"She was never fucking Kipling." Whitman's breath grew short, and his fingers quivered as he lifted another shot to his mouth, knocking it back. The center of his nose prickled, and his eyes grew hot. "I am a prick. I am the biggest fucking prick."

CHAPTER 42

WILDE

"You guys can go. I'll be fine," Wilde told Woolf and Hemingway.

"I'm not leaving you alone," Woolf insisted despite his obvious irritation. A couple more gimlets and he might lose his rapidly disintegrating self-control and drag Whitman across the bar by his tie.

"What if he comes back?" Hemingway said, her eyes still misty.

"Koontz and King are babysitting, remember?" Wilde wasn't ready to return to her bed and her thoughts. She didn't want to waste the effort that Hemingway, Koontz, and King had spent on preparing her for the grand re-entrance by only staying for an hour.

As much as it shamed her to admit it, she longed to see Whitman again. Everyone expected her to be furious with him, but the moment she laid eyes on his face, her heart did a stutter step. The memory of the other night sliced fresh through her, and her confidence evaporated.

Wilde had spent the evening swallowing the hurt that threatened to collapse her body. She pushed her chin up and employed her best bulletproof swagger, praying no one clocked her watery eyes or the tremor in her voice. The moment she had turned from her interaction with Whitman, a tear escaped and rolled down her cheek. He had acted so casually, and she knew she meant nothing to him.

Maybe this was for the best. Whitman would be safe from her and her past. She had spent so many years on her own. Now wasn't the time to start needing people.

If only she could stop wanting him.

"Are you sure?" Woolf interrogated her with his eyes.

Wilde fixed him with a charming smile and placed a reassuring hand on his arm. "Yes. I'm sure."

Hemingway pulled her into a hug. "Talk when you get home?" she whispered.

"Of course."

Hemingway released her and took a steadying breath.

"I'll, uh, walk you back," Woolf said, extending his hand in front of him to indicate that Hemingway take the lead. When they reached the door, Hemingway threw one last concerned glance back at Wilde, like a tearful mother watching her kid drive off to college.

Wilde needed another drink to soothe the brutal racing of her heart that had lingered since Kipling arrived. Panic slapped her in the face at the realization that she had to fetch her own cocktails now. Creeping dread caved her chest, and she dragged her feet in a slow circle to face the bar.

Only Hawthorne stood behind it.

Oh, thank fuck.

She tried to appear unrushed on her way over. Hawthorne assessed her with warm, almost sympathetic eyes. Had Whitman told them what happened?

As she arrived at the bar, they reached below it, producing

a champagne flute with a lemon twist on the rim. They slid the French 75 toward her, and she took a cautious sip. It was unmistakable that Whitman had mixed the drink.

"Just in case you craved an old favorite," Hawthorne said with a grin.

"Thanks." Wilde took her cup of bewilderment and rejoined the party. She tried to drown her insecurities and confusion with another few cocktails and conversations. Whitman remained mercifully absent from the bar, but Hawthorne's French 75s couldn't compare with his.

The party started to die down, and Wilde headed toward the exit.

A strong arm shot out, ensnaring her waist and dragging her into a dark corner. Wilde's body flooded with alarm, activating to defend herself, but her reaction was slowed by the alcohol. Before she could cry for help, a hand clamped over her mouth. In an instant, she was scared sober.

"Don't be afraid. It's just me." The voice was husky. The scent of Whitman's cologne filled her nose, and her heartbeat backed off its sprint. He lowered his hand from her lips and grasped her lower back, pressing her into him. She should have pushed him away, but her longing overwhelmed her, and she yielded to his embrace. He brought his mouth down to hers and parted her lips with his tongue.

Wilde usually found Whitman's kisses intoxicating, but he tasted of straight liquor.

"Whoa, Whit," she broke off the kiss, "I think you and the bourbon have finally become one."

"I didn't want to miss out on that taste you offered. You look just about good enough to eat," he slurred, his breath thick with alcohol.

"I'm surprised you can taste anything but booze."

Wilde's eyes adjusted to the dark, and she got her first good look at him. Whitman's eyes were glazed over, and it appeared the wall he was leaning on was the only thing holding him up. She had seen him drunk before, but never in such a bad way as this.

He swayed, and Wilde caught him, pinning him to the wall. He closed his eyes, letting out a small snort. Then, he opened them and blinked rapidly, trying to get them to focus.

Wilde sighed. She draped one of Whitman's arms over her shoulders and wrapped her arm around his waist. He staggered forward and let out a goofy giggle. Wilde wanted to feel satisfied that this pitiful state stemmed from jealousy. If he were jealous, it would confirm that he cared about her.

She would have plenty of time to think about that during the long walk back to the dormitories.

"Let's get you to bed, Loverboy," she said.

"OoOOoo, your place or mine?" he said, one of his feet slipping on the floor.

She caught him by the waist and steadied him.

"Definitely yours."

CHAPTER 43

WOOLF

The door swung open and hit the wall with a slam. Wilde and Whitman stumbled across the threshold, with Wilde narrowly preventing both of them from face-planting on the polished floor.

"A little help," she shouted.

Woolf set his book aside and rushed over from his bed. Wilde's chest heaved, and her face glistened like a wet tomato as she supported Whitman, who wobbled like a Bourbon Street vagrant, holding one eye closed. His wrinkled dress shirt flopped halfway out of his pants, and his tie spilled out of his pocket. He was shitfaced.

"Jesus, did he get roofied?" Woolf asked.

"I think this was self-inflicted," she said.

They both supported Whitman over to his bed, and he plopped down on his back, feet still on the floor. Wilde took a second to catch her breath, then grabbed the wastebasket by the bed and placed it in his lap. He swayed to a seated position.

"What's this for—" was all he got out before his stomach lost the battle with the booze and all the contents of his stomach stormed out of his mouth into the wastebasket.

"Would you please get me a towel?" Wilde asked.

Woolf snatched one from the sideboard and tossed it to Wilde. She caught it one-handed and started dabbing Whitman's mouth. Whitman slouched back down onto the bed and released a massive sigh.

"Snakes got no legs to stand on," he mumbled before beginning to snore.

Wilde drew a forearm across her forehead, swiping the sweat off and wiping it on the clean part of the towel. She placed the wastebasket back on the ground and lifted Whitman's feet onto the bed. Woolf watched in confusion as she gently removed Whitman's shoes.

She walked to the bathroom and retrieved a washcloth. After moistening it, she placed it on slumbering Whitman's forehead. Her hands moved with meticulous calm, giving Woolf the impression this wasn't her first time taking care of a drunk. He wondered who else she had performed these silent, lonely rituals on. Watching her filled him with a profound sadness, and he ached to go to her and wrap her in his arms.

What did Whitman do to deserve such adoration? Their whole plan was to make him jealous. Judging by his current state, it worked. How did this evening end with Wilde playing nurse, and Woolf playing nurse's assistant?

Wilde filled a glass with water and placed it with some painkillers by Whitman's bedside. Unsure what to do, Woolf poured her a glass of Pinot Noir from the sideboard. She gave him an exhausted yet warmly grateful smile as she took it from his hands, a silent thank you. Those dark walnut eyes sparkled, crumbling Woolf.

Fuck, I love this woman.

He had sidelined his feelings for her out of respect for her love for Whitman, but they still simmered within him.

This was the first time he witnessed firsthand the depth of her feelings for Whitman. No part of her seemed angry, annoyed, or put out by his drunkenness. She did what was necessary to ensure his well-being, appearing happy to do so despite her exhaustion.

Woolf had seen so much pain in her eyes over the last week that it nearly broke him. Every tear, every sob, had torn through him like razor wire. He struggled to conceive of the amount of strength it took to continue loving Whitman after what he put her through.

Fucking Whitman.

How in the world did he deserve a woman like Wilde? She possessed both tenacity and grace, loving her people with an unmatched fierceness. She could charm you right out of your pants, and then hold you until you felt home.

"I'm a little wired. If you don't mind, I'd like to stay for a bit," Wilde said quietly. Woolf would never turn down more time with her.

He nodded and placed a hand on her shoulder. "You know where to find me."

She wrapped her hand over his, sending a tingle of excitement up his arm. "Thank you."

CHAPTER 44

WILDE

Wilde's shoulders relaxed as the soothing warmth from the Pinot Noir spread across her chest. Her heartbeat was finally recovering from the odyssey of dragging Whitman's stumbling body halfway across the Keep. Safely in bed, he snored away.

"We now know oviraptors were not egg stealers," he mumbled to his pillow in a fairly decent David Attenborough voice.

She unlaced and removed King's Doc Martens and tucked her feet under her knees on the couch. Woolf wasn't yet asleep, and she felt his intermittent inquiring glance.

What a night. Wilde hadn't known what to expect. She was under orders to show up, look hot, and torture the shit out of Whitman. Judging by the last several hours of Whit's inebriation and the hangover that would inevitably follow: mission accomplished. In her heart, she wished she were angrier with him.

Anger was useful. Anger felt like power. And she thought she had been angry with him, but the moment she saw him at the party, she felt powerless. She still craved him. She wanted him to be hers. She yearned for his touch, his attention, his taste. Deep down, she wanted to believe she still meant something to him.

"Frenchy," Whitman groaned in his sleep. Wilde's breath left her lungs. She must have imagined it. She peered over at the bed. He turned over, grasping at the comforter. "Wilde, mhm..." his voice drifted off.

Wilde's skeleton froze. Her gaze penetrated the emptiness before her, searching for meaning in the cold room. She struggled to swallow the feelings rising in her throat. Whitman's cry shattered the armor she had built around her unworthiness, and her brain scrambled to pick up the pieces.

No, no, no. Keep it together. It's just more sleep talk nonsense.

Wilde was terrified of opening herself to the possibility that Whitman loved her back. It had taken her great pains to close the door on those feelings. She was not about to sign herself up for more of that hurt. She still grieved the rejection of the other night. How could he have done that if he loved her? She had constructed her defenses against Whitman on the concept that he didn't care about her. That shield left no room for his feelings about her to be ambiguous. Just because he wanted her didn't mean he loved her.

Wilde gulped her wine. Whitman rolled over on the bed, facing her.

"Turtles can breathe out of their butts, you know," he muttered, burying his face into the pillow. Even passed out and three sheets to the wind, she couldn't resist him. Wilde padded over from the couch and settled on the edge of the bed beside him. She wondered what circumstances had converged to create the masterpiece before her. She knew from her own experience that people like them weren't products of happy childhoods. The wittiest among us aren't typically born from nurturing caregivers. If the world had no terrible parents, we wouldn't have funny people.

Wilde's heart flooded with a shared sadness for both of them. They had both committed disgusting, ugly acts to survive. Things they would have to live with forever. They would always be two extremely complicated people, which was why they shared such a profound understanding of one another.

Wilde's heart swelled looking at him, and simultaneously ached to think of the things he must have endured. What terrifying memories did he work so hard to numb?

Wilde loved Whitman. As much as she tried to push it down, she couldn't deny it. All she wanted in the world was for him to be happy and safe.

She lifted his wrist to remove his timepiece and caught a glimpse of herself in the sapphire crystal. She stared into the same eyes she always did, but a new strength emerged behind them, something that seemed impervious to pain. This girl wasn't afraid that he didn't love her back. She could love him, and the odds could be damned.

Wilde knew instinctively, the moment she saw this girl, what it meant for her. She would love Whitman. She didn't need him to love her back. She would accept whatever he was willing to give. Any piece of him was enough, as long as she could stay in his life. She would keep him safe. Always.

CHAPTER 45

WHITMAN

Whitman descended the desolate, stone steps. Arhythmic drips of water ploinked against the slate, an eerie counterpart to the steady thunder of his heartbeat. As he reached the bottom, the narrow staircase opened into a vast subterranean warehouse. Whitman's organs fell out of his ass. Familiar tin and wooden cubes in sickly colors covered the floor, forming a checkerboard pattern.

Drip. Drip.

The first box popped open, sending a jolt of terror across Whitman's forearms. A harlequin clown in a cheap, frayed, nylon costume sprang out and laughed at him, a distorted, rapid giggle, half-clown, half-child, that sounded like it was being played backward from a tinny speaker.

Whitman shuffled through the labyrinth of dented tin and wood and shoved the clown back in the box, shutting it up for the moment. The remnants of its unsettling laugh echoed off the walls. A second, larger box exploded open. The laugh intensified and morphed into Kipling's low chuckle.

Another box burst open, revealing a fat, orange-bearded clown that boomed with Kipling's full bellowing laughter.

A lightning bolt of pain shot through Whitman's leg. He limped to the open boxes and wrestled them closed, as others popped open around him. A Woolf-in-the-Box. A Hemingway-in-the-Box. A Dickinson-in-the-Box. All cackling with sneering laughter. The boxes swelled and towered around him, growing too large for him to shut. They kept opening and opening, creating a deafening chorus of jeers.

"Whitman," Wilde's muffled voice called to him from behind the wall of boxes. He squeezed desperately between them toward the sound, catching a glimpse of her in a small clearing. She stood trapped inside a clear box, wearing her navy silk wrap dress and his dinner jacket. She pounded her fists on the glass when she saw him.

Whitman activated, suppressing the pain and fear, and forcing his way through the erupting cubes. Wilde's eyes scanned the area for any means of escape. He wasn't getting any closer, no matter how hard he pushed. The boxes closed in around him.

At the edge of his strength, he barreled into the clearing and slammed against the glass, desperate to free her. Wilde's eyes flared wide and her pupils narrowed. Her fingers reached up her neck to clutch her throat. Her lips mouthed his name and opened and closed like a dying fish. She was suffocating.

Anguish cascaded over him like a squall. He could not lose her. He would die first.

Kipling's laughter boomed, threatening to explode his head. Whitman pounded helplessly on the glass.

"Frenchy, no! Stay with me."

Despair and acceptance dimmed her eyes. He couldn't save her, and she knew it. She lifted a hand from her throat and placed her convulsing palm on the glass, the violent spasms in her chest growing smaller. Her skin blued, and blood shuttled through the bulging veins at her temples. She was dying.

The warehouse spun around him like a carnival Gravitron, and Wilde blurred out of his sight.

"Nooooooooooo!" he screamed, but couldn't hear it. The floor opened, and the Jack-in-the-Boxes swirled into a vortex. At the center, Kipling's immense taunting face chomped at him. The wrinkles on his sallow skin cracked and glowed like fissures in a cooling lava flow. Massive razor-sharp blades rotated from his mouth, chopping like helicopter rotors. Twisted metal and splintered wood erupted as projectiles from the blades, slashing Whitman's flesh and adding to the deafening symphony of destruction. He scrambled up the descending boxes, but the maelstrom pulled him in.

He searched everywhere for Wilde but couldn't find her.

The grinding and cackling grew until Whitman wanted to tear his hair from his skull. He slammed his eyes shut and covered his ears.

Someone grabbed him by the shoulder and shook him. The grinding continued, but was now farther away and quieter, like rocks grinding in a garbage disposal. The laughter ceased. Whitman cracked one eye open. The Kipling Shredder was gone. The boxes, gone.

Woolf stood over him. "It's just a dream, man." Whitman thought he detected a flicker of concern in Woolf's furious glare.

"Good morning, Angelface," Wilde's bright voice sliced into his ears above the scream of the blender.

Whitman groaned and slowly opened his other eye in the direction of the racket. It was Wilde, alright. She was alive, thank god. Part of his heart relaxed.

He wasn't dreaming anymore. The pummeling pain he

felt grounded him firmly in reality. Suspicion slinked into his mind.

What is she doing here?

Her presence wasn't unwelcome, but that sound sure as hell was. Confused, Whitman pushed himself up to his elbows and rubbed his eyes fully open. His head pounded, and his entire aching body felt like it had been run through a taffy machine.

Whitman tried to piece together what he could remember from the previous night. Had Wilde stayed over? The last he remembered, she was walking away from him, looking sexy something fierce. Her perfect hips switched in those skin-tight jeans, hypnotizing him as she headed toward Woolf and Hemingway.

Oh, and then the shots. All the shots. Fade to black. There was no way he could've snatched a victory out of the jaws of defeat in the state he must have been in.

Wilde poured a chunky, green-brown concoction from the blender into a tall glass. She cracked a raw egg on top and brought it to Whitman's bedside.

"Take those." She gestured to the painkillers and water on the side table. Whitman complied, needing relief and not wanting to pick a fight in his weakened state by being stubborn. "And drink this."

Whitman pulled a disgusted face. Wilde might be the only person he could tolerate at the moment, but even she couldn't bring out the best of him when he was like this.

"Trust me, Love."

Hearing her call him "Love" again felt like a balm on his battered soul. Whitman took a sip, swallowed his gag reflex, and gave her a tight grin. He closed one eye, still not loving the brightness of the room. Had she turned on every single light?

He gulped down the sickening smoothie, feeling the gelatinous egg slide down his throat like a raw oyster chased with spinach and banana chowder. An aftertaste of ginger and black pepper lingered in his mouth.

Wilde produced a shot glass of cloudy green liquid and gave him a reassuring nod. He tossed it back: pickle juice.

Worst pickle back ever.

"Good boy," she teased and patted his head, sending a spike of pain into his skull. His brow furrowed, and his eyes opened enough to glare at her. Last night's makeup had barely budged, and her stunning smile melted the tiniest fraction of his headache.

Oh god, I must look fucking horrible.

He couldn't believe he let her see him like this. Shame rang the alarm, and he burrowed back under the covers, smothering his face with a pillow.

"Range later?" Whitman heard Woolf say on the other side of the pillow. He hadn't realized his roommate was there. The mystery developed further.

"Bet on it," she said. Whitman heard the smile in Wilde's voice, and it tightened his aching neck. He heard the door open and close, and he released a deep groan.

Was Wilde here because she stayed the night with Woolf? Were they sipping gimlets and doing the dirty while he was passed out in the next bed? He couldn't even remember returning to their room. The whirlwind of thoughts made his head swim, and he had to sit up and place his feet on the floor. He crushed and kneaded his forehead with his fingers, trying to form it back into something resembling a human skull.

"What in the hell was Wilde doing here last night?" Whitman needed to know. He assumed from her clothes that she hadn't been back to her room.

"If you must know, she carried your stupid, drunk ass home from the party and poured you into that bed." Woolf's tone dripped with disdain.

"Carried me?! That's halfway across the North Wing," Whitman exclaimed, incredulous.

Woolf raised his eyebrows at him, indicating he was fully aware of the distance.

"Why was she still here this morning?" Whitman pried.

"Beats me. She wanted to stay. Maybe she was concerned you'd choke on your vomit."

Whitman wanted to strangle Woolf for his smug tone.

"You talk in your sleep, by the way. You might want to get that handled before they send you on assignment. If the Director finds out, she's likely to send you to Reprogramming," Woolf warned, tonelessly.

The discomforting thought of undergoing Reprogramming exacerbated Whitman's migraine. In the years Archangel had taught real-life torture resistance, they had discovered the perfect symphony of isolation, deprivation, psychopharmacological, physical, and multi-sensory overload "therapy" that failed to produce torture-resistant cadets with intact psyches. It did, however, achieve a near-perfect success rate in wiping all recollection from the mind, except for muscle memory. A cadet would retain physical ability and some skills, while their personality was reduced to a puddle. It also earned them a lifetime appointment to the Archangel Staff sans compensation or departure privileges.

"Oh god, what was I saying?" Whitman panicked.

"Not much. Just calling for Wilde, mostly."

Fuck me.

Whitman had no idea how he was ever going to look Wilde in the eyes. The searing pain between his temples intensified. Mortification engulfed him and he retreated under his pillow, hoping the world behind it would cease existing.

CHAPTER 46

WHITMAN

Whitman caught up with Wilde in the hallway.

"Hey," he said, trotting to keep pace with her.

"Hey," she replied, not bothering to slow down or meet his gaze. She adjusted the strap of the duffel on her shoulder.

"Where're you headed?" He tried to sound casual.

"Long range," she stated plainly, revealing nothing.

"Do you really need the practice? Aren't you still top of the leaderboard for marksmanship?"

"How do you think I got there? It certainly wasn't by going to happy hour." She threw him a sideways smile. The thought of alcohol tumbled his stomach.

"You're killing it at throwing knives, too." Whitman mentally scolded himself for the feeble attempt at flattery.

"That's more of a hobby. They're pretty impractical as a weapon," she said.

"How do you mean?" At least he had her talking.

"Well, best-case scenario: you land a kill shot. It's pretty hard to kill someone with one stab wound. Worst-case scenario: you miss, and you've just armed your adversary. In both cases, you've thrown away your weapon. At least your enemy can't throw a bullet back at you."

She had a point, and Whitman lost his words for the moment. They walked to the end of the hall and turned the corner in silence.

"Do you need some company?" he managed to ask.

"I'm meeting Woolf. You're welcome to join if you think you can shoot with double vision."

Ouch.

Wilde had struck first blood.

One point, Frenchy.

"Thankfully, that has gone away," Whitman said, stung. "That hangover cure of yours is killer. I'm gonna need that recipe." His recovery from the morning was nothing short of miraculous. He didn't feel fresh as lettuce, but he no longer prayed for death's swift embrace.

"No way. It's proprietary." Her smile warmed, and she shot him a flirtatious glance. "You'll just have to keep me around so I can make it for you when you need it." She nudged a playful shoulder into his arm.

Whitman was unsure what to make of this. She seemed sincere. He was sure she should be annoyed with him, at the very least. And, at the most, downright murderous. Was this a trap? He knew she possessed an exceptional talent for deception, but he felt like he knew her well enough to get a decent read on her. He didn't detect an ounce of malice in her expression or tone. She was being sweet.

Alarms sounded. Not in Whitman's head. In the castle itself. The lights switched from their regular amber to emergency blues, casting an eerie glow along the hallway. Wilde looked up at him with a knitted brow.

"Lockdown protocol," he said, all business. "We need to get behind a secured door, now."

Wilde nodded, and they bolted down the hall.

"Dorms?" she asked.

"We won't make it. The safeguards will be down by the time we get there. I don't think we'll make the library either. Come on." Whitman grabbed Wilde's hand and led her down a side hallway.

The ominous sound of the steel security doors clamping down in front of all the secured spaces chased them down the corridor. They were running out of time.

Wilde tried a door. It was already locked from the inside. Whitman tried the next—same deal.

CLOMP. CLOMP. CLOMP.

More security doors slammed into place.

Wilde's hands clasped on a door handle, and it gave. She pulled Whitman inside, and they quickly pushed the door closed just as the steel barrier hit the floor, sealing them in.

Darkness shrouded the room. Wilde's labored breaths matched Whitman's as they stood with their backs against the door, as if their bodies could provide another line of defense from whatever chaos lurked outside.

The slamming of security barriers ceased, and an expansive silence entombed the chamber.

"Do you think it's a drill?" Wilde whispered, her voice barely breaking the silence.

"I don't know. It's strange to run a lockdown drill on a Saturday, with all the assets scattered and half the faculty gone." Realization dawned on him as the words left his lips, and a cold shiver slid down his back. "But, strategically, pretty ideal for an attack on the Keep."

Archangel was one of the most successful and prolific private intelligence training programs. Any number of organizations would have a motive to attack the castle. He was relieved to be secured behind a safeguard with Wilde. He wouldn't need to spend the whole lockdown worrying about where she was. She was safe with him.

"We should find some light." Wilde's voice snapped his focus back to the moment. She searched the wall and found a switch. With a flick, warm light flooded the room, illuminating a familiar antique four-poster and a star-speckled ceiling.

"No. Fucking. Way," she said, shocked. A playful excitement replaced the apprehension in her voice.

Whitman's mouth dropped open. A kick of fresh adrenaline rushed through his veins. Of all the rooms they could have ended up in, they landed in the fucking Stargazer Suite. Memories flooded Whitman's mind—wonderful memories now tainted with jealousy and guilt. Emotions drenched the room, making Whitman desperate to relive those precious moments with Wilde, but he couldn't bury all the things she had done with Woolf.

Wilde's giggle broke through his thought spiral. She dropped her duffel, kicked off her shoes, and skipped over to flop onto the bed. Gazing up at the ceiling, she spread her limbs as if making a snow angel. A deep sigh escaped her lips. She had the eyes of a child, rolling around in the grass, counting animals in the clouds.

Whitman felt glued to the door. He wanted to take her in his arms and roll around with her under the stars. He realized he wanted to do that beneath every night sky they could find all over the world. He longed for her youthful glee to whisk him away with her, but the thought of Woolf crept around the side of his skull, tightening his jaw.

"Such great memories in this place," Wilde sighed. "Not the worst place to be locked up, nor the worst company." She turned toward him and winked.

"All we're missing is Woolf," Whitman said tightly.

Why the fuck did you say that? What the fuck is wrong with you?!

Wilde rolled back to face the ceiling and sighed, this time sounding more disappointed than contented.

"I'm not missing Woolf a drop. Are you?" she said. She gave him all kinds of bait, and he couldn't bring himself to bite.

Whitman unglued himself from the door and strode over to the ornate bar on the opposite wall from the bed, attempting to project more confidence than he felt. He surmised that the Stargazer was either used as a training module for Program H or a room for esteemed guests. It was more well-stocked than the last time they had visited.

"Speaking of drops, can I interest you in a cocktail? No way of knowing how long we'll be in here. We'll have to keep ourselves busy somehow," Whitman proposed. Anxiety coiled and squirmed in his chest. His fingers trembled as he reached for a bottle of gin, eager to take the edge off.

"Oh, I can think of a couple of ways to stay busy," Wilde said, without diverting her gaze from the ceiling. Whitman still wasn't sure if she was serious, but he was willing to follow her down this path.

Maybe she wasn't upset after all. Perhaps he was reading too much into things, and he was the only one who caught feelings in this situation. It crossed his mind that Wilde might view their relationship as casual, meaningless sex—just a blip on a vast radar. That thought provided him no comfort. He had meant nothing to everyone else in his life. He couldn't confront the possibility that he meant nothing to Wilde as well, even if it might alleviate the burden of having rejected her.

Wilde stretched her arms and legs out sumptuously, sinking deep into the bed with that irresistible feline elegance.

She trailed her fingertips along the silk coverlet as if passing them through the surface of a stream. Whitman collected the ingredients for French 75s and mixed two of them. He hoped she wouldn't be disappointed that it wasn't a gimlet. Jealousy stabbed an ice pick into his side.

"Consider it happy hour," he said with a wry smile. "Not your top choice for the afternoon, but hopefully a rewarding second option."

Wilde slinked off the bed and sauntered over to the bar. She reached for a glass from Whitman, and her fingers brushed against his, binding him in the ache of anticipation.

"I get to drink my favorite with my favorite? That's a very rewarding option." Wilde's eyes twinkled, and her pupils dilated. Her lips parted on the edge of a smile, pulling Whitman in like a tractor beam. He was powerless against this look. He didn't care if it was a trap; he never wanted her to stop looking at him like that. She leaned over the bar so close that her warm breath danced on his cheeks. Her proximity electrified the air around him, awakening all the nerve endings on his skin to her presence.

Fuck it. If this is poison, call me Socrates.

If Wilde was down to relive some good times, he was more than happy to take that ride with her.

"We've got a fully stocked bar and a very inviting bed. We could start making some new favorite memories," Whitman said. He noticed a fleeting emotion in her eyes, and a bit of warmth faded from her expression.

"Tempting..." Wilde said, with a pause. "But I just sewed the buttons back on this shirt."

Fuck.

How did Whitman overlook that she wore the same button-up from that night? Molten shame spilled into the pit of his stomach, and he began to sweat.

"Anyway, those safeguards won't let me leave when you decide that you're finished with me," she said, turning away from him.

"French—"

"Don't call me that." Her tone was quiet and weary, more a plea than an order. Her footsteps stalled, and a shallow sigh dropped her shoulders. She tipped a sip of the cocktail into her mouth.

Whitman had no words. He had regretted that night every day since it happened. Hell, he regretted it as he was doing it. Of all the heartbreaking memories that haunted him, the wounded sound of her voice calling his name as he broke her trust sliced deeper than any other. He had no idea how to repair this. Guilt tightened around his chest like a straitjacket, imprisoning him in his disgrace.

"It's better this way anyway," Wilde threw over her shoulder. "It was a much-needed wake-up call. We should just keep things casual." Every word pierced him. Wilde failed at masking the hurt in her voice, and Whitman loathed every part of himself for it. The last thing he wanted was for things to be casual. The shame in his stomach cooled into a hard mass.

Wilde returned to the once-inviting four-poster and sat on the edge of the mattress. Whitman watched a distance glaze over her eyes.

"We're just two incredibly complicated individuals doing uncomplicated things together." She half-smiled, but neither of them found consolation in those words.

The silence threatened to replace the air in the room, and Wilde stared through the wall.

Whitman could no longer stand the dense space between them. He walked over and sat facing Wilde on the edge of the bed. Her body stiffened, and she avoided looking at him. He reached a hand toward her, then hesitated and pulled it back. Remorse churned inside him. He ached to console her, but didn't know how to start. He was probably the last person she wanted comfort from.

Whitman swallowed hard, hoping to find the right words.

"What if I don't care if things get complicated?" he said. Wilde's lashes fluttered, and she exhaled sharply. A swallow shifted the column of her neck, but she didn't look at him.

"Like thinking I slept with the bastard who broke your leg? That kind of complicated?" she said in a brittle, bitter whisper.

"Fuck," he muttered. "Hemingway told—"

"Of course, she told me," she said with more of an edge to her voice.

Regret punched through his ribcage and dug its steely claws into his heart. She knew.

God, she must hate me. Why do I always fuck everything up? Hemingway's right. I don't deserve her.

As Hemingway's words replayed in his head, renewed anger mixed with his anguish over what she had been through.

The image of Wilde suffocating in his dream flashed across his mind. He couldn't shake that helpless feeling, watching her convulse and reach for him in her last moments.

What went through her mind when Kipling attacked her?

I couldn't protect her, and she knows it.

Not only was he not there for her, but he blamed her for something she would never do. How could he have thought so little of her?

Then he had taken all his torment out on her.

I am such a fucking dick. What the hell is wrong with me?

The swirl of possibilities of what Kipling could have done

259

to her sent fiery comets of wrath across his chest. He needed to know.

"What did he do to you?" he whispered through his thickening throat.

"What do you care?" she hissed, every word a hot blade in his gut.

"You think I don't care?" He cared more for her than anything—more than his friends, himself, his image, his career, and even his own life.

"It doesn't feel like it lately." Her voice dropped, heavy with disappointment.

In that moment, he knew he had demolished any trust she had in him. He wanted to die.

Whitman spiraled into desperate rationalizations. He needed to make this right. Knowing Wilde thought he didn't care about her made him feel like he had fallen into that Kipling Shredder and was being torn limb from limb. His face burned with remorse, and his fingernails dug into his thighs through his trousers. He had to fix this.

I'm probably just gonna fuck it up, like everything else.

His nose stung and his eyes blurred with unwept tears. He swallowed his fear down a burning throat.

"Look. I fucked up," he said.

Her glistening eyes met his, pleading with him not to lean back into swagger and callousness. He never wanted to see that suffering in her eyes again.

"I fucked up," he admitted, just above a whisper.

Her chin gave the slightest quiver, and she pressed her lips together.

"Wilde, I'm sorry. I am so fucking sorry," Whitman said. He found the courage to brush a tendril of hair from her face. She closed her eyes tightly, and a tear escaped down her cheek.

He kissed it away, hoping to soothe some of her sorrow.

She opened her eyes and penetrated his gaze, saying nothing. Behind the veil of pain, a softness returned to her face.

"What I did was awful. And you didn't deserve it," he said.

Wilde choked down a sob. Her eyes squeezed closed, pinching at the corners. A hollow opened around his heart, exposing the fragile place he had been repeatedly unloved.

The silence gnawed at him. He wished she would say something.

"What did he do?" Whitman murmured, afraid of the answer.

She closed her arms, gripping her elbows with her hands, and turned her face away from him, rubbing her cheek on her shoulder and releasing a stuttering breath. "You want all the gory details?" she choked out.

"Whatever you feel like sharing." He had to know how painful he needed to make Kipling's death.

"I don't remember most of it." She returned to staring into the wall in front of her. "It's not a big deal. Nothing really happened in the end."

"It's a big deal to me. I—" *You can't tell her, you idiot. She fucking hates you.* "I really do care about you. I care a lot."

She turned her face toward him, wariness poorly masking her misery. He had never seen her so vulnerable.

Whitman gathered all his courage and placed a small kiss next to her eyelid, whispering more apologies. He wrapped his arms around her, and at first, her body was wooden. He kept apologizing with every kiss, every caress, and she relaxed, melting back into him.

"He will never touch you again. I promise."

They sat like that for some time, Wilde silently weeping in Whitman's arms. He sensed when she started to level out. She stirred and sat up, composed and in control once more. Without words, she reached over and sipped from her French 75 on the bedside table.

"I heard you broke his nose," he said.

"That part I remember perfectly." A sly smile tiptoed out of her tears, sending a flutter through Whitman's stomach. Her brief return to their comfortable banter lifted the weight on his chest.

"Elbow?" Whitman remembered exactly how vicious her elbow strikes were.

"Palm strike," she said, wiping a hand across her cheeks and sniffing.

"Atta girl."

A grin tugged at the corner of her mouth.

Silence descended on them once again, but the tension didn't feel as thick.

Say something, idiot. Anything. She's giving you an in.

I love you.

Not that.

"I know there's nothing I can do to make up for what I did to you," Whitman said. Wilde's eyes surveyed him, neither confirming nor denying the validity of his statement. She yielded nothing.

"However, it could be potentially rewarding if you'd let me try," he said, attempting to inject the moment with a bit of levity.

Wilde tried, and failed, not to smile. Her eyes glinted with a familiar playfulness, and relief peeled a few of guilt's talons from Whitman's heart.

"Only if you promise..." she said.

"Anything."

I'll jump off a fucking bridge if you want me to.

"You promise to try... really hard." Half her mouth turned upward in a mischievous grin.

All the tension Whitman held locked in his muscles released, and a shaky laugh bubbled out of him.

What had he ever done to deserve this perfect woman?

He leaned toward her, dipping a toe in her waters. Her tear-washed eyes fell to his mouth, and she sucked in a breath. After a moment that felt like a month, her eyelids slid closed, and she accepted his kiss.

The tenderness of her lips hit him like a shot of morphine, numbing the consuming ache that constantly wound around his bones. He wrapped his arms around her, devouring her with his kisses. The rest of the world fell away, and nothing mattered but this moment.

"Do you want me to stop?" he whispered against her lips. After their last encounter, he needed to know this was what she wanted.

"Never," she sighed, drawing her tongue up his lower lip and slipping it inside his mouth. He sucked on it eagerly.

The respite from his shame mingled with the freedom she granted him, kindling his desire. She swirled her tongue around inside his mouth, and he relinquished command over his appetite for her.

Whitman hooked his arms under her and lifted her to the headboard, where he lay her down gently on the silk pillows. Desire swam in her eyes, but an undercurrent of pain and uncertainty flowed in the depths. He was only setting his first steps on the road to rebuilding her trust. He would not stop until he saw sweet satisfaction spread across her face.

Whitman freed the top button of Wilde's shirt, the shirt

he had previously defiled. He planted a kiss on her chest behind it, a silent apology. She exhaled and acquiesced to his touch. Her nipples stood taut underneath the white cotton. As much as it drove him wild to see her in lingerie, it unraveled him when she wore nothing underneath, when he could see just a hint of those curves that unknit his sanity.

Whitman fingered another button and skimmed his lips along the margin of her ribcage. The tension in her abs released, and her tender tummy softened under his mouth. She arched toward him, and he swelled inside his pants. He released the final button and spread her shirt open with delicate care, revealing immaculate pink nipples.

Whitman struggled to keep the reins on his lust, but the ache in his cock grew.

Keep it together.

Wilde's pleasure was paramount. He needed her to know how much he desired her, how much he needed her, how much she meant to him. How he felt like he might die if she didn't forgive him.

Whitman opened the buckles on her plum tartan skirt, unwrapping her like a birthday present. He slipped her sheer black hiphugger panties down her legs and off her feet.

She allowed him to spread her thighs wide without resistance, melting into the mattress. Placing himself between her legs, he slid his hands around her thighs and pulled her into his face, exploring her with his tongue.

"I missed the way you taste," he mumbled between her lips. He pulled her sweet clit into his mouth and sucked it, swirling his tongue around as he suctioned around it. She lost her breath for a moment, the sweetest moment.

He ran the tip of his tongue along the inside of her hood. Time stopped. But Whitman didn't. Wilde buried her fingers in his hair and released one of those exquisite whimpers he could never get enough of. He took the opportunity to take a slow suck and drag his tongue from the bottom to the top of her swollen little clit.

"Oh, fuck," she moaned.

Whitman had to unfasten his belt and pants to relieve the pressure on his throbbing cock. He slipped two fingers inside her, and her breath caught in her throat. Her walls were drenched and swollen, and they gave at his touch. He curled his fingers, stroking the ridges there, and her hips writhed to meet his touch. A deep moan emptied her lungs, and she sank farther into the bed.

Whitman stopped for a moment, only to witness the bliss on her face before ramping up again.

Her thighs began to quiver around his face. Sweet little moans surged in succession out of her throat. He sucked and licked and fingered as if his very life depended on her pleasure. She gasped, and her whole frame trembled. He held her tight as ecstasy overcame her, and her euphoric cries pierced the air. She rumbled for a moment in his arms, then took a deep, satisfied breath.

Whitman removed his shirt as he kissed a path up her body, pausing to taste her firm nipples. She hummed.

He slipped into her as their lips met, her glistening gaze colliding with his. Her muscles pulsed around him. When he felt the tip of his cock meet the end of her, his whole spine tingled.

"Fuck, Whit," she whined, sending a twitch to the base of his cock. Other people called him that nickname. But when Wilde half-breathed, half-moaned it, as if she was so enraptured she couldn't get his whole name out, he came undone. He wished he could record it and listen to it on a loop.

"I know, Baby. Just let go and I'll take care of you."

Whitman glided himself out and back in slowly, savoring every inch of her. Tiny aftershocks beat around his cock, hardening him further. She slipped her little hands around his hips and grasped his ass, pulling him into her.

The topside of his cock dragged along her upper wall, sending an exhilarating shiver skittering up his spine to the top of his skull. When her tunnel suctioned around him, drawing out his very essence, he lost control over himself and surrendered all of what he was to her.

CHAPTER 47

DICKINSON

Dickinson sat, massaging her forehead. She yanked open the wooden drawer of her desk and sprinkled a few painkillers from a prescription bottle into her palm, washing them down with the remains of her n^{th} cup of coffee. The grandfather clock ticked the seconds away. Seven minutes had passed since she keyed the code to lift the lockdown into her computer terminal.

The first fingers of the breaking dawn squeezed through the narrow panes of her office windows, casting an orange glow across the room. Her eyes caught the glistening specks of dust that rose in the air as the room warmed, a welcome sight after hours of staring at a screen. She had spent the night scouring the data and CCTV footage in search of a trail that would lead her to the source of the breach.

Raising the lockdown felt like a risk, but she needed help. She needed her team.

A muffled conversation neared the door to her office. Recognizing the voices, she disengaged the lock with the button under her desk.

Faulkner barged in, followed by Fielding. Frost floated in

behind them.

"What happened? How was the lockdown triggered?" Faulkner demanded.

"We had no communication. The encrypted comm network was down," Fielding said.

Dickinson pumped her face-down palm above her desk to encourage them to calm down.

"I triggered it. Someone used Fitzgerald's credentials to log into the system," Dickinson said.

"What?" Frost's face betrayed an uncharacteristic worry.

"From the outside?" Fielding asked. Dickinson pursed her lips, dreading the news she would have to share.

"From inside the Keep. I haven't been able to track which terminal. I disabled the comm network in case the culprit tried to communicate with any accomplices."

"What about the perimeter? We can't risk this element escaping the grounds," Faulkner said.

"Still secure. No one in and no one out until we find this mole," Dickinson ordered. "Any luck finding a replacement for Fitzgerald?"

"Capote and Christie show promise," Fielding said. Dickinson weighed the options. Capote was fresh but fierce, her programming astounding. Christie's reputation for talent was well-established, as was their slight distaste for authority. Christie was in their third year, which gave them a slight advantage in the devil-you-know category. The risk of bringing someone new into the fold to replace Fitzgerald felt overwhelming, but an unfortunate necessity.

"Which one is better with the system?"

"Capote," Faulkner and Fielding answered on top of one another.

Dickinson shifted her gaze to Frost, pointing her fountain

pen at her.

"Did she pass her I.I.?"

Frost nodded. The Investigative Interview chemicals were incredibly potent. The only psychopharmacological compound they administered that was stronger was reserved for Reprogramming. If Capote came through the I.I. clean, that would suffice. It was all they had.

"Grant her the clearance she needs to hunt for our mole, with as few details as she needs to get the job done. And make sure she's supervised, but don't make it obvious."

The three nodded in assent.

"Should we lock Fitzgerald's account?" Faulkner asked.

"I have it flagged. Drop the clearance to Pedestrian, but leave the account active. It may be our best chance at tracking them. Search his office for any leads."

CHAPTER 48

WILDE

Wilde dragged her jelly legs to the library. She had put herself on a grueling training schedule after Kipling attacked her, determined to be ready next time. Thankfully, he had been bizarrely absent from haunting her steps since the Program H party. Wilde plopped her daypack onto a bench at a corner study table. She didn't think Kipling would be caught dead frequenting the library, but she still felt more comfortable when she could see the exits.

She sat down on the bench gingerly. Every muscle in her body throbbed. She had sparred with Woolf for an hour, then with Koontz. Wells had strolled in as she was getting ready to leave, and she snagged him for a quick session. She jumped on any chance she got to spar with her "Big Buddy." She hoped it would give her a better advantage to practice with someone of a similar size to Kipling's. Well, not exactly fe-fi-fo-fum, but taller and broader than Woolf and Koontz. She hoped that counted for something.

She wanted nothing more than to collapse in bed and sleep for a week until the ache subsided. Not an option, as her training schedule had caused her to fall behind in her courses.

She pulled her notebook out of her bag and opened it on the desk. Reaching across, she pulled the gold switch chain on the green banker's lamp, illuminating the broad desk.

Her exhausted brain strayed to Whitman, as it often did. They hadn't spent much time together since the lockdown. A familiar knot of guilt braided around her stomach. Their reunion had been so uplifting, even if her lingering hurt held her back from fully trusting it. She wanted to enjoy it while it lasted, as long or short as that may be. She allowed herself to entertain the fantasy that she meant something to him.

She missed Whitman. She hoped he didn't think she was avoiding him.

Wilde dragged her weary eyes down the page of notes, not retaining any of the blurry words. She caught her head bobbing several times and jerked it up.

"Well, hello, Sugar," a deep voice drawled from over her shoulder, jolting her awake. Kipling's presence radiated behind her, sending a prickling wave of apprehension over the hairs on her neck.

FUCK!

"Shhhh," Wilde ordered.

"Why, cuz we're in a library?"

"No, I just really hate the sound of your voice. If you're looking for the Berenstain Bears books, I think they're on the upper level." She knew being polite wouldn't deter him from whatever he had planned, but she hoped the hushed environment might discourage him.

Kipling placed a heavy paw on her shoulder and leaned down to put his mouth by her ear, his rancid breath blasting past her cheek.

"We're gonna have some fun, you and me," he sneered. He squeezed his hand on her sore shoulder, and she masked a wince.

"I'll have to pass on the fun. I'm trying to quit." Wilde flinched her shoulder out of his grasp and turned to face him, scanning the gallery on her way. Only a few people occupied the space, none of whom she recognized. Her legs stood trapped between the bench and the desk. Kipling's beard curled up, meeting the malice seething out of his eyes.

"Maybe I'll have all the fun then. I could just spread you out, right here on this desk." He leaned over her, his hot, fetid breath permeating her space. Panic wriggled a hot path up her spine.

"Not here," she conceded, darting her eyes to find any means of escape. Silence sailed over the rows of wooden study desks. No friendly face arrived from the expansive rows of tomes. The doom of the upper section loomed—no exits on that level. The setting sun streaked through the windows of the cupola, a promise of freedom cut off from her.

Kipling rolled the proposition around his empty skull for a moment.

"Lead the way, Sweet-cheeks." His voice shredded the remnants of her sense of safety. She slid from behind the bench, dropped her notebook in the bag, and attempted an appearance of normalcy as she slung it onto her shoulder. It held a few books. Maybe a blow from the bag could do some damage.

With wariness, she turned her back to Kipling and walked toward the shelves like a march to the gallows. She rounded the first shelf and picked up her pace, speed-walking. She needed to maintain a distance between them. If Kipling got a hand on her, he could disable her in seconds. Halfway down the aisle, she rolled a book cart behind her, blocking the path.

Kipling closed the gap, reaching the cart as she locked one

of the casters. He swatted and caught her bookbag, jerking her back as she started to run. She shrugged off the strap and took off on a sprint. Kipling's angry grunt followed her, but she didn't look back.

Wilde only made out some of the numbers as she ran down the stacks.

600s.

Kipling stumbled and crashed into the shelves behind her on his warpath. He was gaining.

400s.

Wilde's legs felt like they might give out. Only her flight instinct cranked her limbs forward.

300s.

Wilde flew down the 200s aisle, launching books behind her as she ran, anything to slow him.

250...240...

Her eyes landed on the 230s with relief. She pulled the heavy bookcase open and slipped inside the secret passageway. Slim electric candelabras lined the familiar limestone walls. Her relief died as she saw Kipling reach into the passage as she pulled the bookcase shut. She yanked with her remaining strength, crushing his bratwurst fingers. He wailed and wrenched the bookcase open, tearing part of the door from its frame. Wilde released the door to avoid getting yanked toward Kipling, causing her to stumble back on her ass.

Wilde crab-crawled backward, but Kipling reached her before she could get to her feet. He plucked her up and hoisted her over his shoulder.

Not a great start, Babe.

She wrapped her right arm around his head and underneath his chin, praying she could reach it with her other hand around his immense neck. She caught the tips of her fingers and pulled them, solidifying her grip. She dropped all her weight toward the floor and wrapped her legs around his trunk of an abdomen, cutting off the blood and oxygen to his head. He dropped her before he lost consciousness.

In the moment Kipling took to regain his bearings, Wilde repositioned her feet, grasped his shoulders, and drove the full force of her hip through her knee and into his head, following through with a battle cry that echoed down the tunnel. He tumbled back onto the floor, stunned.

Wilde bolted. If she could reach Fitzgerald's office, she might be able to trap Kipling behind the door or at least escape into the hallway outside Fitz's office. She pulled some of the candelabras that lined the passage across the path as she sprinted. Glass shattered behind her as one, then another, smashed into the wall. Kipling roared behind her. Fire blazed inside her lungs.

She could make it. She had to make it.

She was six strides from the back of the bookcase that led to Fitzgerald's office when Kipling snagged the sleeve of her sweater. She unzipped it and slipped her arm out of the sleeve he held, but couldn't release her other arm before his hands grabbed her by the shoulders. He snorted as he launched her backward into the wall. Her head hit the stone with a crack, and she cried out. Her vision washed out white. Splintering agony fanned out across the back of her skull.

The blow jiggled her bone marrow, and her body lost the strength to support itself. She crumpled to the floor. When her vision returned, sparkling ants danced pathways around the periphery of her field of view.

Kipling's enraged face entered her blurry tunnel of sight. His brawny hands dragged her to the center of the passage, and the weight of his body imprisoned hers to the floor.

CHAPTER 49

WHITMAN

Whitman strolled down the hallway toward Fitzgerald's office. He and Wilde hadn't been able to line up their schedules since lockdown, and he stewed himself in a sludge of loneliness and self-pity. Fitzgerald could usually cheer him up and also offer some sage advice. His confidence wasn't exactly at an all-time high. Wilde dominated his thoughts, and being separated from her was a dragging, persistent torture.

As he approached the door, he checked the box of pistachio macarons in his hand, shuffling it slightly to hide the space where he had eaten one. He could never resist the temptation to indulge in a good sweet.

He gave two quiet raps on the door before entering the office.

"Special delivery. It's your favorite..."

Instead of Fitzgerald's white-bearded smile, he found Faulkner and Fielding rummaging through files on the desk. Frost stood in the corner, sifting through manila folders in a vertical file cabinet along the wall. They all glanced over at him like three raccoons caught mid-mischief in a dumpster.

"You're not who I expected. Where's Fitzgerald?"

Whitman probed.

"On assignment," Faulkner said curtly. He stacked some papers together and concealed them with a folder on the desk. "He requested some files to aid him."

"And it takes all three of you to search for them?" Whitman teased with a roguish eyebrow lift.

"What do you need, Whitman?" Fielding's dismissive tone gave Whitman the sense they wanted him out of the office, and quickly. He sauntered over to the desk, placing the box of macarons on it. He tapped the top of the patterned box with two fingers, drawing the moment out for his own amusement.

"Just a drop-off. Consider me out of your hair," he said, cranking up the charm.

A muffled shout echoed from one of the bookcases along the wall, drawing everyone's attention.

What the hell?

"Frost, don't take me to your office for saying this, but did that bookcase just... yell?" Whitman asked. The four of them exchanged confused glances.

"Get off me, you motherfucker!" Wilde's strangled voice was unmistakable from behind the wall. Whitman had no time to make sense of what was happening. Frenchy was on the other side of that wall, and she wasn't alone. She was in danger. Whitman reacted instinctively, hurtling himself toward the source of the sound. He pounded on the bookcase.

WILDE

Wilde struggled to get a limb out from under Kipling, but his legs pinned hers to the stone floor, and his paws clasped around her wrists. She heard a pounding on the other side of the door leading to Fitzgerald's office.

"Frenchy!! Wilde!!" Whitman's muted shout sent a small ripple of relief through her body.

"Whitma—"

Kipling shoved his hand across her mouth, cutting off her yell, but freeing one of her arms.

Wilde chomped down on Kipling's meaty pinky until her teeth met bone. Hot blood poured into her mouth, hitting the back of her throat and making her cough. Kipling's enraged bellow reverberated off the walls. Wilde shot her free hand across Kipling's face, gouging her nails into anything she could reach.

CHAPTER 50

WHITMAN

Faulkner shoved Whitman out of the way, opening the false bookcase.

Pull, not push. Oops.

Kipling had Wilde pinned to the ground, her face covered in blood that appeared to be pouring out of her mouth. A wildfire erupted in Whitman's chest, and runaway rage blazed through his veins. He flew at Kipling, tackling him off Wilde. She scrambled to the wall. Kipling threw Whitman off him with a guttural howl. Whitman rolled back into a crouch, placing himself between Kipling and Wilde.

Kipling stalked toward them. Whitman dodged his punch and shot a kick at his ankle. It achieved grazing contact, but not enough to take him down. The brute took a long stride and a half, his second step interrupted by Wilde's outstretched leg. Kipling tripped, then partially regained himself, building momentum as he shoved Whitman back through the doorway into the office. Whitman pitched over an armchair, rolling backward onto the floor.

Kipling's hulking frame dwarfed the doorway as he entered the office, eyes trained on Whitman.

Before Whitman could rise to meet him, a small fleshy snake ensnared Kipling's neck. In the span of two constricted breaths, Kipling's eyes filled with shock, then stupor. His head drooped, revealing an impeccable auburn victory roll followed by a pair of winged eyeglasses. His massive form tumbled into a heap on the ground, unveiling Frost balancing in her Cuban-heeled spectator pumps on a Kimball mahogany rose parlor chair.

There's that Program K training.

She hopped off the chair, her heels double-clicking as light as a fawn's hooves on the glossy hardwood. She removed what looked like a small ballpoint pen from her skirt pocket. She uncapped it, revealing a stubby needle. Kneeling daintily beside Kipling, she jabbed the pen without mercy into his neck. Whitman sat on the floor, transfixed.

"He's set for transport," she said to Faulkner with her customary sweetness. She glanced at her watch. "With his mass, I'd wager about ninety minutes. Two hours, if we're lucky."

"You didn't disinfect that," Whitman teased in a deadpan.

"Oopsie," she said, her perfectly painted pinup lip spreading into a devious smile.

Whitman focused his gaze on the passageway. Fielding had her fingers around the back of Wilde's neck and head, probing gently. She brought a blue-gloved hand back red. Whitman's blood chilled, and his throat thickened.

Wilde lifted her head, and she opened her eyes. She was conscious.

Thank god.

The buzzing in Whitman's veins quieted some, and worry took the wheel. What had that bastard done to her?

"Are you cut in there? Missing any teeth?" Fielding asked

Wilde, referring to the blood that traversed down Wilde's neck and laterally across her cheeks. Her sports zip-up hung halfway off one arm and spilled onto the floor. Blood ran in a delta from her mouth, across her disheveled sports bra, and down past her navel.

"It's...not mine," Wilde rasped. She blinked slowly, her eyes rolling in a circle as she reopened them. Her eyebrows closed in on each other in a wince. Wiping her hand up her forehead like she wanted to rub it off her skull, she exhaled a frail groan.

"Did you hit your head on anything?" Fielding asked.

Wilde nodded. "The wall... and maybe the floor. I'm not sure."

"Does it hurt?"

"On a scale of one to Nine Inch Nails? It's a Johnny Cash," Wilde mumbled.

Her head swayed. Fielding asked her what date and day of the week it was. Whitman needed to be with her. He rose to his feet to walk toward them, but Faulkner's hand shot out to stop him.

"You were instructed not to engage with Kipling."

"No way. That deal is off. LOOK at her!" Whitman gestured to Wilde. Fielding evaluated her and questioned her gently, assessing her for injuries. Whitman darted his eyes back at Faulkner, making sure he took in the sight of Wilde's state. If Faulkner wanted to brush him off, he had better know damn sure what side he was choosing.

"Jacket. Arrow. Pepper. Cotton. Movie," Fielding recited to Wilde slowly, prompting her to repeat the sequence of words. Whitman recognized this as part of a standard concussion assessment.

"Jacket...Arrow...Um...Movies." Wilde lost the trail.

Whitman's worry intensified his anger. He wheeled on Faulkner.

"I agreed to lay off Kipling because you guaranteed to keep her safe," Whitman accused, advancing.

"Clearly, my assets didn't expect Kipling to be in the library," Faulkner replied, standing his ground.

"I made her a promise, and your incompetent assets made me break my word." Whitman's vision clouded, and the blood rushed in his ears.

"Careful," Faulkner warned, his piercing gaze narrowing like a predator. "You risk treading near the ledge of my leniency," he said, enunciating each word with severity.

"I could have PROTECTED her!" Whitman's voice rose.

"You would have killed him." Faulkner crossed his arms, an unflinching barricade of authority.

"So WHAT?! She would be SAFE right now!" Whitman's voice cracked under the weight of his outrage.

"You would risk the consequences of eliminating another Archangel asset, the least of all is Reprogramming, for—"

"Fucked if I care about the consequences," Whitman seethed in a carefully controlled tone.

"You wouldn't remember who she was," Frost interjected, her tone rueful.

"You won't remember who you are," Faulkner cautioned with an undercurrent of threat.

"But she'd still remember me," Whitman said, determination etched on his face. Faulkner's eyes drilled into him, appraising his resolve.

They could erase me like a wrong answer, and I'd still fall for her the moment I laid eyes on her.

"Kipling's not worth it," Frost said.

"Well, she is!" Whitman's cutting tone drained the color

from Frost's face.

A wounded whimper slipped from Wilde, snapping Whitman's focus to her. His worry for her surpassed all other thoughts, and he abandoned the argument with Faulkner.

Fielding ushered Wilde to her feet and waved Frost over. Wilde's eyes slowly blinked wide, looking like she might be sick. She puffed her cheeks and exhaled slowly through her mouth, closing her eyes. Whitman's heart writhed in his chest. Fielding and Frost lifted Wilde and supported her into the office from the tunnel.

"She's concussed. I'm taking her," Fielding said, neither asking for permission nor forgiveness. She stepped gingerly with Wilde and Frost toward the door.

"I'm going with them," Whitman said, his tone leaving no room for debate. Faulkner's iron fingers closed around his arm.

"Give Fielding and her team time to do their jobs," Faulkner ordered. Whitman lasered his eyes from Faulkner's hand to his face.

You wanna go, Grandpa?

"I understand your concern. She'll heal better without you getting in their way," Faulkner added, the militancy fading from his voice. "She'll bend, but not break." His gaze landed on Wilde, and Whitman witnessed an unfamiliar emotion pass through Faulkner's eyes. At first, it looked like resignation. Or disappointment.

Failure, perhaps? Your team fucked this one up.

Whitman failed her, too, and it killed him to think about it. He had promised her.

Faulkner's uncertain gaze tracked Wilde. Could it be worry? Did Faulkner care for her? Was he capable of care? Who could be so special that the King of Crotchediness himself would descend from his tiny throne to give a fuck about them?

If anyone could melt that black heart, it would be Wilde.

Wilde gave Whitman a weak smile as Fielding and Frost assisted her out the door toward the infirmary.

Whitman turned his fury back to Faulkner. "We have quite a few things to discuss." His eyes must have betrayed their murderous intent.

Even at a head-and-a-half shorter than Whitman, Faulkner's presence filled the room. "I don't need to remind you whom you're talking to, Mr. Dawes," Faulkner threatened. The use of Whitman's real name felt like a cooler of ice poured over his head. His ribcage trembled with rage.

Only the hostile hobgoblin in charge of my future in this program.

"I suggest you cool off, rediscover your lane, and remain there," Faulkner said with stern finality.

Wrath puffed in and out of Whitman's chest.

Faulkner's face relaxed to a less authoritarian scowl. "Get some rest, James. She's going to need you."

CHAPTER 51

WILDE

"I'm sorry I wasn't there. I'm supposed to watch your six," Woolf said. Failure and self-inflicted disappointment turned his eyes a glossy mossy green. Wilde hated to see him in this state.

"It's not your fault. You can't be with me 24-7." She took his hand and gave him a reassuring look. Woolf shot her a challenging gaze to demonstrate that he would prefer that option.

Woolf sat on the edge of the hospital bed. Wilde had recently been permitted to sit up, and her morning meds were finally dulling the piercing band of pain squeezing her skull. She could now enjoy the comfort of the beige walls in addition to the beige ceiling. And the all-you-can-choke-down beige buffet that was trayed into her at regular intervals.

Fielding and her staff wouldn't admit her guests until this morning. Yesterday, they performed all the tests: blood, urine, X-ray, MRI, CAT scan, assessments of unknown origin, you name it—everything except a visit with Frost.

Woolf's face had soothed her anxious heart when he had walked into her room in a cobalt sweater holding a bubblegum-pink bouquet of stargazer lilies. She felt like Judy Garland walking out of her sepia doorway into a world of color.

"What happened?" Woolf asked.

"I don't remember it all." Wilde struggled to filter the memories out of her buzzing, throbbing brain. "I remember fighting with Kipling. And then, somehow, Whitman was just... there. And then Kipling was gone. I think he saved me."

"I guess he deserves the nicer set of cufflinks for Christmas," Woolf admitted.

"Careful. For the price of what he considers nice cufflinks, you could buy a used car."

"Well, he deserves my gratitude. I'm not ready to lose you just yet." Woolf's eyebrows drew together in concern.

He climbed onto the bed to sit facing her and gently wrapped his arms around her back, pulling himself closer. Careful not to disconnect her IV port or the pulse oximeter on her index finger that kept the machine next to her beeping away, she crawled into his lap and wrapped her arms around him. She rested her head on his shoulder and breathed deeply. She was safe.

"I'm right here," Wilde whispered. Relief filled and emptied Woolf's lungs.

CHAPTER 52

WHITMAN

Whitman had been denied the chance to see Wilde thrice, by three different orderlies on three separate shifts. The fourth time, Fielding herself came out to address him.

"She's still being assessed. We're keeping her for observation tonight, probably for a few days. Why don't you get some rest and come back tomorrow?" Fielding's eyes were kind but firm.

Whitman hadn't been able to eat or sleep, so he resorted to drinking. Hawthorne didn't try to joke him out of it. Instead, they provided concerned glances, deep sighs, and a consistently filled snifter.

He woke up late the next morning, showered quickly, and headed back to the infirmary, where he was finally admitted. He rushed down the hallway to Wilde's room. The vertical blinds hung half open, slightly obscuring the view. He peeked through, eager to catch a glimpse of her.

On the bedside table, he noticed a bouquet of lilies.

Fuck me, why didn't I think of getting her flowers?

Beyond the blooms, Wilde and Woolf were sitting on the bed together. She was in Woolf's lap, her arms and legs wrapped around him in a skimpy hospital gown. Woolf held her tightly, as if he couldn't get his arms any farther around her, but he still tried. Whitman's heart climbed into his throat, and his nose and eyes stung.

How could he have been so foolish? They spent all their time together now, "training."

She'll never be mine.

Whitman was still reeling from nearly losing her. She was alive, but was she ever really his to lose in the first place?

She was never mine.

After taking one last watery look at them locked in their embrace, Whitman trudged out of the infirmary.

Whitman steeped himself in scotch and misery. He longed to return to the brief honeymoon period with Wilde during the lockdown. Their stolen hours under the stars seemed to transcend reality. She made him feel whole, like the missing piece he had searched for his entire life was finally locking into place. When he saw how hurt she was, he harbored the fantasy that she felt the same way about him. Their reunion felt sublime.

Then he saw Woolf and Wilde wrapped around each other after the attack, and those fantasies dissolved. He was back to being a broken, incomplete mess. He had done everything he could to protect her. *He* tackled Kipling off her. And yet, Woolf showed up with flowers, and she chose his shoulder to cry on?

Whitman questioned everything. Was it all an act? Was she the same way with Woolf? They spent a great deal of time together, always talking and always laughing. Were they laughing at him? He felt like a man on the rack, his soul's joints pulled and torn apart.

Whitman sorted through his emotions, but failed to find any sense. How could she give herself so openly to him, making him feel like he was all that mattered to her, only to turn to Woolf when it mattered most? Whitman tried to weigh the pain of losing her to Woolf against his current torment. His anguish at sharing her devoured him from the inside.

Woolf entered the dim room and strode to his bed. Whitman landed his glass on the table heavier than he needed to.

Woolf startled. "Jesus Christ, Whit! Ever heard of lights? You scared the shit out of me."

Oh, I can scare you worse than that. I'm just getting started.

Whitman's thoughts darkened.

"Look. Wilde told me what you did. I just wanted to say tha—"

Whitman cut Woolf off before he could finish his sentence. "You two talk about everything, don't you? Or do you have us bugged?"

"Don't be paranoid. And yes, Wilde and I talk about a lot. Occasionally, you are the topic of conversation," Woolf said.

Whitman's skeleton turned to iron. "Does she give you ALL the gory details of what we do together?" he jabbed, hoping to inspire some jealousy.

Woolf's jaw steeled. "No. She spares me those." It appeared to have worked.

"I'm sure you can fill in the blanks." Murderous thoughts flooded Whitman's brain, and he hoped Woolf would take the bait.

Woolf opened his mouth, then closed it. He exhaled

forcefully. "You can be a real fucking asshole sometimes, you know that? I don't know what she sees in you."

"Likewise," Whitman hissed. "You're always following her around like a puppy dog."

Woolf's eyebrows snapped together, and he took a few steps toward the edge of the bed. "We spend time together because we're FRIENDS. You might understand if you had the emotional capacity to build relationships deeper than drinking buddies and slampieces," he spat. "Oh, wait. I forgot. You also have a thriving friendship with a bird."

"Don't bring Pattycake into this."

Blood pounded in Whitman's ears. The insinuation that Wilde was no more than a slampiece made rage rise from his gut. Hot bile scalded the back of his throat. He loved Wilde more than Woolf could ever understand.

"I'm capable of..." Whitman was on the verge of losing himself to his anger. He took a measured breath. "You know what? I don't have to justify myself to you." There was an irritating shiver in his voice that he hoped Woolf couldn't detect.

"No, you don't. But you know who you should justify yourself to is Wilde. She gets viciously attacked, and you ghost her? And I'm the one who has to watch what it does to her," Woolf said.

"Oh, and I bet you love every minute of it. Just fuck the pain away."

Woolf threw his hands up. "You are so off base. You really have no clue what's going on here, do you?" he said.

"Oh yeah? Well, why don't you enlighten me? Tell me all about your romantic weekend."

"You're still on that? She didn't leave her bed for three days!" Woolf yelled.

"Yeah, I fucking heard!" Whitman slammed his glass down on the desk and gripped the edge.

"You know what, I don't need this. You are so incapable of breaking out of your bullshit for five fucking seconds to get a goddamn clue," Woolf yelled as he stormed back toward the door.

"There you go. Run on back to her like a good boy," Whitman sneered at Woolf's back.

Woolf spun around on the spot. "If you have such a fucking problem with what Wilde does with her time, why don't you go and TALK TO HER?! You might actually learn something by listening, for once. You're acting like a jealous prick."

"Jealous?! Of you? That's rich." Whitman clung to the shreds of his superiority.

Woolf's hands opened and then curled into exasperated claws. Whitman's spine straightened, priming for the possibility of a fight.

Woolf took a deliberate breath. "Get over yourself," he said, slamming the door on his way out, leaving Whitman in the turmoil of his thoughts.

CHAPTER 53

WHITMAN

"Let me get this straight: you're gonna break it off with a woman you..."

"Don't say it."

"...*Care about* because you can't stand the thought of her being with another man. And that's not jealousy. What are we calling it, then?" Hawthorne asked. They smoothed a glossy lock of hair over their ear and set their Negroni down on the polished bar top of the Program H Common Room.

"Jesus Christ, whose side are you on?" Whitman did not need the cherry of judgment on top of the shit sundae of emotions overwhelming him.

"Cool it, Whit. I'm not taking sides. I'm just saying Woolf has a point. I think you should talk to Wilde."

Whitman threw a hand up in acquiescence and used it to knead his brow. "And say what, exactly?"

"I don't know. You've been hopelessly in love with the woman for months. But if you can't admit it to yourself, you've got no hope of confessing it to her. You're right. Go on then. Break her heart, and then you'll be free to die alone." Hawthorne sipped their cocktail and tunneled their smoky

Eliza Begrave

eyes into Whitman.

"What the fuck, Thorne? I came to you for a little comfort and understanding." The throbbing bass of his heartbeat thudded across his sore skull.

"I'm flattered you think that's in my wheelhouse. I'm your best friend, not your wet nurse." Sympathy was not on today's menu at Chez Hawthorne.

Whitman slipped the last sip of his drink into his mouth and slammed the glass on the table.

"THAT is Waterford crystal. Destroy your own life, fine. But destroy my barware, and I will never forgive you," Hawthorne scolded. Whitman murmured an apology. He surveyed the tumbler, checking for cracks.

"Doesn't this stuff have lead in it?" he said, peering through the facets of the glass.

"I'm gonna fill *you* with lead if you insult my grandmother's crystal again." Hawthorne cracked a half-smile. Whitman appreciated the attempt to lift the mood.

"Look, you care about Wilde, right?" Hawthorne asked.

"You know I do," Whitman mumbled, defeated.

"And you promised to tell her if you caught feelings. Don't you think she deserves to know how you feel?"

Whitman fell silent, lost in thought. Of course, he felt that Wilde deserved everything. He wasn't prepared for the possibility that he didn't mean as much to her as she did to him. What if she rejected him? If he broke it off first, he would never have to face that possibility.

"Honestly, if you're gonna end it anyway, what are you even risking by telling her you love her?" Hawthorne asked.

Only his heart.

CHAPTER 54

WILDE

The door closed behind Hemingway, and Wilde chucked her half-eaten brownie into the wastebasket by her bed, unable to stomach another sweet. As relieved as she was to be back in her room, having traded Fielding's watchful eye for Hemingway's stress-baking, fuzzy-blanket-providing, everyday-sleepover style of care, she grew weary of being treated with kid gloves.

All she wanted was to see Whitman. He hadn't visited her in the infirmary. In fact, every one of her friends had except him. Hemingway had transferred all the bouquets, stuffed animals, and gifts back to their room, and it resembled a pastel teddy bear garden. Except, of course, for the black mamba petunias from Koontz and the stuffed Baphomet from King that Wilde kept at her bedside next to Woolf's stargazer lilies.

Wilde unscrewed the orange prescription bottle and rattled out another Ativan for the searing headache that now kept her constant company. Fielding felt comfortable releasing her once she could walk on her own, but she ordered Wilde to rest—no screens, no mentally taxing activities, and no training.

The door swung open.

"I need to talk to you," Whitman said as he stepped inside.

Wilde's heart lifted at the sound of his voice, but that joy quickly faded when she laid eyes on him.

Matted curls hung over Whitman's brow, and his wrinkled clothes hung loosely on his frame. She rose from her bed and approached him. The scent of whiskey seeped from his pores, and his lower eyelids were puffy and dark. It was noon, and there was no sign that he had slept.

"Are you okay? What happened?" Wilde asked, her heart tightening in her chest. Whitman furrowed his brow, rubbing the heel of his palm against the center of his chest. He shook his head, leaving her uncertain if he was dismissing her question or signaling that he wasn't alright. The ground felt unstable beneath her, and her throat dried out.

She moved closer, eager to comfort him, every part of her being on high alert, but he stepped back from her. Had she done something wrong? What had happened that day that she couldn't remember?

"Just stop... I need you to listen," Whitman said, keeping her at a distance.

Wilde raised her hands in surrender. "Okay. I'm listening."

"I can't do this anymore," he confessed. His words hung in the chasm between them, a chasm he had created.

"Can't do what?" she asked, confusion mingling with dread. A wave of dizziness swirled around her head, and she closed her eyes, willing it to go away.

"This... us... I just can't," he said, his shoulders slumping. The spark in Whitman's eyes dimmed like a flame reaching the end of its wick. When it extinguished, it pulled Wilde's heart into the darkness with it. What had she done wrong?

"What did I do?"

"You didn't do...I mean, I don't know," he said. He blew

out a long exhale. "It's just..." His eyes glazed. "It's over."

"Whit... I..." Wilde struggled to find the right words, desperation turning to despair. "Please don't do this." Whatever turmoil he was facing, she hoped they could work it out together. She searched his face for any clue, but he refused to meet her gaze. Her chest caved. "Not again," she whispered.

"Just tell me you're in love with him," Whitman said, resignation thick in his voice.

"With who?" The dizziness intensified with her confusion, and her head throbbed, shrinking her patience.

"Don't fuck with me, Wilde." The edge in his voice set a match to her irritation.

"Don't fuck with you? You're one to talk. You anger fuck me and tell me to leave, then apologize. Then you save me from Kipling and disappear. Now, you're brushing me off again. What the hell do you want, Whitman?"

"I want you to be honest with me. Do you love Woolf?" His interrogative eyes finally met hers.

"What? What would even make you think that?" she said, concealing the wince caused by a fresh jolt of pain in the back of her head. She fought the nausea growing in her stomach. Standing up may have been a mistake.

"I'm not intrigued anymore. I am fucking jealous. I can't STAND sharing you with Woolf, and it's ripping me apart." Whitman's voice broke, and a tear rolled down his cheek.

The shock held Wilde frozen to the floor. "Did you talk to Woolf?"

"Yes, very loudly." Whitman raked his hand through his hair.

Wilde chose her words carefully. "What exactly did he tell you?"

Woolf knew everything about the situation, and Wilde

didn't understand how Whitman could be so upset if he had just spoken with him. She needed to know every word Woolf had said to him.

"He told me I was acting like a jealous prick. It's infuriating that he was right about the jealous part," Whitman admitted with a defeated look.

Wilde felt a slight ping of relief at his admission of jealousy, but it was overshadowed by her need to understand why he was so upset.

"What did he tell you about me?" she pressed.

"That you three spent three days in bed together."

"What?!" Wilde couldn't contain her fury. Whitman saw the rage in her eyes, and confusion spread over his face. "*I* spent three days in bed. Woolf and Hem were NOT in bed with me." She was going to rip Woolf to pieces the next time she saw him.

"Why would you be in bed for three days, then?" Whitman asked, bewildered.

Wilde's anger broke free of its worn tethers.

"Because you broke my heart!" She raised her voice to him for the first time, and his eyes widened like she had struck him across the face. "You made me feel like everything to you, and then you made me feel worthless."

Horror replaced the shock in Whitman's expression.

"I am *not* worthless. I am not just a slut, or an operative, or a weapon, Whitman." Tears burst the levee of her eyelids and streamed down her cheeks. "I am a woman, with emotions and needs, and I'm done denying it to make everyone else comfortable. I want someone to love me and fight for me. Not just toss me away when I'm no longer of use to them."

"Wilde, I..." Whitman took a step toward her, eyes glistening.

"Now, if you'll excuse me, I need to go kill Woolf." She

pushed past him toward the door, but the dizziness reared its head, and she lost her balance. The room blurred, and she tumbled toward the floor. Whitman's arms clasped around her, and she landed in his lap on the parquet.

Their lips sat inches from each other, and his thick, bourbony breath kissed her skin. His tentative, plaintive eyes searched her face and lingered on her lips. His hot skin sent echoes of excitement through her. Her stupid body betrayed her.

How could he still look at her like that?

"I thought you loved him," he whispered.

She shoved him away. "I love you, you asshole," she seethed, staggering to her feet and wobbling over to the couch.

"Whoa whoa whoa, careful." Whitman hovered his arms around her, bracing in case she fell. His eyebrows crinkled his forehead in a mixture of shock, confusion and something that looked like deep-hearted concern.

Realization flowed over her like a tidal wave. Wilde exhaled through her nose and shook her head.

Unbelievable.

"He didn't tell you," she said. Knowing Woolf, he would have preferred her to share her feelings with Whitman directly. Woolf would have felt he betrayed her trust if he had disclosed her love to Whitman. She hadn't realized that he would intentionally mislead Whitman into believing they were still sleeping with each other.

"Tell me what?" Whitman asked, his expression dropping as he awaited the revelation. He remained on the floor in front of her, sitting back on his heels.

Wilde took a deep breath.

Time to let it out, Babe.

"I haven't been sleeping with Woolf. I haven't been

sleeping with anybody. Except you."

A swallow shifted Whitman's throat, and he blinked rapidly, lips pressed tightly together.

"I broke it all off when I realized I was falling for you." Tears stung the corners of her eyes as the words fell from her lips. It was out.

Whitman dropped his chin to his chest and released a swift exhale. He lifted his head and met her gaze with tear-drenched eyes.

"I'm actually all yours. I have been for a while," Wilde managed to say.

Whitman let out a sound that was half cough and half sob, then rose from his heels and enveloped her in his arms. She buried her face in his chest while he rained frantic kisses on the top of her head.

"Why didn't you tell me?" His voice carried a mix of desperation and betrayal.

"I was going to—"Wilde took a deep breath and steadied herself "—that night I came to your room."

"Oh, my god." Whitman's eyes flared with recognition. "And then I?!" he huffed. "Jesus, FUCK!" He broke off their embrace and stood. He walked away from her, running his hands through his hair. "I'm so fucking disgusted with myself."

Wilde's anger returned. "And now you're just another person I love that I have to watch walk away. I'm so stupid."

Whitman spun on the spot and walked back toward her. "French, no. You're not stupid."

Wilde stood. "Then tell me, why am I still here? You showed me I'm nothing to you, and I still held on to hope. But you don't want me."

"No. No." Whitman grasped her upper arms and drilled

his eyes into hers. "I want you so much it is destroying me. I've wished you were mine every day. Every fucking day."

"Then why are you leaving me?" she said, all her hurt strangling her voice.

"I'm not." He wrapped his arms around her. "I'm not. I won't ever leave you. I'm so sorry, Baby. I misunderstood everything. If anyone's stupid, it's me."

Wilde wanted to believe him, but the blazing brand of that night still singed her heart.

"This is all my fault. Please let me try to fix this. I know I have a lot of work to do, and I don't deserve it. But you make me want to be better. I want more than anything to be good for you." He stroked and kissed her hair. "Let me show you I can be good for you," he whispered. "Please."

Wilde choked on a sob. Whitman released her and cradled her face in his hands, wiping a tear away with his thumb. He gently swept the hair off her forehead and gazed into her eyes. "I love you, Frenchy." Tears streamed down his cheeks as his breath caught in his throat. "I love you so much I almost destroyed us."

Warmth spread through Wilde's chest at the sound of that word. He had never said it before. In that moment, she realized that all her fears of being insignificant to him weren't real. He loved her in return. They loved each other, even though neither of them was perfect. Overwhelmed by the surge of emotions, tears refilled her eyes.

She brushed a tear off his cheek with the backs of her fingers. "Nothing can destroy us, my Love."

CHAPTER 55

WHITMAN

Whitman's fingers traced lazy circles on Wilde's arm. Her head rested in his lap, eyes closed. Whitman was grateful to drink in her beauty. He could stare at her forever. He tried to memorize every curve of her face, hoping to recall it perfectly whenever she was away. Each moment spent with her made him feel renewed, and he almost didn't want to break the silence.

"I've overheard Capote call you Ali. I know I'm not supposed to ask this, but is that your real name? I know you two knew each other from before," he said.

Wilde smiled without opening her eyes, an amused laugh escaping her nose. Whitman marveled at how gorgeous she was.

"Nothing gets past you, does it? It's not my real name. G and I have known each other for a long time. She's the only person on the outside I'd consider a friend. But we've never known each other's real names. We both value our anonymity," she said.

"G?" Whitman asked, puzzled.

"I met 'Capote' when I was first trying to get false papers. She told me she'd been forging fake IDs ever since she was a lowercase g."

Whitman chuckled at the Montell Jordan reference.

"At that time, we were both lowercase g's. But since then, she's been G." Wilde nuzzled her head into his lap, and he struggled to keep his thoughts focused on their conversation, shifting his legs to avoid disturbing her.

"Why Ali, then?" Whitman pressed, his curiosity getting the better of him.

"It's short for 'alias' because that's all she's ever known me by. She helped me acquire all of my identities. She's extremely talented."

Whitman felt a pang of jealousy at the thought of the time Capote had shared with Wilde. He wondered what she was like outside of Archangel. Why would she have needed multiple identities? Her skill set was vast, especially for someone her age. At times, he thought she was overqualified for Archangel, as though all the material was a review. But where could she have possibly learned all of this? She remained a mystery to him, and he wanted to know everything.

"I left Ali behind when I got here. I'm not the same person I used to be. None of my old names matter, because I'm not any of those people anymore," Wilde said, opening her eyes and gazing up at him. Her rich brown eyes sparkled as they connected with his.

"What matters is who I am right now. And right now, I'm your Frenchy. I'm Wilde."

A rhythmic buzz erupted from the bedside table. Wilde groaned and rolled over, leaving a lingering kiss on Whitman's lips. She picked up her phone, took a cursory glance, and then set it back down on the nightstand. Rolling back, she planted a kiss on his chest.

"I have to go. Capote needs me," she said.

Eliza Begrave

Whitman raised an eyebrow in challenge.

"It's not like that," she replied, kissing him again. He pulled her close, kissing her deeply, and groaned softly when she pulled away.

"But I haven't had the chance to dangle my new girlfriend in front of Woolf," he whined. His fingertips grazed the soft skin of her sides while he drew her hips closer to his. "Look at you; you're so dangle-able." He tried to be so adorably enticing that she wouldn't want to leave the bed.

"You're evil," she said, unable to suppress a smile.

"Do you want me to walk you?" he asked, concerned that her concussion was still affecting her.

"No, I'm good. It's a short walk. The dizzies are gone, I promise. See you tonight?" she said with a playful smirk.

"Nothing and no one could keep me away," he promised. She lifted from the bed and headed toward the door, pulling his heart with her.

CHAPTER 56

WILDE

Wilde swung open the door to Capote's room, their long-standing camaraderie having rendered formalities like knocking a thing of the past.

"This better be good. I was in a very warm, very comfortable bed," Wilde said.

Capote sprang from behind her desk, her eyes sparkling with enthusiasm.

"I want you to meet someone," she said. She glanced over Wilde's shoulder at someone Wilde had no idea was in the room.

Before she could turn to look, a powerful arm wrapped around her, and she felt a piercing pain in the side of her neck. All the strength emptied from her legs, and the arm lowered her to the ground. The last thing she saw before her vision closed was Capote's horrified face.

Wilde's head throbbed, and an acrid copper tang spread across the back of her tongue. Pain stabbed the back of her skull, and her eyelids felt like kettlebells. She labored to crack them open. She saw nothing in the blackness. Her heartbeat ignited first, thrumming an accelerating knock against her sternum.

Fluorescent light flooded the room, blinding her.

"Wake-y wake-y, eggs and bake-y," a soft voice called from the corner of the room. The voice resonated a hair lower than she remembered, but there was still no mistaking it. Wilde's heart dropped into her stomach. She opened her mouth to speak, but no sound came out.

Wilde's forearms were duct-taped to the arms of a metal chair. She wiggled her legs. They were bound to those of the chair. She wasn't gagged, so she assumed he wanted to talk.

Soft footfalls padded toward Wilde and stopped five or six feet short of her. She wrenched one eye open. The piercing light sent shockwaves of pain radiating from the center of her forehead.

"Still sleepy, Peanut? I might've overdone it on the dose. If memory serves, you're pretty hard to put down." The man's voice stole all warmth from the air.

Wilde forced her eyes open to the scalding pain of the light and fought to allow them to adjust. A lanky figure began to take form in front of her. The details of the man's outline crystallized in her returning vision, confirming her suspicion.

"P...Pasha," she croaked.

"Aw, you remembered. I'm touched. It's good to see you, too." Pasha's face came into focus. He leaned on an aluminum table facing her. His lips stretched across his teeth in what would have been a rather charming smile, if not for the malice that lingered behind his eyes.

"I've waited a long time for this," he said, lifting from the table and walking toward her. He knelt in front of her and seized her chin in a leather-gloved hand. "Wasn't expecting this look. The hair suits you, I suppose. But the schoolgirl get-up is... surprising. I think Vasily would've loved to see you like this."

A deep rage surged within Wilde, clearing her thoughts for the first time. Her eyes flew open wide, glaring up at him from beneath her eyebrows. Her jaw locked, pushing her chin forward defiantly. Pasha smiled at her, clearly pleased with the reaction he had provoked by mentioning Vasily.

Through the veil of her wrath-watered eyes, Wilde got her first good look at him. The years hadn't changed him much. His growth seemed to stall around the age of fifteen. He was one of those men who would probably look like a teenager until he hit forty. He looked impeccable—not a mark on him indicated that he ever experienced a moment of violence. Not a single flaw revealed itself on his perfectly moisturized skin. Starched, expensive clothes clung to his thin frame, and he sported a stylish, cropped hairstyle that must have required both significant cost and daily effort to maintain.

Whenever her thoughts had landed on her brother over the last decade, she had hoped he was still alive. Helleborus was far too secretive for her to find out what happened to him after their first and last op. Seeing him now, and taking stock of her current predicament, she assumed he had continued to work for Helleborus this whole time.

She understood his anger. The last time they were together, she knocked him out, abandoned him and their mission, and took off with the target. And he had the last ten years to stew over it. Had they sent him to kill her?

Wilde remained silent. She took two consciously measured breaths to reground and calm her flaring nervous system. She needed to think. She scanned the room for any means of escape.

Stark cement walls enclosed them. In the center of the wall to her right was what she could only assume was a one-way mirror. She saw no door, so she surmised it was behind her. The air smelled damp and stale. This room made Frost's interrogation cell look like a beachfront Malibu condo.

"Looking for an escape? I guess that's what you're good at. But there is no way I'm letting you slip through my fingers this time. You can scream. You can fight. But you're leaving this castle with me."

Leaving?

They were still at Beverstone. Wilde wasn't aware there were cells like this inside the Keep, but it made sense if she thought about it. More importantly, he hadn't taken her to a second location. There was still a chance she could get out of this. She only needed to outsmart the highly trained Helleborus asset in front of her, and he happened to be the one person in the world who knew her better than anybody.

"Oh yes, we're leaving. For some stupid reason, they still want their precious Xiphos back. Honestly, I hope you give me trouble, so I get to kill you instead. I've proven to them I'm ten times better than you ever were."

The thought that Pasha wanted to kill her tightened Wilde's chest. He used to be the most important person in her life. There was a time when he was all she had.

"How did you get inside?" Wilde surveyed the room. A black duffel sat on top of the table next to Pasha.

"Hoping to keep me talking? And here I thought they'd teach you something new at this silly school. So much for Archangel's reputation." Pasha always excelled at being difficult. He knew, by instinct, how to ferret out someone's buttons and then mercilessly push them.

"No one knows you're missing yet, so you'll have plenty

of time to tease out my nefarious plot while you plan your escape." Pasha breathed a disappointed sigh, and his eyes drilled into her. "You're supposed to be the fearless one. When the hell did you get so soft?"

CHAPTER 57

WOOLF

Whitman strode through the door of their room with a grin plastered on his face. At least he was in better spirits. Woolf's muscles tensed. It had taken all his strength not to beat the dumbass out of Whitman the last time they spoke. He didn't know if he could hold it back if Whitman started back up.

"What's with the smile? Did Frost test too many drugs on you today?" Woolf asked.

"Cease fire, white flag, and all that," Whitman said, throwing his hands up with a smile of submission.

Woolf eyed him from over his book. He took a breath and willed the fight to leave his muscles. If Whitman and Wilde reconciled, she probably wouldn't take too kindly to him handing Whitman his ass.

"Did she straighten you out, or are you still on your bullshit but drunker?" Woolf asked.

"Off my bullshit. Scout's honor. We good?" Whitman looked sincere and uncharacteristically humbled.

Woolf wasn't ready to relinquish his anger, but Whitman didn't admit he was wrong often—or ever, now that Woolf thought about it.

"We're good," Woolf ground out. He still had Whitman to thank for Wilde surviving Kipling's attack. "You're still a dick."

"I know." Whitman sauntered over to his desk. "Has she been by?"

"She wasn't with you?" Confusion descended on Woolf.

"Nah, I was at happy hour with Hawthorne." That explained the carefree attitude and easy admission of guilt.

"I just got in myself," Woolf said. He directed his attention back to his book, not desiring to continue the conversation. Whitman wandered to his desk, looking for a brandy snifter, likely.

"What the fuck is this?" Whitman's tone sounded shocked and angry. Woolf rushed over to the desk. Whitman's laptop stood open. A cursor blinked at the end of a message on the screen.

"Wilde has been taken. Put your comms in. -C"

Woolf's anger dissolved, and fear slid into its place. He dashed to his bedside table as Whitman pulled his earpiece from his pants pocket and plugged it into his ear. Woolf retrieved his comm from the drawer and inserted it.

"Capote? Is that you?" Woolf said.

Capote's answer was quiet. "Yeah."

"What the fuck is going on? What do you mean by taken?" Whitman practically yelled. "Who has her? Kipling? Where are they?"

"There's no time. Lockdown is about to drop in the Keep. Your only chance of getting to her is to stay outside the secured areas. Otherwise, you'll be locked in, and you won't be able to do anything."

"How do you know there's going to be a lockdown?" Woolf asked.

"Because I'm the one initiating it. Get out NOW. Take whatever you need with you."

"Where is she?" Whitman demanded.

"Thirty seconds. I'm not fucking around. You two need to MOVE," Capote urged.

"Whitman, come on," Woolf said, dragging him out the door by the arm. As they exited, Whitman grabbed their coats from the rack.

CLOMP.

The safeguard slammed down behind them.

CLOMP. CLOMP. CLOMP.

They watched as the steel doors closed in succession down the rest of the hallway. Woolf glanced at Whitman, whose face held a mix of worry, confusion, anger, and fear that mirrored his own.

"Well, now what? You need to give us some answers," Whitman demanded of Capote in a quieter tone, but the threat was clear. "Who has Wilde?"

There was silence on the other end of the comm.

"G!" Whitman hissed.

A moment passed in silence on the channel.

"The Deathstalker," Capote said, resignation in her voice. Woolf's blood solidified to ice in his veins, and he watched the color drain from Whitman's face. Woolf couldn't think of any reason the Deathstalker would be after Wilde, but he also didn't know much about her life before Archangel.

What have you gotten yourself into, Wilde?

"How do we get to them?" Woolf asked, shifting into operation mode.

What's the next step?

"I'm trying to find out where he has her. I may be the best hacker alive, but Archangel's lockdown protocol is a fucking beast, even for me," Capote said. "I suggest you try to improvise some weapons."

"The armory is out," Whitman said, locking eyes with Woolf.

"It is. And I can't open anything for you. I'm stuck in view-only mode. I'm trying to crack into what he's accessing, but I can't manipulate the code. Try the gym. It's not locked down," Capote said. Whitman said nothing before he took off toward the gymnasium.

"Wait, how is he accessing anything?" Woolf asked, pulling his coat on as he chased after Whitman.

"The Director has an encrypted keycard that allows her to access any area in the castle at any time. He has it."

"Then, how did you initiate the lockdown?" Whitman asked. There was a pause.

"I'm at the Director's terminal," Capote said.

"You're in Dickinson's office? Can you get her to lift the lockdown?" Woolf asked.

"She's um... not conscious. I'm working on expanding my access inside the system, but he only gave me the initiating code."

"You're helping him?! Why the fuck would you do that?" Whitman's anger returned.

"Because he's the fucking Deathstalker!" Capote yelled, exasperated. "What the fuck do you expect me to do?"

CHAPTER 58

WILDE

Wilde had lost sense of how long she had been in the cell, which she knew wasn't a good sign. She needed to keep Pasha talking. The heated argument they were having seemed to be doing the trick.

"She was only a child," Wilde argued, gritting the words out of her mouth.

"So were we!" Pasha's voice emerged in a strangled snarl. "You were all I had! When you left, I had fucking nothing!" For the first time, she saw hurt in his eyes, which he attempted to conceal. He tried to regain his calm demeanor, but the betrayal surged out of him. "We kept each other safe. How was I supposed to be safe without you?"

Wilde's ribcage squeezed in on her lungs. She knew they had been everything to each other. But there were things he couldn't protect her from, and ways she failed him, too.

I left him. I left him all alone. I chose to save Dominika, and I abandoned my brother. How could I?

"Why did Dominika deserve to be sheltered from the ugliness of the world any more than we did?" Pasha's eyes fell to the ground, weighted by the heaviness of his words. "It gets everyone in the end anyway."

A flicker of the young man she once knew resurfaced, and Wilde's heart cracked at the sight of what he had become.

"You know she would've grown up to be a piece of shit, just like her father," Pasha rationalized, regaining his control. His energy cooled.

Wilde's anger at his switch flipped hers. "What, like you did?" she snapped back, furious that Pasha had let Helleborus form him into another callous asset.

The back of Pasha's hand impacted the side of Wilde's face like rebar. Her mouth filled with blood. The blow filled her ears with a loud, high-pitched whine, and her eyes blurred with tears. She probed the inside of her cheek with her tongue and wiggled a loose molar. Pasha's small stature always belied his nearly inhuman strength. His body was as iron as his will.

Wilde spat a mouthful of blood on the toe of one of his Testoni oxfords. His eyes darted down at his shoes, and a glimmer of intensified rage passed over them. His predator's pupils narrowed on hers.

"You think you're so much better than me, don't you? You think Archangel won't make you kill for them when they find out what you are?" Pasha's voice grew. "You're a killer. Just. Like. Me." He punctuated the last three words with a slow tone that mocked her with every brutal syllable.

"I'm nothing like you," Wilde spat with as much strength as she could muster.

Pasha's activated frame relaxed into a measured aggression, and a leisurely smile spread across his lips.

"You sound so certain." His voice lifted in a soft, melodic tone. He crept forward and placed his mouth at the entrance of her ear. "But I've watched you kill," he whispered. "The precision. The carefully controlled rage. Your eyes never left his

313

as his life drained out of his body all over you." Pasha's words dug into her very soul. "You were satisfied... pleased, to watch him die. You wanted it so. Very. Badly."

Wilde's strength faltered. She couldn't refute him. As she had watched the last shivers of life leave Vasily's eyes, she finally felt safe. His warm blood had drenched her skin and nightdress, baptizing her in crimson hope.

Pasha's eyes lit up as he watched Wilde's face fall. "It was downright inspirational," he said.

Every word twisted into Wilde's deepest doubts about herself. She remembered the look of horror on Pasha's young face when he found her in Vasily's bed, covered in blood. She was a killer before he ever was, and she feared she always would be.

But she wasn't like him. She wasn't just another Helleborus pawn, killing on command. She needed to save Nika from her lustful father. Save Nika like no one saved her. Everything she did, she did to protect. Every one of her kills was to save someone, herself included.

"I don't torture people." Wilde's vision fully cleared from the blur.

"What do you think they did to me?!" The pained rasp emerged from Pasha's curated coolness like a wild horse escaping its bonds.

His words stunned her silent. She had never allowed herself to give much thought to what happened to Pasha after she fled. She had been so focused on staying hidden from Helleborus. She never thought they would punish him for her disappearance. No, that wasn't entirely true. That was the convenient story she told herself to avoid feeling guilty about leaving him. Now Helleborus had succeeded in turning him into a weapon.

Or maybe *she* had done it.

"What do you think *he* did? When I came home from a failed mission? How do you think he took it when I told him you escaped with the target? And you think you hold no responsibility for that?" Pasha brought himself so close to her face that she felt his hot breath on her cheek.

"Pasha, what did he..."

He walked back toward the table and unzipped the black leather duffel.

"Oh, you'll find out. I'm going to put you through every single moment of what I went through after you abandoned me." Pasha slid brass knuckles over gloved fingers. The leather squeaked as he closed his fist. Wilde's mind raced. She knew full well of their father's brutality. Guilt spiraled through her insides. This happened to him because of her.

"I want you to know I took my time with that little brat. You helped her escape for nothing," Pasha said, knocking Wilde out of her thought spiral. Wilde's throat felt thick, and a knot formed in her chest.

No. He can't be. Not Pasha.

She carried the guilt over Dominika's death for a decade. She assumed the Deathstalker was a seasoned, high-level asset. Pasha was so young.

"Pasha, no. You didn't... Tell me you didn't..."

"Oh, I did. And I'd do it a hundred times over. I have that spoiled snot to thank for jumpstarting my whole career. And I guess I have you to thank as well. She would've had a clean death if we had finished it together. There's more than Vasily's blood on your hands."

Pasha pulled a small glass vial of liquid from the bag. It clinked as he set it down on the table.

"Why..." Wilde's stomach hardened, and she started to

feel lightheaded. "Why did you do it like that?"

"Where do you think I had just learned it?" he said, turning over his shoulder and cocking an eyebrow at her.

The thought of the torture Pasha had been through horrified Wilde. Maybe if she had just carried out the mission and continued the Xiphos program, their father wouldn't have twisted Pasha into becoming the Deathstalker.

But if she had stayed in Helleborus, she knew she would have become something even worse.

Wilde needed to focus, but the pain in her head clouded her thoughts, and grief consumed her.

FOCUS!

Wilde took a deep breath and stock of the situation. Her reality at this moment was that she was locked in a room, a hostage of the most notorious and widely feared assassin in the world. The only advantage she hoped to have was that she once knew the boy he used to be.

He wasn't the only one in this damn family who knew how to push buttons.

Get him on the ropes. Force him to make a mistake.

"Come on, Pash... The Deathstalker?" Wilde faked more strength than she had. She was trying to provoke him. He may have learned control over the years, but impulsivity ran in his veins. It was braided into their family's DNA. "You're just taking credit for someone else's kills. Come on. Like you could ever..."

"Oh, I fucking COULD. And I DO. And..." Pasha took a breath and composed himself. He nodded, seeming slightly amused at the rise she was able to incite in him. His calm returned.

"Deathstalker. I always liked that name. Wish I had thought of it myself. Stupid newspapers. If they only knew how sophisticated my cocktails have become. You see, I'm a bit of a mixologist now. Like your little boyfriend."

Ice jolted down Wilde's spine at the mention of Whitman. How close had Pasha been watching them? Did he have Whitman imprisoned somewhere as well?

"If they only knew what I use. Well, actually, I have several different formulas, depending on what I want to extract from my companions. Why stick to just scorpions when the world is full of venomous creatures with much more...entertaining effects? You'd be surprised how inept and unmotivated the average medical examiner is, especially when the victim's family doesn't care for the details of their death to hit the press."

Pasha gazed down at his gloved and brass-knuckled hand like a bride admiring her wedding ring. His eyes shot up at Wilde, under the half-veil of his eyelids. In all her years knowing him, she had never seen such malevolence. Her dwindling chances of making it out of this alive drifted over the fine hairs of her skin and off into the ether.

"But, Deathstalker venom has its place in my arsenal. It has a nice sharp kick to it while I wait for the Irukandji syndrome to settle in. And it won't usually kill an adult human," Pasha said softly as he picked up the glass vial and loaded it into the end of a silver pistol he pulled from the leather bag. He smiled at her as it met its home with an ominous hiss.

"It just hurts like a bitch."

Pasha eliminated the distance between them with two steps and pressed the gun to the side of Wilde's neck. She felt a scorching pierce. Once the burn of the injection wore off, she took a deep breath. Her face still throbbed worse than this puny neck wound.

317

"Is that all you got, you little..." The words barely left Wilde's mouth before every nerve in her body became lightning inside her muscles. Her limbs turned to lead. Sweat broke out all over her body, and she could scarcely will herself to draw a breath. She heard the deafening thrum of her heartbeat in her eardrums. Darkness crept over her being, threatening never to leave her soul. Her stomach twisted into a snake's nest of painful, curling knots. Something was coming up inside of her, and she couldn't stop it. Wilde retched and vomited over the side of the chair.

"You were saying?" Pasha chided.

Her vision blurred, and sweet blackness enveloped her.

Wilde's shallow breaths sawed in and out of her lungs. Pasha kept her conscious with the occasional hit. A sharp stab pierced her side with every breath, confirming that the last blow of the brass knuckles had fractured at least one of her ribs.

Her vision blackened around the edges, and her fingers tingled and shivered. She bit back a groan, struggling to stay aware. Pasha's voice sounded farther and farther away with every passing moment, but the continued beating confirmed his proximity.

Wilde needed to stay awake. She couldn't let him take her away from Beverstone.

Her eyelids could only crack open to a blur of faint light.

A calling emerged from deep within her. A call to home. A white, purifying light. Death couldn't be that bad; the relentless pain that consumed her would be cast away forever.

If she died now, her last chosen vision would be Whitman telling her how dangle-able she was and kissing her like he never wanted her to leave. And those sweet words, "I love you," lingering on his lips.

I don't want to leave him behind. I want to be with him. I want to live.

"You made a mistake, Peanut, thinking I was a good person," Pasha's buttery timbre drifted into her ears, shocking her into consciousness.

Pasha will never let me keep him. He will always hunt us.

"I don't think I ever was," Pasha continued. "I only played that part for you."

CHAPTER 59

WHITMAN

Whitman and Woolf scoured the gymnasium for anything they could use to defend themselves.

"What the fuck am I supposed to do with ninja stars?" Woolf said, his frustration bubbling over.

"They're called shuriken, and if you don't know how to use them, you probably shouldn't even be touching them," Whitman shot back. He also struggled to find anything useful. There was nothing particularly practical for fighting the Deathstalker. They needed to find something. They had come across mainly workout equipment, martial arts pads, and recreational weapons. His hands landed on a fencing rapier.

Fucking useless. More fucking useless garbage.

Not only was it dull as Woolf's personality, but Whitman was dogshit at fencing. He knew his way around small blades, but the only ones available in the gym were throwing knives. At least they were sharp. He attached a holster with a set of three onto his belt.

Wilde's words rang in his ears: *"They're pretty impractical as a weapon."*

Well, they were all he had at the moment. Impractical was

better than facing an accomplished assassin empty-handed.

Whitman glanced over at Woolf, who picked up a compound bow.

"Alright, Legolas. You gonna shoot the Deathstalker with a fucking arrow?" Whitman teased. Woolf flipped him off without looking up.

"Kinda short on options here," Woolf said with disdain. He put the compound bow down and picked up a crossbow, glancing over at Whitman and shrugging.

"Better," Whitman said. It was better than nothing.

"Guys, I found them," Capote's voice crackled over the comm. Woolf's eyes met Whitman's, and they headed for the door without a word.

"Where?" Whitman demanded.

"The last thing he accessed was a cell in the dungeon under the Keep," Capote said. "I can't get you in, but I can get you into the adjacent observation room."

"How do we get down there?" Woolf asked.

"I'll have to baby-step you through it. The schematic I'm working off is insane. Head toward the Program K Wing," she said. "The service elevators are all locked out, so it's about to get real weird."

"Should be your fourth door on the left," Capote said. Whitman tested the door, and it opened. They both stepped inside. The small cubicle had a one-way mirror on the wall to their right. What Whitman saw on the other side of the glass stole his breath. The walls of the cramped room advanced around him.

Wilde sat bound to a metal chair inside a concrete cell. Whitman instinctively put his hands to the glass. He brought his face as close as he could to get a detailed assessment of her state.

She slumped forward in the chair, her hair hanging in a curtain over her face. Her head swayed back, and he got his first full look at her. Her cheek was deep purple and bleeding, and one of her eyes was nearly swollen shut. She had a round knot at the corner of her mouth, and half her lip puffed out. Whitman felt a pinching pain in his chest.

Woolf's voice drifted over, sounding much farther away than it was. "That little twerp is the Deathstalker?"

Whitman scanned across the room to the man he hadn't even noticed was there. He was a scrawny thing, clean-cut and well-dressed. He projected a chilling sense of calm as he appeared to casually speak to Wilde. She seemed barely able to keep her eyes open. Worry and fury flooded his chest, and his skeleton caught fire.

"I'm gonna kill this fucker. I'm gonna fucking murder him," Whitman muttered. Never in his life had he wanted to harm someone more than this skinny little motherfucker.

"Would you shut the fuck up? I'm trying to figure out what they're saying," Woolf said.

"It's soundproof, idiot."

"I can read lips, asshole," Woolf said, his gaze locked onto the Deathstalker's face, who seemed content to yammer on nonchalantly. Whitman didn't know Woolf could read lips. He was full of surprises. It was becoming increasingly difficult not to like this guy. Maybe he didn't need to hate Woolf just because they loved the same woman. His feelings for Wilde were making him a motivated partner.

"He thinks she has something called Xiphos. Or knows

where it is. What's Xiphos?" Woolf asked no one in particular.

Something clicked in Whitman's brain—something from his days when he worked jobs on the fringes of organized crime.

"Wait, I've heard of Xiphos. Some of my old contacts would talk about it. It's a Helleborus weapon they started developing twenty-something years ago. But it's been missing for years," Whitman said.

"Why would Wilde have it?"

Whitman's unease grew. His knowledge of Wilde's past was alarmingly restricted. He was starting to wonder just how little he knew.

The Deathstalker sauntered over to Wilde and crouched in front of her. He appeared to be speaking in hushed tones.

"What the fuck?" Woolf whispered. "He's talking about some op they were on together," he said, eyes wide with shock.

"Wait, they know each other?" Whitman didn't want to believe it. If they worked together, did that mean she was tied to Helleborus? Was she an infiltrating asset? How much had she been keeping from him?

"Who the hell is Vasily?" Woolf murmured, still scrutinizing the Deathstalker intently.

Cold rage flashed across Wilde's face as she opened her eye to glare at the Deathstalker. She spat a mouthful of blood onto his face, the red clots and tendrils trickling down the side of his flawless cheek. If her one good eye could breathe fire, it would have. Despite her injuries and the enormity of the threat before her, her spirit and tenacity remained unyielding.

That's my girl.

Was she, though? Whitman didn't know anymore.

A muscle in the Deathstalker's jaw fluttered. He stood up and drew a long, measured breath. With a caustic grin, laced in barely-restrained rage, he wiped the blood from his face with a leather-gloved hand. That was when Whitman clocked the set of brass knuckles across the back of his fingers. Without warning, the Deathstalker delivered a brutal punch straight to Wilde's abdomen.

Whitman's throat caught fire, and time slowed. He helplessly watched Wilde's mouth open and close as she tried to draw breath, just as she did in his nightmare. She gasped and coughed, blood coming out in splatters from her mouth.

Whitman pounded on the glass, wishing he could break through and tear that runt piece of shit limb from limb. Mostly, he wanted to wrap Wilde in his arms and take her away from here.

The pounding must have shaken the glass because the Deathstalker's sharp gaze darted toward them. If Whitman hadn't known this was a one-way mirror, he would've thought the man was staring directly at him.

The Deathstalker walked over to a leather duffel on the table and calmly placed a few items inside, closing the zipper. He prowled back to Wilde, who was still gasping for air, struggling to catch her breath.

The man produced a switchblade from his pocket, and Whitman feared it was the end. Instead of turning the knife on Wilde, he cut her free of the duct tape bonds and lifted her limp body over his shoulder. It took surprisingly little effort for someone with his frame. He slung the duffel over his other shoulder before pulling out a keycard, opening the door, and exiting the cell.

Whitman and Woolf rushed to the door of the observation cell only to find themselves locked inside.

"FUCK!" Whitman yelled.

"Capote, we need this door open!" Woolf yelled into his

comm. "Now!" A shadow of panic simmered beneath his anger.

"It's a security measure. When one holding cell opens, all the other doors in the hallway secure themselves. It's to prevent the possibility of a breakout. The locks won't open until he exits the door that secures the hallway from the rest of the dungeon," Capote explained.

"Is there a workaround?" Woolf asked, futilely yanking the door handle.

"Not that I can see. The safety measures are in place to ensure the Director's safety during a lockdown. He has complete control," Capote said.

Whitman spiraled. He couldn't shake the image of Wilde's battered face, coughing and gasping for air. Somewhere in between his rage and powerlessness, a moment of clarity descended.

"Capote, you can see what he's accessing with the keycard, right?" Whitman asked.

"Yeah," Capote said.

"Then we can track where he's going," Woolf said, catching up with Whitman.

Silence met them on the other end.

"Capote!" Whitman demanded.

"I already know where he's going," Capote said quietly.

The sound of the lock disengaging distracted Whitman from his confusion at Capote's admission.

"He's out. Head back up the hallway you came in. He's going to the outer grounds." Capote shifted back into mission mode.

"When this is all over, we're gonna need a serious debrief," Woolf said, sternly. Whitman agreed that Capote had a lot of shit to answer for. The two marched out of the cell and

Eliza Begrave

sprinted up the hallway.

CHAPTER 60

WILDE

The wind bit at Wilde's skin, but it held no candle to the lightning that electrified her nervous system. The Deathstalker venom had overtaken her body. Pasha hauled her across the wet grounds and out into the night. Each of his steps sent splintering pain across her chest and abdomen, allowing her only shallow sips of breath.

Pasha possessed extreme strength and relentless stamina, but eventually, he needed to let her off his shoulder. He hooked an arm under her armpits and dragged her across the wet grass, her limp legs slogging behind her.

"Jesus, you got heavy," he said with a brotherly sigh.

Wilde possessed no strength to retort. The nerves on her right side, where he had broken her ribs, had surrendered, leaving her no control over them. Her muscles vacillated between extreme pain and an excruciating, dull, numb ache. Her body was dead weight.

Fucking good.

She wanted to make it hard for the motherfucker.

Wilde felt Pasha's frustration grow with every step she couldn't take. Her head raged with pain like a pair of red-hot blacksmith tongs encircled her skull. But any opportunity to hinder his escape served her.

The chopping of rotors tore through the deafening wind. Wilde mustered the strength to look up into the night. Between the swirling clouds, a tungsten grey, unmanned helicopter banked back and forth in the gale about a hundred and fifty feet above the whipping grass. Its wake cast circles of disturbance on the grounds.

How the fuck did he get a Helleborus stealth drone into this airspace?

Wilde knew she shouldn't have been surprised. Hellebores pioneered stealth tech and excelled decades beyond what any government contractor offered for the lowest bid.

Fuck it.

Even if Pasha got her on board, she could distract him and crash the helo. Kill them both and end this. It would all be over soon.

"Land the fucking drone, G!" Pasha yelled into his comm. From the recesses of her brain that still held shreds of thought, Wilde wondered about G's involvement. The horror on G's face had betrayed both her complicity and the appalling realization of what she was into. Wilde dreaded the possibility that G would have betrayed her knowingly.

But why would she be surprised? Your enemies can kill you, but your loved ones can make you wish you were dead. Pasha's movements toward the helicopter grew increasingly frantic. Was he panicking? Wilde's foot hit a slick spot, and she fell, lacking the strength and will to stop herself.

"STOP!" shouted a voice from behind them.

Woolf?

It couldn't be. Wilde prayed she was hallucinating under the venom. Woolf should be safe under lockdown in the Keep.

Pasha snagged Wilde up viciously and turned her toward the sound. His arms squeezed around her, and a bolt of agony crackled across her torso. He could only raise her to her knees, and her eyes rose to meet something worse than the pain.

Not only was Woolf there, but Whitman sprinted beside him. His perfect curls swirled around his chiseled face in the wind, and murderous intent barreled out of his narrowed hazel eyes. Her heart free-fell into the damp earth.

No!

They should have been safe—safe from Pasha, safe from her and her past. Yet here they were, chasing down a ruthless Hellebores hitman, risking their lives... for her?

"One more step, and she gets a maximum dose." Heavy breaths heaved in and out of the Deathstalker's sneering mouth, but there was no mistaking the danger in his tone. He coiled his arms around Wilde's body like a ravenous python. She felt the business end of the silver venom injector meet her jugular.

Whitman and Woolf stopped in their tracks, struggling to catch their breath. Whitman doubled over, placing his hands on his knees, but keeping his eyes trained on Pasha.

Woolf planted a foot forward, aiming a crossbow at Pasha's head. Whitman took on a fighting stance and flipped a throwing knife into the air, catching it by the tip. Wilde vowed that if they lived through this, she'd teach him to throw from the damn handle—way better accuracy.

Pasha pushed the injector into the meat of Wilde's neck to deepen the threat. She watched the blood drain from Whitman's face.

"Give her up, man. There's no way you're getting out of here in this wind," Whitman warned. His voice and face dripped with pure hatred and malice. Woolf's stalking eyes never left his target, not even to glance at Wilde. He looked more lethal than she had ever seen, even armed with that silly crossbow.

They had come for her.

Wilde's head swam as the venom coursed through her, triggering another surge of nausea. Underneath the agony, the small glimmer of Whitman and Woolf coming to her rescue bolstered her soul. That glimmer began to grow, sparking a flame of strength within her. In front of her stood the two men she loved most in the world, and they hadn't come to hurt or betray her. They came to save her. Even if it was a gloriously outgunned, foolhardy attempt that would likely end in all of their deaths, it was the thought that mattered.

Wilde refused to let Pasha extinguish their hopes. She had to fight. She would rather struggle and risk her life to save those she loved than allow fear to take over. The time for running was past. She would stand and fight to protect her loved ones or die trying. Well, she would kneel, stumble, and fight, if she could.

The Deathstalker chuckled in earnest at the two men with recreational weapons threatening him from the lower ground. The injector gun loosened the tiniest increment from Wilde's throat.

It opened the moment enough to score Wilde a lapse in Pasha's concentration. She landed a vicious elbow on his face, busting his cheek open. He released an aggravated snarl and tightened his arm around her ribs. Pain shattered her core, and she crumpled, unable to stop the blood-curdling cry that loosed itself from her lungs. The Deathstalker lifted Wilde back to her knees, and she dry heaved over the grass.

"Little sisters can be so annoying sometimes," he sneered, just loud enough over the wind for Wilde to see it land on

Woolf and Whitman's faces. His snicker in her ear seeped into her brain like poison.

"The Deathstalker is your fucking brother?!" Whitman said, incredulous.

"Tell us he's lying, Wilde." Woolf couldn't hide the plea inside the gritted-out order, even with his eyes still trained down the crossbow.

Wilde's shoulders hunched, and she gazed back at them weakly. They would hate her for this. Losing them was inevitable now. Whitman detected the shame in her eyes, confirming the truth. His eyes widened with shock, and a deep, betrayed sadness lifted his eyebrows. For a moment, he appeared paralyzed by the recognition.

"I'm taking this little nugget back home to Helleborus," Pasha added with a sly grin in his voice. "Oh, she didn't tell you she was Helleborus from the day she was born? She's practically royalty in our circle. And here I was, thinking you were all so close." The Deathstalker twisted the mental knife.

"God damn you, Pasha," Wilde sobbed. Nothing he had ever done to her, including the events of the last several hours, could compare to the cruelty of this moment.

Whitman's eyes pleaded with Wilde for reassurance she couldn't provide. A cold heaviness spread down her body, and she watched a shadow fall over his heart.

"He already has, Peanut," Pasha whispered in her ear. That last word stabbed. The pet name he had called her their whole childhood. When he was her Pashka and she was his Peanut. How they would comfort each other through all the darkness and trauma. How he would stay with her on the nights she drifted into his bed after surviving Vasily's. He would give a whole foot of space in the bed but hold her pinky finger with his as they fell asleep, knowing that she could only stand to be touched in ways she could control. They protected each other. Now, he turned it against her. That name made her skin crawl worse than the venom rushing through her veins.

Tears blurred into the black spots in Wilde's vision. Her entire soul cracked open, the heartbreak surpassing her physical torment. She stockpiled her strength to glance at Woolf, knowing this betrayal would cut deep. They had grown so close. She feared she had lost any chance of keeping that kinship.

Woolf still leveled the crossbow on the Deathstalker. A red glassiness filled his eyes, and the crossbow trembled in his hands. He pressed his lips together, and a tear rolled down his enraged face. The Deathstalker's grip shook with his near-silent laugh as he savored every moment of their pain. He was the only one enjoying this.

Another jolt of anguish rippled through Wilde's muscles. She knew that the minutes she had left were slipping away. Even if Whitman would never look at her the way he used to again, and he stopped loving her—or if Woolf turned his back on her—she was not going to give up. She would fight for them, die for them, and prove to them that though she might be a murderer—a monster, even—she was their monster.

Pasha would learn how dangerous it was to underestimate his baby sister.

"Look at you two," the Deathstalker mocked, gesturing toward them with the injector gun. That little window was big enough for Wilde. She dropped her weight, ducking her head down. Reading her perfectly, Whitman threw the knife without hesitation. It whizzed past the Deathstalker's face, nicking him in the ear.

Pasha dropped Wilde, and his shocked glare followed the path of the knife. Rage filled his eyes as he turned back toward them.

"I can't believe you're making me stoop to this," Pasha sighed. Before Wilde had any time to react, she heard a snap release, the hammer of a pistol click back, and a gunshot over her head.

The shot hit Whitman square in the chest, blasting him off his feet. His body crumpled to the ground. Wilde's heart and brain screamed, but her mouth could only open and make no sound, trapped in time like Munch's famous painting. From her position up the hill, she could see only his boots.

Woolf took advantage of Pasha's distraction and fired the crossbow, missing by a whisper of air. Woolf scrambled to reload the crossbow as Helleborus' most lethal assassin bolted toward him.

Free from Pasha's clutches, Wilde clawed down the hill toward Whitman. If she could steal any last moments with him, she needed to. She struggled to steady herself on her trembling hands and knees as darkness enshrouded her vision. She'd be luckier than a ladybug fucking a dragonfly on top of a four-leaf clover to make it to the man who she was tethered to, heart and soul.

CHAPTER 61

WOOLF

Woolf tipped the front of the crossbow to the ground and jammed his foot into the stirrup. He pulled an arrow from its housing on the side of the bow as the Deathstalker charged down the hill toward him.

Shiiiiiit, shit shit shit shit.

Woolf had never loaded a crossbow. Whitman had loaded the first bolt. The opposite of the business end of it somewhat resembled a rifle.

Can't be that hard.

The helicopter banked low across the grounds, and the rotors grazed the grass, carving trenches into the soil.

CHUNK CHUNKCHUNKCHUNKCHUNK.

Through the blades, the Deathstalker stared at Woolf with malevolence. Woolf took the extra few seconds he gained from the bladed barrier to pull the bowstring toward him. Shit was damn heavy. The blades lifted, and the drone stabilized above the ground.

The Deathstalker leveled the barrel of the pistol at Woolf and winked. Woolf glanced over at Wilde, who was crouched over Whitman's body. If this moment were to be Woolf's last, he would spend it on her. In every lifetime, for eternity.

A piercing screech cut through the roaring wind and the rotor's hum.

"Ow, fuck!" the Deathstalker cried, pulling Woolf's focus back. Pattycake's wings flapped rapidly around the Deathstalker's face, blocking Woolf's view. The man fired the gun in his best guess of her direction. With one strong pump of her massive wings, she caught a gust and disappeared into the charcoal sky.

The Deathstalker wiped blood from a deep scratch on his face and regained his bearings when a black tactical ladder unfurled from the drone. One of the carbon fiber rungs collided with his arm, knocking the gun out of his hand. It tumbled down the hill, too far for Woolf to retrieve. The Deathstalker fumbled, half caught on the ladder.

Capote's voice emitted from a speaker on the helicopter.

"I fucking did it!" the speaker blasted, Capote's proud celebratory cry echoing through the wind-whipped valley.

"Goddamn it, G. We are on comm! You don't need to use the speaker," the Deathstalker yelled. "The feedback is gonna make me go deaf." He ripped his earpiece out and rubbed his ear.

"God, you are ALWAYS so critical! I'm learning to fly this thing as I go, and I'm making this crosswind my bitch, but it's NEVER good enough for Mr. Perfect!"

The Deathstalker freed himself from the ladder's ropes just as Woolf nestled the plastic fletches of the arrow into the crossbow's firing mechanism with a satisfying click. He had him.

CHAPTER 62

WILDE

Wilde reached Whitman's motionless body. As she hauled herself across the grass from his boots toward his head, he groaned. He was alive.

My love.

"Where are you hit?" Wilde searched for blood. She needed to get pressure on that wound if he had any chance. Whitman's eyebrows crunched together in pain as he reached into his breast coat pocket. He whimpered and pulled out a green leather book embossed in gold.

"Saved by literacy. Do you think the library will make me pay a fine for this?" he murmured.

He handed Wilde the book. The bullet had mushroomed on impact, embedding into the cover.

Thank fuck for hollow points.

Wilde turned the small book over: *Leaves of Grass* by Walt Whitman.

"I guess I proved them all wrong. I finally did save myself." Whitman looked up into Wilde's eyes, and she detected a familiar mischievous twinkle. Even the Deathstalker couldn't dampen Whitman's swagger.

Woolf's scream pierced the air. Whitman and Wilde's heads snapped in his direction. Woolf had succeeded in reloading the crossbow just in time for the Deathstalker to disarm him of it and shoot him point-blank through the leg, pinning him to the ground.

"Feel like saving someone else?" Wilde questioned, testing the waters of Whitman's strength. She lacked the ability to save Woolf, but she couldn't lose him either.

"Permission to kill your brother?" Whitman groaned as he rose to his feet. He pressed his palm to his chest and winced.

"Granted. Nothing would please me more."

"I don't know. My pleasure game is pretty strong. Challenge accepted." Whitman smiled at her despite his obvious pain. Time paused, as if the gravity of the moment couldn't compare to what flexed and stretched between them. Despite all the odds stacked in piles against them, and being shot, he could still break the moment just to let her know he always wanted her.

The Deathstalker stood up and gave Woolf a dismissive glance, as if to say he wasn't going anywhere. He trained his sights on Wilde and Whitman.

"Less flirt. More kill," Wilde said.

Whitman slipped his fingers around the back of her neck and kissed her with excessive gentleness.

"I love you," he whispered against her ear.

"I love you, too."

"Don't tell Woolf I was reading."

Time slowed as Whitman and Pasha stalked toward each other. The blackness encroached in puddles and plops around Wilde's sight, but she fought it. The sweet taste of oblivion teased her mind, promising an end to all her pain. A lifetime of agony blinking to an end with a single last breath she had prayed for countless nights over the years. A blissful death. And a Great Forgetting. A final exhale when her heart would release the acts of violence enacted on her soul.

No! I don't want to forget!

Wilde wanted to live, for once in her life. For herself. She wanted to stay. With him. With both of them. With all of them. She resisted the Great Forgetting: that beautiful bliss that felt like going home to an old friend. She knew she could weather the storms of her memories for one sweet chance to spend another precious moment with him.

Wilde's senses reignited, and the pain with them. She grounded herself in the excruciating agony. She couldn't stand. She could barely lift herself off the ground. Wilde grasped the earth, grass slipping between her fingers. She fought to rise.

CHAPTER 63

WHITMAN

Whitman fumbled with the snap on the holster at his hip. He pulled one of the throwing knives out, as the other two tumbled out and disappeared into the cold grass. Whitman pulled back and loosed the knife into the night air. It caught wind and missed the mark by several feet. The Deathstalker reared his head back and laughed into the sky. Whitman scrambled to find one of the other knives on the ground in the dark. Just as his fingers closed around a handle, the Deathstalker lunged at him.

Grappling with the man, Whitman sensed the family resemblance. The Deathstalker shared Wilde's exceptional training in hand-to-hand combat. She was faster and more graceful, but what the Deathstalker lacked in speed and artistry, he made up for in power and brutality.

Whitman struggled to maintain control of the knife, attacking with it when he could. He landed a grazing slice on the Deathstalker's shoulder. The man looked down and fingered the shreds of the cut on his sleeve, his eyes seething with fury. He appeared more enraged that Whitman ruined his shirt than by the fact that he was bleeding. The Deathstalker landed a savage front kick on the top of Whitman's bad thigh, reawakening that old pain and knocking him to the ground.

The Deathstalker pounced on him, and they rolled across the grass away from Wilde. He tried to strip the knife from Whitman's hand. In the struggle to hold onto it, Whitman lost his advantage in their grapple. The Deathstalker trapped him on the ground and wrapped both of his wiry hands around Whitman's neck like a noose. In moments, Whitman's vision tunneled.

A quick whipping sound sliced the air above Whitman's face, and the grip around his neck loosened. He opened his eyes. The three inches in front of the Deathstalker's left eye were replaced with the stainless-steel handle of a throwing knife. The blade was embedded perfectly into the center of his eye socket.

The man's form collapsed onto Whitman's body, and he shoved it off him. He rolled over onto his stomach in the grass away from the body. Glancing up, he saw Wilde staring at them both, arm outstretched. Flawless fucking follow-through.

That's my girl.

Wilde fell back down upon her hands. Whitman stood up to run to her, and a bolt of pain shot through his leg. The Deathstalker got him good with that kick. He assessed himself quickly. It wasn't broken, but it smarted something fierce. Taking extra caution, he hurried back to Wilde, noticing that her complexion had turned pale.

"Can you stand?" Whitman asked.

"I'm good. I'm good. I just need a minute to catch my breath. Go check on Woolf," she said. Whitman glanced over at Woolf, who fought to unpin himself from the ground.

Shit.

Whitman looked back at Wilde. She smiled some reassurance at him and nodded over toward Woolf. Whitman started to move toward Woolf when Wilde grabbed his shoulder.

"Whatever you do, don't take that arrow out," she said, pushing him with both hands toward Woolf.

By the time Whitman reached him, Woolf had freed himself from the ground and formed a makeshift dressing from his shirt. The arrow had pierced the meat of his quad, and he was wrapping the dressing around the wound. He had lost a decent amount of blood, but it wasn't arterial. Otherwise, Whitman would have run up on a corpse.

"What can I do?" Whitman asked. Woolf appeared to be experienced in field medicine and had self-administered care quite well.

"I could use that tie," Woolf grunted between pained breaths. Whitman took a reluctant glance down at his tie. It was one of his favorites: the one with the little beagles on it.

"But it's Drake's," Whitman whined.

"Whitman," Woolf warned in a low growl. Whitman exhaled in disappointment.

"Fine." Whitman rolled his eyes. He stripped off the tie and handed it to Woolf. He must have been starting to like this guy. Woolf cinched the tie onto his thigh above the arrow in a makeshift tourniquet.

RIP, doggy tie. I'll never get Woolf's stupid blood out of that hand-rolled silk.

"Alright, let's get you up. Do you think you can walk?" Whitman asked. Woolf gave him a firm nod, biting back a groan. Whitman wrapped one of Woolf's arms around his shoulders and ushered him to his feet.

CHAPTER 64

WOOLF

Woolf and Whitman turned back toward Wilde. Her motionless form was heaped face down on the ground. Cold dread smothered Woolf. They hobbled over to her in a three-legged race, Whitman half-supporting Woolf, and dropped to her sides. Woolf rolled her over. Small blades of grass freckled her pallid face. She was breathing, but barely conscious.

"Frenchy, stay with me. Look at me. Can you hear me?" Whitman said. Wilde's eyelids fluttered. Woolf put her arm around his shoulder to lift her to a seated position. Her body was dead weight.

"Whit?" Wilde's voice was weak.

"I'm here, Baby. Tell me where you're hurt," Whitman said, his voice faltering. Woolf searched for a trail of blood. With half the exposed parts of her battered and bruised, it was difficult to assess the worst injury. Her eyelids feathered open and closed again, and Whitman kept trying to rouse her.

Woolf slipped his arms under her shoulders and knees to lift her. Her agonized scream stopped them both dead.

Woolf laid her back on the grass. His heart stalled in his chest. He couldn't lose her.

"Keep your eyes open, French. Come on." Whitman's voice trembled with urgency, and he tapped the side of her face gently. A groan lost breath as it left her mouth. Her head lolled over, and Whitman slipped his arm behind her limp neck, cradling her head and leaning closer to her. Woolf wracked his brain for a solution. They had to save her. He didn't want to live in a world without her.

What's the next step?

There was no next step without Wilde.

"Baby, NO. Don't you dare leave me," Whitman pleaded. A heavy tear dropped from his eye. Woolf's heart fractured watching them. This couldn't be the end.

Assess the injury. We have time. We have to have time.

Woolf lifted the bottom of Wilde's sweater. A big blue bruise bloomed across the side of her torso, sending a cold chill down Woolf's spine. He checked her wrist. Nothing.

"She has no distal pulse. She's bleeding internally. We need to get her to the infirmary NOW." Woolf shifted into crisis mode.

Whitman's gaze shifted from Wilde's ashen face to her bruised torso, and all semblance of color drained out of his skin. He took Wilde's head in his hands, smoothing her hair out of her face.

"Frenchy, you said you were good. I don't understand. Why didn't you tell me?" Whitman's voice cracked, and tears plummeted from his eyes onto Wilde's cheeks.

"Whit, there's no time," Woolf urged.

That knocked Whitman back into the moment. He wiped his face on his sleeve and collected himself. He scooped Wilde's nearly lifeless body into his arms, careful to avoid her middle as much as possible. His arms pressed into her as he lifted her from the ground, and she yelped.

"I know, Baby. I'm sorry, I'm sorry, I'm sorry," he whispered as he cradled her. Whitman settled her into a position that seemed less excruciating, and her head crumpled onto his chest. Determination filled his face.

"We need to get that lockdown lifted, or she won't stand a chance," Whitman said, stalking back across the green toward the Keep.

"On it," Woolf said, activating his comm. "Capote, do you copy?"

"I'm here," she said, shame choking her voice.

"Wilde is dying. She needs Fielding," Woolf said, hating the words as they grated out of his throat.

"The Director's keycard will get you back into the Keep. Get to the drone. I can fly you there faster." Capote's voice trembled.

Woolf was already limping his way to retrieve the keycard from the Deathstalker. His leg felt like it was on fire, and every step sent piercing jolts of pain radiating from the arrow wound. He reached inside the pocket of the Deathstalker's pants and pulled the keycard out... in two pieces.

"Um, Whitman," Woolf called. "Small Problem." He held the two useless halves of the keycard up.

"Fuck!" Whitman yelled. "The keycard's toast, Capote. Lift the damn lockdown, now."

"Only the Director has the code to do that," Capote said.

"You better find a way to wake her ass up then," Whitman shouted.

CHAPTER 65

WILDE

Wilde opened her eye to the blinding light and tried to blink away the intensity. Something soft covered the other eye and cheek. She felt floaty and groggy, like awakening in a cloud.

"Hey, look at you," Woolf's soft voice was the first thing she heard.

"Why do I have half a face?" she asked.

"You have a whole face, Baby." Whitman's velvety baritone danced into her ears like a lullaby. "You've just had a... few surgeries. The bandages are there to help."

As Wilde's eye adjusted, she dragged her gaze around the room. Woolf and Whitman stood on either side of the reclining medical bed to which she was restrained. Woolf steadied himself on crutches, while Whitman's matted curls frizzed around his concerned face. His wrinkled clothes looked several days from fresh.

"You two look like shit," she croaked.

Woolf chuckled, but Whitman's face remained drawn with concern. Wilde's thoughts began to unscatter, and reality poked a few fingers into her experience. She remembered.

"Where's Capote?" she asked, recalling the memory of

Capote's face just before being tranquilized. She pieced together during her time with Pasha that he was the new boyfriend Capote had been talking about, and that she had managed to sneak him past Beverstone's security.

Whitman and Woolf exchanged a glance. Wilde attempted to sit up.

"Whoa, whoa, whoa. Take it easy. They've kept you sedated for six days. It wouldn't kill you to take it slow," Whitman said, his expression softening with concern. Wilde was fortunate to be alive. If Pasha knew where to find her, Helleborus wouldn't be far behind. Archangel had every reason to want her eliminated at this point.

Realizing she didn't have the strength to sit up, Wilde lay back down. All moisture abandoned her mouth, and she felt the corners cracking as she spoke.

"Capote," she insisted, short of breath. She needed to know Capote was okay.

"Frost and Fielding are interrogating her..." Woolf said. "Considering her involvement in the attack..."

Wilde did not envy that experience.

"And the fact that she stabbed the Director with epinephrine to get her to lift the lockdown," Whitman added.

"Jesus," Wilde squeezed out. How had they let things get so far out of hand?

"Now that I think about it, where'd she get the epi while locked in Dickinson's office?" Woolf said.

"She's deathly allergic to Brazil nuts. If only they made an EpiPen for Brazilians. It would've saved her a lot of heartaches when we were in São Paulo," Wilde said. Her thoughts returned to her current predicament. "I guess I'm probably next on Frost's list."

Woolf glanced down at Wilde's restraints and didn't meet

her eyes. "You are being considered a significant security risk."

"They're sending you to Chaucer." Whitman's voice was tight.

Wilde had heard very little about the Board of Directors and its Chairman, Chaucer, none of it good. To achieve that high a level in Archangel, you either had to be providing an amount of funding requiring at least nine zeros or be an excessively accomplished spook. Likely both. The Board was the pinnacle of people not to be fucked with. Most faculty members would serve their entire career without meeting any member of the Board of Directors. Unless, of course, they messed up royally, and that meeting would likely be their last.

An audience with the Chairman of *that* Board?

"Outstanding," Wilde grumbled. The drugs started to wear off, and a throbbing grew in her head.

I'm as good as dead. I should've just let Pasha kill me.

Wilde's gaze traveled to Woolf's eyes. Those emerald beacons shone true.

But then Whitman and Woolf might not be alive.

Wilde glanced up at Whitman. There was a guardedness to him, but he couldn't mask the hurt and betrayal in his eyes.

"Is it true? Is what he said true?" Whitman's quiet plea shattered the splintered windows of her strength.

If Wilde was dead anyway, there was no harm in coming clean. They both deserved to know what she truly was.

"That he's my brother?" The words stung her mouth, and tears pricked her eye.

Whitman pressed his lips together, and the top of his jaw flexed above his temple. This truth would hurt all of them.

"Yes. And that I was Helleborus? That, too."

Whitman and Woolf's faces fell. Add two more to the list of people she loved and disappointed. She should be used to this by now. May as well rip the whole Band-Aid off.

Woolf surveyed the room. "You don't have to... this room is probably..." He shuffled on his crutches.

"It's a school run by spies, Woolf. It's most definitely being surveilled. I don't care anymore. Frost will get it out of me anyway. And if Helleborus can reach me here, they can reach me anywhere. Archangel can't protect me. And why would they guard a threat? I'm as good as dead."

Whitman grabbed her hand, his love breaking through the armor of his hurt. "I won't let that happen."

She knew he couldn't save her. Not from everything that must be coming for her. It was over.

"I'm tired, Whit," she said. "I'm tired of running. I'm tired of lying. You deserve to know what I am."

A swallow worked its way down his throat, and his jaw ticked. He gazed at her with a weary expectancy, steeling himself for what was coming, as if the inevitability of those you love hurting you was just as commonplace as another dissatisfying breakfast.

Wilde's heart—a heart she used to doubt was there, a heart she didn't believe could break any further, a heart she never trusted until she met Whitman—withered as the brilliance faded from his eyes. Her heart had already fractured, shattered, and imploded. All that remained were dying embers, desperate for oxygen.

Wilde took a deep breath. A piercing pain shot across her torso, and a cry escaped her mouth. Memories of Pasha's beating flooded back, reminding her of her broken ribs.

Whitman grasped her arm, and his face lost its color. She gave him a reassuring glance. She drew a shallower, ginger breath.

I may as well face my death telling the truth, for once. I'll die free of the lies. At least they'll know.

"Pasha—the Deathstalker, as you know him—we grew up together in a Helleborus training program. Whether we're biological siblings or not, he's the only brother I ever knew. We were programmed from birth to be deep-cover sleeper assets. It was an experimental program. The training was intensive. The programming was... inhumane. The initiative was executed by two high-level Helleborus assets, whom we knew as our parents. Suffice it to say, my father and mother made Faulkner and Frost look like Ward and June Cleaver. I escaped the program ten years ago, and I was on the run until I got here."

"That's why the Death—Pasha came for you? He said that you have some weapon called Xiphos?" Woolf asked.

"Xiphos was the name of the program that formed me. I'm the only person who has ever completed it. I'm the weapon. I'm Xiphos," she said. Both Whitman's and Woolf's eyes widened.

"Does that mean they can activate you as a sleeper?" Whitman asked.

"Maybe. I don't know how deep my programming runs. But the first time they tried and failed. I killed the wrong person and escaped with the target."

"So, Pasha was Xiphos, too?" Woolf asked.

"Initially. But the Xiphos experiment was a colossal failure. I abandoned my directive, so they scrapped the program. They took a different tack with Pasha after I left. They tortured him and twisted him into something... else. They created the Deathstalker. That thing we met is not the brother I knew."

The truth hung in the air. At least it was out. Part of Wilde felt relieved to tell the truth finally. She closed her eye. She didn't want to watch the love leave Whitman and Woolf's faces. She couldn't bear to see how they looked at her now that they knew her past.

Time stretched between the moments as silence lingered.

"Who is Vasily?" Whitman asked.

Wilde's skin crackled like lightning at the sound of that name exiting Whitman's lips. She was accustomed to sweet things coming out of that mouth. That name felt like a mouthful of poison spat in her face. It wasn't Whitman's fault. There was so much he had yet to know. Wilde's eye welled, and she willed the tears not to fall, but the center of her nose prickled.

Full disclosure time, Babe.

She cleared her throat. "Vasily Volkov is the man I murdered." His name tasted worse than bile and blood. There was no going back now. Wilde would be a monster in their eyes forever.

"I started my first deep-cover assignment at the age of ten. Pasha and I lived at Vasily's estate for four years. We ate at his table. I played with his daughter. She was four years younger than me, and I became her protector, of a sort."

Whitman and Woolf stared at her in shared shock and horror, but she continued.

"Pasha and I didn't know the nature of the assignment. We were just sent to live with them. When the time came, we were ordered to eliminate Vasily's daughter, Dominika, to manipulate Vasily into a specific political decision. When the directive came, I couldn't go through with it."

Whitman and Woolf had no words.

"Pasha found me moments after I killed Vasily. He wanted to complete the mission, fearing the consequences of our failure. I knocked him unconscious and fled the estate with Vasily's daughter."

"What happened to her?" Whitman asked.

Wilde's memory snapped her back to the day she found Dominika:

Dominika's ankle split at a right angle inside the boots Wilde had lent her. They were too big for Nika, but she wanted to wear them anyway. Now, she would wear them forever. Her other booted foot lay unnaturally far across the floor, neither of the legs making sense with the spinal column bent to a nearly bobbin-pin angle.

The grief that dominated Wilde's life for the last ten years descended on her, blending with the realization that her miserable life would end very soon, just as she started to want it to continue.

Rotten timing, Babe.

"After our father completed his training, Pasha caught up with her and executed our original directive. She was the Deathstalker's first confirmed kill."

"Jesus fuck," Woolf whispered.

Silence blanketed the room as the weight of this knowledge pressed down on Whitman and Woolf.

The silence and awkwardness must have gotten to Woolf because he started to scan the room for a means of escape.

"I'm going to... get a coffee. Can I, uh, get either of you anything?" he pushed out.

"Yeah, could I get a pineapple Jell-O with a side of the key to these restraints?" Wilde said with a snarky grin, lifting her wrists in the jingling shackles, attempting to lighten the conversation. Woolf tried not to smile. The jab worked.

"I'll take a doppio macchiato and a Drake's tie," Whitman threw over at Woolf.

Tough crowd. Poor Woolf.

"Fuck both of you," Woolf said, smiling before he left the

room.

"Too late," Wilde chimed after him, her underused voice cracking.

"Only one of you, technically," he hollered over his shoulder before disappearing into the hallway.

Wilde laughed, and the stabbing pain in her side returned. Whitman grasped her hand, and worry furrowed his brow once more. The betrayal dissolved from his face, leaving only concern, and something she hoped was still love—a love she hoped against hope she hadn't destroyed by being what she was.

"You had us scared there," Whitman admitted.

"'Us?' You and Woolf are an 'us' now?" Wilde teased. Whitman rolled his eyes at her.

"I'm under sedation for six measly days, and that home wrecker steals my shiny new boyfriend? Now, I understand why you were jealous," Wilde said, desperate to lift the mood. Whitman couldn't help but grin. Even with everything that needed to be said between them, they fell back into their old banter with ease.

"Shouldn't you be saving your strength or something?" Whitman scolded playfully.

"So I can beat Woolf off my man with a stick, sure," Wilde said, keeping the game going.

"Shut. Your. Mouth," Whitman whispered, fighting to hold back a smile. "You almost died. You could dial back the sarcasm."

"And demolish a pillar of my charm? I'd rather die. So what, are the two of you besties now?"

"I'll admit, for a wet blanket, the guy's not that bad." Wilde felt relieved to see that Whitman was starting to warm up to the Woolf she knew and loved. "Apparently, his love language is combat, so, for better or worse, I think we're bonded for life or something. I don't know. He didn't give me a battle buddy manual."

A smile claimed Wilde's lips, activating a dull ache in her cheekbone.

"I guess it's not unlike being jumped into a gang," he added.

"And you would know all about gangs," she teased.

"You don't think I could have been in a gang?" he said in mock outrage.

"Please, you look like you'd need a chauffeur for a drive-by."

"How dare you impugn my street credentials, madam." Whitman clutched his invisible pearls.

Silence fell over the two of them.

"I'm sorry," Wilde said. "For everything."

"Don't..." Whitman pleaded.

"No, I knew when I fell for you that all I would do was put you in danger, and I did it anyway. I put both of you in danger. It wasn't fair for me to do that. It was fucking selfish, and a mistake I will not repeat," Wilde said, rising off the bed. Whitman placed a gentle hand on her chest and pushed her back down. His eyes glassed. He pursed his lips and took a measured inhale through his nostrils. He spoke slowly and deliberately.

"We... were not a mistake. If that's what you feel after all this..." He inhaled sharply. He sat on the edge of the bed, and his eyes fell. "If we were a mistake, it was the best mistake I ever made. And I would make it again. Every day of my life."

He still wanted her? Wilde never entertained the possibility that he would discover the truth about her and not leave. Her heart swelled and burst open. She reached for

Whitman, forgetting her hands were shackled to the bed. The handcuffs rattled, shaking Whitman out of his moment of despair. He looked at her, his face drawn with hurt.

"You... we... were never..." Wilde said, trying to swallow her feelings down before they overwhelmed her. "You're the first good thing, and the best good thing, that's ever graced my whole crooked fucking life."

Whitman choked back a tiny sob, and he smiled with a furrowed brow. He took her closest hand in both of his and squeezed it tight. They were two complicated people, sorting through complicated feelings, walking forward together into this complicated life.

They sat in silence for a few moments.

"I want to ask you something," Whitman said, his voice tentative and quiet.

"Anything, Love," Wilde said.

"Why did you kill Vasily?"

Whitman may as well have dumped a bucket of ice water on her head. The painful memory of Vasily combined with the crushing realization that she had become her worst nightmare. Wilde killed Pasha. She had become the monster she feared for so many years. It felt like it had been her inevitable destiny all along. She never stood a chance to avoid this outcome. Murder flowed in her veins. She felt stupid for believing she could have a normal life or authentic love. Wilde's fingers started to tremble, and Whitman squeezed her hand.

"You don't have to talk about it. I'm sorry. I never should have asked," he said.

Wilde's breath shuddered into her lungs. How could Whitman still love her? Even after finding out she was a murderer?

"He was going to do to Dominika what he had done to

me. She didn't deserve that." Wilde's voice broke. She had never put words to those feelings in front of anyone else. She had prepared herself to bury those emotions underneath her own grave.

Whitman's eyes filled, and his eyebrows knitted. He fought the quiver in his lip. He reached for her and slipped his arms behind her back, squeezing her gently. With her hands bound, she couldn't hug him back. She felt like an iron skeleton, unable to express all the emotions threatening to escape her body.

"Neither did you, Baby," he whispered in her ear. His arms tightened around her, and her frame melted. "Neither did you."

There in his arms, she fell to pieces.

"I'm a murderer. How could you ever love me?" Wilde wept in his arms.

"I already love you. It's too late for that." Whitman loosened his squeeze and sat back, gazing into her eyes. He wiped the tears from her cheek.

"I wouldn't be sitting here if you hadn't thrown that knife. You saved my life—and Woolf's. When you killed Vasily, you saved Dominika from him. You have killed to protect the people you love. That doesn't make you evil. That makes you a hero."

"You don't think I'm a monster?" Wilde's tears blurred her vision, and her nostrils started to close.

"Never. How could I? Just because you've done some dark things in your life, that doesn't mean you don't deserve to be loved. You could massacre half the people in this building, and I would still love you." Playfulness re-entered Whitman's eyes. Relief soothed the rock in her stomach at the sight of his walls collapsing completely. All she saw was love. And all she felt was love.

"Our kills don't define us," Faulkner's stern voice came from the corner.

"JESUS CHRIST!" Whitman gasped. Wilde could have sworn his ass left the bed. "Haven't you heard of knocking?"

Shock and surprise pumped through her body, and her nostrils cleared. How long had Faulkner been in the room?

Faulkner walked slower than his regular, fierce, short-legged gait over to the bed.

"Unless we let them." Faulkner looked deep into Wilde's eyes. "Some people kill." He produced a key and unlocked one of Wilde's restraints. "And others become killers. We choose if it becomes who we are." He unlocked the other restraint. "We get to decide if we retain our essence beyond the actions we are required to take." Faulkner's eyes pierced into Wilde with an uncharacteristic softness.

"It's easy for an average person to say their actions define them. But that is because they are afforded the luxury of electing from many options. They possess the privilege to choose their destiny. Some of us have paths chosen for us. We are thrust into situations where the only alternative to murder is annihilation. That is no choice. Thus, people like us are not defined by our actions. We are defined by our character."

Wilde sat stunned, her eye cleared by the shock. She rubbed some of the ache from her wrists, but couldn't pull her gaze away from Faulkner. It was the best damn lecture she'd ever seen him deliver. And it was a welcome one, for once. Whitman stared at Faulkner as if his face had burst into a hundred eyeballs.

"Character is everything," Faulkner said. He gently picked up one of Wilde's hands with both of his. "You get to decide who you are and what you stand for. You choose if you become a monster." Wilde's breath feathered in her chest, and tears stung her eye once more.

"Let's get you up, kiddo," Faulkner said, pressing a button on the bed's remote. It whirred as it lifted her into an upright position. Her head became light. Faulkner and Whitman steadied her. Wilde had never considered before that maybe Faulkner's harsh demeanor resulted from all the terrible things he had seen and done. She assumed he popped out of the womb as a grumpy, murderous garden gnome. Underneath his gruff personal armor, he retained his essence. Inside Faulkner resided tenderness and grace.

"Kiddo?!" Whitman shot across the bed at Faulkner, poking at the casual fatherlike pet name. Faulkner gave him a look that told him if he ever breathed a word of this to a soul, he'd meet a true monster. Whitman retreated with a sheepish glance.

"I'm to deliver you to the Chairman," Faulkner said, the usual graveness returning to his voice.

"Now?" Whitman didn't even attempt to mask the shock and worry in his voice. Panic's icy tingles settled into Wilde's extremities, but she didn't dare show it. Faulkner nodded, resigned. He helped Wilde shift her legs over the side of the bed.

Everything hurt. The pins and needles returning to her limbs felt like jabs and stabs. Hotness, coldness, numbness, and searing pain coexisted like a churning pool of anguish enveloping her entire being. And that was just the physical.

If she could have mustered the power, she would have razed her emotional landscape to ashes to avoid feeling the complex mix of emotions that overwhelmed her spirit. Her need, her love, her shame and guilt, and everything else she had refused to feel until she came to Archangel—until she opened herself up to the people who taught her what love was meant to mean.

For the first time, she wished she had more time. Instead of hoping the minutes would waste and wash down the hourglass, taking her with them, she wanted to savor them. They had become precious, and she had so few left.

A strange calm fell over her. The end was finally here. No more running. No more lying. At least she would face her death knowing who she was. She was Wilde. She loved and was loved. She had Whitman. She had Woolf. She had Hemingway. She and her people were fierce champions for each other. She killed to save them. She would not be defined by what she had done or what had been done to her.

She readied herself to face death as a whole person. She wasn't broken. She chose wholeness. She decided to be deserving of the love she knew she had, imbuing her with unbreakable strength.

Helleborus couldn't control her. Vasily would no longer haunt her flesh. She left behind being afraid. In killing Pasha, she killed all the previous versions of herself. All the fake names and stories that were never truly her. Wilde was all that remained. And Wilde was ready to face the music.

She peeled the medical tape from the back of her hand and pulled out the IV needle, internally gagging. Faulkner took her by both hands and gave her an encouraging look, trying to get her to test her legs.

Whitman's eyes widened, and heavy tears fell. Wilde's heart opened and broke at the same time. Fear and sadness dampened the pierce of his hazel eyes until they turned into grey pools. His already heavy eyelids seemed weighted further. She hated to leave him behind. She dropped one of Faulkner's hands and grabbed Whitman's, squeezing it. Whitman pushed

Faulkner aside, which he surprisingly allowed, and scooped Wilde up with all the gentleness possible. She wrapped her arms around him, swallowing the pain that wracked her body. She needed to be in his embrace one last time. She kissed him long and slow.

"What am I gonna do, Frenchy? I can't be without you," Whitman sniffled into her shoulder. She kissed his hair and squeezed him tight. She brought his face up and gazed into his eyes.

"You're going to live, Love."

She rested her forehead on his, and they passed one final moment together in silence.

"But am I gonna laugh?" Whitman's small joke broke the silence, and they both giggled through their tears.

CHAPTER 66

CHAUCER

The Chairman of Archangel's board had searched for Xiphos for ten years. It was intended to be the weapon that eclipsed all others Helleborus had designed. After all these years, she was finally going to be in the same space with the weapon. Councils of people had tried to convince her that this weapon would pose a significant threat to her life.

Surprise could not explain what the Chairman felt when she found out Xiphos had fallen into Archangel's possession. Despite multiple demands to see the weapon, her requests up to this point had been denied, citing security concerns. She took advantage of Dickinson being in a weakened state to push her case with the Director's subordinates.

Chaucer wrung her fingers as she made her way through the greenhouse toward the exterior garden. She pushed open a gilded stained-glass door and stepped out into the fresh air. Her feet crunched on the gravel between the stepping stones on the path. She smelled the dampness of the earth. The crisp bite of the air made her clasp her Kennington trench coat around herself, just as the flowering herbs curled their petals inward for protection against the chill. She pitied the ferns for not sharing the benefit of a custom cashmere lining on the inside of their leaves.

The hedges stretched tall around the bricks and borders that housed the mulched beds of flowers and herbs. The breeze whistled through the tall purple fountain grasses, causing them to sway in rhythm to some unwritten song.

The Chairman came upon a young woman on the path. The woman's back faced her. She wore an oversized white waffle-knit bathrobe, baggy beige cotton scrub pants, and brown rubber Wellington boots. She stepped with care and a deliberate slowness. The Chairman detected a slight limp, not due to a leg injury, but a wince that came with each movement.

A raptor's call rode the wind to the garden. The young woman cocked her head to the side, listening. She exhaled with a relieved hum. Despite what looked like considerable pain, the woman stretched to her full height, raised her face to the sky, and took a deep breath.

A massive, speckled, white bird landed with grace on a short plinth next to her, startling Chaucer. Xiphos lifted a tentative hand toward the regal falcon. Instead of pecking her eyeballs out, like Chaucer expected it might, the bird dipped its head underneath the woman's fingertips, nuzzling her hand. Xiphos scratched its head, ruffling the feathers. She giggled, then winced in pain. The bird screeched gently and lifted into the air, and the woman's eyes followed it into the sky.

Chaucer stood planted to the spot on the garden path, captivated. The woman began to walk down the path, trailing her fingers through the tall feather grass. Chaucer had never witnessed another person so completely engrossed in a moment, at least not since her children were babies. The woman knelt to pull a blossom to the tip of her nose, inhaling its fragrance as if it were her first breath—or her last.

The young woman stood up, her back still facing the Chairman. She had gotten so big.

"If you chose here as the place for me to die, I thank you," Xiphos said quietly but firmly. "It's beautiful."

The Chairman had not realized her presence had been detected. Her heart blossomed open. She had no intention of killing this young woman. After ten years, Chaucer had finally recovered Xiphos.

"Has any one supposed it lucky to be born? I hasten to inform him or her it is just as lucky to die, and I know it," the woman said in a tone both wistful and rueful.

Chaucer recognized Walt Whitman's words, as she had recited them many times. She ventured to speak, though the words resisted leaving her lips.

"I celebrate myself, and sing myself,

And what I assume you shall assume,

For every atom belonging to me as good belongs to you," the Chairman recited from *Leaves of Grass*.

The words hung in the garden like mist.

The young woman exhaled sharply and stumbled sideways onto a raised bed of flowers. Her entire body trembled as she turned her face toward the Chairman.

"Mama?"

ACKNOWLEDGMENTS

First and foremost, massive accolades to the love of my life, Hubs the Great. He has loved me through every phase of this crazy adventure we call existence.

He was my first alpha reader, biggest non-judgmental brainstormer, and might actually deserve co-writing credits for some sections. He is my Whitman and my Woolf, and all the love that inspires me to write about devotion so fiercely. It sounds trite, but I could not have done this without his support and love, and if I had, I would be a much meaner and uglier person.

He has stood by while I rearranged story beats on index cards like a conspiracy theorist, and grieved with me as I tortured my favorite fictional people. Anyway, I could go on and on about the guy forever, but that would increase my printing cost.

To Stacy, my first writing partner. The woman who climbed her way out of the darkness, and left me a ladder that saved my life. She championed me when I didn't want to live, and gave me a community that helped me face my shit and heal. She is the best big sister that we all deserve, and I hope each and every one of you finds a Stacy in your life.

Bestie. Shanni-Banani. My heart. My best friend since diapers was the person who I think first loved me unconditionally and proved to me, through consistent care, that I was worth it. I cannot overstate the value of that love. I wouldn't have learned how to love me without her example. I hate that we're so far apart. I will make the most book money ever so that we can live on a complex in the woods together with all of our favorites.

To my first beta readers:

Franzi: You devoured my book with a ferocity that I hoped everyone would, but I was always disappointed when they didn't. And I wish I could have recorded your fresh reactions. You will always get my first beta copies.

JenJen: Your gentle feedback was essential to my edits, and your desire for more Koontz and King content has been echoed by others and heard. It's coming. Keep reading. I have a whole spinoff planned.

J.L. Brown: Thank you for being such a great cheerleader, always supporting me through every step of the process, and keeping an open mind while you read through a book that was beyond your spice level. I will never forget you when I get famous, so you can put those anxiety dreams to rest.

To my readers: I hope you either treasure this book like a trusted friend or chuck it across the room in scathing hatred. I just want you to feel something. If that something involves a down-low throb, even better.

Love and smooches with a consensual ass grab,

Eliza

ABOUT THE AUTHOR

Eliza Begrave is a Capricorn sun, a Leo moon, and a Sriracha rising. She lives in Orlando with her husband, who is a certified Rizzly Bear, as we think the kids are saying nowadays.

Her love of suspense began with Michael Crichton after the movie Jurassic Park captured her heart at the age of eight, and she subsequently inhaled his entire body of work. Her love of romance started with a weathered copy of *Gentle Rogue* by Johanna Lindsey she borrowed from a friend in high school. She followed up by reading every novel in the series.

She writes for the readers who think romance could use more action and suspense could use more boning.

She daylights in the world of circus theatre, spending her evenings ensuring the acrobats are wearing the proper color of spandex before they fly through the air with the greatest of paycheck.

She dislikes fudge and marzipan, but would go full Deathstalker for a sushi boat.

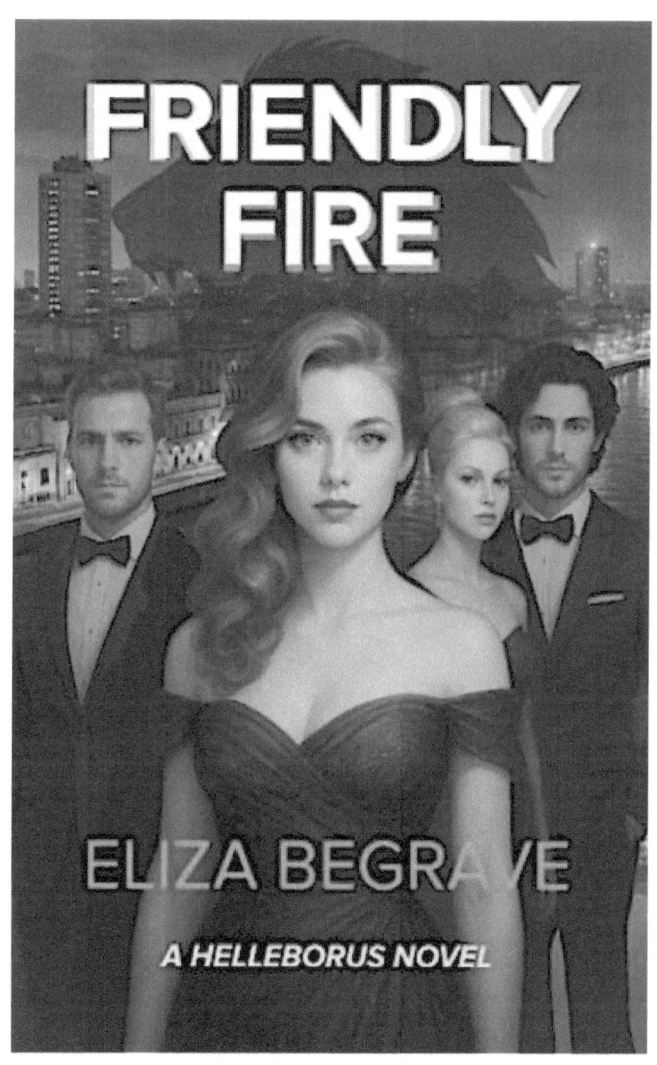

FRIENDLY
FIRE

ELIZA BEGRAVE

A HELLEBORUS NOVEL

THE ADVENTURE CONTINUES SOON

Keep reading, my loves.

www.ingramcontent.com/pod-product-compliance
Lightning Source LLC
Chambersburg PA
CBHW020547120726
47903CB00001B/167